Operation Wolfe Cub

THE TIME TO TELL

Book I

H.C. WELLS

Operation Wolfe Cub is a work of fiction.
Names, characters, organizations, businesses, places, incidents, and interpretations are products of the author's imagination or are used fictitiously. Any resemblance to actual events, locales, persons,
or entities, living or dead, is entirely coincidental.

Copyright 2012 by H.C. Wells

All rights reserved.

Printed in the United States of America.
No part of this book may be used or reproduced in any manner whatsoever without written permission except in the case of brief quotations embodied in critical articles and reviews.

The Time To Tell series, logo and marks are trademarks of H.C. Wells

Information about the author and the continuing books in *The Time To Tell* series:

Wolfe Odyssey

http://www.hcwells.com

https://www.facebook.com/pages/HC-Wells-Author

henry@hcwells.com

ISBN-10: 1480242551
ISBN 13: 9781480242555
Library of Congress Control Number: 2012921041
CreateSpace Independent Publishing Platform
North Charleston, South Carolina

Acknowledgments:

Michelle E. Trigger, Esq............................Primary Editor
Jen Myers ....Secondary Editor
Raquel A. Wells..................................Cover Illustration
CreateSpace..Publishing Team
Christina Cortino..........................Biography Photograph

    Finally, to my only love, a dedicated reader of all genres, a former librarian's right hand and nurturer of my stumbling passion. She is my wife, Sherry M. Wells, an unmistakable extraordinaire who stood up to prevent me from abandoning my work. Time and again, since 1995, she saved this entire project through her discipline and unwavering support. Without her, *The Time To Tell* might never have been told.

To all those who have suffered, or are suffering,

the hardships of war, both at home and abroad.

Prologue

The story you are about to embark upon may startle you. Read on and see why. This dramatic account didn't just begin once upon a time. It began only one way: the way a story begins that was never, ever told. But told it was, told the way it was.

It's a gripping chronicle of one earthly soul who was involuntarily thrust into an almost impossible journey against the worst of odds. This single mortal's beginning on earth marked a terrible time of catch and run, massive devastation, and conflicts of culture and belief. It could have been said that philosophy stood on its head. Lines were drawn in the sand. Bygones were bygones possibly, but no, not so fast. It was they.

Minds of people spoke a strong language about what they thought was right and wrong. The pivotal change set course through the majesty of the moments. Time would tell, but where this chronicle began was where the stepping-stones grew into an unsuspecting legend, moving forward year after year. As mystifyingly magnificent as one could dream, the infinite numbers of souls could not have expected the consequences.

Oh, but the "one thing that perpetually exists" did expect the consequences. The limitless thing called "eternity" would look back and say, "This is where it began." Within the simple marking of years and within the confines of conflict among simple souls was where the most powerful forces were unleashed.

The Second Great World War could have been professed as the time and origin, another war between good and evil perhaps. In a spiritual sense, this particular collision against corruption within the minds of moral judgments was perceived as the very miracle from where this story's glory spawned. Then again, maybe the spawning of it wasn't so glorious. Maybe it wasn't a miracle either. Maybe it marked the repercussions beyond the wildest perceptions of both believers and disbelievers.

The times were real. The facts were there, but in a heretical sense, so much was stricken with bias and religion that the ideals of what people *thought* could have gotten in the way. Yes indeed, populaces caught up in their ways of judgment and righteousness were part of it. But there was more. Far more than anyone knew—or could have known.

It was not just a matter of simple beliefs. The simple-minded, with their own little versions of victors, were not what they seemed. Differences were made. Naturally, sides were taken. Ultimately, history was carved out of the rubbish everyone resided upon. After that, the little line in the sand was washed away. Pay attention to this story for what it's not. One may judge again after it is told and done, out in the sun, for everyone to see—as clear as can be.

Spiritual forces beyond the simple, man-made texts in biblical proportions were, in fact, unleashed. That is, man-made terms spelled out by the so-called prophets speaking to God were in for a rude awakening. Meddling with it was the only sure thing that could have been counted upon.

If only the truth could tell. For the sake of the world, corrupt or not, one or many might even say in more fundamental terms that this was where the unmistakable truth began to shed light. The truth began to track the lonely, lost trails across the land and seas on this ever-so-tiny haven called "Earth."

The most troublesome of truths were tangled with complexity, making the hiding place for facts seem like fiction. Simply put, this terrible tale had spawned and been nurtured through history in a horrifying way. Slowly but surely, every intelligent human being unknowingly faced the facts laid down before him or her. Now, even the blind will see the telling, because—the time to tell has come.

And so, let it begin, as it deserves to be told in an epic way through the lifespan of just one living, breathing human being who survived as part of some grandiose master plan to create worldly peace once and for all. "Nonsense—that's *fiction!*" one might quickly spit out. Think again before tossing such nonsense into the freak shows of fiction. Read along and see, for the time to tell is in this writing. History attested, as the events miraculously lived on. It didn't matter, for hardly anyone cared enough to believe or believe what *wasn't*. The masses, whose ways of life were lived and controlled by these events, told it their own way. They chose the path, and not a single soul could prevent the outcome. Does history deceive? Did "true" history happen or not? The most magnificent men and women reserved their right to answer such questions.

To their own misfortunes, magnificent minds came to be commonplace. In all reality, magnificence is what almost everyone wanted. They came in droves. They came by the thousands. Then they came by the millions. Call it whatever it was. When it came down to it, that's just the way it was.

As a result, philosophies and beliefs from all different corners of the world broke out in seemingly the dawn of human conflicts *of all kinds*. The faithful idea of a God-given world was in the minds of almost everyone. Few took heed to a little-known fact, unfortunately.

THE TIME TO TELL

This forever-gigantic world was changing to what seemed obvious. The aging planet seemed to be getting smaller as years marched by without any God ever coming yet. Those who call earth home, with all of the vast open spaces, had, in fact, begun to suffer. Obvious too was the prevailing sense of arrogance and self-centered mindset, dominated with the fright to fight in this ever-closing arena getting smaller by the year. Sure, there were wars from before. Keep in mind that it was the time of yore that revealed only the beginning of more gruesome wars yet to come—and they did come.

There are many kinds of war, but all of their mighty lessons come hard. So what about the fate of the United States with those seemingly unforeseen wars that mysteriously sprouted up from within? Where did they come from? Did they hitch a free ride while *we the people* stayed focused on what we thought wars were all about? Did anyone fail to mention that wars come in different forms? Answers to such questions seemed so wildly elusive they could have been thrown in the stockpiles of fiction too. After the Great War, the thoughts were unified, then solidified. There *were* none of those foreseeable wars to worry about. Should anyone stand up tall and say, "Can anyone see?" The star-spangled flag was still there. Victory was felt from every little corner of the young country—from sea to shining sea.

More importantly was what was unforeseen beyond the wildest of dreams. Forces not of this world not only remembered the methodical beginning; they were rudely awakened with their powers and almighty concerns. Behind the backdrop of everyone's lives on this speck of a planet, the happening was too big to ignore anymore. Truly, there was no turning back. What was done was done, as described for the simple minds in their homes of the brave. Bear in mind, something else happened which nobody knew. This was what threw the world into the arena of a true war; a supernatural war too horrific to comprehend. That was then. This is now. Enough said. This page must be turned in order to avoid the intricacy of utter confusion that war has come to be known for. *Now* is the time to tell.

Sincerely to you,

Henry Charles Wells

Chapter 1

This extraordinary story began on a stormy winter's night in 1944 during one of history's most trying times. The loathsome carnage of the Second World War had spread across the lands like an plague, affecting almost every major continent around the globe. The gruesome consequences of what some people thought might be close to the end were far from over. Nobody really knew what lay ahead for the world at the time. What the multitudes of people standing by their countries did know was they had to belong to a side in order to survive. Those opposing would have to face the fate of utter decimation. It was truly the ultimate battle of good versus evil.

Total blackness of the night left little to describe the surroundings of the barren, rocky landscape. A periodic flicker of the lightning in the sky showed only glimpses of the few people engaged in their little ad-hoc plan. The wind, rain, and distant crashing of waves from the ocean were the only sounds heard above the thunder of that dangerous night.

None of it seemed quite right. It was eerie. The small group was out there in a torrential downpour of rain, but somehow they didn't seem alone. Somehow, it was the hot feel of the storm's air that brought on their troubled looks. Odd it seemed, for the forlorn warnings of the storm were so horridly close to their backs. Nothing looked more out of place. It was as if the weather itself tried to track them down and do away with them. Troublesome as it was, the most frightening of all were the mammoth thunder cracks and deadly lighting strikes the storm harnessed. Every so often, one of the stray charges would fry the very ground upon which these few desperadoes had shuffled across just moments before.

There were four of them. That's all there were. Their faint silhouettes seemed to be lost or wandering, but that wasn't the case. Their roundabout wondering had a distinct direction. They had only one dim lantern carried by the front-runner leading them away into the abyss of the wet, rainy night. Perhaps they didn't want to be seen.

Sounds of an air raid whistle off in the distance might have offered at least some explanation as to why they were in such a hurry. Muffled thumps of massive, earth-shaking bombs lit the sky like thunder and lightning too. At first there were only a few bombs, but then came several. Echoing quakes from the blasts behind them shook across the territory as if they were out of control, blowing almost everything to smithereens about a mile or two away behind the bluffs.

Instinctively, all four of them stopped to look back and gawk at the flickers and to feel the thumps that rumbled up through their feet. After that, they peeled back around and picked up their pace. Presumably, they had been running away from the subtle glow of civilization being bombed. Just then, those lights faded as the air assault grew heavier and heavier.

Regardless of their surroundings, they were determined. They kept in loose stride with one another as they crept closer to what sounded like the violent spills of waves at a nearby ocean beach. The men were German, from the sounds of their speech.

The third man, known as "Dr. Wycliffe," shouted over his shoulder to the last man running in back, "How far were those bombs, Wolfe?"

Wolfe did not answer.

THE TIME TO TELL

Dr. Wycliffe looked ahead to the two in front, "Hey! US-1, US-2! Wait up!"

The two men up front with the rather odd code names appeared to be the strongest and youngest of the four. Quite frankly, it was too dark and stormy to tell exactly what they looked like, for the nighttime conditions prevented any clear identification of who they were. However, the lightning did offer some subtle silhouettes to fit together at least some description. They were escorting officers, strategically armed and dressed for combat in solid, flat black.

Oddly enough, they didn't wear any sort of traditional uniform of German or European style. Their Denison coats did, however, resemble a special operation of some kind. They were dressed with officer hats and tall, black, shiny boots that resembled German military attire of some sort. No identification was seen on their clothing whatsoever, except for a unique symbol that glimmered once in a while when illuminated by the lightning. It resembled a badge. Really, it was hard to make out any details other than the fact that it shone beautifully with the glisten of gold with every spark of lightning that reflected upon it. One of the men pulled down his hat over his blond crew cut in an effort to block the wind and rain that was pelting him as he ran through the darkness.

Dr. Wycliffe wasn't suited for such a run, due in part to his age or a physical condition. The poor, round-faced man with the soaking wet, white smock, carrying a plastic-covered clipboard and satchel, clearly belonged inside a laboratory or other professional facility somewhere and not out in such dire conditions. Besides being drained and drenched head to toe, he sported no kind of hat at all, which he could have used to shield his bald head and spectacles from the rain. To make his state of affairs worse, he kept wiping his lenses off until he eventually bent his frames, which made him have to stop more frequently.

The man named "Wolfe" was obliged to stop with Dr. Wycliffe, even though he seemed to be the one carrying the authority. Not speaking too much, and in much better physical condition than Dr. Wycliffe, he seemed hardly deterred. Occasionally, he took a grip on the bill of his fedora and pulled it down to shelter his eyes. Suddenly, a break came when a series of lightning strikes revealed the bottom portion of his jaw. It wasn't much, but he continuously clenched like he had the determination to see almost anything through. Literally, come hell or the high water of the storm, he was going to do what he was going to do.

Other than that, there were really no other immediate explanations regarding the purpose of the man in the rear other than listening in on the conversations of Dr. Wycliffe, who piped up and said, "I know this was your idea, but I don't understand why you wished to be here. We have this under control." He went on, "How do you expect to do your job being here anyway?"

Wolfe didn't say a word. In spite of his indisposed presence in back and the eroding economy in Germany, he was very well-dressed for such an event. From the looks of him, his attire must have come from some of the finest tailors in Europe. His clothing was protected with water repellant. It had to be, since the water beaded down every strip of his double-breasted, black trench coat and black fedora like a finely-waxed surface.

The Reichsmark, or literally the *Reich's mark,* was currency at the time. Inflation had its way, shoving the mark's worth down so far it had become a worldly joke. It might have taken suitcase loads just to buy what he wore that night. The mysterious man could afford to dress up that evening, and did so, regardless of the awkward timing and weather.

Perhaps he dressed up for the occasion of what he was gingerly protecting in his arms. It was plain to see that what he was carrying was very dear to him, as he carefully slipped around the jagged rocks, making sure not to fall with his bundle. It was a baby, of all things; the sweet little sounds of a muffled whimper gave it away. As determined of a German as he looked, there must have been a soft side to him too. In a very heartfelt, worried way, he kept looking down at the newborn cuddled away in baby blankets.

The men continued onward, shuffling, bobbing, and tripping across the barren land of jagged rocks and hard, wet sand without a single soul to see them. An occasional splash of a puddle or the sound of a boot striking a boulder could be heard now and then during their desperate skirmish. Dr. Wycliffe's breath intermittently whistled as they slowly made their way closer to a much stronger sound, which soon deafened almost everything behind them, the unmistakable sound of the open sea. Surprisingly, as they got closer, the sounds calmed the tiny nighttime team. They occasionally stopped and smiled, listening to the wild waters as if the ocean was exactly the safe harbor to which they had been running.

Dr. Wycliffe coughed and yelled with every ounce of his tired breath inside the howls of wind and ocean over his shoulder, "I assure you, Wolfe! Nobody has seen us! Our new work in the ODESSA[1] project was well financed! Well organized! It guarantees the baby's top-secret departure." He gasped for air. "Also, just to be sure along the way, your secret baby was marked with our symbol hidden on the back of his head beneath his hair!"

Wolfe stopped dead in his tracks, "No! He will be discovered!"

Dr. Wycliffe backpedaled, "Sorry! We needed positive identification to get him through! The marks are difficult to see! They may fade in time!"

---

1 ODESSA: "Organization Der Ehemaligen SS Angehorigen" is a clandestine organization that helped German military officers and special members escape capture during World War II, using various hidden routes. Rogue members of the Catholic Church assisted them.

Wolfe tried to see the marks for himself, but it was too dark.

Dr. Wycliffe went on. "No worry. All of the other scientists knew he was The One! He will secure a new, peaceful world. For good! As you've said, peace, once and for all! Peace for at least a thousand years! Forget the mark! It's up to the baby now—just as you planned."

Wolfe seemed so disturbed he hesitated before continuing.

Dr. Wycliffe begged, "Please...the B-B route to the Italian port of Bari was hard to get through for the baby's emergency departure. You wanted him undetected. He's going to the safest place on earth, remember? It should not matter."

Wolfe blasted out, "Fool! Review now!"

"Our network, *'Die Spiner,'* was alerted of the special condition...the mark wasn't good enough. Some did not know what it was, so *ODESSA* was placed on his head too! This assured them he was the one...The Chosen One!" He went on, "Absolutely all aspects of this operation were given no chance of mistake...total secrecy. You have to believe me."

Wolfe settled down, then pointed ahead, "And them?"

"Who? Our two special officers? They are never to speak their names again. Their names are US-1 and US-2 from now on...I'll complete their training aboard the vessel. They know their mission. That's all. Nothing more."

Wolfe warily nodded then flagged Dr. Wycliffe to move on.

Just ahead, the two officers stopped briefly to let Dr. Wycliffe and Wolfe catch up. One officer, US-1, smiled cockily, with hardly a loss of breath. He held his lantern up high, signaling where they were. Just then, the lantern's light swung across the chests of their jet black uniforms revealing their symbol once again, except more vividly. It was most unique, glistening in a darker shade of gold, but of a design unlike any other. It was simple, looking like nothing more than perhaps a rolling star encased in an outline of a circle, like an authoritative badge might conceivably look. Interestingly too the golden symbol proudly embossed itself to the left of their chests—right square in front of their hearts. No doubt, it was a symbol dear to them, for they both glanced down at it whenever they got the chance. As Dr. Wycliffe closed the gap between him and the officers, he labored to talk further over his shoulder: "All—*Christ, it's hard to breathe*—all of the equipment and rations are on board the vessel. It was checked—verified by separate technicians—without knowing any details of the mission."

Wolfe caught up with him, "And the medallion?"

Dr. Wycliffe paused to think and then continued jogging: "*Ah*, yes. We used the chain to secure the baby's medallion. It's permanently locked on the baby's ankle." He continued, "All—*whew*, forgive me. I'm not used to this running. I have to stop momentarily."

As he caught his breath, he raised his head up to Wolfe. "Forgive me. All the other scientists were troubled. How do you expect the baby to know with certainty how to get there? More importantly—when to get there."

Wolfe didn't answer, so Dr. Wycliffe began to panic. "Christ O'Mighty—how did you choose him? He's just a baby."

Wolfe lashed out beneath the shadow of his rain-drenched fedora, "He will succeed!"

From the tone of Wolfe's voice, Dr. Wycliffe knew he had overstepped his bounds. Just then, the men became mildly distracted by the sounds of sirens fading off in the distance and the bombs, which had stopped dropping. Coincidentally, the wind and rain had also died down, as if the squall itself wished to hear what was being discussed. The oddity of tempest turning to silence was so overwhelming that all four of them scattered in a loose line, stopping briefly to wonder what happened to their surroundings.

US-2, next to US-1, held his hand out, feeling the air. "It's warmer than it was before."

US-1 stuck his lantern out to shine into the darkness, but saw nothing from any direction.

Farther back behind them, Dr. Wycliffe wasn't shaking off the odd feeling too well either. He grabbed his weak chin, for the secure sense of thinking, perhaps. He then glanced back to Wolfe with a look of fear. Through the borderline of pure darkness, he tried to chuckle. "Odd weather, I guess."

Wolfe himself seemed just as puzzled as he stepped up closer. He stared directly at the ground with a little sense of lost hope. Slowly he brought himself to realize it was just the weather.

Dr. Wycliffe asked again, "Well? All of us back at the lab—back at the facility of—Thule![2] Christ O'Mighty—the whole world depends on this. Who's the boy?"

Wolfe blindly looked around through the dark as he became angry. "Quiet...we've said too much."

Even though he couldn't be seen, he caught his simmering temper with a long, exhausted exhale, like he was tired of it all. He then dropped his face all the way down, revealing more of his regretful sadness. Slowly he lifted his shadowy head, as if clinging to perhaps what little bit of pride he could muster. His pride was in short supply, for he looked to the ground for composure again with a quivering, clenched fist. Desperately, he sought comfort in the midst of his lacking pride and conflicting thoughts. It must have been with great difficulty that he searched through his mind for answers in the pit of the sadness with which he so obviously looked to be troubled.

---

2   Two locations exist when referencing the island of Thule. One is recognized as an actual location, and the other is considered mythical. The recognized one, part of Antarctica, is the southernmost land of the South Sandwich Islands, called "Southern Thule." The mythical one is believed to be at the opposite end of the world, where "Hyperboreans," an Aryan race, lived and where the sun shines twenty-four hours a day.

THE TIME TO TELL

Dr. Wycliffe caught his disturbed silhouette. "Hey! It's just the war! The war's to blame—we haven't died yet!"

His supportive words must have worked, but something else worked too. Through a single flash of lightning, Wolfe caught a tiny glimpse of the baby's bright, blue eyes shining some sort of message that whatever he was dealing with was okay. Surprisingly, the child hadn't been disturbed through this trying time. In fact, the child even returned a smile.

Wolfe let out a hard breath as Dr. Wycliffe suddenly looked relieved too. He took time to pause, wipe the rain from his glasses, and think about Wolfe's hidden problems. Then he hunched closer to the baby. "He's not your baby, is he?"

"No!"

Suddenly, from out of the nowhere, *Cra-crack-crack!*

The shrilling shock of thunder and lightning struck from behind, just beyond the bluff. US-1 and US-2 immediately shook their curiosities aside to sprint ahead again while the weather still allowed.

As the rain and wind eerily emerged again, Dr. Wycliffe and Wolfe paused briefly beside one another. In that very moment, their troubles seemed to fade. Even though they were standing in an increasing torrent of rain all over again, both of their harsh realities seemed subdued by the tiny, magical prospects of the baby and their mission.

Wolfe looked sharply ahead and then began to march forward as Dr. Wycliffe tried to catch up, "Okay, I don't care who he is—Christ O'Mighty—how can we be sure this operation will work?"

Wolfe kept marching, then raised his fist. "It is desire! He will have the strongest desire in the *world!*"

Another hurling crash of thunder and lightning raided their conversation.

Dr. Wycliffe hunkered down. Instinctively, he raised his clipboard and satchel to shield his head against the ambush of electrical fire. In just seconds, continuous bolts of blinding light blasted down across the barren landscape across their path to destiny by the shoreline. Just then, all of them caught their first glimpses of what was chained and anchored against the brunt of the elements. Their vessel was waiting lifelessly, rocking at the edge of the violent sea. She looked desperately like she wanted to save herself, but without a crew to pull her anchors from the seaside, she had nowhere else to hide.

She was stark, cold, and flat black, looking more like a menacing machine than a floating vessel. Such a seagoing vessel could have elicited the curiosity of almost anyone setting eyes on her. Her wraithlike image appeared and then disappeared through the lightning, leaving her first onlookers, US-1 and US-2, begging out loud for more lightning just so they could keep seeing her. Finally, their hardest sprint slowed to a walk.

"We're going to climb aboard that thing?"

"It's not a thing! It's a *she*...and she's beautiful."

Another flicker of bright white lit up the sky, helping to show her entire hull up close, causing US-2 to feel the hair tickling from the nape of his neck. "Su-so...so far, so good—you think?"

US-1's shivering grin widened with the same sort of superficial tickle. He nodded uneasily before turning back to signal with his lantern, then yelled, "Over here! We're here!"

US-2 paced back and forth, looking on with amazement. He then gazed off into the darkness of the cold, black sea in anticipation of what was in store for them. A trip through the great, wide-open unknown, with the sea ship of all sea ships, dazzled his mind. "I can't believe this...I...I mean, look at her."

US-1 stayed still to say in a daze, "She's really something. I can't get used to it...she looks so...so—"

"I know what you're thinking, US-1. They called her the *Wehrwolf* because that's what she is."

THE TIME TO TELL

US-1 smiled and turned back around. "What's taking them so long?"

Though Dr. Wycliffe was still a little way off, he could see the vessel too. He was equally impressed as he gazed upon only a portion of the sleek, angles of the bow where US-1 swung his lantern. He whispered to himself, "What a she-devil. I'll never get over her, I suppose."

He seemed to be the one taking the most pleasure in admiring the look of such a special ship waiting for them. He swallowed tenderly and licked the rain from his lips. With a swift turn of his head, he looked back to the man who continuously conspired to be his inspirational source. The man he gazed back at, carrying the baby, was a trusted friend of his, for he beamed with delight, smiling his biggest smile for the first time that evening.

He couldn't make up his mind which way to look after that. First, it was at the vessel, but then he looked back at Wolfe. Finally, he made up his mind by paying another glance back at the fearless-looking, black figure floating there no more than eighty meters away. He turned back to Wolfe, cupping his mouth to yell, "My whole life has been one wild ride with you!" He went on, "This is it—my ultimate journey. Hope to see you again, my friend—someday or somewhere!"

Wolfe stepped up, quietly shaking Dr. Wycliffe's shoulder with a little dose of confidence and inspiration. His charisma soon grew contagious. Dr. Wycliffe lifted his head as if that was all it took for him to smile again. His emotions ran high, shedding a tear. "I'd better move ahead before the coward shows up in me again." He then shook his fist in the air without an ounce of despair. "This *will* work. I can *feel* it! It *will*! I'm telling you!"

Juiced with confidence once again, Dr. Wycliffe turned and sped into some form of a symbolic victory sprint, just like a youth defying all odds, before slowing back down to realize his age. He turned back to Wolfe, grinning ear to ear.

"The baby must be very special! My associates are working the Island of Thule! They will be coming home—for good now!"

He went on, "We are talking about the impossible journey. Impossible, I said. *Ha haaa.* Oh, and by the way, cutting off all lines of communication is a good idea! Our ship here—the US *Wehrwolf*—she'll be the most fabulous ship on the sea that nobody ever knew! Nobody will ever know."

He carried on. "This is the beginning. The heavens gave us science to bring us peace. Peace for the world." Just then, a powerful bolt of lightning shot down from the sky, startling him. "Oh my God—Christ O'Mighty. If I didn't know better, I'd say we're fighting against the storm too. That was close."

Wolfe slowed down to a stroll as he watched Dr. Wycliffe walk the rest of the way down the beach to meet up with the others. It seemed as though he already knew what his crew was on—an artificial high that wouldn't last for long. Nevertheless, he stayed focused while saving a little sense of amazement just for himself. Reality came down to pinch him on the side. Indeed, he was finally there on scene with his tiny team, in front of his wondrous-looking warship.

He took in the final moments he had apparently been waiting for with strong, deep breaths, but the man deflated down to the lonesome sadness he'd tried to shake off earlier. He gathered his last moments for thought, for reasons known only to him as he touched the nose of his tiny baby. He whispered, "Your mother wished to say good-bye."

All too quickly, he clenched his jaw. Whatever anxiety he had to overcome made his knees buckle. He gasped with the feeling of petrifying pain, but no physical encounter was the cause. Surely, it must have been his own contemplations that railroaded his mind. It had to be a clash of emotions, hammering him from out of the black of night while holding such innocence in his arms. Wildly, he started seesawing, as if he himself didn't know what he was going to do next. Desperately, he twitched back and forth as if one part of him wished to call the mission off, while his countering side wished for him to continue.

His conflicted thoughts slowly subsided. Within a few more battling breaths, he calmed down and looked straight ahead once again. Not much farther down the last stretch of dark and lonely beach, he saw his comrades' silhouettes dancing around the single lantern. They looked so excited, hooting in the night and expressing their fathoms of fun as if they were a wild tribe getting ready for the adventure of their lives. That seemed like enough. Cut between his pinned-up divide, he broke free with one thing on his mind: to follow through with the mission. Operation Wolfe Cub wasn't dead. It was very much alive and well.

Without even a second more, he double-checked the baby's medallion beneath his tightly-bundled quilt. Just like Dr. Wycliffe said, it was locked onto his ankle. He opened the medallion, revealing a hidden locket. He reached inside his suit pocket to pull out a neatly-folded piece of paper. Once more, he felt for the locket, stuffed the note into it, and shut it back tightly, as quickly as possible. With his thumb, he felt around the perfectly-mated surface, making sure it was sealed without a clue about its contents. Decisively, he marched forward, basically forgetting all about what he just did. Nothing could have stopped him after that.

In the interim, all three of his comrades continued frolicking in awe next to their magnificent ship, even though their only lantern might have been ready to go out at any moment from the wind and rain. No doubt they were excited, so excited that US-1 didn't care. He picked up the lantern and flung it out into the sea as if the light of the lightning was good enough to see by itself.

His impulsive stunt was shocking to the others at first. All three of them paused with absolutely nothing to say, except to try and mutter their irritated grievances in the dark. Just then, a little piece of the moon emerged from the clouds, casting slight visibility onto the vessel once again.

Dr. Wycliffe pointed straight up. "Christ O'Mighty…look at that. An omen…this is it. A moon in the storm! I can feel it now."

US-1 and 2 locked at each other and then busted up with laughter while Dr. Wycliffe looked puzzled enough to ask, "Wha-wha…what's wrong? Don't the two of you believe in Christ, the Mighty?"

The two officers slapped their knees, staggering: "*Ha ha*…yeah sure."

"The moon's full too. Can't you tell? Just look beyond the clouds…and we're boarding the US *Wehrwolf, ha ha!*"

Their confidence seemed to grow by the second as they quieted down their laughter all at once. Suddenly, all became serious as they had the chance to see the vessel in its entirety, courtesy of the moon. It took their breath away as she rocked in the waves like no violent ocean could ever disturb her. They seemed hardly scared, but they should have been. The comfort of their vessel distorted the reality of what they failed to pay attention to.

Indeed, perhaps a true omen was above them. From just above in the unadorned, black sky, the violent storm mysteriously paused in the middle of their jokes while they hardly noticed. Far from funny was the fat chance that maybe such an anarchic event circulating around them was, in fact, something to be feared beyond their comprehension. It was there and could have been seen circling, but none of them bothered to look up again, including Wolfe himself.

Perhaps it was just happenstance, like the moon that had appeared. However, the moon was quickly vanishing again. What they didn't see kept them leading on with bravery, and the vessel they were next to fed their fires of desire. Their spirits soared to a new level of celebration as the moon slowly succumbed to the ever-increasing swirls of troublesome, black clouds.

"*Whowa! Hoo-hoo-hoo!*"

"I can't believe it. We're really going to go!"

"Believe it. We're here! Look at what's out there waiting for us!"

"Look out, big, bad ocean, 'cause here we come!"

Dr. Wycliffe calmed them down. "Okay, okay...don't lose your heads...this is it. Remember what you are here for, please." He then looked over his shoulder to Wolfe walking up. "Okay, I want to see respect...quiet. Here he comes. *Shhhh, shhh, shhh.*"

They quickly sucked down to silence as they watched their superior taking his time to walk up from behind. Rather confidently, he swaggered right up a few feet away then stood there straight as an arrow at attention. Obviously, he already heard the dishonorable hoots and cheers. He tried to forget about them for a moment by taking in the smell of the sea, but that ended quickly. Immediately, he focused on each one of them as if he were a drill sergeant looking over a loose platoon. Abruptly, he pushed his way past them to step in front of the vessel and examine its hull.

Dr. Wycliffe stepped closer too. "She's a beauty. At first I thought this was nothing but a dream. I had touched the vessel too. This is all...this is all very real."

US-1 and US-2 quickly stepped up to feel the vessel too. "That's right! We can't believe it either. We can never let it down; we swear it until our flesh becomes the earth."

"Our promise will not fail. We mean it on our lives. Never will we forget the day you gave us this chance."

Dr. Wycliffe held them back. "*Shhhh!* Talk only if he asks, as I instructed." He then turned to Wolfe. "Please excuse them. I regret to say they are still in training. I must say, there was such a diminutive amount of time to get the mission together."

Wolfe seemed undeterred as Dr. Wycliffe stepped up closer to his side to whisper in his ear, "Vessel's complete... she's not fully tested yet, but she will get the baby safely to our US destination. You can be sure...I am positive...if the US *Wehrwolf* malfunctions in any way, it will be because of my crew and me—not you."

Wolfe had heard enough. He stepped back to get a better look at its sleek, serpent-like profile for one last observation, then tended to the baby's whimper as if wanting to hear more. Still, he looked troubled, so Dr. Wycliffe anxiously stepped up. "The vessel's a first generation, I know, but I—I—I assure you...she's the best vessel this world has ever seen...I swear to you she should not fail above or below the water...her submersive capabilities were accelerated above and beyond by me personally. There's no other except for the other prototype we used for additional parts." He went on, "And we will not be discovered, I can assure you that to my grave. The special weapons panel has been verified and checked."

Wolfe ignored the comments as he kept looking over the ship.

Dr. Wycliffe convincingly carried on, "Yes, yes...look at her. Nothing else will ever see her again...nothing, I assure you. You have my word—may Christ have mercy on my soul."

Only then did Wolfe start to relax as he looked back to the two young crew members in the dark. Dr. Wycliffe stepped in front of him. "I promise you. It's just two men, but their training has exceeded my expectations. It would be impossible not to trust them now...you've seen their selective process yourself, no?"

Wolfe looked the other way, pondering with silent cynicism, so Dr. Wycliffe stepped in front of him once again. "I know what you're thinking, but please. They—know—nothing—else. Final training has to take place at sea now. There is no other way, considering the circumstances. They will fight too; I assure—fight to the death."

Wolfe looked down to Dr. Wycliffe's hands, which were holding a radio-controlled, metal box of some kind, with two antennas he had just pulled out from his satchel. Dr. Wycliffe looked down too, realizing what he didn't say and gulped. "Oh, *um*, no it's not what you think it is…it's just a control box, which I can demonstrate. All communications have been aborted from the ship, per your request. We have absolutely no assistance from the outside world. Please, climb aboard and see."

Wolfe didn't bother.

Dr. Wycliffe continued, "My crew has been informed too. No radio means we will engage hostile waters—against either side if we have to." After pausing, he said, "Our top priority is defense only, of course. No combat unless the baby's life is in jeopardy."

Wolfe looked back at the ship, presumably for a final once-over, though he hardly looked convinced. Dr. Wycliffe circled him, continuing on, "Yes, yes. I checked everything myself. She's ready…we are ready. We have no more time. We must go before the tide goes away. We still have to navigate the reefs. I must apologize, but the time is now, my friend…the time to go is now."

Wolfe brushed his chin, then blew out his deep-held breath. "So be it…let it be forever done…carry on."

The peep show of faltering flickers of lightning looked surreal as they repeatedly revealed the danger of what lay in wait out in the ocean just beyond. The rage of the white caps alone looked almost impossible to overcome by any kind of vessel. It was reckless, but the ship braved them, nevertheless. She did indeed fair through the massive waves pounding against her stern so far. Just two chains anchored her down to keep her from floating away on her own. Each heavy, iron link yanked together tightly, testing their iron strength with each passing wave.

This brute of a vessel bore a few more merits worth mentioning. She looked to be a shocking engineering marvel, yet menacing-looking by any ship standards. She was a design of surprise. Clearly her looks were ahead of the times, if one could get past her sinister shape.

Her 1940s construction was evident throughout. Most noticeable was her surface, heavy-laden with crown-headed rivets the size of nickels. Her entire hull mastered the French curve in every way and from almost every angle. Size apparently didn't matter. From the tip of her bow to the bulk of her stern, she wasn't much longer than a school bus.

Her main deck crowned downward slightly at the bow all too beautifully, yet the deck was well-suited to walk on. Presumably, aerodynamics was the answer. Straight down from there on each side toward the stern was a pair of aerodynamically-designed, sturdy fins that resembled dwarfed airplane wings. This pair of eye-openers must have had a purpose beyond making someone look twice, though aesthetics without function began to have notorious effects during the era. Much more remained to be seen of the wings. They spread themselves away from the hull all too gracefully, resembling a modern-day jet more than a watercraft. They gave the impression of being much too short for flying.

Wings and things seemed like only the beginning. Just below these unproven fins were small, glass, oval observation portholes. Accompanying each porthole were smaller portholes beside them without any protective glass at all. They contained the most troubling feature found through the darkness: stout war cannons, looking too intimidating to reveal themselves just yet, so they remained inside. Concealed next to them were other holes. One could call them all "pocket cannons," except the smaller ones contained twin-barreled guns loaded up for double the trouble. Whether she was truly a scientific marvel still remained to be seen, but so far, she resembled the likes of a small, sexy, seagoing warlord.

THE TIME TO TELL

Her space-age cockpit was another example of idiosyncrasies hard to relate to back then. For starters, no space age at the time gave them the ideas. Space craft never really took off the ground until after the war, or did they? If fiction were fact, then there it was as plain as being under a glass bonnet of nighttime sky. Her hatch began with a neatly-contoured, almond shape that barely stuck above the deck. Quite frankly, the drivers inside couldn't see what the engineers were thinking there. However, it did favor a risky style in back toward the stern. What protected the navigators inside seemed like very little. The hatch was nothing more than a sleek, oval bubble of clear glass, which one could only hope wouldn't break. It looked very fragile, but surely had to be tough enough to take on those huge waves gathering momentum behind her at the time.

Deeper inside, size may have mattered more. The entire cockpit itself had plenty of elbow room, with a spacious, well-designed seating area for three elaborate captain's chairs, each of which had its own navigation controls. However, the center chair contained more. It was the one with an optical overhead on top of the glass cockpit.

Another oddity succumbing itself to the character of this free-flying idea of a vessel was her large vertical center fin at the stern. It might have been one of the first things to notice when the men walked up to her. It gave her that cocky, "fair-warning" look of a massive predatory monster relating to a behemoth mechanical shark.

All in all, the most shocking part about her appearance did not relate to super marine crafts or predatory fish. Rather, she struck an idea as far-fetched as the stars. From the pointy bow, all the way back to her sleek trio of fins at the stern, she resembled a miniature, black version of the very first United States Space Shuttle, *Columbia*.[3]

---

[3] The United States space shuttle, Columbia, was first launched April 12, 1981. It has been argued that at least some of its design originated from 1930s German concepts.

Wolfe's shadowy postures expressed serious calculation for his prototype design. He carefully looked over her hull as the flickers of lightning permitted, when suddenly he saw something he didn't like. He hardly jumped for joy when he discovered that the same peculiar golden mark found on the two officer's coats was also on the wings of his vessel. In fact, the golden emblems contrasting against the black body made them quite hard to miss.

Wolfe pointed to the one up on the center fin, which was the size of a large dinner plate, and immediately barked, "Remove it!"

Dr. Wycliffe hesitated. "Please, reluctance chains me. We are proud of it."

US-1 and US-2 stepped up: "No, you mustn't, please. Peace—it's in our hearts as it is on our coats. It should remind us while on our ship."

"Yes, please. It's all we have to look forward to."

Dr. Wycliffe shook his hands, begging: "Please, it's the vision. It's our vision too now. Please, the ship, it will self-destruct. I swear the ship and the symbol will disintegrate by my hand. Give us this guidance to go across the great seas. Please, I beg you."

All three of them paused with little more to say except to wait and see what Wolfe might decide to do next. Suddenly, a strong wave caught their attention as it crashed up beside them. As all of them watched the sudsy foam coast up the beach through the fading moonlight, Dr. Wycliffe sadly wiped the rain from his faced and then readied his remote control box as if he wished to move on. "Please, the tide is moving away. We may come upon dry land soon. We have to go."

Without saying much, Wolfe bowed in utter regret, as if all he'd done up to that point was just short of one great, big, bad idea.

The storm gave them little time. Once more, lightning struck down at a distance with vengeance. At the same time, bright white light shed down on the entire ship, revealing the mysterious golden symbols once again. They gleamed so brightly that Wolfe had no choice but to glance at them for the last time. "So be it...go!"

Dr. Wycliffe quickly focused his attention on the remote control box, pointing the two antennas toward the watercraft. Nervous from his excitement, he turned one of the toggle switches on and waited for a long, few seconds. "Excuse me. It's the tube filaments inside. They take a while to warm up... *ah* yes, here we are. It's coming on now."

A red bulb slowly lit up on top of the box, and chattering noises escaped from the port bow, revealing a gangway ladder extending down onto the beach.

All of them, with the exception of Wolfe, jumped with joy. Quickly, Dr. Wycliffe struck another toggle switch, sending the cockpit hatch spewing a pressurized vapor. Slowly, the hatch opened up, extending an exciting invitation to climb aboard, which they did.

Wolfe looked on from the beach as Dr. Wycliffe came back and reached down from the ladder. "All systems go. Time to give up the baby." As Wolfe hoisted the baby up safely into his arms, Dr. Wycliffe raised his eyebrow as he took the baby away. "Christ O'Mighty, so now he decides to cry...he's acting like he's leaving his father."

He then gingerly took the baby into the cockpit and pressed his controls to close the hatch. At the very moment he sat down, a huge spill of lighting lit up the entire area. Thunder immediately followed, rumbling up through his feet. Everyone inside felt it too as they looked out through the glass. Shock and awe kept them glued to their chairs as they got a good look at their leader left on the beach, silhouetted in the forefront of the lightning show.

Dr. Wycliffe spoke softly to his comrades as they all instinctively tooled with the components of the launch sequence. "Say good-bye to the man that made this possible."

He further muttered, "He's playing God if you ask me," but neither of his comrades heard it, so they begged his pardon to say it again.

Dr. Wycliffe quickly snapped out of his daze and turned his attention to them. "Oh, nothing...it was nothing. Say good-bye to him. That's all I said."

Immediately, he flipped on more of the cockpit lighting. With a brief sense of thrill, he and the others danced their eyes across their instrumentation like children in a candy store. Before indulging, they slowly looked at one another with an awe-inspiring sense of what to do next. Quickly, they continued with their launch sequence, speaking out to one another:

"Closing cross shutters...locking in vapor redundancy."

"Repressurizing bonnet...humidity check done."

"Moisture lowering to normal, five minutes...God that was a lot of rain. Look at our instruments."

"Setting dehumidity levels higher. Better switch to eight or nine...let's get this place dry."

Intriguingly, the triangular seating they were arranged in appeared to work quite well around the panel of components. Directly in front of their view were varieties of brass toggle switches, brass buttons, and three rows of T-handles that pointed to "Navigation," "Transmission," and "Subversive." Ahead of the T-handles, presumably for steering or navigating, were crafty gauges protected in round bubble glass covers, tastefully outlined in brass rings.

Each captain's chair station featured a number of other instruments they seemed to be diligently feeling out. Through their tooling around, one of them quickly repositioned his recliner, while another tested his chair using his shiny, brass wheel cranks just below the cushions. Chair maneuvering seemed to be what he was trying out. It worked as smoothly as a well-oiled wheel with the assistance of ball bearings.

The controls on each of their armrests might have been the reason the chairs move as swiftly as they did. Each of them was furnished with a flip-up pistol grip, complete with a trigger, making the men smile when they tried them out. They were thinking of fun and guns, but they still needed some way to aim. Of course, their source of aiming came from optics, which was hard to miss. They were brass too, intricately crafted with the same touch of class as the rest of their instrumentation. Each was fortified with its own set of crosshairs inside spotting scopes, tucked away in the back of the headrests. Evidently, they just had to flip them in front with a blind grab of the hand.

Dr. Wycliffe's control panel and dashboard were virtually the same as the two navigators on each side of him. He did have a few additional configurations worth mentioning too. His extra controls looked like master controls and labeled above them were the words "Master Override" printed in brass German lettering. They gave every indication that the center seat navigator was capable of operating the entire ship alone.

What seemed to be most intriguing about his master controls was yet another unique set of larger brass push buttons, which looked as if they were designed to be noticeable and easy to press. Without question, these huge controls, the size of small saucers, were intriguing beyond just their size, but the crew didn't pay much attention to them. In fact, they stayed away from them as best they could.

After the formalities of the launch sequence were almost complete, they strapped themselves in quickly and began to relax and look around.

Dr. Wycliffe was the first to carry on by carefully leaning forward to flick on another two switches, turning on an overabundant set of external lights. Slowly, he sat back, pausing a moment to take a breath. As he tended to the baby in his lap, he cast a long look through the rain-speckled glass, as if pausing for thought, then commanded, "US-1—port...start up sequence...activate engines one and two."

First, the rumbling of one, then two large, gas-blasting engines sounded with a shock of hair-raising flare. From the outside, the monster tune of the exhausts sounded like something wildly unexpected.

In contrast was the quiet inside their cockpit. The intrusive sounds found outside were heard far less. The crew felt the rumbling more than anything. Each of them exchanged smiles and snickers like their vessel had just turned into a beast, rumbling with hair-raising vibrations, feeling like music to their ears.

US-2, the one with his foot on the gas, gave a quick test of the throttle. Instantly, the tachometer raced up to the edge of its needle. The mighty engines roared all the way down the beach in both directions. Obviously, the vessel was coupled with double the power, hardly sounding like a coward.

Dr. Wycliffe continued, "US-1, bring in the ladder and sickle anchors...stage sea buoyancy sequence."

US-1 reached forward and methodically flipped a couple of toggle switches, sucking the sickle anchors up into the hull with a huge clunk. At the same time, the ladder chattered back into hiding at the bow, "Externals in."

He patiently waited for the green light to glow and then ceremoniously put his index finger down for a few memorized taps on the sea buoyancy controls, as if he was playing a favorite piano tune. All the while he kept a cocky eye on US-2, and then sarcastically smirked.

Dr. Wycliffe rolled his eyes. "Not this again, you two." He went on, "US-2...activate reverse—slow, damn it! Remember, it's touchy."

US-2 returned the sarcastic smirk to US-1, except with more laziness on his grin. Slowly and tenderly, he pulled his T-handle back as if he was pulling off his first girlfriend's shoe. Just then, a soft jolt of the automatic torque converters kicked in, and a green light began to glow. Ever so gently, the ship removed itself from the sand bar and glided out to sea as free as could be.

US-1 balked. "*Ha*...you made us move. What a surprise."

Dr. Wycliffe scuffed in his chair. "No monkey business. Get serious. Christ O'Mighty...we've wasted enough time. The reefs are higher than ever now."

Without anyone saying another word, the two officers pierced curious looks over the long, sleek bow to catch their last glimpses of where they were just a few minutes ago. As their vessel continued rocking back against the waves, they kept a close eye on the man they had just left behind on the beach.

Wolfe stood there like a black statue, not moving a muscle, as US-2 pointed back to him. "Hey, look...he's finally moving...he must be going away."

US-1 squinted. "I can't see very well. Looks like he's—he's—what's he doing?"

Dr. Wycliffe dropped back in his chair, looking for something with which to wipe off his rain-drenched face and spectacles. "He's not going to do anything. He's going back home—to his tomb. May Christ have mercy on his soul."

US-1 and 2 gasped. "What are you talking about?"

"To his tomb? You mean he's going to die? We should turn the ship around to save him if—"

"Silence, you two! It's true, so best get used to it now. Our homeland's done. Most of Europe...it'll be gone. Consider both of you lucky to be on this mission."

US-2 sat up to the edge of his chair. "Wait, I thought we were on a mission to end wars."

Dr. Wycliffe seemed bothered. "We are. It's the war going on now. That's the problem. You wouldn't understand. It would take me days or weeks to explain what's at stake here...I've got no time for that."

US-1 looked perplexed. "But I thought this was the final peace mission."

Dr. Wycliffe jumped. "It is, and I mean it! I have no time for this. Maybe later...all you two need to know is that it's all up to us...and this baby here." He then pointed outside to the beach. "Wave good-bye to the man of vision before he leaves. Not that he'd wave back...I know him all too well." The two officers waved through the dim, beaded glass.

Wolfe hardly saw them in their dimly-lit cockpit, beaded down with rain in the distance. Their external lights were fading quickly into the turmoil of the blackened sea. He did return a minor self-sense of triumph, however. Calmly, he took off his fedora and faced the troubled sky above him. He looked relieved, but then again, maybe he noticed the sudden temperature swirling around had drastically changed too. In any case, he let the rain pelt down upon his face in the middle of his windy, wet solitude.

For a moment, he looked as though he might have even tried to look beyond the heavy barricade of the solid nothing staring back down on him. At least for a moment, he looked as though something was way up there above him. Showing some concern, he reached up into the distilled sky at what wasn't there—only to draw his hand back down then rub the rain in the empty palm of his hand. Quickly, he shook the feeling off, putting his fedora back on while he continued to unwind with a long, tired, overworked breath. His spirit, on the other hand, wasn't nearly as tired. Methodically, he raised both his hands high into the sky, gesturing the victory of his little accomplishment, it seemed.

Operation Wolfe Cub was indeed underway with some success. Even if this was what Wolfe was so proudly standing there for, his little victory stance could have been misunderstood. Just then, a most unusual surprise came about which could have trampled the beliefs of almost anyone. Evidently, he had no idea of what lurked directly above. If one could see through the nighttime sky, it whirled about with a potently powerful presence. It was the eye of the storm looking down on him and his vessel both.

Wolfe showed no signs of suspicion or fear. The occasional warnings of lightning strikes barely caused him to flinch. He looked like he had something more earthly on his mind at that time. Perhaps he was feeling the minor success of their mission's beginning, and rightfully so. If this were the case, then he did what any winner would have done: he showed pleasure in his small triumph and hoped for further triumphs in the future.

One thing seemed almost too strange, however. It was the weather that became so unnerving, which led up to this lonely, victorious moment of his. It could have been described as being just beyond the imagination. Once more, it was too hard to discard as merely chance or happenstance. It was the beginning of what seemed to be something unforgettable.

Whatever it was, it seemed to follow them through their continued travesty inside the storm that evening. It filled the nightscape with fire and ire, sending chiseling charges of blinding lightning so bright that anyone might have taken it as a signal. It caught up and then quaked beneath their feet so deep that anyone should have stopped to think. It was so bizarre that it could have even challenged the worst of pessimists to question their bounds of believability. No paradox this profound should have existed along that stretch of beach within the vast sights and sounds of merely the forces of thunder and lightning. But it was there. It was preposterous to believe such a quantum leap was possible, or worse yet— unleashed.

If the truth was known, something else horrific and unknown besides Operation Wolfe Cub began that evening. It was unlike anything baring a resemblance to normalcy— far from it. It was as if some *thing* reached into the facets of existence where the very fear of reality actually resides here on earth. Petrifyingly so, its shrilling existence echoed from out of the thin, black air, but could be seen—absolutely nowhere.

Ssssskakaka Ka Kaaaaaaaaaah!

Inside the warm, dry, and nearly soundproof cockpit of the US *Wehrwolf*, the crew heard only the crashes of thunder mixed in with muscular-sounding exhaust. They saw only what was there outside. The three of them all gazed in awe at the light show, which, by then, encircled the beach before them. The spectacle just came and went without leaving a sign behind. It was as if nature and whatever other forces were working performed a vanishing act before their very eyes.

Through the safety of their ship's cockpit, US-2 rested his head back on his headrest in a sort of collapsed state of shock. He withered down in relaxation to say, "Wow, did you see that?"

US-1 asked, "See what? I didn't see anything."

US-2 saw that his comrade's face was buried in a towel. He withered again in his chair and then lit a cigarette with his silver lighter. "What do you mean 'what?' You couldn't see a thing with that towel on your face…the lightning out there. Wolfe, or whatever Dr. Wycliffe called him…he didn't even move a muscle when all that lightning struck. He must have nerves of steel."

US-1 rocked back into his chair then stared into the night. Another flash of light lit up the cockpit when he looked over his shoulder. "Was that really him, Dr. Wycliffe?"

US-2 had to add, "Yeah, was that really him? Neither of us could see a damn thing all night."

Dr. Wycliffe, while holding the infant in his arms, took a deep breath and then felt for something in his upper pocket. He took out a small, silver flask that flashed their faces. He unscrewed the cap then took a quick mouthful and held it. With closed eyes beneath his foggy glasses, he swallowed in relief. His small drink might have given him food for thought.

Finally, he nodded, then grabbed US-1's towel to dry his face next. "You mean you two never saw him before? That was he, my boys."

He then wiped off his spectacles while he whistled a soft breath of relief. As the cockpit began to warm up a little more, he slowly moved to click on the small metal blade fan in front of him. "*Ahhh*, that's better." He closed his eyes to let the warm breeze dry his face while US-1 and US-2 looked at each other as if they were not going to let him off the hook quite so fast. "Why do you call him Wolfe?"

"Yeah, why is he Wolfe? Is it a code name like ours?"

Dr. Wycliffe carefully put his spectacles back on then took another small sip, with no apparent hurry to answer their curious query. He squinted then swallowed again. His comrades' stares weren't going away, so he looked back at the two of them and shook his head, smirking. "Because that's his name. Besides, I think deep down, he sees himself as a wolf."

US-1 rebutted, "But I thought—"

"You thought nothing...I'm in command here. He chose you two, didn't he? Give the dead man what he wants, for God's sake."

Dr. Wycliffe quickly explained. "Okay, now, as hard as it may be for both of you, I'm qualified to be in charge—fully. First, let me start by saying that you should call me 'Doc.' I don't feel like being too formal anymore. Second, stop thinking this mission is too big—even though it is." He muttered to himself, "Christ O'Mighty, *this is big*. What am I saying? Erase what I just said...do your job as if it is the most important thing in the world."

US-1 and 2 both nodded.

"Yes, Doc."

"Okay, Doc, no problem."

Doc went on, "My first line of business...US-1 is the midshipman—"

US-2 threw his arms up. "*Ah,* I knew it even before we even got on board."

Doc politely waited, then tried to finish his sentence. "As I was saying …Number One is the midshipman who will be in charge should something happen to me. Now, as for you, Number Two, if you would be so kind as to continue backing into the waves so we can turn around and get out of here."

Doc shook his head as if problems had already started when they hadn't even begun. Still, he shrugged it off and began commanding: "Go ahead and turn her around in thirty seconds…then get us in drive…we've got to make time. Number One… set the sonar and depth-finder…check the underwater reefs…give me some depths. And Number Two? When the time comes, set the forward navigation controls on automatic…fifteen knots until we break the waves."

US-1 reported. "Checking…reefs are barely going to clear, Doc."

Doc moaned. "*Hmmm*…sounds a little rough going out. Be sure buoyancy is set to maximum."

Just about then a good-sized wave hit the stern, barely rocking the ship. They looked overhead and watched the suds silently coast over the glass.

Doc took another nip from his flask and said with a changing smile, "Well, US-1, US-2…here's to you two and the US *Wehrwolf*…oh, and this baby here too, of course. We're headed for—where?"

US-1 and US-2 chuckled. "The United States."

"Yeah, *ha ha*…Theee United States of A-mericaaaa! I'll drink to that."

Chapter 2

While Wolfe still stood on the beach, he watched the vessel quickly vanish through the smashing waves until nothing of it was left to see. He stood there for quite some time afterward, long enough to at least notice the storm this time. The brunt of the storm had quickly vanished out to sea with the vessel. While choosing not to be in a hurry, he took his time to turn around and begin his long trek back to wherever it was he had to go.

He didn't get very far when he sensed an unexpected presence inside the nightscape just ahead. Upon second glance, he apprised himself that it had to be an intruder directly in front of him no more than twenty meters away. Once he got a focus on the person's faint silhouette, he also noticed that the intruder was watching him from the vantage point of a small bluff.

Quickly, he threw back the flap of his trench coat and drew his Luger pistol to fire when he heard the voice of a woman cry, "Don't shoot! It's me!" Unpersuasively, she cried again, "Please! I know you have a gun! It's *me*!"

He must have known exactly who she was because he slowly relaxed the tension off his trigger finger. He drew back, holstered his pistol, and looked down in shame. Though terribly disturbed, he quietly asked, "Why are you here?"

"I *had* to come. The baby's mine too."

Their encounter seemed quickly revealing. Both of their silhouettes looked like wilting tree stumps stuck in muck, ready to rot the rest of the way into the lifeless ground beneath them. It was an awkward moment that dragged on for some time in utter silence. Their shadows pondered before either of them really knew what to do or say to one another.

Finally, a remnant of life gave Wolfe some reason to look back up after he heard the sounds of the whimpering woman growing too loud to ignore. She scared herself when she turned on her flashlight. The light was so dim, it looked like it had been on all evening. She couldn't get it to turn off, so she dropped it to the ground and muttered, "It's morning time now." Without the aid of her flashlight, she staggered and tripped over the rocks toward Wolfe.

Their futile, lost feelings seemed mutual, for Wolfe had already begun making his way directly to her too. They knew each other all too well, for their reactions to come to one another went without saying. At the last second before their embrace, he opened his arms just in time to catch her limp body collapsing completely. She was the one slated with pain the hardest. Her mourning seemed to escalate into misery with just the touch of his hands. Their dreadful midnight meeting came at a great price, for her weeping and sobs swelled into outbreaks of cries that sounded like they'd last forever.

She broke down gingerly, thumping on his chest. "I know I was supposed to be far away. I made a mistake, an incredible mistake…I never should have let him go."

Wolfe replied, "How did you find me?"

She sobbed, "Dr. Wycliffe told me. He made me promise not to say. I didn't…I'm sorry. I just had to see our…our son…one last time…he's gone, isn't he? Say something, will you? Is he gone? You said he wouldn't really be gone. He's really not gone—is he? He's going to be a fine boy someday? Please, tell me again. He's going to live. He will live, won't he?"

Wolfe looked out to the sea of darkness. The moonlight barely reflected the angry mood in one of his blue eyes. "He will live."

THE TIME TO TELL

"How can you know?"

"He now has the desire...even if he has to go to hell and back, he will look and find. I'm counting on him."

She gasped. "The note! You said you were giving him a note. What's it about? You didn't tell him we were not—we were not—"

"I did not. We will marry...our wedding will be soon—if it's the last thing I do."

Further out to sea, inside the cockpit of the US *Wehrwolf*, US-2 was deeply devoted to navigating, slowly turning the ship around, but before he could get the vessel about, a massive wave came into sight along the port side.

Doc yelled out, "We're testing again! Hold on!"

Swoooooosh!

The ship barely even rocked as the wave completely engulfed their vessel.

Separately, the crew opened their eyes, spewing their relief. All was pleasantly dry inside their cockpit, of course. As treacherous as the storm tried to be, all they could see was the beautiful, pure white foam drizzling down off the glass in front of them.

US-1 and 2 broke out just short of shouts. "Wow! It's okay. We're okay. Our ship is taking the worst of it."

"Oh wow, you didn't cover this in training?"

Doc smiled as he tended to the baby. "Yes, indeed. It caught me by surprise, though. We should be able to withstand a lot more than just a storm. Wait and see, my good friends. Wait and see."

US-2 reported, "We're about face, Doc...straight ahead, doing fifteen knots."

Directly in front, within view of their front floodlights, another wave, twice as tall as the last, came up way too fast. Doc held onto the baby as he strained to watch. "Brace yourselves...another incoming."

Swoooooosh!

US-2 scratched his chin of blond whiskers, grinning. "You know...I could get used to this."

Doc carried on. "Set a base course, US-1"

"Okay, I'll get on it."

Doc quickly unbuckled his safety belt then got up with the baby as if he was unexpectedly leaving when US-1 asked, "Where you going?"

"Well, my cheerful two crew members. *Ahem*...it's time to put this here baby to bed down below. I think you boys can figure out the rest of the evening without me." He turned to walk away then turned back again. "Well...can you?"

Both officers smirked all too confidently.

"Yes, Doc."

"No problem, Doc. All under control."

Doc nodded away his disbelief and slipped down below, but before he went totally out of sight, they stopped him again. "Wait, Doc...what's his name?"

"Yeah, our precious cargo you're taking away. He's got a name, doesn't he?"

Doc looked coy as he pondered for a moment. Actually, he looked as if he'd almost forgotten. Finally, he sputtered, "*Uhh, um*, the name...Christ sakes, I just had it...his name is *err um*—oh yes...it is Randolf. Yes, yes, Randolf's his name."

US-2 held back his laugh. "What? Rudolph?"

Doc glared. "No...it's Randolf. Don't be silly now...get serious on this mission."

US-2 smiled. "Oh, Raaandolf, I see...Randolf."

US-1 unbuckled himself then reached out with a smile looking more like joy than jokes. "Can I see him, Doc?"

US-2 caught on quickly, unbuckling himself too. "Yeah, I'd like to see who it is we are transporting here."

Doc studied the two faces dubiously before finally giving in. "I suppose it wouldn't hurt anything...here you go. He looks like a skinned toad if you ask me."

THE TIME TO TELL

US-1 grinned. "*Aw, nah*...ladies think he's a cute thing. He smells like a toad, though. I'll give you that. *Whew*...he needs a change."

US-2 handled him next. "So he's the lucky boy with the one-way ticket out of hell like us, *huh*?" Randolf grabbed his pinky finger. "Oh, look at that! He's a strong little bugger... good grip...he's a man."

Doc gently took him back. "Yes, yes, yes, healthy, strong boy. He's had a healthy, hard night too. Time to go below before our luck runs out. Mark my word, he'll probably start crying. So far we're lucky he's not...now you both know what to do when we hit open water?"

US-2 quickly sat back down and got back to business. As he tapped his fingers, patently showing no patience, he finally answered, "Yes, Doc, we know. Engines off...go to stealth propulsion and submerge."

Doc kindly asked, "And what else, may I ask?"

US-2 blew through his cheeks. "Automatic navigation... I'll remember."

US-2 yawned with boredom all too quickly. "Yeah...we know."

Suddenly, Doc poked his head back up on deck. "And they recline too. Christ, what's that smoke?"

US-2 took another drag from his cigarette then leaned heavily on his armrest while US-1 felt the sealskin on his chair with his fingertips. "Don't worry, I turned on the oxygen filtration."

Just then, Doc popped his head back up on deck, sort of surprising them this time. "Oh, I forgot. US-2...you're on first watch tonight."

US-2 turned back to face him. "What? I thought you said US-1 was midshipman. He should be first watch!"

US-1 smiled as he reclined his chair. With the purpose of bothering his comrade next to him, he put his hands behind his head then smiled even more. "*Ah*, yes, I can begin to like this."

Doc then tried to remember something else, but he couldn't quite put his finger on it until he snapped his fingers. "Oh, yes…one more thing. Don't forget to hit the scale shutters over the glass before you go to sleep."

Both officers looked at Doc as if they might never get him off deck. Doc, on the other hand, looked a little worried when he saw them acting a little too complacent. "No, I'm not kidding, you two…you'll get the Holy Christ scared out of you if you don't…do what I say, I mean it."

US-2 gave a halfhearted German salute with his cigarette between his fingers. "Yeah, sure, not a problem for me."

US-1 symbolized his lack of concern with a dainty salute of his own. "Okay, Doc, I'll see to it our buddy here, Number Two, will shut the shutters. Is that right?"

"Right, Mr. Midship."

Doc studied them with a peculiar eye before shrugging his shoulders. As he again went out of sight, he muttered, "I told you anyway…nothing too damaging, I suppose. Trust me…you literally may see what I mean, soon enough. Okay, good night, sleep tight, don't let the big fish bite."

Back down the ladder he went with Randolf. Just a few more short steps further through the bulkhead, he strolled his way right up to a sophisticated bubble contraption, which turned out to be a baby crib in the main sleeping quarters. He felt the glass to see if it was the temperature he liked, and it was. Next, he changed the baby. Immediately therafter, he turned on a couple of brass wheel cranks just above, released the pressure inside, then opened up the door and placed Randolf inside the nice bed of white linens already made for him. In addition to routine matters of tucking a baby in bed, he strapped him in securely with built-in safety belts. Finally, Randolf was ready to go to bed, so he closed the lid, turned the brass wheel cranks to pressurize the crib once again and then read the gauges to ensure optimum conditions. Tucking Randolph in for the night seemed finished after that.

THE TIME TO TELL

In no time at all, Doc hung up his white smock and clothing and placed his shoes in the billet next to the baby and plopped down on a bed of his own, which looked much more normal than Randolf's. Apparently, this was all it took for him to fall sleep. Within a minute, he began to snore away his day of alacrity.

Back on deck, the other two crew members proved to be just as exhausted. They leaned more and more toward lethargy.

US-2 yawned then put his cigarette away in a nearby ashtray, "How's the echo sounder?"

US-1 yawned back at him, while he labored to stay awake. "All clear down to twenty fathoms."

US-2 then pushed his lazy hand forward to hit a few of his kill switches. "Switching engines off....take over. I'm done."

"Okay, taking over...submerging sequence...preparing for stationary dive...initiating negative buoyancy."

After US-1 nearly completed his tasks for submerging below the surface, he looked over to his comrade. "You watching this?"

"Watching what? You playing like a *submarine boy* or something?"

After US-1 gained his comrade's attention, he methodically rolled his fingers onto his T-handle, as if he was about to begin a submersion ceremony. He then pushed gently forward with a quirky smile. "Submerging to the underworld, my friend. The goddess of blackness appears before you to take you away *hu huuu*...you're going dowwwn, US-2...you're going all the way dowwwn."

US-2 spewed as he shook his head from such nonsense. To answer him back, he just reclined his chair and rolled over on his other side to look out his part of the glass. "*Shhhhh*, get over it. You're the ass-wipe going down, not me."

"Hey, Number Two, you have to stay awake, remember? Close the scale shutters."

"Yeah, yeah...I'll get around to it."

Soon thereafter, jokes were set aside for something more soothing. Their thoughts quickly lent themselves to more lethargy as they watched their ship slowly begin to dip beneath the surface. In no time, the ocean's restless waves washed over the deck and up to the rim of their cockpit glass. Surely, it raised the minor thought that they were sinking. In a sense, it might have been the ocean's pretense to poke them with a sinking joke. Neither of them spoke a single word while they submerged. Only after they submerged completely could one see the bliss in their eyes. It was the abyss that captured them most.

US-1 almost looked like he purposely waited a good while before he finally turned the underwater lights on.

US-2 quivered with goosebumps then jumped to snicker about it. "*He he,* yeah, *whu-ho*...yeah, *he he*...if you're trying to scare me, it didn't work, you prick. Are you forgetting? I get off on this kind of shit...is it great or what?"

US-1 reclined his chair then relaxed with his hands behind his head. "*Ahhh* yes...smooth as glass, Blondie...life doesn't get any better than this. First we're on top, now we're not...all in the nice, warm comfort of our sealskin chairs... so, the lights didn't scare you *huh*?"

US-2 huffed, "You're going to have do better than that, Curly...*ahhh,* life doesn't get any better than this...hey, listen real hard...so quiet."

US-1 switched the rest of the lights on, completely lighting up the empty, dark, watery scenery around them. Slowly and willfully, a few small schools of tiny fish drifted past, soothing their eyes as they rocked back and forth with them. In the midst of almost being hypnotized by the little fish, US-2 muttered, "How different two worlds can be. Who woulda thought I'd get this chance. And you? What about you?"

US-1 didn't really answer immediately. Instead, he reached for more controls then flicked a few more toggle switches. "Okay, this should do it. We're deep enough... switching to stealth propulsion...right about...nowwww. There now...all good, set to gyro-pilot for the evening."

US-2 barely heard a word. He almost fell into a daze, looking out into the haze of blue as far as their lights could see. He muttered, "So, what are you going to do when we get to America?"

"Who me? I haven't really given it much thought."

"I know...you'd better find a job because you'll be out of one when we land."

US-1 put his hands up behind his head. "I suppose you're right for once. *Hmmm,* maybe I'll start a business or something. I don't know. What about you?"

US-2 started picking his fingernails, thinking. "Hey, I know. I'm gonna track me down one of those American women—maybe get a farm. You know, settle down or something."

US-1 snickered. "What? You? Settle down? When hell freezes over."

"What? You don't believe me? Well, maybe I'll try out a few before I settle down first. I read about it. That's what they're starting to do over there. There's supposed to be bright lights, dancing girls, big cars. I mean *big*. And money everywhere...I can buy whatever I want."

US-1 shook his head, spewing, "Free to do as you wish, I guess. You should fit right in."

"What's wrong with that?"

US-1 ignored him, basically thinking himself into a trance before he began to yawn. He closed his eyes, only to struggle with opening them again, and then yawned through his speech, "Buoyancy set on automatic...depth set to fifteen fathoms."

As their vessel began to slow, the schools of fish caught up with them again, except this time they tried to look inside the glass porthole closest to where Randolf was seen sleeping in his crib. Then suddenly, without explanation, the entire school of fish swirled up to the bow of the vessel and began to dazzle themselves on top of the deck where the underwater lights shone the brightest.

US-2 pointed out the fish. "Hey, look at those silver sides. Looks like they're playing…maybe they like me or something, *huh?*"

"*Naaa*…not you…got to be the baby. They came to greet him, you clown. Get off it."

US-2 carried on, "No, it's me…the last one they want to see is you. Try not to scare them off with your face, will you?"

US-1 smiled. "If they came to see me, they'd be stuck to our glass, kissing it. Then they'd jump in my frying pan after I snap my fingers."

"*Ho ho*…whatever you say. Looks like I've got a dreamer on deck."

US-1 reclined in his chair, dipping further into a daze as he watched a larger school of fish swoop in to try to eat the smaller school.

US-2 looked mildly surprised. "Dog-eat-dog world out there…look at those bigger fish trying to gobble up those poor, little guys. What kind are they anyway?"

US-1 yawned. "Don't know…some kind of sea bass. Say, are you all right staying awake? I mean, I can maybe try to stay awake for you."

"What? You kidding me? I'm fine."

"Are you sure?"

"Sure I'm sure…go to sleep if you have to…we've got a big day ahead of us tomorrow."

Immediately, US-1 took him up on it. Within seconds, he was out like a light.

Surprisingly, US-2 didn't last nearly as long as he thought he would. Almost as quickly as his comrade, he dozed off in his chair too.

THE TIME TO TELL

Soon, both of them slumbered below the wide-open, titan sea. Blackness gloomed everywhere beyond their lights as they glided through the water on autopilot, steady and straight. Their vessel was only a speck in the immense abyss just outside their cockpit.

Safely tucked in and warm inside the US *Wehrwolf* was the supposed guardian crew, holding the baby golden egg of world peace. They were quite a special team, it seemed. Now they dreamed into no-man's-land while their vessel cruised along seamlessly, without a wakeful pilot to guide them.

Though there was quietness of the great ocean beneath, all wasn't quiet inside the vessel. While all the snoring was going on, the baby was lucky to be isolated in his capsule where he couldn't hear too much of anything. Randolf was the one among them who didn't seem sleepy at all. To the contrary, his eyes were wide open, bright and blue, looking for something fun to do. It didn't take him long to find it either. Just outside his porthole window, something shadowy was keeping up with the vessel.

It was immense enough to completely shade the multitude of navigation lights on the port side of the vessel all at once. After several more of its shady passes, it revealed only a portion of its scarred-up, white underside before unintentionally showing its huge rows of chiseled teeth.

It was a monstrous great white shark, which revealed more of itself when it swam up to the cockpit of the vessel to take a better peak inside. Much to the old shark's delight, two healthy-looking men were lying motionless, wrapped up in real sealskin chairs. It didn't take long for the shark to want a bite of them, but it soon discovered an invisible bubble of glass. Still, the shark was determined, so it began bumping into it with its nose.

Bump. Bump. Bump.

US-2 moved to his other side, mumbling, "Knock it off... trying to sleep."

US-1 kept snoring when suddenly he heard it again.

Bump…bump, bump.

He opened one eye. "Knock it off, I said…what? *Aaaah-AAawwwww!*" US-2 crashed out of his chair and immediately backpedaled until he fell again all the way down to the cabin below, next to where Doc was sleeping.

Craaaaaassssh!

US-1 woke up to the same ugly sight. "*Aaaah-AAawwwww!*" He cried out too before backpedaling and falling right on top of US-2.

Thud! Crash! "*Guuuuuuuuch!*"

Doc jumped out of his bed, looking like the entire ship was sinking, until he saw his crew tangled up with each other on the floor. Without saying a thing, he looked at them for clues, but all they could do was grab their heads and moan. As quickly as he could, he rushed up to the main deck and looked around, but nothing was there. The controls, their chairs, the deck, and even the scenery outside were all clear and fine.

US-1 hobbled up on deck, rubbing his knee then pointed out into the abyss. "It was out there—a monster shark."

US-2 poked his angry face up on deck. "Son of a bitch… you fell right on top of me, you bastard, you!"

US-1 helped him up on deck. "It's your fault, Mr. Carefree…you didn't flip down the blinds like Doc said!"

Doc looked back and forth. "Shark? What shark? Blinds? *Ohhhh*, the shutters? *Hmmph*, I see. You two left the scale shutters open! *Dummkopfs!*[4]"

US-1 pointed his finger to his comrade. "No, not me… US-2 went to sleep and forgot. I told him to shut the damn things down."

US-2 blurted, "Who cares! It was a monster shark. His head was gigantic! I mean big enough to swallow all our chairs right there!"

---

4 "Dummkopf" is German slang for a clumsy, unintelligent person.

THE TIME TO TELL

Doc whipped his head back, then squinted out into the abyss without his spectacles on, "*Hmmm, dummkopf*....there's nothing out there. Can't you see?"

US-1 walked up to the edge of the glass and looked out. "I'm sorry about this, Doc, but—I—I saw it too. It was maybe twenty meters long—as big as the front of this ship."

US-2 stepped up from behind, "More like twenty-five or thirty meters long, damn it. It was huge—right there—in front of our faces."

Doc moved aside chuckling. "I don't have time for fish stories."

Just about then US-2 spotted another shark, half the first one's size, circling the bow. "Look, Doc, see?"

Doc hissed, "*Pssss*, that? Get a hold of yourself, Christ O'Mighty. You two are beginning to worry me already." He then pushed a button on the control panel, closing the scale shutters, "I told you two to close the shutters. Now don't forget next time."

Just as Randolf began to cry below deck, Doc scolded, "There, look, see what we did? We woke him up...one of you stay on watch. I don't care who it is. I've got to go down and try to quiet the poor lad. We've got a big day ahead of us—don't forget...I'd best be gone for now to get some sleep."

Chapter 3

The next day's bright, early morning spread itself across the wide, open sea. No discernible trace of light, however, was readily visible inside the US *Wehrwolf* beneath the surface. A sound came into the cockpit before the sunlight did. An alarm clock suddenly sounded off at the feet of both officers on deck, who were sleeping all too deeply. To the irritated and foggy dismay of just one of them, it kept ringing.

US-1 was awakened by it first. It took some time before he realized the dreadful clanging sound intruding his dreams wasn't supposed to be there. It was coming from somewhere on deck. Slowly, he began the dizzying task of finding the noisy nuisance. Since his eyes didn't want to open too well, he felt around for the alarm clock first. That didn't work, so squinty-eyed, he staggered to the more plausible areas where the obnoxious alarm clock should have been. It wasn't anywhere in sight, so he relied more on his ears, which were rattling from the sides of his head. Unfortunately for him, the entire cockpit sounded like an alarm clock.

Frustration bubbled, until finally, he started to get used to the ringing. In the midst of his mild quandary, he glanced over to US-2, only to be splashed by a new frustration. Jealousy must have looted what little bit of good feelings he had, as he noticed his comrade was still fast asleep. To make matters worse, he even looked comfortable while the alarm clock kept up its ear-piercing assault.

Finally, US-1 found the clock. It was hidden in one of the most inconspicuous areas on the floor, beneath the control panel and in a place where he could barely stretch far enough to grab onto it. He spewed with disbelief that it was actually there until he got ahold of it. After shutting it off, he looked at it for a short time, wondering why someone would set it in such an area in the first place. The puzzling idea wasn't worth the weight of the clock itself, so he pitched it aside and nudged his comrade. "Hey, wake up…it's. It is oh-six hundred hours…did you bring the stupid alarm clock on board?"

US-2 rolled over, stretching. "No…Doc must have brought it…you took long enough to find it. You're so lame."

"What? You mean you were awake? Why didn't you get up and find it yourself? It was right next to your feet!"

"Because I knew you would."

US-1 opened the scale shutters. "Well, I guess that's all the relaxation we're going to get for now. 'Tis another day of glory and greatness to be put to rest for Operation Wolfe Cub."

"What's that supposed to mean?"

US-1 shrugged his shoulders then scratched his armpit. "Oh, nothing. You wouldn't understand. Wow, look…look at the instruments. We covered a lot of distance last night."

"Yeah, well I'm curious to see what the weather's like above us…that was one spooky storm last night. If I paid attention to myself any more, I'd swear the devil was riding in on it."

"Wild comments you have…it's called 'sixth sense.' Anyway, you don't have it."

"If I don't have it, nobody's got it…why don't you get yourself on your submarine controls and get us up to see the damn daylight."

US-1 positioned himself in his chair more appropriately and began switching toggles and turning on knobs. "Okay—sounds fine with me. Switch on a few lights and—okay, got it…a switch or two here and there—got it…sequence is set.

Buoyancy control next... almost done...we are headed up to see the surface right about...nowww. Stealth propulsion is good...you ready, Blondie?"

"Well, yes, that's what I was saying."

"Stand by for your part when we get there. We're preparing a stationary ascent."

"How far do we have to go? How deep are we now?"

"Just about seven fathoms to go, looks like."

US-2 grabbed his pack of cigarettes, lit one, and cocked back in his chair, thinking. Mildly amused with himself, he blew his first thin stream of smoke and watched it curl up across the glass of the cockpit. "*Ah*, yes. It looks like it's sunny up there to me."

"*Huh?* How can you see? Looks like smoke and fire."

US-2 took another drag from his cigarette. "There's no fire up there. What are you talking about?"

"I meant your cigarette fire."

"Oh, does it bother you?"

"Not yet." US-1 leaned over to switch on the fans, dissipating the air throughout the cockpit.

Soon, the sunlight's rays became overwhelming the closer they got to the surface. The splendor of sparkles raised smiles across their faces as colorful prisms of light started to cast all over inside. Right at the surface they crested into the brightest point, which sparkled so intently that it was difficult for them to adjust their eyes.

When their vessel broke onto the surface, she did so quickly, leaving nothing more than gleaming streams of water trickling down her flat, jet-black surface. The day was grand. Even last night's wind was gone. In fact, almost all of the morning's beginnings were cheerful, from the clear blue ocean to the silver-lined clouds. It looked like a wonderful day to come.

Both of them were still without Doc on deck, who was presumably still sleeping. They seemed not to care, for they were too busy glancing around at the prevailing sense of goodness that surrounded them. US-2 rocked back in pure pleasure as he felt the sealskin of his seat. While he played with a puff of smoke, he tried hard not to speak his mind, but then he grinned. "Are we still on stealth propulsion?"

"Yes, of course we are, why?"

US-2 quickly buckled in his safety harnesses. "I thought so…shut it down. We need to pick up some real time."

"What?"

"Yeah, look out there. The ocean's flat."

US-1 grinned then buckled himself in too. "I thought you'd never ask…okay then…buoyancy is normal…stealth propulsion now off…take over, Blondie. Let's see about your job now." He then leaned back in his chair with his hands folded behind his head. Before he got too comfortable, he looked over his shoulder. "You don't suppose Doc is awake do you? Maybe we shouldn't—I mean, you know. Don't get too crazy on your controls."

US-2 saw his comrade chickening out all too quickly as he put all of his controls into motion. On a whim, he wiggled his cigarette to the side of his mouth as if he was an old pro-operator in the brand-new prototype ship of theirs. While scratching on his whiskers of his day-old beard, he obliged his comrade briefly to answer. "*Naaaa*. He'll sleep through it…maybe he needs a little alarm clock too. Don't you think?"

US-1 contemplated the question, then raised both his eyebrows, snickering, "A wake-up call, you mean? We might not find him hiding his clock beneath our feet anymore."

That was all that US-2 wanted to hear. At least for now, the inaudible mischief-maker returned his gesture with more pointless overtures and then took his cigarette out of his mouth. He gazed at its burning ember, then blew on it, making it brighter, before muttering, "Did I catch that or am I just hearing things?"

US-1 looked like an angel hiding behind a thorn bush. "Catch what? I didn't say anything."

US-2 immediately attempted to turn their special mission vessel into some kind of fun-filled, radical hydro-jet boat before its time. As he turned and sparked up one of the engines, he grinned. "Oh, I've got the guts, my buddy… the question is—do I have enough petrol to prove it?" He started up his second engine then rumbled with the foot throttle just a little too much.

By then, US-1 started to look as if perhaps what they were racing into might be a little too fast. With every thrust of US-2's touchy gas pedal, the mighty vessel's side tipped down deep into the water, showing off her torque.

Just a tiny bead of sweat looked like it wanted to escape US-1's forehead when he glanced over his instrumentation. Tepidly, he looked straight down the long sleek nose of their new jet boat-to-be and thought twice about saying, "You sure you want to do this?"

"*Aw*—how nice of you. I thought you'd never ask."

US-1 swallowed carefully. "I mean, I don't know if this is such a—"

"How's it looking out there? Over the bow—see any whales or anything in my way?"

"Wha-what?"

"Haven't got all day. Get serious, how we looking—or are you really second in command?"

US-1 took a deep breath as he smiled with regret. "Okay, if you say so…this is the Midshipman. Our signaled course is set. We're in the Mediterranean on a bright, beautiful, wonderful day. Test time conditions seem optimal."

"*Huh*? Damn it to hell! Are you ready?"

US-1 nodded tentatively. "You heard me…we're good to go—dead ahead—for a few kilometers anyway."

"That's what I want to hear. Blasting for the Strait of Gibraltar is what I know—all the way."

THE TIME TO TELL

"That's right, Gibraltar here we come. Let 'er rip!"

"Then it's to the Atlantic."

With one big stomp, US-2 dropped his foot on the gas, unleashing the misery of burning combustion into not one, but two, wild-sounding engines at the same time.

Booowaaaaaahhhhh!

Massive amounts of motor hunkered down somewhere in the back. The power of horses collided with forces. From gas blowing up into combustion, the power punched its way down to those poor, little fellers called propellers.

Waaaaaaaaaaahhhhh!

"The US *Wehrwolf* had every intention of leaping out of her skin, but not without testing her engineers, who wished to keep her together first. From a standstill she blew, instantly slapping her two rear wings into the water. Her stern barely stayed above the water when pure power came to meet with the smooth, flat ocean. Something had to give, and it wasn't their ship. Two huge jet streams blasted high into the sky behind them. She took off all right, looking like she'd turned on a pair of fire hydrants to full blast.

In their surprising launch, neither one of the officers could move a muscle, but the neighboring wildlife sure did. Seagulls fled for their lives, and the fish did too. While the forward force kept them stuck to the seats of their pants, nothing else escaped them, except ear-shattering yells:

"*Aaaawwhhhh!* Holy *shhhheeaawh!*"

"*Yeeeeaaaaaaw!* Son of *beee-aaawh!*"

Down below deck, Dr. Wycliffe's deep sleep must have felt like it was getting mugged by his worst nightmare. Gravity didn't go where it should have, yanking him off his bed and slamming him into the back wall of the bulkhead.

Boooooof! "*Awwwh!*"

Then came the inertia of his boots, spectacles, clipboard and whatever else he didn't put away.

H.C. WELLS

Whack! Crash! Kabang! "*Awwwhh!*"
In the midst of the roaring engines, the gravity that didn't work, and flying objects, God only knew what he was thinking, so he barely had time to ask, "What the God's Christ name is happening?!"

Back up on deck, US-1 tried to pull away from his seat, but gravity must have given him an unfair shake from the planet Jupiter. Finally, he gave up, for it was too hard moving against the force. However, he did manage to pull his head over to see what US-2 was doing in the middle of their wild exhibition. It wasn't good, and it wasn't good at all. All he was looking at was a strained copilot, feverishly holding on for dear life with an oily face, a mania for more speed, and teeth looking longer than they should have. They even looked like fangs, clenching down on his cigarette; he could have bitten through a brick with them.

Seeing all of this must have cooked US-1's thoughts together, leaving him gasping. "Stop! You're going to get us killed!"

To make matters worse, US-2 just let go one of his controls to take his cigarette out of his mouth and shout, "I can't hear you! What did you say?!"

US-1 looked down at the instrumentation. "Holy shit. We're ninety knots 'n climbing fast!"

As the steering flirted off course, US-2 quickly caught it. That must have been cause for celebration, for he quickly threw a fresh cigarette in his mouth but didn't know how he could light it after the force threw his lighter out of his hand.

Lighting cigarettes in distress might have been the least of his worries. Suddenly, the whites of his eyes grew when he looked out just few seconds ahead, which could have meant it was a quarter kilometer away. Rolling along was a gift rising up from the sea that offered no path for detour. Two parallel waves looked so perfectly intrusive that there was only one thing left to do. At 130 knots or better, US-2 barely had enough time to yell, "Look out dead ahead!"

US-1 ducked while US-2 closed his eyes, but the US *Wehrwolf* kept going as if nothing was there.

Swoooooooooosh!

She took the first wave with about as much grace as a squirrel flying out the end of a circus cannon. Off the crest of wave she went, yet to the amazement of her rooky navigators, she glided like she was meant to before returning smoothly to the sea.

US-2 opened his eyes as he kept working his navigational levers. "Oh, so that's what this one's for!" He looked up again just in time to see the second wave fast approaching. "Here comes another! Look out!"

Effortlessly, on the next takeoff she glided even farther than the last one before landing on the water again.

US-2 dropped his jaw with excitement. "Wow! It's like this thing can fly almost. *Ha haaaa!*"

US-1 screamed, "Shut it down! Shut it down, now!"

Instantly he backed off the throttle, sending their vessel into a nose-skidding slowdown. "Wow…seventy knots now… Good God…feels like we're standing still, doesn't it?"

US-1 quickly took off his safety harnesses while gasping for air. "*Shhhh*, you scared me—*maniac*. If I'm ever in charge you better not ever do that again."

US-2 lit his cigarette as they kept slowing down. "Do what?"

"Do that! You know, fly! I saw it right out there. We were stuck to our seat—sailing over who knows what at a hundred knots."

US-2 simply ignored him as he looked down at the new pair of controls he just found. "*Hmmmph*, how about that, air navigations…says so right here. Did you see that before?"

"I don't care what it says. Whu-what? Air what? You're a hazard."

US-2 bit down on his cigarette, grinning as he pretended to be flying again with his controls. "Shit, I can make this thing do *anything*. Hey, look, here's something new too. Look at these big buttons. I wonder what—"

"Don't touch them! Don't even think. The Doc hasn't explained those yet either."

As their vessel slowed to less than thirty knots, her bellowing exhaust continued spewing long, rattling rasps. She sounded as if she could have done it many times more without a problem. Slowly, she calmed down to twenty knots, then ten, before she rocked steady all the way down to a wandering, gentle float.

Large tail waves quickly found her stern and splashed over. When she leveled off in the ocean, steam spewed high into the air from the pressurized engine bays. Water hissed at the touch of the blazing-hot edges of her exhaust peeping out the sides. While she idled to cool herself down just above the water, she resembled the relaxed turn of a surprise test ride that went without a hitch.

US-2 slapped his knee with joy. "*Ho-ho*, this thing has big *hoden!*"

US-1 looked shocked. "Yes? Yes, wow, big *hoden*."

"Did you see my launch back there? And then we kept fuu-lying, *he he*, yeah—flying!"

US-1 quivered. "No…I mean, *I know*—"

"No? No way soldier man…we were—fuu-lying! Wow, where are my cigarettes? I got to get me another."

US-1 threw him his pack like he'd like to shut him up. "Here, knock yourself out. Don't forget to light it this time."

US-2 kicked his legs up on the controls. "*Whoweee*, if I can only figure out how to steer better. Hey, I just thought of something! When we get rough water? Maybe I can float the handles next time to grab more air, *ha*! That's it. Yeah that's what I'll do."

---

5 "Hoden" is a German word for testicles.

THE TIME TO TELL

US-1 bit his lip. "Oh, God, that's it...you could have got us all killed. I can't believe I'm hearing this."

US-2 tapped on his controls as if he were playing drums. Ashes and red cinders fell from his cigarette while he did so. "I got power. I got tools, yeah—"

"Knock it off...you're dropping your ashes all over the place! Now you're a fire hazard too."

Just then, thumping clunks and clangs bellowed from below deck, which drew their weary concerns. Sure enough, it was Doc, kicking things out of his way just so he could get to the ladder to get up on deck. "Son of God's Christ O'Mighty! What in the name of?! Why I ought to—*Christ!* Oh holy boy, *Jesus!* You two had better be ready! This has *got* to be good! *Christ*—O'Mighty! Did you hear that, my lord? They are cooked potatoes in a fire!"

US-1 and 2 looked at each other like lost muskrats captured in a cage. "What do we do, US-1?"

"You're asking me? You're the self-made smart one, not me."

"You're the midshipman. Of course, I'm asking you."

US-1 shrugged his shoulders, looking the other way. "I wasn't at the helm. Get yourself out of this."

"You gave me the command, damn it. I heard you. Wait, maybe a warship was chasing us?"

US-1 crossed his arms, shaking his head. "No lies, Blondie. He won't buy it. Can you hear him coming?"

Doc popped up on deck, beet-red in the face and panting mad. As he tried to get his bent spectacles to fit over his eyes, he barked out, "Okay, US-2 on engines...get yourself out of this!"

"Well it was like—"

"I already don't like your answer!"

Doc looked outside while he tried to put on his tangled-up white smock with baby milk spilled all over it. He then focused on US-1. "You're the partner in this behemoth crime. Where's the danger out there? I don't see it. What's your story, *huh*? Speak up! Speak up, *huh*?"

"*Uh*, it was an exercise, I believe. You could call it an exercise."

Doc could have slapped himself. "Exercise? What!? What exercise?" While he adjusted his smock, he took his handkerchief out to wipe the sweat from his forehead and neck to think. "*Hmmm*, continue, US-1, but if I hear any lies I shall personally give you a life raft and send you away—to General MacArthur!"

"Yes, Doc...we wanted to see what this thing could do in case of a surprise engagement of combat."

US-2 jumped up. "Yes, it was an escape! We thought of it before heading out into more troubled waters. Look, we have smooth conditions right now with nothing out there."

Doc glanced back and forth, seeing nothing but calm in their eyes. He gave up being mad and looked over to the side where his pair of binoculars were sitting and grabbed them. After straightening his spectacles, he calmed down a little more. "Well, that is precisely the only foreseeable answer worth the attention...I might let you by on that test analysis—but just once." He then rushed to the edge of the cockpit glass, looking out to sea, frantically. "Quick now, open the hatch and shut off those noisy engines. Do it—*now*!"

US-2 quickly killed both engines, then hit the switch, depressurizing the hatch.

Speeeeeewwwwww.

As fast as Doc could manage, he lifted his pudgy body up to the edge and then crawled up on the outside deck where he began casing the area.

His two copilots just looked at each other as if their new captain in charge was perhaps lost or something. They shrugged their shoulders before they too crawled outside. They stretched and yawned as they kept their eyes on Doc, shuffling from one end of the vessel to the other. "Sooo, you think that shark was big last night, eh, my boys? *Ha!* Wait until you see a U-boat armed with *torpedoes* the size of sharks... Christ O'Mighty, forget that...God forbid. Wait until you set your eyes on a *Destroyer* with—God forbid—*cannons* and, and *torpedoes!* Dozens of them—yes."

He slowly put his binoculars down as if he'd just been spooked. "Worse yet, a fleet of U-boats, even. You did it! They're nothing but a bunch of—*barracudas.* Christ O'Mighty, you boys." He went on, "The Italians, British—our own Germans even. There all out here—like sharks stuffed with mouths of gun powder—*bombs* in their bellies! Oh, holy one. I can feel myself being blown apart already."

US-1 stepped forward, opening his arms with all due concern. "We didn't mean any harm, Doc, really...what can I say? We're sorry."

As Doc cased the area, he carefully said, "Didn't you hear back on the beach, or did we not make ourselves perfectly clear? We're—on—our—own. No radios. No nothing. We're clay targets in a skeet shoot—except we can't fly."

US-2 muttered to US-1, "Destroyers, U-boats, battleships? He forgot planes."

US-1 wasn't quite so amused. "Doc...I looked on my sonar...there's nothing out here, really."

Doc stepped up to them, "Don't you—neither of you understand. The scatter tails of water you *spastis*[6] kicked up were more shocking than my dead mother's casket!"

"Yeah, but—"

"Don't you 'but' me, US-2...those engines you sunk into sounded like the Battle of the Atlantic...no...we're in the Mediterranean, I suppose....Battle of the *Mediterranean...* Christ O'Mighty....God. Those cockroaches can hear us from ten kilometers away by my calculations. Wait, I believe maybe more."

---

[6] "Spastis" is an offensive German word that deliberately insults somebody with a mental illness or disability.

He went on, "They have sonar too, maybe better!" You sow ears sent knuckle signals vibrating all across this ocean that said, '*I'm over here on a special mission.*' No, we might not see them now. Just wait…wait and see is all we can do, God forbid."

US-1 spoke earnestly, "Look, Doc, you told us about the operation. It's safe. There isn't supposed to be much going on here in this vicinity. Look in your binder. It's all there like you said. I'm sure…nothing…no planned engagements. There's nothing, right?"

Doc stopped casing for a moment then looked as if perhaps he was over the top. "Yes, I remember…didn't see anything out here anyway. Okay, I'm satisfied now." He continued more kindly. "Okay, one of you—fetch my binder and clipboard please."

US-2 darted inside the cockpit then quickly came back and handed the requested material to Doc, who said, "Let me see now—going over my notes. Yes, here we are…this is a good time as any I suppose, don't you two boys think?"

His officers pondered. "Good as any?"

"What you got in mind, Doc?"

Doc glanced as if they were supposed to know. "To finish up your training. It's a good day, wouldn't you both say?" After he found the place in his notes, he paused and crossed his hands with his material against his chest. "Okay, what would you like to know next?"

Both of them eagerly stepped forward, starting with US-1. "We want to know what's under this thing!"

"Yes, and I want to know why this bastard's so fast. What about the wings here too? Tell us about those. This thing fuu-lys."

Doc thought for a moment as he gazed up into the spotty clouds. "I thought you might like to know all that. Come, come over here. Follow me." He then reached down on deck in back of the cockpit near the stern and cracked open the sealed twin engine bunkers, sending air spewing out. "There they are. Two Rolls-Royce Merlin[7] aero-engines—water tight—modified to my specifications for marine use."

US-1 asked, "Rolls-Royce? I thought this was a German vessel."

Doc snickered. "Oh, yes, it is. We stole them from the United Kingdom. That was the easy part."

US-2 dropped his attitude. "You stole them?"

"Yes…the hard part was smuggling them back into Germany with the war going on. The only time we could do it was in the morning. About three o'clock as I recall."

US-1 looked confused. "Aero engines? Aren't those for planes? Why didn't you use German engines?"

ΩUS-1 recalled, "What about those United States-made Ford engines you told us about in the training lab?"

Doc smiled. "What I said to you was true. He's our good friend and longtime supporter. Henry Ford. He sent over a couple of 1940 Lincoln Zephyr[8] V 12s, but we couldn't give them enough boost. The Americans call them 'stinking heifers,' and now I know why. Anyway, when we got them tuned in to going four hundred horsepower or better, they went *poof!* Yes, *poof.* Their crankshafts were too long to harness the torque effectively."

Doc then pointed down into the engine compartments. "Now *these* engines were the predecessor of the legendary Rolls Peregrine and Kestrel seven hundred horsepower engines from the British…have you heard about their Super Spitfire racing planes? No? How about the Hawker Hurricanes? Oh well, doesn't matter for the purposes of Operation Wolfe Cub. When we cranked up the superchargers you see here with octane boost, they tipped our meters at eighteen hundred horsepower."

---

7   Merlin engines were aircraft engines of the World War II era, built by Rolls-Royce.
8   Ford Motor Company's entry level luxury car from 1936–1942 was the Lincoln Zephyr with a V-12 carburated engine.

US-1 and 2 grinned as Doc kept talking. "Oh, but you haven't seen anything yet...take a look at this over here." He rubbed his knuckles, and then tugged on another sealed hatch next to the engine bays. As soon as he cracked it open, vaporized fog rose from within. He then paused to wait for the fog to clear before opening it fully. "Our Aero engines are used for fast takeoffs and getaways, as you already found out...here's what will get us across the ocean with less fuel. It's our underwater power too...the first advanced propulsion technology that works seamlessly—well up to twenty knots."

Both officers looked eager when Doc motioned gladly with an open hand. "Questions anyone?"

"Yes, we have a lot."

"What is it?"

A: "It's the first fully successful accomplishment from our flying disc engineers of our top secret spacecraft division."

Q: "Oh wow, I heard about flying...real flying saucers that fly. Am I right?"

A: "No, no, no. Funny you mention. Our flying discs are ridiculous as far as I'm concerned. They never could get them to fly straight—so they crashed. Sure did wonders for keeping everyone on their toes guessing about them though, I must say. Our Foo Fighters were not meant to be, I suppose."

Q: "Why's that? Why don't they work?"

A: "It was their centrifugal problem, among other things. Steering was impossible to master under the twisting force. None of us were able to figure out how to control them, so we kept crashing everywhere."

Q: "No way to control them, *huh*? I get it, so couldn't you do something else?"

A: "Yes. We worked on drones for a while with some degree of success. We couldn't arm them, though. They were quite harmless, so I suggested they light them on fire and send them out to opposing aircraft anyway. It was a funny distraction we all laughed about. *Ha*, their minor success gave them cause to nickname our joke."

Q: "Oh? What was that?"

A: "I told you, 'Foo Fighters.' The British and American pilots didn't know what to think. Some of them even contracted emotional trauma, from what I understand."

Q: "I heard about them, I believe. Balls of fire, jetting across the sky—at night usually. Was that them?"

A: "Those are our Foo Fighters, my friend, but nothing compared to what you see here right now."

Q: "Nothing? Maybe you can make them better? Isn't there any time?"

A: "Oh no. There's no more time, I'm afraid. They'll be gone like the rest of our work, sad to say."

Q: "What's wrong, Doc? You look like you're attached to all this."

A: "Yes, I suppose I am. My people are still slaving on those discs back home, underground right now as if there was no war at all...God bless their souls—years of hard work. All will be gone soon."

Q: "You're really someone special, aren't you? What exactly did you do?"

A: "Who me? It's not all about me. An unforgettable amount of genius was in our spacecraft division. Our V-Rockets were going on their third phase. I even thought that one day we could go to the moon. Blame the war, maybe. Better off with mice than men, I suppose. Christ, all of them came to a halt before I could really say good-bye...I never said good-bye...so long...just about a week ago was all it was."

Q: "What do you mean? I thought we were doing something about this right now. Aren't we making a difference?"

A: "You two really can't surmise what's going on. I'll tell you again, as sure as probability digs my grave...the war finished us—for good. Remember what I say. The good of all mankind depends on the success of our work."

H.C. WELLS

Q: "Let me ask something for once, US-1...okay, Doc, so let me get this straight. Flying saucers were in the garbage, so a bunch of you crazy scientists took over those ideas then somehow made some of it work right here in this vessel?"

A: "Well, you're only partially correct, US-2. We're not crazy. Our ideas made this operation possible too. The technology from the works of Arthur Sack A.S. 6 Experimental Haunebu Disc[9], or 'flying saucer' as you might call it, was combined with Viktor Schauberger's turbine research, among other things. You're looking at a revolutionary Electro-Magnetic-Gravitic Engine here that's modified, which is an improved version of my friend, Hans Coler's, free-energy machine."

Q: "Wait a minute, Doc. Free energy? I mean is that a little, *uh*—"

A: "That's exactly what I said, US-1...*free energy perpetually*. This is only part of the equation. We cruise the *Wehrwolf* on free energy up to twenty knots underwater and above it if we have to... it's an energy converter coupled to a Van De Graaf band generator,[10] precision crafted and mated seamlessly to an improved and modified version of the Marconi Vortex Dynamo.[11] Such an accomplishment of—"

Q: "What? A Mussolini and Diana ma-ho, *who*?"

A: "Forget it, US-2. It's too complex. It's a pressurized, spherical tank of mercury. That's what it is, and that's all that matters to you now."

---

9   Arthur Sack built the first manned saucer-type craft called the *AS-6* in 1943–44. After World War II ended, American troops entered Brandis Air Base to confiscate the *AS-6* technology, but supposedly did not find completed examples of the crafts.
10 The Van de Graaf Generator was invented by Robert J. Van de Graaf in 1929 and uses electrostatic forces to harness millions of volts with a high-pressure tank of sulfur hexafluoride gas.
11 Marconi Vortex Dynamo is associated with the truth and myth of Nazi UFOs. The German SS-IV occult "Order of the Black Sun" set out to research alternative energies before their time. It is a spherical tank of mercury, which, along with the Van de Graaf Generator and Electro-Magnetic-Gravitic Engine, created powerful rotating electromagnetic fields that affects gravity and mass.

THE TIME TO TELL

Doc looked back and forth at them with supreme concern. "I didn't lose you, did I? I may be short and hairless, but I am a good teacher. My vision is for you both to become my apprentices, should anything happen to me. Did you follow all that I said?"

Neither of them would answer, so Doc slowly moved his hands into a circle. He liked this idea, so he began talking with his hands, swirling them around and making circles bigger. "Like this...it's a powerful, rotating electromagnetic field that affects gravity and reduces mass...do you understand me, boys?"

They just stared at Doc as if a blanket of fog had just moved in between them. US-2 opened his mouth as if he wanted to shout about his confusion, while US-1 squinted into the sun. Doc soon realized that perhaps he wasn't a good teacher after all. Somewhat frustrated, he shook his head, turned his back to them, and touched his finger onto his cheek.

Suddenly, he lit up with an idea. "*Ah* yes, I have it!" He then spun back around to face them. "You know, sort of like our older version of the Triebwerk[12] ...no fuel except to kick it up. You know, *free energy.*"

Suddenly his newfound apprentices awkwardly faked a few gestures of confidence before they came around to say, "Oh yes, that's really great. I see nowwww."

"Really great...*um.* Free energy. Lasts longer...less fuel across the Atlantic. This is good, perpetically."

Doc suddenly looked relieved. "That's called *perpetually*, US-2, meaning 'everlasting'...I can go on then...this Triebwerk we're using here, I call the '*Trieb Tachyonator Two.*' Our land-based versions were going to be called the '*Trieb Tachyonator Ones.*' Our planes were to be the '*Trieb Tachyonator Threes.*'"

---

[12] The result of the Electro-Magnetic-Gravitic Engine, Van de Graaf Generator, and Marconi Vortez Dynamo working together to produce free energy was referred to as the "Triebwerk."

H.C. WELLS

"Oh, Doc...I'm not into this sort of thing."

"Don't listen to US-2...please tell us more. I can't believe the amount of work you must have poured into this."

Doc began to teeter back and forth. "You mean you understand, US-1? What you don't know then is I'm saving the best for last. I haven't told you what else we stumbled across." He continued as he stirred himself up in circles. "Oh, it is big—really big. It's bigger than you know!"

US-2 turned away, but US-2 kept on.

Q: "Doc, I have newfound respect for you and—you and everyone else involved, but what could possibly be better than this?"

A: "Oh, *ho ho*...it was discovered quite by accident. You see—how can I explain this? Oh, yes. We've discovered a new frequency to interphase a grandiose technology. And then, and then...we combined the unique sources of energy. How shall I say this simply? At a *monumental* scale, much larger than what you see here in a primitive propulsion system. We had to create a safe, controlled environment, of course. Actually, the supreme perfect sphere worked quite nicely. Then, of course, there was the problem of protecting the subject with an intermixture of elements."

Q: "Scales, spheres, protecting elements. What?"

A: "Yes, to protect our subject from harm...we found it quite by accident, too. It came to us inside of a meteorite, believe it or not. We ran lab tests—compatibility tests. Nothing like it on earth, actually. The answer was right before our very eyes! That's why your symbol on your uniforms is the color gold, yes. It was gold of all things. That's what completed our magical enigma. Magical it was! Oh, it is scientific—don't get me wrong. I just wish I understood it better."

Q: "You're—you're losing me again, Doc. Why can't you explain what this operation is really about? I mean, maybe US-1 likes this, but I couldn't care less about it if it doesn't have anything to do with…what's all this got to do with us and the kid? The baby—down below."

A: "What? Oh, that's classified, US-2. I can't tell you."

Q: "We're out here in the ocean all by ourselves on some crazy ship nobody's ever seen, and that's all you can say?"

A: "I can assure you, this operation begins with your mission, which you vowed to fight to the death for. It's worth it. Between the baby down below and the technology we've comprised, our world depends on this operation. I've said enough now. It's way beyond you and me."

Q: "Yeah, yeah, I heard you before. You said world peace forever, which is hard to believe, so what's wrong with telling us a little more. Right, US-1?"

A: "I didn't say 'forever.' I said a thousand years. It's a pretty good start, don't you think?"

US-1 looked Doc in the eye with intense interest while US-2 whispered in his ear, "I can't believe I'm hearing this crap."

Doc overheard his whisper. Immediately, he dropped his smile as if his feelings were hurt. Slowly, he closed the engine bays and secured them shut with very little to say.

US-2 thought nothing of it. Casually, he walked onto one fin of the vessel and stood there right on top of the emblem of the golden rolling star. He looked down, not at the symbol, but at the entire fin assembly, and then jumped up and down as if testing its sturdiness. "What's this thing made of, Doc? This thing's pretty strong."

"Aircraft aluminum and Victalen."[13]

US-1 felt it. "Victalen? What's that?"

"It's a Frozen Smoke, we call it. It's the armor and frame of the ship. We had to find something strong enough to withstand what this vessel is capable of doing. The greatest difficulty my metallurgists had to endure was how to lighten it up. They did it."

---

13 Victalen is a special alloy associated with the truth or myth behind the German occult, SS-1V, Triebwerk, and Haunebu Disc.

When US-2 was through testing the fins with the weight of his whole body, he asked, "These wings. Tell us about these funny wings."

Doc looked as if he couldn't believe US-2 was testing his patience too. He faintly shook his head then with a friendly false face, he sorely corrected, "They're called 'aqua fins,' thank you very much...not wings. Wings belong on planes."

US-2 huffed, "Yeah, but this thing looks like a plane. I mean, look at it."

Doc glared. "She's not a 'thing.' She's a 'she.' You didn't think we put those aqua fins on for looks did you?"

US-2 laughed. "No. I guess not...I flew a little ways already."

Doc grew somewhat irritated. He stepped over onto the fin with US-2, weighting down his playful bounce until he stopped bouncing. "They do a lot more than just raise the weight off this vessel at high speeds...they reduce the hydrodynamic effect of sucking down the stern taking off, caused by propeller thrust. They also enable the driver to land softly so they don't look like spastis or lose control when they're speeding—for no reason."

Doc walked away and then turned back around. "Oh, and by the way, my good friend...she doesn't 'fuu-ly,' as you so eloquently put it. She glides. When she leaps into the air, she sails back down like she was designed to."

US-2 complained, "The fins hit the water when I took off. Felt like I was dropped on my ass on concrete!"

"See what I mean? You could be smart...you already discovered their secondary function and you didn't even know it. You know what we call it for inevitable navigators like yourself?"

"No."

"It's called 'punch and go.' They are for real, live situations, US-2, not just playing around."

THE TIME TO TELL

US-1 quickly walked over. "So that's what happened when Blondie goosed it? I never would have guessed."

Doc cleverly nodded. "That's right, simple physics. When you *punch and go* with this unusual amount of horsepower, she wants to suck herself under the surface. She contains the insatiable urge to throw her bow straight up in the air. Trust me, we didn't overlook a thing when it came to this operation...you can count on her to escape from any situation, and she can do it fast. No sinking and no shooting to the moon either...once she pulls out of her split-second chaos in takeoffs, she's gone across the ocean."

US-2 stroked his whiskery chin. "*Hmmm*, I have to give you something...I didn't think eighteen hundred horses could do that much damage."

Doc smiled. "You look compromised for once, US-2... correction, however. It is eighteen hundred horsepower to each propeller—per engine, my friend. Add it up again."

US-2 suddenly looked more humble. "*Ahh*, Dr. Wycliffe... I'm really sorry about this morning. I didn't know..."

As Doc gathered up his clipboard and notes once again, he licked the end of his pen to scribble something down. "That's okay. It's good that you threw out your incongruences and got it out of your system...by the way, just so you know...I was informed well that you were the wild one. You're lucky to be here as far as I am concerned...Wolfe said you might be necessary for Operation Wolfe Cub... strange as it is to me. He said you might be a component to success."

US-2 beamed. "Yeah, I knew it! Did you hear that, US-1? Take my two and shove it 'cause I'm the Number One."

Doc added, "Don't get ahead of yourself. Both of you are essential. The facts remain with my beliefs, however... I thought someone like you could be catastrophic...just do me a favor and prove me wrong for once." Ever so sadly, Doc stepped back down into the cockpit and then peeked back out to his two officers. "Well, it's time for weapons review and my last lesson. Shall we get a move on?"

US-1 and 2 snapped out of their thoughts then swiftly stepped inside too. Once all three of them harnessed themselves up securely in their captain's chairs, Doc opened his binder. Casually, he made a few notes then thumbed through his bell book log. 'So, US-1...how far did we glide when US-2 hit maximum speed?"

US-2 interrupted, "Oh, wow, that must have been—"

"I said for Number One to answer my question, thank you."

US-2 fell back in his chair just as US-1 politely answered. "It was at least a hundred meters I estimated. I kept an eye on the gauge as best I could, but we were moving too fast."

Doc made a quick note, and then he looked over to US-2. "And now for you...how fast were you going?"

US-2 sprang up to the edge of his chair. "It was a hundred sixty knots, at least. She wanted to go higher—I could feel it!"

Again, Doc made a quick scribble in his bell log while muttering to himself. "*Hmmm*, really now...one hundred fifty knots sounds about right." He then hung his pen behind his ear and moved onto the next page where he referenced a chart. "Interesting...eighty-nine meters is the farthest she's ever glided...I'd say that was a record. You have anything else to say, US-2?"

US-2 looked like the cat that just ate the canary and didn't say a word.

Doc rolled his eyes then continued. "Okay, then, now for review of standard weapons and secondary weapons, shall we? First is the MG 81Z. The 'Z' stands for "Zwilling Twins,"[14] as you both know. They're paired up on one mount capable of what US-1? Quick!"

---

14 Zwilling Twins is a German belt-fed machine gun.

THE TIME TO TELL

"That's easy. They're specially designed with explosive bullets. We've got thirty-two hundred rounds per minute, with specially shortened fifty-one-centimeter barrels and flash hiders and no sound suppressors. There are two sets on port and starboard sides. Limited ammo is on board, so we have to use them sparingly."

Doc nodded convincingly. "Very good. Now for you, US-2...continue on with the auto cannons please."

US-2 dropped his arms then labored to talk. "*Ah,* Doc, do I have to answer it the same way?"

"Why, yes, of course, go on."

"Oh, all right...they're the BK37s...two on each side, with specially-shortened ninety-two-centimeter barrels, I guess." As he paused to yawn and pick his fingernail, he finished. "One slug will down an aircraft or disable a small vessel... limited quantities of lead in the trunk...oh, and the lead is specially designed with gunpowder to blow craters in their asses on contact."

Doc tapped his pen looking irritated. "Lead in the trunk? Asses? I see...are you practicing American culture already? Is there anything more you care to add, besides bricks in your pants?"

US-2 looked as if they were ganging up on him. "Bricks? I didn't say that...okay, I'll continue...the BK37s were originally designed for the Messerschmitt aircraft.[15] They fit on board the *Wehrwolf* even better...we know all this already. Can we learn something new for once?"

Doc chewed on his cheek for a second then closed his binder. "Very well, I'll skip most of it...it's not that easy by the book, I can agree with you...since you haven't engaged in real arms fire, we'll have to go over accessories for engagements quickly. Nobody's getting out of this important session."

---

15 The Messerschmitt Aircraft was one of the most famous German fighter planes in World War II.

He went on, "As you already know, any one of us can move to my center captain's chair. All you have to do is switch to 'master control.' This allows for operating the vessel completely alone. There may come a time when one or two of us are—"

"Yeah, yeah, injured, we know."

May I continue, US-2? Thank you. As I was saying, heaven forbid if one or two of us should fall off the vessel, die, or get eaten by marine life. You both need to be prepared to take over at any given time...questions?" Nobody replied so he continued. "Okay, to your right armrest is your pistol grip; that operates almost all of the weaponry, as you know—"

US-1 raised his hand, "What? You said 'almost all.' I thought this was all we had."

"Let me finish...remember to toggle the weapon you wish to use before you go duck hunting with the crosshairs inside the optical provided behind your headrests. I assume you both know how to position yourselves quickly, spin your chairs and line up your targets. We must move on now, shall we?"

"Yes, Doc, ready to move on."

"Yeah, sure, Doc, what else you got in that book of yours?"

Doc paused then continued. "Very well. You see these large brass buttons on the center dash of the master controls? They are our secondary weapons...one of them is experimental. It's there if you need it in case we run out of standard munitions. It's a single KSK[16] that operates solely off the vessel's power source, which is the modified version of the Triebwerk spoke of."

US-2 snarled, "What the hell's that again?"

"I knew you would be the one to ask, US-2...it's a Strong Ray.[17] The muzzle blast from the projectiles looks like a laser

---

16 "KSK" stands for "Kraft Strahl Kanone," or "Strong Ray."
17 Strong Ray, also known as the "anarchronism gun," was an incredibly powerful gun, disputed by physicists and thus regarded as a myth.

gun, but it's not. It's also called an 'Anachronism Gun,' like it says here on the control panel—"

US-2 lazily flagged his hand. "Wait—wait, what did you call it again?"

"An Anachronism Gun. Anachronism, meaning 'nothing like it' or 'chronological error.' Call it the 'Strong Ray.' That's what I call it. How it works is simple: it's made up of abnormal metal balls and tungsten spirals. The Triebwerk-connected balls form cascade oscillators that are connected to a barrel-shrouded transmission rod—precision made into a tungsten spiral or coil to transmit a powerful energy burst. It's powerful enough to pierce, or even obliterate, one hundred millimeters, or four inches, of solid steel armor…listen up…it's good for one shot. It's slow to start, and it takes forever to recharge the vessel's system, rendering us temporarily vulnerable."

He paused to see if they were listening. "Very well, it looks like you two heard me well…well then. Let's see how good you two are. Give me an example of what it's good for."

They both replied simultaneously.

"Battleship. Nothing else floats out here with skin that thick."

"Destroyers. The big gunners. Turrets and guns almost as long as our ship."

Doc nervously nodded. "That's right. Any large ship over three hundred meters is a good candidate for the Strong Ray."

US-2 seemed mildly interested as he reached for a cigarette. "How far is it good for?"

Doc answered, "About one point five kilometers, or a mile perhaps, but it's testing is sketchy and unpredictable. It could go further since it is tied to our surprise technology I mentioned on deck."

US-1 snickered, "Wow, a mile. We're invincible. Nobody can expect that with a vessel our size."

US-2 chuckled as he lit up his lighter. "When in doubt, blow 'em out…I could get into that all day long."

Doc disrupted their laughs. "No! Listen up—it's dangerous! It's there in case of an emergency only. You better ask all your questions now, this very minute."

Q: "Okay then, how dangerous?"

A: "The Anachronism Gun is integrated into our advanced system, as I have said."

Q: "So...what's so dangerous about that?"

A: "Oh, *ho...ho ho ho*, you only know the beginning, my friends."

Q: "Beginning? Lay your cards down, Doc."

A: "The tip of what I'm saying is bigger than all the battleships and the Bismarck too! This is all you should know for now. You best take my word for it."

Q: "Doc, how can you teach us about your secret gun unless you tell us why it's so dangerous? I mean, why use it at all?"

A: "Well...my teachings put me at a supreme disadvantage with secrecy, I suppose. *Hmmm*, very well...what you saw back there...you saw it in the engine bays."

Q: "Yes, the Triebwerk. The *Tachyonator 2, err um*, the mercury dynamo thing with the fog. What's so big about that?"

A: "It's not meant to be a weapon, but it's viable for the protection of this venture across the sea. It's—it's, *uh*—"

Q: "Come on—no going back now. What's so special about it?"

A: "*Ahh*, I suppose giving away a piece of it won't matter too terribly."

Q: "Say it, will you, Doc? We're out here all alone."

A: "This is not to be repeated...what we discovered can unleash a tremendous amount of power."

Q: "How much power? The power of ten bombs?"

A: "No! Nothing like that. Different power...the power of the universe, I guess you could say."

Q: "How did you and your scientists determine that?"

A: "Oh, that's very hard to explain. What we have on board here is but a tiny fraction of what it can do. The very least I can say is—we are somewhat safe on this operation because of it."

Q: "Somewhat safe, you say? Can you tell how safe?"

A: "Oh, did I say that? I did, I guess. Yes, safe to some degree… anyway, that's why it's dangerous now. That's all I have to say. I've said too much. It jeopardizes too much."

Q: "It's about this mission of the operation again, isn't it?"

A: "Yes…if I say more, it could surely jeopardize everything. Just remember what I said about using it in an emergency. It must be destroyed with this ship when our mission is successful."

Both officers carried on with two different reactions; boredom struck US-2 square in the face. In no time, he readied himself to forget about it. US-1, on the other hand, stuck his hands in his pockets and thought about what Doc said. Clearly, he was intrigued. "I'm beginning to get this. *Hmmm*, so this modified Strong Ray…where is it?"

US-2 suddenly became interested too. "Yeah, I can't see it anywhere. Where's Mr. Ray hiding? I don't see anything anywhere."

Doc nervously poked his nose over the control panel then slowly pointed a shaky finger to the dead center of the bow. "It is right there…up front…underneath the lid…below the deck. Look hard. See the hatch? It's flush with the deck. You can't see it, but believe me, it's there."

US-1 stroked his chin. "How do you determine last-minute engagement before using it? The big brass dishes are control pads?"

Doc snapped out of his fear. "Oh—why, of course. It's a firm decision process…it won't engage unless you've definitely decided. The controls are punch pads, designed this way for the definitive purpose of eliminating uncertainty. Feel them…it, as well as the others next to it, are hard to press down. You have to strike it with your fist. After that, you'll know. Engagement is transferred automatically to your pistol grip. When you're ready to shoot, the optics behind your seat will provide the same assistance for accuracy."

US-1 continued, "I see. Sound's simple enough. That's it?"

An eerie moment of silence broke out among them as Doc kept running his eyes back and forth between theirs. Almost mystified thinking about it, Doc carefully chose his words. "Yes. One more thing…we don't understand it fully. Just plead to the heavens on your life you don't have to use it. Maybe nothing will become of it. I wish I knew. It had destructive consistencies while we tested it for conventional uses, so its home here on the US *Wehrwolf* is well-founded for your mission." He went on, "Any more questions? We have to get a move-on—there's more."

He continued, "Okay, next to the 'Strong Ray button,' is the 'self-destruct button.' It operates the same way. You strike it with the ball of your fist, hard. Afterward, you have forty-five seconds before the vessel completely obliterates itself… this is a must once we've reached our destination. Hopefully, none of us will be in it. It can be used for two things: as a last line of defense and to complete our mission fully. This brings me to my last and most important detail, which I must reiterate."

Doc paused a moment. "Let me make myself very clear. Once the baby is delivered to the United States, this vessel must vanish from the face of the earth. The success of this operation hinges on it. More importantly—the secret contents you two just learned about on this vessel must never be discovered."

US-1 questioned, "Wasn't there another vessel just like this one back home hidden underground?"

"Yes and no…it's the one with the Ford engines. We salvaged all we could from it so that we could complete this one ahead of schedule. This one is fully functioning and one hundred percent successful, I might ad."

US-1 went on, "I get it. The other is just a dumb derelict now...wait a second, Doc. What about the flying saucers?"

"What about them, US-1?"

"Well, I mean if the war is lost like you say, won't they fall into enemy hands? Any valuable technology lost there?"

Doc shut his binder, closing his concerns. "They can't fly right anyway. All their power sources have been dismantled and melted down already for just that reason."

US-1 smirked as he looked at the ember of his cigarette up close. "Soooo, nobody will ever know the truth about anything... not us, not this vessel, and not even the baby."

Doc nodded firmly. "Yes, they'll never figure out what my team of special physicists and I have uncovered...they will live to find that Operation Wolfe Cub never existed either."

Suddenly out of the blue, ***Boom! Boom-boom!***

Utter shock gave way to huge bursts of water blasting up several meters high in the air, landing so close they couldn't help but see the spectacle of spray engulf their vessel. Each of them stood up from their chairs to see what it was. Fear rushed through Doc's eyes as he froze in his shoes. "Christ O'Mighty! It looks like—no it can't be."

Shortly thereafter, a huge crack of cannons sounded off, catching up to the incoming blasts. Then more bursts of water splashed the daylight out of the sky.

Booom......Booom-Booom......Booom!

Doc quickly grabbed the periscope above him and yanked it down. With a swift motion, he feverishly surveyed the seascape, and within an instant, he gasped, "Holy-holy, we're being fired at! Three o'clock!"

US-1 snatched up his binoculars. "It's got twin turrets.... big ones....lots of guns...all over the deck. Look! Submarines too! I can see them!"

He then looked at Doc. "They're escorting U-boats, I believe! Doc! They're submerging already!"

Doc picked his binder and thrashed through his pages then scrolled his finger down. "Oh no...it's the German Kriegsmarine Zestorer.[18] The only destroyer in the Mediterranean, and she's got us in her sights. We've got to get out of here. Fire on engines, US-2. I'm driving."

US-2 threw his cigarette down as he quickly shifted his chair toward his controls. "Zestorer!? They'll chop us in half if we don't get out of here."

Suddenly, two more monster splashes cratered the water again.

US-2 fired up both engines. "Shit! That was closer yet! The next one won't be so pretty!"

US-1 pulled his binoculars down, shouting above the engines, "Hatch is sealed. Next one's going to land in our laps!"

Doc quickly swiveled his chair toward his controls. "Switching engines to master controls. US-2, go below. Secure the baby for battle."

"Got it!"

Doc secured his safety harnesses. "US-1, harness on."

"Already there."

"Good, guns on starboard side. Switch to auto cannons and prepare to return fire. We've got to buy some time."

"Right away."

US-1 cranked his chair around and pulled his scope down. Within seconds, he held steady on his trigger. "I got him, Doc! What's our distance?"

"Stadimeter on periscope says two kilometers...fire when ready."

Outside the starboard side, two shining cannons clunked out of their porthole faster than stiletto blades in a knife fight.

---

18 German Kriegsmarine is the German navy and "Zestorer" refers to one of their most heavily-armed battleships, usually accompanied by armed fleets of submarines for additional protection.

THE TIME TO TELL

Booof! Booof! Booof! Booof! Booof! Booof! Booof! Booof!
US-1 commenced firing, rocking their boat and sending blistering rounds of forty or more straight across the ocean with a deadly hit.

Immediately, the crew of the Zestorer scattered across all of their decks. Red-hot rounds from the US *Wehrwolf* sliced their way through metal walls with a rude awakening. Gaping holes exploded up from out of nowhere, sending calls of calamity across their tower, bridge, and pilot houses. Stray projectiles ricocheted everywhere.

Twang-Twowwww! Crash-Cheooowwwww! Twang-Crash!
Every assailant inside the Zestorer's tower and control quarters, including the *kapitanleutnant*[19] hit the ground as he cried out into his megaphone, "This is *Kapitanleutnant* Hans Hildagard! All decks! Take cover! Sound the alarm!"

Immediately after, brutal bellows of deafening bullhorns sounded off from all corners of the ship. Hundreds of crew members held their ears, looking around in fright as if hell came to knock through their walls. More alert crew members flooded to their stations, giving every ounce of energy they could toward cranking their ten-ton, slow-moving guns over to the little speck in the sea that returned fire.

The US *Wehrwolf*'s crew hardly looked the same. Her scrambling crew of four, including a baby, had no more than buckled in when Doc set the twin engines free to full throttle.

BoooWaaaahaaaahhh!
Her propellers twisted tornadoes of torque, shooting up fountains of water flow while the exhaust let the rival know the US *Wehrwolf* was making a fast escape. With a squat and lunge, she left with a towering stream of water falling back down to the ocean as if their rainy day had just been left behind them in a big way. Just then, two incoming rounds made their way right where the ship had been just a second

---

19 "Kapitanleutnant" is the German word for "captain."

ago. Quaking blasts upended the water into a spectacle of twin water towers.

US-2, who was harnessed in his chair by then, looked back. "Son of a *bitch*, that was close!"

US-1 tried to steady his aim back at the Zestorer when he lifted his hand from his trigger and smiled. "She stopped firing, Doc!"

Doc wasn't in the mood for saying much, but his perspiration said quite a bit. He was quietly busy looking straight ahead, to nothing else but calm, blue sea, clipping by faster and faster as the seconds ticked by. A bead of sweat trickled down his bald head as he twitched and said, "Don't worry, they'll come again. My spectacles, where are they? What's our speed?"

US-1 carefully put his spectacles on for him. "Eighty knots—wait—no, ninety...we're still climbing."

Doc gained a smidgen of relief. As he reached for another control, he glanced at US-2 to see if he was paying attention. "Switching to glide rudders...take note of this and watch, US-2...it is good past one hundred knots...switching right—now."

US-2 felt for the same control in front of him. "Oh, wow, I can feel it...so smooth."

Back on the decks of the Zestorer, the picture wasn't quite the same as it was moments ago. Most who had taken their battle stations were hidden flat out on the deck behind their guns. Slowly, they got back up on their feet. Some of them gazed at the holes riddled across the walls—telltale signs of close calls.

In the control room, Hildegard looked so angry he could have spit nails at every one of his crew members. "Shut off the alarm on deck!" He turned to his two subordinate officers. "*My* crew? This is *your* crew! They're nothing but *spasti arschloch!*[20] Look at them! Why didn't they keep shooting?!"

---

20 "Arschloch" is a German slang word similar to "asshole."

THE TIME TO TELL

He quickly moved to the bridge as the two subordinate officers followed. All three of them jockeyed for a vantage point to see what they could see with binoculars. Immediately, they caught up with the tiny black speck heading west in a fountain stream of glory.

Hildegard looked even more preposterous when he saw the little, black, wedge-shaped thing with airplane wings arch up into the air in a jet stream at least four times its own height. Not only that, it was hard to ignore the sound he thought he heard. He cupped his ear out to sea. "Listen to it...*hmmm*, that's no sitting pigeon. She's armed and noisy too."

One of his subordinates asked, "*Kapitanleutnant* Hildegard. Is it some kind of water rocket or something?"

The other subordinate next to him lowered his binoculars. "Never heard such a noise. I can still hear them."

Hildegard tried yanking his frustration down with his binoculars. Death signals quivered from his eyelids as he watched the tiny-but-mighty black speck magically get away. "*Hurenshohn*[21]...a water rocket? Don't be funny, *Einfallspinsel!*[22] We missed them—can't you see?"

The chief of the crew skipped up on the bridge to ask Hildegard, "Shall we send out a U-boat scout to trail her?"

"No! It's too fast. I doubt they'll return anyway...*hmmm*, they're going somewhere. I can tell."

The chief lowered his head and began to make his way back to the control room, when Hildegard shouted, "Wait!"

"*Jawohl, Kapitan?*"[23]

"Take a countermeasure...they're heading for the Strait of Gibraltar...our U-boats—are they still sleeping somewhere along the opening?"

---

21 "Hurenshohn" is a German slang word similar to "bastard" or "son of a bitch."
22 "Einfallspinsel" is a German word for "idiot."
23 "Jawohl, Kapitan" is a German phrase meaning "Yes, Captain."

The chief stepped forward, rather excited. "Yes! They're right off the Shores of Morocco...we have four that could position an ambush."

"Good. Radio and tell them *Kapitanleutnant* Hans Hildegard of the *Zestorer Z91* wants to seek a countermeasure against a small, unidentified warship. Tell them to set an ambush at the Pillars of Hercules and stagger all four of them."

"*Jawohl, Kapitan!*"

Hildegard continued, "And tell them to stay submerged close to the surface and spot from their conning towers. She's a high-speed, floating craft with guns—that's all."

"*Jawohl, Kapitan*...anything else?"

"Salvage the ship, if possible. We need to see what kind of enemy it is."

Hildegard pulled his binoculars up to his eyes once again, speaking more calmly. "Commence firing until they're out of sight."

"*Jawohl, Kapitan.*"

In the midst of making time and skimming across the ocean, US-1 kept an eye out through his binoculars. It wasn't long before he saw the distant ship light up her turrets once again with heavy cannon fire. "Incoming, due any second!"

Huge rounds made a sinister sound as they hurled down close by, splashing the waters several hundred meters behind them. Doc looked back while navigating still. "*Ha haaa*! We're free!"

Just as US-1 and 2 began to celebrate, Doc interrupted. "We're not out of this yet...US-1, how far to the Strait of Gibraltar if we run steady at one hundred knots?"

US-1 grabbed his pencil and notepad, made a few calculations, and then spun the eraser in his mouth. "We should get there by dusk."

THE TIME TO TELL

"Good. US-2...take the controls. I'm too old for this."

"I thought you'd never ask, Doc."

Doc strained as he nodded. "Very well then...at the count of three, ready US-2?"

"Ready."

"Okay, then...one, two, three." The Doc switched his master controls off as US-2 took over. He then fell back into his chair in the company of his own exhaustion.

US-1 grabbed the Doc on the shoulder. "You okay, Doc? That was some kind of excitement back there."

"Yes, thank you. I'm all right. Just a little dizzy from age I suppose."

Something came to mind to Doc right about then. He looked around before he finally felt his upper coat pocket to find what he was looking for. Quickly, he reached for his apparent long-awaited reward, his shiny silver flask, and gave a tiny toast in the air. "*Ah*, yes. My scotch...here is to us... through the Gibraltar—then it's the Atlantic."

US-2 grinned with the unlit cigarette he'd recently teetered into his mouth.

Doc took another swig and glanced over to US-2. "You learn easy, my irritating good friend."

He then switched a glance over to US-1 and gave him a silent nod as he unbuckled himself. "I've got to go below and check the baby." Just before he left, he stopped for a second to turn around. There on the floor was US-2's cigarette lighter, so he picked it up and cordially lit his cigarette for him.

"Thanks, Doc."

Doc put the lighter in US-2's shirt pocket and patted him on the back. "Just do me a favor. Don't dump your ashes. Keep your hands on navigations."

"Don't worry about me, Doc. I'll be fine."

The Doc slowly made his way down to the lower deck, where he quickly opened Randolf's protective capsule. To his surprise, he was sleeping well—like a baby. Without much delay, Doc then stepped through to the small galley to grab a bottle of milk. When he came back, he felt Randolf's little bottom and sure enough, another mild chore needed tending to as well. A diaper change was overdue, so he went about his business of waking him up, feeding him, and then diving into the diaper changing last.

Apparently, Doc didn't know exactly what he was opening up. The look on his twisted-up face was priceless. A stench of boiled eggs and rotten potatoes instantly permeated the air. Its fragrance must have lingered with a vengeance too, as Doc wiped the tears from his eyes. His face would have looked better if he'd been peeling onions. Suddenly, he backed off, but not so much from the rotten smell. Randolf had given him a surprise fountain stream of urine too.

As he wiped the baby and the floor clean, he muttered, "*Whew*, God's Christ O'Mighty—worse than sea battle. At least we could run away from that."

Eventually, the unpleasant aroma made its way up to the vicinity of the two copilots, diligently minding their own business. US-1 looked back at the hatch where he last saw Doc. The smell coming up from below was so sour, he thought he could see it too, but nothing was there. Still, he kept looking for it. He must have thought a grotesque pile of dung had to have sprouted out from the corners somewhere. He even looked under his shoes before he barked his confession out loud. "*Eww*, what's that smell? Hey, Doc! You, old man, close the head down there!"

US-1 then turned his attention to US-2, but US-2 could hardly do a thing. He just shook his head and looked at his cigarette as if it didn't look all that appetizing to smoke anymore. "It's not me…wow. Maybe I'd better put my cigarette out before this place blows up."

Doc's voice rang out from below. "Christ O'Mighty—I've got to throw it out! This'll kill aquatic animals, I estimate!

THE TIME TO TELL

The child has secret weapons I didn't know about! Next time one of you up there has to change him!"

He then climbed back up on deck and strapped himself without much else to say to US-1 and 2 except to groan. He began feeling his controls, fingering everything in sight. Suddenly, he stopped as if he had the overwhelming feeling that he was being watched. "What? Oh, I washed my hands. Christ, it's true, don't you two believe me?"

US-2 leaned over to smell him. "What's that I smell on you, Doc? Baby powder?"

"Yes, foo foo dust, it is. Don't you worry, either of you… after a few more days, you're both going to be asking me for some too."

Chapter 4

Many hours came to pass. Late afternoon caught up with the crew of the US *Wehrwolf*, almost as quickly as the speed at which US-2 was assigned to travel. Even though he began to show cramps on the leg of his acceleration pedal, he stayed at one hundred knots for the better part of the day.

As the day drew toward sunset, the sky wasn't allowing them to see across the sea as far as they could before. Slowly, shades of reds and ember all across the rims of the scantly stretched clouds appeared, reminding them of their normal day-to-day lives, despite the mission they were on now.

US-1 took a double take at his instrumentation, and then tapped on the petrol gauge as if he thought it might be stuck. "Strait of Gibraltar less than fifteen kilometers, and we're riding as scheduled with petrol low on target, Doc."

Doc woke himself up in his chair then pinched his chin, thinking. "Shut us down, US-2…we'll let US-1 take over." He continued as he turned to US-1, who was catnapping. "Wake up, US-1—we need you."

"Yes, Doc? Did I hear something about petrol?"

"No, it's not that…prepare for a slow-running dive while US-2 finishes up."

Just as US-2 decelerated, miles of smooth, colorful twilight ocean received the intrusions of their long-lasting rasp of exhaust, when US-2 seemed puzzled. "We still have enough petrol to get to our fueling drop in the Atlantic, don't we? What's wrong, Doc?"

THE TIME TO TELL

"It's not the fuel I'm worried about." Doc hesitated as he kept looking outward into a sea of clear, calm nothing that shone with a beautiful, warm, crimson color. "If there's any place for us to get in trouble, it would be at the Strait of Gibraltar. Uncertainty chains me. The beauty out there deceives me too—I must say."

As US-1 slowly took their vessel underwater, Doc quickly instructed, "Reduce detection US-1...go to stealth propulsion, set buoyancy a few fathoms below periscope, and no lights...I want battle lights only."

Within seconds, the dark world beneath the sea reappeared with a dim, eerie, red glow.

"Battle lights on, Doc." US-1 quickly grabbed a spotlight handle on his far side and tested it before he softly said, "Sonar says it is clear...we are approaching the bottleneck in seven minutes."

Doc tried to swallow his concern, as he tried desperately to see ahead into the abyss. "US-1, set your Naxos and Aphrodite[24]...we need to confuse enemy instruments now, if there are any out there."

US-1 looked at his instrumentation. "But, Doc, I'm showing nothing but—"

"Just do it anyway. Set them now, I'm telling you."

Moments later, US-1 coughed. "Doc...I was wrong...I'm reading a large object dead ahead. What should I do?"

"Plot time to intercept, US-1."

"Looks like five minutes."

Doc tried deciphering his instrumentation. "What in God's name is it?"

US-1 looked closer on the screen. "I don't know. It can't be a ship. It's too big...too irregular."

---

[24] "Naxos" or "Naxos FuG 350a la" was a new German scrambling technology. A newer 3-cm version was scheduled for production, but World War II ended its advancement. An "Aphrodite" was a decoy balloon that floated at the water's surface that gave off echo signals similar to a German submarine."

Doc rattled off quickly, "Quick, shut down all controls... stealth propulsion set to *low*—now. Adjust forward trim... left...see if it reacts...well, did it react?"

"No."

Doc stood at the edge of his chair. "Easy...easy does it now...go easy."

While gathering whatever clues he could, Doc dared to draw a breath of fresh air. Still, nothing erroneous could be seen outside their observations, so Doc leaned closer to the dim light of US-1's sonar screen. A green glow reflected from the instrument to his face, revealing that they weren't in such a happy place. He didn't really want to budge except, perhaps, to move his lips cautiously. "Trim left a little more...the battle lights are too dim to see out very far... slow it up a bit and keep scanning your spotlight, will you, US-1?"

All three of them tried desperately to look out beyond the bow of their vessel, but little could be seen through the thick wall of utter blackness coming upon them all too quickly. Inside the dim, red ray cast out by US-1's spotlight, a few particles of seaweed floated up to the bow and over the cockpit glass.

Quickly US-1 balked. "Du...Doc—look at this. The big object. It's now multiple objects and they're still dead ahead and not moving."

Doc leaned over for a closer look. "What? Are you sure? I can't see it, but you can?"

"Believe me they're there...right ahead about fifty meters or less. I'm slowing down seven knots."

US-2 stood up to the glass to be the first one to get a glimpse at whatever it was. He got his wish in a terrible way. Right out of the blindness of the black, a horrifying object of immensity emerged. "Oh no, I...I think I see something."

Doc bellowed out, "Slow to *full*, US-1!"

THE TIME TO TELL

Nothing but a barricading bulge of crust, rust, and iron mixed with barnacles came forth to show itself from out of the abyss.

Doc pulled US-2 back in his chair. "It's another vessel. Get back."

It looked like the underside of a massive rock, except it was a keel of a submarine twice their size. Not only that, it was about to rip its way right up over their port bow and into their cockpit.

Doc yelled, "We're still going too fast. Pull down *full*, US-1! Hard right. *Hard right!*"

US-1 was already on it, tilting his controls as far as they would go, which was all he could do through their next few excruciating seconds.

Doc and US-2 just gripped their chairs and looked away from the grotesque mass of metal while US-1 kept his eyes looking straight at it. "I got it...I got it! Hey, look...it's okay now." Slowly US-1 leveled their vessel off and fortified some distance between them as they began to float by.

They gazed in awe at the reddish black and gray iron skin. She'd been in the ocean for a very long time from the looks of her. Her tubular bow, which looked to be designed to ram other massive ships, had already passed them by, but there was still plenty more of her to see.

Doc hardly move his lips as he muttered in shock, "Look at her...she's been on many missions at sea...look at her ramming scars...I think I know what she is. Did you see her bow cap, US-1?"

"How could I miss the torpedo chambers staring straight at us a second ago?"

Doc pinched his chin as he quickly thumbed through his binder. "She's a submarine, of course, but nothing here says they shouldn't be here. They must be scouting from their tower above the surface—looking for a ship, perhaps. I show no record...remarkable they haven't detected us yet."

US-2 seemed relieved. "Good call submerging, Doc. We were up there with them a few kilometers back."

Suddenly, the unmarked submarine's port wing slowly came into sight, offering yet another menacing obstacle to maneuver away from.

Doc put his binder down. "Steady now—that's a sub bow plane ahead. See it? Trim down further, US-1."

US-1 quickly adjusted. Shortly after, he twisted his spotlight to port quarter to get a better look at the sleeping sub's bow plane. "She's a *Rudeltacktik*.[25] The most brutal in the *Kriegsmarine* fleets. There could be more."

US-2 flatly stated, "That's doesn't tell me a thing."

Doc added, "A *Rudeltacktik*? She's from homeland Germany—a type Seven, I believe—isn't that right, US-1? Godly thing is loaded with enough torpedoes to blow us to hell and back if we'd kept cruising on the surface like we were. She's three times our size too, but slow."

US-2 smirked then leaned back in his chair smiling. "*Ha*, I knew it…We should surface and blow them to China?"

Doc glared. "I might have guessed you would say such a thing. That's not our mission. We don't stir up any trouble if we can help it. Besides, we can't miss our fuel drop, which is now vital. She may be slow, but she would follow us like the tortoise meeting the hare, except they could catch up to us with a full volley of guns and torpedoes—enough to set the ocean ablaze."

Out of curiosity, US-1 flashed his spotlight the other way and immediately saw something that made him let go and jump back. "Look! Another one! She's idle—over there."

Doc took a look. "*Ah haaaaa*, yessss…just what I thought… look, she's surfaced too. Sends me chills to think how she's waiting like that…waiting like the deadly Moray eel in her cave. Waiting for someone like us to drift by so it can eat…

---

25 "Rudeltacktik" refers to a group of World War II U-boats orchestrating an attack on a single vessel.

there are others around here I can fortify. Be very, very careful, US-1. Trim down a little more. I wouldn't be surprised if there were four—maybe more. God-forsaken German *wolfpack* is what we may very well be into."

US-2 quickly pointed in the other direction. "I think I see another—way over there. You see it? I saw a light blinking in the dark."

Doc fell back in his chair, brushing thoughts away from his nose. "They must be waiting for us. The *Kapitan* of the Zestorer this morning...he must have radioed for them to intercept us...they must have traveled over here. That's why I have no record of them...we have to be more careful from now on, my boys."

US-2 lit a cigarette. "I'm not worried. Nobody can touch us. We've got stealth propulsion, Aphrodite, guns, all this power. Face it...we're too smart too. Don't you think—"

Doc blurted out, "Quiet! We're just lucky. Learn from this. We submerged on a guess. It wasn't my predicted calculations of science. These are trained military tactics, unlike us with no radio contacts. Next time might not be this lucky."

US-2 glared at the both of them as Doc glanced over to US-1. "Look ahead, Number One. Anything you see on sonar further out?"

"No. All clear."

US-2 suddenly grew more perturbed as he grinned. "It's not luck...by my warlord calculations, I feel fearless. Sorry if anyone feels different. I mean, we can practically fly with this thing. We got jet marines, submarines...guns, twin guns, cannons... we got Strong Rays and stingrays, so *ha*! Grab the crotch of your pants if you want to see what I'm talking about."

Doc and US-1 both glared at US-2. Neither of them was entertained by his remarks in the slightest.

US-2 kept on, "What? It's true...come on, give me a break. Can't you two lighten up? Don't make me feel like I'm traveling with weaklings, okay?"

Doc went about his commands to US-1, as if he hoped US-2 would shut up on his own. "Maintain speed until we get out of danger, US-1. After that, establish the signaled course for our fuel drop...stay on stealth propulsion, but kick it up when it's safe...go to gyro pilot for the evening. That should be all...we should get there by morning if my calculations are correct."

Doc then looked over to US-2 and waited to see if he knew what to do. He was sitting there picking his nail, so Doc poked him to get his attention. "We're entering the Atlantic for an abrupt change of sea, Number Two...would you be so kind as to read the bathythermograph and adjust our vessel?"

US-2 put his cigarette out to get to it. "Got it. Reading... change is fifteen degrees...salinity has increased....adjusting for thermohaline effect."

After US-2 finished, he relaxed a little too quickly. A minute later, he suddenly woke himself out of his daze with an idea. Eagerly, he rubbed his hands together.

"Hey didn't you say it was someone else's turn to go below and stay with the baby for the night? You two can stand watch? How 'bout it?

Doc and US-1 seemed surprised with his apparent generosity. Happily, they agreed.

"Sure, I don't have an appetite for bottles and diapers. Do you, Doc?"

"No, can't say I do...thank you, Number Two, but remember. You have to think about changing a number two when you get down there."

US-2 shrugged his shoulders and headed down below. "Not a problem. It can't be worse than the shit we see up here."

A few feet along the way, before he slipped down the ladder, he saw Doc's alarm clock over at the corner of the deck. Curiously, he picked it up then smiled with another one of his little mischievous faces. "Hey, Doc...catch."

THE TIME TO TELL

Doc turned around just in time to see his alarm clock lobbing directly at him in midair. Barely in the nick of time, he caught it through an exorbitant amount of juggling around like a clown. "Why, thank you…a minor cause for 'alarm,' to say the least…by the way, did the alarm help anyone this morning?"

US-2 retorted as he slipped down the ladder. "Didn't bother me a bit…but, ask your number one man. He's the one who couldn't find it."

Doc looked over to US-1, who didn't comment right away. "Oh, yes, it got us right up."

Doc smiled cordially then wound it back up. Content, he placed it at his feet below him. Then with the careful, slow moves of an older man, he adjusted his seat to the recline position and closed his eyes with his arms crossing his chest. "Good…no time for sleeping-in aboard my ship."

US-1 hollered to US-2 below. "Hey, I smell something…close the hatch if you're going to change that diaper, will you?"

US-2 yelled up, "I didn't change him yet. What do you mean? I'm on the head."

US-1 shook his head. "Never mind…it's just you then."

"Can you hear me up there? I said I'm on the head."

"Yeah, we can hear you."

A minute or two went by before US-1 glanced over to Doc, who had fallen asleep all too quickly. He grinned as he looked up through the wide-open view of their glass cockpit underwater. Very quietly, he leaned way over to Doc, and then shouted, "*Hey*! Forgetting something!?"

"*Ahhh*! Christ O'Mighty! They're coming! *They're coming!*"

"Wake up, Doc."

"*Whew*, felt like I got shocked by an electric eel. Did you say something, or was that a dream?"

"I said, the scale shutters…are you forgetting to shut them down?"

"Oh, why sure…thank you for being so kind. I must shut them down here now."

"Don't know why. Not much could scare me after today. What about you?"

"I suppose you're right, my good friend. Insurance is cheap, so I'll do it anyway. There we go…*ah* yes. I feel better now."

"You know, Doc? You're all right."

"Oh? Well you're quite friendly too. Something just came to me before you so kindly woke me up out of an apparent bad dream."

"What's that?"

"Well, how should I say without striking too much alarm? I'll just say it, I suppose. Do me a favor if this is not asking too much."

"Yes, what's that?"

"When we get to America and part our ways, I wish for you both to stay in touch with me while I take the baby."

"Doc, I realize this mission was a last-minute plan, but new plans keep surfacing that you never—"

"No, I surely mean this…I want you to see our mission through to its entirety."

"Of course, Doc. I always see things through…like Blondie said, we've got it made."

"No—no, I mean getting the baby to the United States and giving him a good home. The point is moot, I suppose. Any one of us is capable of taking care of the child, but I surely know about everything."

"Blondie is a concern of mine, but I think he would live up to his oath of whatever it takes…as for me, you have nothing to worry about. I can easily see anything through. For me, it would be nothing shy of an honor. You'd just have to tell me what to do with him when he gets older."

"Yes—yes, but not now. The part about US-2 concerns me too…pardon my brutal honesty, but I don't know if US-2's head is in this."

THE TIME TO TELL

"Why was he chosen for the operation anyway? I mean, it couldn't have been that much of a hurry, could it have been?"

"The war came upon us too fast as you know, but the selection process was unilateral, actually. It had to do with the Aryanization Program. He was the Nordic one, in case you wish to know."

"Oh, one of those blonde, blue-eyed Aryans? I see now."

"He's not what you think. Nordics have strong tendencies to defend even though they are eccentric. The rebellion in him speaks of it too, quite noticeably."

"So...what makes him so great? He hasn't proved a thing as far as I'm concerned."

"He's a true, blue warrior, so to speak...no other warriors in the pool of a hundred came close."

"Oh, so he was bred to be that way?"

"No, actually not. He's like you. He's a natural—and in his prime too, I must say...I got a good look at him in the exhibition trials. Quite impressive."

"Aryanization program? I know little about it. Where did the idea of Aryans come from anyway, if you don't mind me asking? I mean their beginnings."

"My, my—it is older than you think...*Sanskrit*, it is. Aryan origins go clear back to the ancient Indo-Iranians, who inhabited parts of what is now known as Iran, Pakistan, India, Bangladesh—even Scandinavia."

"Oh, really?"

"Yes, really...its philosophy over the years has changed somewhat. It made its way into Europe, where Aryanism is said to have been perfected."

"You seem like a religious man in a world of cutting-edge science...how can you even relate to Aryanism with your two beliefs?"

"Oh no, there's a lot of Christian believers on my side, ironically. Not just Christians, either. Aryanism is also intertwined with Hinduism, Jainism, and Buddhism in the back sides of time. The striving urge is the philosophy to move the soul to divine consciousness. By the way, Jainism describes a path of nonviolence—to *all* living things, actually to say one aspect. We are an inherently self-centered species, I must say. A most difficult perspective to sustain with all variables considered. It is very old, you know."

"*Hmmph*...I wouldn't have thought you would...can something so *old* still have relevance?"

"Oh, it is very relevant. Its attraction is hard to deny. Perfection is everlasting. Science and religion both agree with this. Aryanism is as old as the people of the world itself... so why do you ask about US-2?"

"I was just wondering. You picked me, right?"

"Two totally different matters, US-1. But, yes, I had some say about you."

"Why me then?"

"Quite simple...we had to deal with a formula called 'diversity.' We had to have it in a tiny bottle too. The bottle is this vessel...the operation has to succeed. We have to protect the baby at all costs."

"Yes, but how can we rely on someone like US-2? I mean, you're seeing his mishaps for yourself."

"Not for you to decide...I think we came up with the right combination."

"I hope so then...you and your brains have to decide that, I guess."

"Yes, I hope so too...okay now, get some sleep. I will proceed with my rest, too. Hopefully, I won't get woken up again—if you know what I mean. I'm tired and I'm turning over now."

"Hey, Doc."

"Yes, US-1?"

US-1: "Thanks for choosing me. There's nothing on earth that would make me more proud to be instrumental in delivering peace—for the world, I mean."

"You're very welcome. Just thank me when we get to the United States. Thank me by taking care of the baby if something happens to me. I'll tell you about him later as a backup."

US-1: "I have to say, I had a dream. Ever since I was old enough to remember, I had a dream."

Doc: "A dream? Is it something of interest?"

US-1: "Yes, it is…I dreamed to be a part of something big—as big as the world itself."

Doc: "I know. It stood out in your profile documents. You're in the right place."

US-1: "You took note of that? Was that why you chose me?"

Doc: "Yes. One has to dream before believing in themselves. A very powerful tool in one of my specialties of science called *Synchronicity*.[26] Okay, now go to sleep. This is enough for one night."

US-1: "Synchronicity?"

Doc: "Yes, synchronicity. That is precisely why I think it is one of you who will see our mission through, not me."

US-1: "Interesting…so there's no chance of going back home?"

Doc: "You aren't having a change of heart, are you?"

US-1: "No, not at all, I mean—"

Doc: "Good. That is why you had to be single. Nothing to gain; nothing to lose. US-2 is no different. You *do* remember that part of the strict criteria, don't you?"

US-1: "Yes, that one stood out to me. I remember. At the time, I thought the only way to be on this mission was to be by myself. I mean, a married man wouldn't have stood a chance for this opportunity, right?"

---

26 Synchronicity was first described by Swiss psychologist Carl Gustov Jung in the 1920s as an experience of two or more events, unrelated or unlikely to occur together, yet they occur meaningfully or with a cause. Such striking occurrences can be viewed as merely coincidental. Mr. Jung's three other concepts need to be present, such as *Causility*, *Indestructible energy*, and *Space–time continuum*. He illustrated all four concepts with *Synchronicity* in a four-sided cross diagram.

Doc: "Not when it comes to warlord assassins and journeys of no return—the problem in this synthesis is we have a baby. The baby is our mission. See you in the morning. Go to sleep."

US-1: "Why is it a baby anyway?"

Doc: "I said I would tell you more later. You best be on your way to beddy-bye. The days will be more strenuous as we carry on, I assure you."

Swiftly thereafter, Doc dropped back off to sleep, but US-1 did not. A lonely sense of sadness suddenly came over him just then. Somewhere after the Doc's last few words about him being single was when his smiles turned to dust.

As he sat in his chair, sulking, more of the sorry look about him came to light in the dimly-lit cockpit. Secretively, he pulled out his wallet and opened it up to the first thing inside—a picture of himself, posing as happy as could be with a beautiful young woman wrapped around him. On his other side, wrapped tightly around his leg, was a very tiny boy with a leather ball at his feet. In the backdrop was nothing much really, just a rundown house so small that all of it fit inside the picture too.

What little could be seen or known of the picture, a conclusion might have been drawn that everything in the wrinkly-edged, black-and-white picture was his. The house, the woman, and even the little boy must have been what he cared about enough to make him so sad just then. He sobbed before putting the picture away, ever so tenderly back in his wallet. Shortly thereafter, he tilted his chair back and fell asleep, leaving one last lonesome tear to trickle down his cheek.

Chapter 5

By next morning, the US *Wehrwolf* and her crew were somewhere deep in the Atlantic, still submerged. It was around 0600 hours when little drops of rain inaugurated the ocean's surface above. Their touchdowns were delicate at first, until they began to pour down from the sky.

A couple of nearby whales were the only visitors, spewing water high up into the air at the surface. After they saw what they wanted to see, they gracefully dived back down again, out of sight. The only thing they left behind was a small wave good-bye with their tails. Shortly thereafter, loneliness crept back over the ocean's drizzly surface, and the silence of the next few moments was mystifying.

The clouds were equally mystifying, filled with shades of gray. They spread across the sky in all their glory that mild morning. A few small rays of light could be seen way off in the distance toward the sunrise, but none significant enough to change the solid pewter color that was present almost everywhere as far as the eye could see. Nothing else protruded above or in between, just the mood of the sky and ocean until, ***Spew-wooooosh.***

Forming up from the soft ocean top, tapped by rain, a round mound of suds and air escaped. An uprising pool of bubbles followed, looking all too familiar. Indeed, she was the US *Wehrwolf* making her recognizable ascent before she could be seen.

A lazy fountain of water in the center of the bubbles grew and grew until her pointy black bow quickly appeared, seemingly from nowhere. The rest of her menacing shape quickly followed, as a feathery fan of water gave way beneath her keel, hull, and, finally, her fins. Steadily and silently she rose to greet the wide-open, gigantic Atlantic once again.

The hatch safely broke away from her seam, letting out a hiss before opening the rest of the way, revealing a very ambitious crew inside. They were ready to receive the thrills of the new day, rain or shine.

US-1 was the first to crawl out with his binoculars, where he eagerly began to case the area. In the moments that followed, he happily told his comrades without looking at them, "You're right, Doc! I see it...it's over there...one o'clock... about four hundred meters."

Off in the distance was the fuel drop they'd scheduled themselves to find. It was a large, black, round tank floating and bobbing about, with a small, white handkerchief-sized flag flying high above. On the face of the flag was the strange golden symbol of the rolling star—the same one found on the fins of their vessel and their coats.

With US-2 navigating inside the cockpit, they idled their way over to the fuel pod while the hatch was still open and US-1 still standing on deck. When they got to the fuel pod, Doc pitched him a rope to secure the vessel to one of the shiny, bronze bollards near the tip of the bow. Once tied off, they began their fuel service procedure. US-1 was still mainly involved with that. With a small hop over to the top of the fuel pod, he gingerly popped open the manhole-sized lid and connected the fuel line apparatus to their vessel, except a minor problem occurred. He tried to work the pumping apparatus, but it didn't budge. "It won't move...the hand pump. It's jammed or something."

Doc stuck his head out from the open glass hatch and placed his hands on the main deck, looking puzzled. While he felt the healthy drizzle of the weather's sideshow, he wiped his hand off with his handkerchief to bide his time. "Still no luck? There's a locking mechanism on it...did you disengage the mechanism?"

US-1 fiddled with it for a while longer before he stood up on top of the fuel pod to give the mechanism a swift kick with his heel. Still, he had no luck, so he looked over to his onlookers and shrugged his shoulders.

Doc adjusted his spectacles, thinking for a moment while US-2 unbuckled himself and started to crawl out to see if perhaps *he* could do something. Doc grabbed his arm. "No—no...not necessary. I designed it. I'll go out there."

With a cumbersome hop outside to the main deck, Doc shuffled over and exchanged places with US-1. Shortly thereafter, it was he who fiddled with the stubborn mechanism for a long time before he too seemed befuddled. "Holy bejeezus...it's jammed." He went on, "Quick. Get me something to knock it loose."

US-1 quickly received a hammer from US-2, when suddenly something else out in the ocean caught his attention. It whizzed by just beneath the surface, and all he saw was its trail of sudsy white bubbles before it disappeared.

US-1 dropped the hammer on the main deck. "I heard something—no I saw something! It was fast, hissing. Yeah, it was hissing!"

Doc adjusted his spectacles to look around for it in the water. "I don't see a thing. What was it?"

US-1 picked the hammer back up off the deck. "It was too fast for a fish—maybe thirty or forty knots. It looked like... scared me. Didn't you two hear it?!"

Doc jumped back then looked all around as if the ocean was splashing with man-eating fish of all kinds. "Christ—thirty or forty knots? That's too fast...that's—that's a—Holy boy Christ. Did you say it hissed?"

US-1 and 2 cried out, "What is it?"

"Say it—what is it, Doc?"

Doc replied, "Well, from US-1's description, it sounds like a—a *torpedo!*"

US-2 jumped around in the cockpit. "Where? Where did it come from? Where did it go?!"

Doc gathered himself up and then took a knee to look around for himself. He couldn't see a thing, so he quickly waved his hand for US-1 to come closer. "Give me that hammer. I need it now. *Now*, I say!" After US-1 gave it to him, Doc quickly ordered, "Get back inside and have US-2 start the engines." He quickly dislodged the mechanism then frantically began pumping fuel. "US-2! Put down those binoculars and start the engines—I said, *now!*"

In the meantime, US-2 kept scanning the area, when he suddenly spotted a tiny object off in the distance. "Battle cruiser! She's behind you, Doc! It's flag looks like it might be Royal Navy!"

On the double, Doc kept pumping. Like a scissoring jack, he worked the apparatus until he almost lost his breath. He paused only to look over his shoulder. "Looks like sixteen hundred meters away! Holy bejeezus. Battle cruiser? She's the demon of the sea...oh, holy God's Christ O'Mighty. Put down those binoculars! Get ready to leave, *now!*"

US-1 and 2 strapped themselves in. "Come on, Doc, hurry!"

"Forget the petrol! Let's go!"

Doc's motions let the two of them know his solemn choice. As he wheezed with exhaustion, pumping faster than ever, he stuttered, "O'Mighty, O'Mighty *God*...please! Christ O'Mighty, can't this thing pump any faster?"

He went on, "She's almost there. I can do this! *Whew*! O'Mighty, O'Mighty....*Christ*! O'Mighty, O'Mighty...get this done, please."

US-2 fired up both engines with a mighty roar.

Through the yelling of his comrades to hurry it up, something terribly wrong overcame Doc. Suddenly, he looked confused. Trepidation and exhaustion flooded his veins. He stopped pumping for just a second, feeling his heart, and then began gasping for air. Sweat coated his face almost instantly before he turned completely white. In the midst of wondering whether he could carry on, he looked to his two crewmembers, who were frantically waving their arms.

"Come on! Jump!"

"Forget about it…jump! We gotta go!"

Delusion quickly got a hold of him and glued him down right where he was. He tried to move his arms and legs, except they were anchored by his mind too. An agonizing apathy of hopelessness seemingly strapped down almost every muscle in his body. He looked as though the twitches of his mind reeled faster than ever, until finally he broke free. Something triggered his thoughts, allowing him to move once again, except he turned his head the opposite way. Clairvoyance must have tortured him to take one last look over his shoulder to see what he thought he knew was coming next. Sadly so, two hundred meters away, and closing in fast, was another terrible torpedo swirling right toward him.

Forcefully, he pounded through his prison of peril to sputter, "The mission…my God, the mission! We've got to get the baby clear!"

Doom struck him deep in the blacks of his eyes, but before he could plan something else, his spectacles dropped off his slippery face and into the water. Blindsided again, he took off his smock to jump and swim for it, but he suddenly stopped in a freeze of stuttering panic.

US-1 and 2 kept yelling.

"Juuuump!"

"Cut the rope! Jump!"

He couldn't.

Tears flowed from Doc's eyes as he sat back on the black crown of the fuel tank, as if he'd just given up. He barely muttered, "I can't swim."

Salvation and sacrifice quickly stepped in, offering up what little bit of calculated courage he must have had left. With one big, angry jerk, he yanked the fuel nozzle from the ship and unhooked the rope from the fuel pod and threw it clear.

While he wiped his eyes dry, he sat back down, waving them on. "Get out of here, *now!*"

US-2 put it in reverse and blasted away as both of them yelled back.

"We'll spin back to get you, Doc!"

"Hang on! We'll distract them!"

US-2 barely got any distance before he locked it into a full turnaround in the middle of his massive wake. "We gotta get him."

US-1 yelled, "He saw another torpedo coming! We've got to get more distance!"

"No, there's still time!"

"Can't you see what he saw? Obey him now!"

"I didn't see anything."

"You're going to get us killed, damn you. *Go!*"

In the midst of their arguing, they had no idea history had launched its course. Dr. Wycliffe was no longer part of it. The feeble-looking, pudgy, old man they'd once called "Doc" looked back at them with barely half a chance to raise his hand good-bye.

The torpedo struck its brutal bull's-eye.

KaboomBOOOOOOOM!

Below his bottom, on a pod of fuel, all hell broke loose with a double blast. Up from the ocean, a raging mushroom appeared within the blink of an eye. Blackened blazes of fire, particles, and water filled the air immediately with it.

The blasting shockwave slammed up to greet the US *Wehrwolf* with such ripping force that she should have met her fate right then and there. Somehow the vessel shunned the continuing blast. She held together, but not without a great price. Instantly, she was thrown, capsized, and then speared into the sea. While the bomb monstrosity kept raging above them, she laid silent, blacked out, and motionless several meters down.

The blaze of the bomb might have ended quickly, but its party of hellfire continued to dance on top of the ocean in a terrible twist of turbulence. Every last drop of fuel from the fuel pod ignited in the scattered blaze, like it was a hungry ghoul wishing for the water to keep burning.

Finally, the catastrophic horror of the fuel and bomb-filled torpedo settled down to only a few floating fires refusing to dissipate. All that was left was the disfigured tail of the US *Wehrwolf*, which barely bobbed back up to the surface. Her aqua fins, bearing the mark of the rolling star, could be seen, but not for long. The last few flames, still fueled by floating petrol, hung around to burn off two of the three golden emblems as a final affront of the blast. The only one that remained was hidden under the protection of the oil-slicked water.

As far as the proud vessel's crew, they seemed trapped for sure. But beneath the peaceful, quiet insulation of the sea, the proud vessel seemed like she wished to remain alive by staying afloat. As badly as her hull was marred, her glass cockpit was intact. There were no signs of light, or life for that matter, inside. In the murky darkness, a few short circuits sporadically flickered along with the tethers of a few tiny, red warning lights that flashed.

A closer look inside the cockpit revealed the subtle sounds of an unattended baby whimpering and the seemingly lifeless bodies of US-1 and 2 still harnessed in their safety belts. At least Randolf was okay, but the situation of his two remaining guardians was questionable. They looked to be helplessly hanging from their seats like rag dolls. Inevitably, the force of gravity invited itself to pull on their limbs and heads, exacerbating their grave predicament. Gravity, with its odd manner of eternal persuasion, had bigger plans. The bottom of the sea was where it wanted to take them and their vessel—straight down to the uninviting kingdom of black abyss.

Apparently, the baby offered an unsuspected gift of consciousness to one of his sentinels. US-1 moved first with the twitch of his fingers, then his eyes. His senses arose more vividly when he noticed that he was not seated correctly. He was hanging vertically downward instead of sitting properly in his chair. In time, he realized he was still strapped in, hanging from his safety harnesses in the dark. He had to do something quickly; the harnesses were cutting off his breath. He finally freed himself, only to fall straight down onto his controls instead of the deck. Nothing seemed to be where it should have been, so he began to feel around for his controls to gain a sense of his whereabouts.

Something eerily quiet overcame him. For just a moment, queer feelings of curiosity spoke out loud, causing him to stop and take a look straight down through his protective glass cockpit and over the bow, which faded into the blackness beyond. The horror of it caused him to almost choke. "*Ahh!*"

Nothing was there except a tunnel of darkness. Immediately he suffered a sickening spell of vertigo. Not knowing what else he could do, he closed his eyes, which saved him for at least a moment. Like a blind man, he felt for his buoyancy controls which, by chance, were blinking danger signals and begging for attention. At the very least, he was on the right track. He then pressed them in sequential order, along with a few others he'd apparently memorized, then whispered, "Reset buoyancy…pu-pu-please work."

Slowly his efforts began to payoff. He opened his eyes with relief as the ship began to level off underwater, but something wasn't quite right. The ship began to descend slowly, causing him to lose what little bit of spirit he'd gained. In the midst of the sinking, darkening surroundings, he struggled for at least a minute before feverishly stuttering, "It's not working. It's not working. Where'd I go wrong? Lights…lights, where are the *lights*?!"

He found at least one light to click on, which was barely enough for him to take a quick glance at his depth gauge. It most certainly wasn't what he expected, so he tapped on it, thinking it must be several fathoms wrong. Suddenly he heard something all around him begin to twist and creak. "*Aaawwh*! We're imploding!"

Quickly, he switched the stationary stealth propulsion to "on," except it didn't work. Quickly again, he switched it back and forth until finally, he got results. "It's on!" Instantly, the vessel shifted its descent and began to rise. As he kept tapping his depth gauge, the needle slowly returned to the green, causing him to collapse back into his chair.

By this time, the baby was screaming at the top of his lungs, so he scrambled below deck to tend to him. As soon as he calmed him down, he rushed back up to tend to US-2 who, by then, had regained consciousness and was sitting in his chair with a lit cigarette.

US-1 almost looked like he wanted to hug him. "Thank God you're okay. You…you are okay, aren't you?"

US-2 wasn't, apparently. Something was deeply wrong with him as he sat there, crouched over with his hands and head sagging between his knees. "He's gone." He looked up, repeating, "Dr. Wycliffe…Doc…he's gone."

US-1 fell into his chair. The horrid image of the brutal blast flickered back in his mind. He then dropped his head. "Oh no. He's gone…yes…he's gone."

Neither of had much to say, really. The only thing that seemed to work for them right then was to sit motionless and mourn the loss of a very big part of their tiny crew. It was hard to imagine exactly what they were thinking. Despair seemed to paralyze them for a minute or two, until US-1 heard a most unusual sound.

"What's that?"

"*Shhhhhhh*, quiet...I hear it too...listen...it's getting closer, I think."

It was there, but very faint at first. A small sound was coming from outside their cockpit, somewhere out in the water. Ever so slowly, it approached them with deep baritones, like a repeating, obnoxious, alien-like sound. It was disturbing the way it resonated through the water and then up through the soles of their feet to the ears.

Wooov-wooov-wooov-wooov-wooov-wooov—

It got louder as it got closer.

Wooov-Wooov-Wooov-Wooov-Wooov—

US-1 panicked. "I can't stand it...I—I—I can't stand it. We gotta get out of here!"

US-2 grabbed his arm. "No! Don't try a thing. We can't. It's here, whatever it is...we have to think. Quick—how deep are we?"

US-1 spun his chair back to his controls, whispering, "Seven fathoms...we're still idling on stealth...we haven't moved a centimeter."

US-2 spun his chair around, looking over his entire control panel. "Good...setting Naxos, scrambling all signals, now...your sonar. Why is it out?"

US-1 tapped the screen and tried switching it on. "It's shorted out."

Suddenly, the colossal wavering sounds stopped, but only to be replaced with rickety iron, flexing from all directions, ringing throughout their cockpit and causing them to hold their ears.

Hoooowwwl-screeeeeeech! Groooaaaan! Eeeeeeek-eeeek-eeek-eek!

Instantly, US-2 looked up and stared into nothing but blackness. "Your spotlight...is it working?"

"I don't know."

"Check it and shine it straight up, will you?"

THE TIME TO TELL

US-1 dashed for the control handle then cranked it straight up and turned it on. "*Ahhhh*! It's right there! Hit the deck!"

"*Oh* shit, I can't look! It's gonna smash us!"

Uncontrollably, they jumped out of their chairs as if convulsions were to blame. Blocking their entire view directly above was a rotting mass of monster steel, encrusted with sea urchins and skeletons of barnacles as jagged as an upside-down reef.

US-1 dared to look again, "God...a massive keel of a colossal ship. It's right on top of us—without touching."

More monstrosities of massive steel revealed themselves as they gained the nerve to look in front of their bow. Two behemoth propellers, looking more like massive iron windmills, stood still, right out in front of them. They were barely visible, yet ready to turn themselves back on at any second.

US-1 quietly gulped with nothing to swallow except for a dry drink of fear. He tethered his tongue around his dry mouth, feeling the need to speak softly. "Look at—look at that. What are those?"

US-2 looked across the span beyond their ship. "Too dark to tell...they look like propellers—except the size—the size of our ship."

US-1 kept scanning with his spotlight. "That's what they are...if they turned, we'd be ripped to shreds...it's got to be the cruiser...the one that shot at us."

US-2 threw his cigarette down and lit another. "Must have been the *woof woof* sound we heard."

"I don't know, and I don't care...thank God they shut them down."

US-2 chuckled, "Son of a...could've been fish bait."

"*Shhhhh*, keep your voice down, damn it...they came to look for us—maybe finish the job...she's surveying, I bet—reading for signals...maybe they think we're a sub. Yes—they think we're a U-boat."

US-2 flicked his cigarette ashes. "I don't know about you, but we need to get out of here before they fire those two twin choppers up...put it on stealth propulsion so we can stealth our way out of here."

"No...they'll litter the sea with depth charges the second we give ourselves away. Any sign of us fifty meters out, and they'll blow up everything in sight."

US-2 paused. "*Ah* yes. They think we're dead right now. They've got nothing on sonar...directly underneath them is the safest place to be...it's cat-and-mouse for now."

Five minutes passed before US-2 muttered, "He's a seasoned captain. I'll give him that."

"He must be, Blondie...they're waiting for the slightest movement...he still might blow the ocean to smithereens for an exercise...Doc never did tell you about shock waves from depth charges, did he?"

"No way. I would've remembered...from the looks of this glass bubble thing we're in, I'd say he didn't want us to know. You think?"

"Yes. Afraid so—and then some. Ever see what those underwater bombs can do?"

"That was your specialty...I was primarily special operations in everything else. So what do they do?"

US-1 huffed, "I'll save your stomach...well maybe you should know. First you bleed out your eyes and ears, provided this glass holds up, which I doubt it would. If it doesn't, our eyes—wait—maybe our skulls will implode—"

"Shut up—I got the picture. We survived the torpedo blast, didn't we? We can survive depth chargers if we have to."

Nearly five more minutes went by before US-2 relaxed a little more. After he realized his cigarette had gone out, he reached in his pocket and flipped open his lighter, sparking a dim light in front of his face. As he looked deep into the flame, his eyes slowly grew overwhelmingly clever "You should've taken my advice...we could have strolled a hundred meters out without detection...our equipment worked against that pack of subs, didn't it? They didn't see a thing."

He finished lighting his cigarette and continued after blowing a smoke ring. "All we have to do is surface—me on the Strong Ray. I'd put the sons-a-bitches on the bottom of the ocean before they could blink an eye."

US-1 glared. "*Huh?* That's what their captain wants...he somehow knows we might still be alive...he's got hundreds of men on post—looking in all directions, I figure...all of them have their fingers on triggers, just itching to fire on something like you."

US-2 twisted his cigarette between his fingers, looking amused. "Yeah, I suppose you're right. Sure sounds good though, doesn't it? After what they did to Doc, I'd like to deliver a big fat paycheck back in their face...speaking about Doc, what are we going to do now that he's gone?" US-1 didn't answer immediately, so US-2 looked around the cockpit. Down below him, he saw Doc's binder, so he picked it up and curiously thumbed through it. "Well? What do we do? Let me see here—hmmm."

"Complete our mission, that's what."

US-2 snapped the binder back up. "Did he ever tell you how the baby was going to end all the fighting in our big, bad world?"

US-1 smirked. "No...I suppose we'll never know now that he's gone...let me see that binder....thank you...hey, look... Doc's got everything in here...he even knew about the ship above us, it looks like."

"What did he say about it?"

"Says here it's Royal Navy, all right...an HMS Cruiser[27]... she's supposed to be escorting a convoy of merchant supply ships across the Atlantic. They've been having trouble with

---

27 HMS Cruiser was a World War II British battleship.

U-boats attacking them, according to this. I told you that's what they think we are. *Hmmm*, she's not supposed to be in this area, though. Doc's got his route way north of us."

US-2 stroked his two-day-old beard. "Maybe they know about our mission?"

"Don't be ridiculous. We're so secret. Our own German ships know nothing about us."

US-2 quickly put his cigarette out, then glared. "What's the bastard doing clear down here then? The ship was alone. I saw it with my own binoculars."

US-1 shrugged his shoulders. "Don't know. Maybe they sent them down on a reconnaissance mission—maybe seek and destroy potential, U-boats flanking from the south. That would put her right here, I suppose."

"How big do you think she is?"

US-2 kept thumbing through the pages. "Don't know... Doc didn't specify in his notes. As long as ten of our ships combined would be a good assumption."

"That's about right...all I could see through the binoculars were those massive guns."

US-2 relaxed up against the back of his chair before he let his mind drift. "What do you know about the baby?"

US-1 took a cockeyed double take before answering. "Baby? I know about as much as you. What do you mean?"

"Why is it *this* baby and not another? I mean, this whole thing sounds crazy to me."

US-1 paused to study the curves in his comrade's face. "I don't want to get involved with you on this. Remember our training. Everyone—hell, the world depends on us. Look at this ship we're in, for Christ sake. Have some faith."

US-2 leaned over, rubbing a stiff part of his neck. "Yeah, I guess. We even have countermeasures— against ourselves. Did you get the same training as me?"

US-1 shook his head with dismay. "Don't bring it up...of course I did."

THE TIME TO TELL

"So, *uh*—"

"Look, Blondie, we can't turn back now. We *have* to continue."

"Oh? Why's that? Please enlighten me...tell me about that."

US-1 pulled out one of Doc's maps. "We're in the middle of the Atlantic...more petrol's ahead, not behind us.... besides, we're free in America. That was the deal, or have you forgotten? By the way, I'm taking over the baby now, not you."

"Sure thing, Midshipman. You get the baby. What I was saying is this all sounds too good to be true. I mean, how can a baby make world peace—then keep it that way? Doesn't it sound a little funny to you? Sounds like Jesus or Mohammad or something. I mean the kid's no prophet; I can guarantee that."

US-1 quickly folded his map and shoved it aside. "Look, I don't know how he can do it or how you wish to think about it. We just have to stick to our mission. That's all I know... that's what we were sworn with our lives to do...it's life or death. Not that you *care,* it sounds like. Besides, Doc made me promise again before he died. He believes, or believed, in what he was doing. I could tell."

"Oh? So what?"

"Listen, Blondie...get whatever it is out of your mind. We'd *die* if we turned back now. What are you thinking? Listen to me."

Silence crept in between their differences as US-2 chewed on his cheek. "Not thinking nothing. Slow down...what did they see in you, anyway?"

"What do you mean by that?"

US-2 nonchalantly played with his lighter, looking like he wasn't very convinced. "I don't know. Maybe I'll see it later... I just don't see it in you yet."

US-1 leaned over in his face. "Okay, big shot. Tell me what it is they saw in you?"

"That's easy...I know that I'm right in whatever I do. It's not my problem everyone else is wrong."

US-1 fell back in his chair almost laughing. "Oh, great. Better think again on that one. I'm sure that answer never got you anywhere."

US-2 then blew another smoke ring straight up. "You asked. I'll keep it to myself next time and let my anger brew like a pressure cooker. That'll give you something else to deal with—besides getting us killed."

"*Ah* shit, take some time off with your wise cracks. It's just the two of us now, so why be bothered?"

"What? You want me to thank you later for getting us out of here? A big thanks in heaven maybe—or hell."

In the midst of silence for almost a minute, US-2 turned on a dime to humble himself. Earnestly he threw out his long-held breath. "Okay, I give up...I don't know what they saw in me...there, are you happy?"

Then, without hesitation, he reached for his pack of cigarettes and poked one in his mouth without lighting it. After he chewed on it for a while, he kept to himself, letting his built-up anger do his talking.

US-1 said, as he looked the other way. "Go ahead...add me to your list of petty problems you already have. That's all we need right now."

US-2 blurted, "I know why they chose you...because you're so damn loyal. If I didn't know any better, I'd say you're married—even though you're not supposed to be."

The baby below began to whimper. They looked at each other as if they'd forgotten about him.

US-1 dropped his hands down both sides of his chair, looking tired and fed up. "I checked the kid while you were hanging around in your seat unconscious. It's your turn, if you don't mind."

US-2 groaned as he lazily got up to go down below, but before he ducked out of sight, he threw his cigarette aside, letting it burn on deck. "This is going to be a bitch without Doc...you know that, don't you?"

US-1 waved him off. "Oh, change him too, will you? Don't throw anything around. Be quiet about it. We don't want any chance of our enemy picking up your angry noises."

US-2 spoke up from below. "Anything else? I mean, I guess you're the new Kapitan, right?"

"Yes, there is. Bring us up some food. I'm starving, aren't you?"

About five minutes later, US-2 quietly strolled back up to the cockpit and threw his companion a bag of military rations, narrowly missing his head. "Here you go. I ate mine already. They're not all that bad."

"Thanks for handing them to me. Hope I can count on more of your pleasant surprises."

US-1 was poking and picking through his rations when he stopped to listen. "Hey, did you hear that?"

"Yes, I did...that's not what I think it is, is it?"

Sure enough, out in front of them, through the murky waters, US-1's spotlight was the first to catch a glimpse of the grimacing fact. The mega-props from the ship began to move. US-2 shouted, "Drop us now!"

"I'm already on it...buoyancy falling, falling...faaaalling. Come on. *Damn* this thing—it's too slow."

"Come on! We haven't got all day!"

Both of them watched through the ill-fated comfort of just one dim spotlight the giant swaths of the massive propellers slowly cranking up. More agonizing yet, their race to descend their vessel may as well have been placed in underwater space, as slow as it was. But when the US *Wehrwolf* decided to descend, she did. She did, barely in the nick of time, through a massive wake of turbulence that rocked their ship until the mighty battle cruiser chopped the waters over the top of them, leaving nothing but massive swaths of a narrow miss. As they watched the blades fade away into the sea, their long-held breaths spewed with relief.

"*Whew*, that was close, eh, Blondie? We're settled down now at thirteen fathoms. What are your readings? We healthy?"

"All resets on par… reading temperature…salinity stable…thermohaline effect still stable…she's all working over here—how about you?"

"Like a dream…we're just a little scuffed up, it looks like. All's well."

US-2 hit the lights. "Hopefully, there are no more surprises. Don't think I can live this way all the time…you?"

"Hell no…let's get our heads into this….so it looks like we're behind schedule for our next petrol drop."

"No hurry. If our engines still function, I can run over a hundred knots until we run out of gas. Then we can coast the rest of the way on stealth."

"Come again?"

"Yeah, like Doc says, we have free energy up to twenty knots…we can go the rest of the way to the United States if we have to."

US-1 paused as if he didn't quite hear right. "That's fine, but it would take us eight or nine more days at twenty knots. We don't have enough water or rations for us and the baby on that kind of watch. Best stick to the next petrol station."

"So how long to get there, you figure?"

"Let me see now…about twenty-nine hours by my calculations, with our delay included."

"Not a problem. I can do it. We're only behind schedule by a couple hours."

US-1 hesitated. "That's a problem. It's Doc's security measure he never told you about."

"Oh, he told you and not me? Why is that? What security measure?"

"Maybe you're not loyal enough. The petrol pods begin to sink after so long."

US-2 shook his head. "Okay spit it out then…how long do we have before it sinks?"

THE TIME TO TELL

"I figure we should get there with a little time to spare. You've got to do your job and kick it up a little more though."

US-2 motioned sarcastically. "Okay, I can do that...if you have any more secrets, you'd better tell me because—"

"There's no more, believe me...so save it, will you? Doc told me about the sinking of the pods by accident last night... he had a bad feeling about him dying. Stop getting upset."

"I can deal with being upset...but he was right about dying. What was he—psychic or something?"

"He blamed it on synchronicity among other things...so I take it you're back in this?"

US-2 pointed his finger, pulling his trigger thumb. "You're the new *Kapitan*. What are we waiting around for?"

"You read my mind. Setting base course....setting stealth propulsion to maximum...preparing to surface on the go. We are getting there, good to go. You ready on engines?"

"I thought you'd never ask."

Back on the ocean's surface, a bubbling mound of water appeared. Here she came, with her bow breaking water on the run. As they looked in all directions, both engines fired up in stride, roaring echoes across the barren seascape.

They may not have looked as good—battle scarred, burned at the stern and all—but the US *Wehrwolf* was back in business. A few minor bent fins and a few more dents down her sides didn't hurt. Other than that, she didn't look all that bad.

Nothing else had really changed since their close call, except for perhaps US-1's new demeanor. He was at the center helm where Doc once was, feeling around the armrests, periodically pausing to take in his new position. The thought of their lost captain must have crossed his mind and settled in, for an overwhelming rush of sadness clobbered him. He looked pale and clammy, when he should have been relieved. A huge migraine must have been thrown in too since he rubbed the side of his temple. Most definitely, he was still stuck in a trench of relapse rather than forethought.

One thing was sure: in the midst of the terrible turmoil, he was the one now making the commands and calling the shots in an operation he knew little about. His depression showed, to the point that it caught his comrade's attention as they started to gain speed across the ocean. "It's all right. America, remember? We're gonna be all right."

US-1 looked back then smiled lightheartedly. Quick comments didn't seem to help, for he spiraled back into his daze, rubbing his temple again.

US-2 suddenly looked like he felt sympathetic. As he sped along, he swallowed and offered a smile. "Hey, I'm in it with you to the end. .I can't lose you, damn it, so listen…I can be loyal too, when I want to be." He went on, "Soooo—what's my command?"

US-1 came around. "What? What did you say?"

"You know. What do I do—*Kommandant?*"[28]

US-1 coughed himself out of stagnation, then smiled. "Get this thing going…let's see one hundred ten knots or better."

"I thought you'd never ask." US-2 surged on his throttle a bit. "She's thirsty for gas…can you feel that? Can you feel it, *Kommandant?*"

US-1 placed his arms back up on his armrests, then pointed his finger out to the bow and beyond. With a fake finger shot, he pulled the trigger. "Let 'er rip."

They took off like they were standing still, disrupting almost everything nearby. Aquatic strangers, once again, fled the scene. Seagulls flew for the lives, fish busted away from their schools, and a distant pack of whales even changed

---

28 "Kommandant" is the German word for "commander."

course. In no time, their vessel danced and skipped across the wakes without a care in the world.

Inside the US *Wehrwolf*, the atmosphere was all business, unfortunately. Forces of nature, along with their miniscule friends of the feather, gave little reprieve for these disciplined sea travelers. The Atlantic did what it did naturally, regardless of what kind of rhythm they were in. It just so happened that the waves and wind steadied, fortifying the luck they needed while making good time.

Midway through the day, US-1 and 2 had found a rhythm of their own with the assistance of a little radio they'd discovered hiding in the instrumentation. They turned it on to a station of static with a hint of music from the foreign land they knew little about. The song was in English, so their German ears couldn't understand much. They didn't care. They flipped their heads around and snapped their fingers, singing in some odd mix of English and German that would make sense only to the intoxicated.

As the hours dragged on, US-1 succumbed to napping now and then, while US-2 had no such benefit. Fatigue settled in on him too, but from something else besides the monotony of navigating. He kept looking down on his steering mechanism, trying to grip it a little harder each time. His controls had been pulling against him all day. Apparently, the damaged rudder had finally taken its toll, making his job more laborious than ever. Eventually, he made the mistake of looking over to US-1, who had dozed off, looking all too comfortable. He seemed bothered by it, so he took the opportunity to summon his comrade back out of complacency. "Hey!"

US-1 barely even moved. Instead, he rolled over, looking more content than ever, so US-2 yelled, "Heyyy! Wake *up*!"

US-1 popped out of his chair grabbing his pistol on his holster. He quickly realized it was his comrade messing with him.

US-1: "What? Couldn't you tell I was sleeping?"

US-2: "Slow down on the trigger. If I can't sleep, neither can you."

US-1: "Thanks for letting me know. You bother me—you know that?"

US-2: "Who said I was here to entertain you? The baby needs a little attention, and so do we. Can we shut down for a minute or two? I've been on the go, holding this damn steering too long."

US-1: "Well, *uh, hmmm*. We've been making good time, looks like."

US-2: "We should be about ten minutes ahead of schedule now from the looks of Doc's alarm clock."

US-1: "Yes we are. Good job. Everything's holding up too, I see."

US-2: "All except for my steering. I can't go on much longer without a break."

US-1: "What's wrong?"

US-2: "The blast damaged it, I think...I have to go outside and see why we are pulling so hard."

US-1: "Okay, let's do it then...hey, look. Our sonar's back on."

US-2: "I know. I fixed it while you were sleeping."

US-1: "How'd you do—oh, never mind, I don't want to know. Well it looks like good news...sonar says we are all clear."

US-2: "What? Speak a little louder...engine noise."

US-1: "I said the sonar works! Go ahead, shut down!"

US-2: "Slowing down right—now."

US-1: "It's so calm outside. I can't believe it...a good a place as any since it all looks the same."

US-2: "You read my mind...beautiful days...keep 'em coming."

US-2 backed all the way off his throttle, sending their obnoxiously-loud rasp across the barren, sleeping ocean. Her noise drove the usual marine animals to escape the scene,

THE TIME TO TELL

but didn't affect a new group of creatures deep down below the surface. To the contrary, these animals were intrigued by their presence. In fact, they actually turned around to swim back toward the direction of the noise.

These creatures could hardly ever be seen beneath the dark waters, but they revealed themselves to be menacing. They were the apex of the underwater kingdom—a feast-or-famine type of family.

In times of yore, they were called the "Evil Black Fish of the Sea." The only name they should have kept. "Unnerving" might have been another way to describe them since they were most definitely unafraid. Their most troubling aspect was their supreme intelligence. It showed, through their eerie alien-like clicks and whistles of echoing communication beneath the water.

Soon, they quickly summoned their loose pod more tightly together. The larger one demanding the lead was, without a doubt, the devout matriarch. Somewhere along their brutal bloodlines, their females had become the leaders. This leader was no exception. She didn't just happen to be the wicked one out front—she looked to be taking a demanding role of leading her presumed siblings all the way.

Like the pure predators they were, they slithered up close to the bottom of the US *Wehrwolf*, completely encircling her without being seen. As their encrypting messages of clicks gained frequency beneath the waters, so did their anxieties. Then, with the click of their last little creepy sounds, they ducked down into the murky depths directly below.

US-2 took another look at his sonar just to be sure nothing was lurking in the waters. "Wait…I thought I saw something."

"What is it?"

US-2 tapped the screen. "I don't know…I think it still has a short or something. First I saw something big below us, but then it went away."

US-1 brushed his hand away from the controls. "You never fixed it…forget about it."

US-2 nodded as he felt the tingling of his hands from holding his steering too long.

His comrade was equally sore. He got up, feeling the numbness of his buttocks.

A little relaxation and recuperation was on their minds as they looked at each other. Just being motionless was good enough. As they lapped up the still serenity for just a moment longer, US-2 was the one to press on. "Go get the baby. I'll try to find some tools around here."

"Tools?"

US-2 paused. "You know, *tools*. Those things we use to fix things. Something's bent outside. Hopefully, we can do something about it…if we can't, we'll be in trouble steering this thing beyond a few more hours."

US-1 nodded and then went to grab the baby down below, while US-2 found a toolbox hiding in a compartment.

After warming up to the idea of fixing things with a freshly lit smoke, he flipped open the cockpit hatch and leaped onto the main deck to look about. While he scratched, stretched, and yawned in the comforts of the wide-open, he soon became distracted by the stern behind him. The steering rudder mechanism was damaged a little worse than he'd apparently thought. Nevertheless, he prepared for the idea of physical labor by taking off his Denison coat, cracking his knuckles, then stretching his arms and legs as if he were preparing for a serious workout. He crammed his cigarette to the side of his mouth and puffed his way over to the vessel's top center fin where the problem was. It looked about as bad as a flopped-over dorsal fin of a crippled whale.

He stopped and muttered. "So that's got to be bent back." While glaring at the damage, he took a long drag of his cigarette and blew his disgusted thoughts out with the smoke. Things didn't look much better after that, so he turned his back to it and talked out to sea. "How in the *hell* am I supposed to bend that back?"

US-1 came up from behind, holding Randolf. He too looked at the damaged apparatus and somewhere between being acerbic and downright dumfounded, he said, "Wow, you can't navigate this thing that way, can you?"

"That's what I've been trying to—where were you when I—oh, well. You've got to help me on this."

US-2 reached down into his toolbox and rummaged around before he finally found a pair of tools that suited him. "Here we go…put the baby down and take this, will you? I'll take this other one."

US-1 gingerly put the baby down in a safe place on deck. "Okay, what do you want me to do…what's this you handed me?"

"It's a pipe wrench…you get on that side of this…what did Doc call it?"

"The center aqua fin, I believe."

US-2 started to get ready. "Okay, whatever. You take it up here with the jaws and pull back, and I'll get over here on the other side with mine…I'll push at the same time. Got it?"

US-1 contemplated with his wrench. "Jaws? What jaws? I thought you said it was a pipe wrench."

US-2 looked at him, wondering if his comrade was serious. He flicked his cigarette out to sea and used his own wrench to demonstrate. "Look here—these here things that go up and down? They're jaws. They go right here on this bent piece…okay, now. We're going to use leverage. You pull this way while I push with my wrench the same way…got it?"

"Yes, okay, leverage. I know about that…sounds good. Got it."

They both started together with a slow, mighty tug and push. Gradually, they began to put their whole bodies into it, without holding back in the slightest.

Their lone spectator, the baby, was in a prime vantage point to watch their fair amount of blunders. Not only was he watching, but he seemed to be enjoying every minute of their seesawing show once they got the hang of it. Occasionally, they stopped just to hammer on it with the backs of their wrenches. This might have made things look crazier in the eyes of an infant; two big men jumping, crawling around on top of, and then pounding on the apparatus did look odd.

US-2 grunted, "What in hell? What's this made of? We're getting nowhere with this…that's it. At the count of three, you heave, okay?"

This went on for quite a while as they struggled with the last bit.

"*Geeyawwwh!*"

"*Rawwwh!*"

Once they finally straightened the fin, US-2 brushed his hands and put the tools away. "There now…all done."

Suddenly, the baby squealed and giggled before US-2 pointed. "Well, at least we know the kid's fine—look at him. We must've looked pretty funny?"

US-1 nodded and looked around to observe just how calm the weather and sea were. Staring back at him was nothing but the serene water and gray, ghost-like clouds. Then, for no apparent reason, he stripped down to nothing but his briefs.

US-2 had no more than put his tools away when he got a glance of the final stages of US-1's striptease act. With a preposterous glare, he asked, "What are you doing?"

"What does it look like? I smell bad—haven't had a bath in days." Without further warning, he took three big steps and sprung off the port aqua fin as if it were a diving board. Almost as surprising was the poor quality of his dive; he went head first and crashed into the water, split-legged and all.

US-2 seemed appalled. In a sort of fed-up way, he strolled over to the cockpit and reached way over inside to grab his

THE TIME TO TELL

Luger pistol, of all things. In the same fed-up manner, he walked back over to the port side where his companion made his dive and took a cocky stance with his gun in hand.

When US-2 popped his head up out of the water, he looked at his comrade holding a gun and suddenly became nervous. "Hey! What are you doing?"

"Watching over you. What does it look like?"

As US-1 swam around, he smiled and asked, "Come on out and join me. What's wrong, can't you swim?"

"Of course, I can. Don't be pulling this. I'm the joker around here, not you. Get back up here."

US-1 treaded water briefly. "I think that's what happened to Doc. He couldn't swim. What do you think?"

"I think you're right. I'll throw you a rope. Let's go."

US-1 looked at the gun, "What were you thinking about with the gun? You wouldn't think of shooting me, would you?"

"No, jackass, I'm looking out for you. Something I shouldn't think about. Let's go before you become shark bait."

"Sharks? There are no sharks this far out...okay—okay, I'll swim back. Just give me just a second...you said you wanted to relax so—*relax*."

US-1 floated up on his back on top of the water. "*Thud-ho-ho*...this is great. It'll wake you right up...you should join me!"

US-2 turned him down again, but something else from the deep had already extended an invitation of its own. In the cold, dark, murky waters, several fathoms down, the big, female black fish, more commonly living up to her name as the "Killer Whale," must have seen what she'd been waiting for. Quickly, she encircled with her big, black, torpedo-shaped body. Within an instant, she turned on a dime, as if savoring her last seconds. She rocked her black body, pointing straight up to the surface where US-1's splashing shadow sparkled with edges of sunlight. In an instant, and out of the abyss, she gave out one last signal—one cryptic click—before bolting up to the surface to greet him.

Thawoooosh!

Before a warning could be uttered, she exploded up like a six-ton marine missile breaking through the surface. She left a massive geyser of water behind her as she continued her launch with US-1 clamped down, deep inside her jaws.

US-2 turned around, barely in time to witness it, "*Ah!*"

The only thing either of them could wish for was a catch and release. Horror came without shame, as far as the wicked female whale was concerned. She celebrated her keep with a horrendous backflip back into the sea and then vanished.

US-2 aimed his gun, but before he could take a shot, he screamed, "Orcaaaa!"

A massive sheet of water engulfed the deck, grabbing everything in sight. US-1's clothes and the baby quickly washed toward the edge of the vessel and began to fall out to sea. US-2 made a remarkable dive across the deck, catching the baby by just his blanket. Without haste, he quickly placed him back into the safety of the cockpit and then rolled back out on deck with his pistol ready to fire.

As he lay there, belly down with his gun pointed at the receding bubbles of where US-1 once was, he gasped, "Just one chance! Show me…give me one chance…damn you! Show yourself!" He got what he wished for. The big female whale popped up on the surface once again, thrashing wildly, exhibiting it was too late. Only part of US-1 was left between her jaws.

US-2 immediately unloaded his magazine.

***Blam-blam-blam-blam-blam-blam-blam!
Blam-blam-blam!—click.***

He tried to reload his pistol, but stopped to acknowledge the fact that his comrade was gone. He must have felt hopeless as she thrashed her meal on the surface even harder, using the whipsawing motions of her teeth. US-2 turned away and closed his eyes, but he couldn't turn off his ears. Behind his back, he couldn't help but hear the gruesome sounds of rock solid bones cracking.

When the shocking incident was finally realized to its fullest, US-2 hung his head low. He tried to move away as far as he could, but avoiding his paralyzing predicament was hard to do. He escaped to the far side of the vessel, but it wasn't far enough, unfortunately. He was marooned there in such a call of quietness that circulated around him like bindings on a miserable life raft. It seemed so wrong; he could only cry out in horror, "*Ahhhhhhhhhh!*"

When he finally opened his eyes out to the calm sea again, another gruesome sight surfaced right before him. The smaller sibling whales surfaced with the other half of US-1. His torso was so mangled that it was hard to imagine that the half body was once human. They paid no attention to US-2 on deck, as they savagely fought for their share, splitting him into yet smaller pieces. Quickly, they too disappeared into their watery hideout, leaving no trace of such a demonic disgrace.

US-2 fell to his knees, collapsing on the deck as if he were hell-struck. Every muscle in his body went loose and lifeless, momentarily letting the waves push him around, right along with his vessel. It was as if he too had been caught up in the killing, but in a different way. He was caught between reality and incredulity, it seemed.

When US-1's blood lapped up to the side of the vessel, US-2's mind was made up with a rude awakening. He was duped into thinking that it didn't happen, somehow. But it happened, all right. It was as authentic as the blood he touched in the water with his shaking hand.

Thereafter, he sobbed while softly tapping the butt of his pistol against the deck. It didn't make his feelings go away, as he would have liked. He later fought back emotions of anger, trying to rid himself of the despair he was in, but the only thing his anger brought on was fatigue.

Exhaustion crept into him so heavily, it seemed to loot whatever energy he had left. To get past his saddened impasse, more time had to pass. As time trickled on, he caught himself inadvertently slipping off into an involuntary sleep. He knew this, so he struggled in his last conscious moments to crawl to the center of his vessel, where he simply collapsed on his back. Within seconds, he passed out, leaving very little desire to open his eyes

In his sleeping moments with Randolf crying in the background, he took himself away from the echoes harkening of the horrendous scene. He may have felt peaceful, sleeping as he was. However, in the real world outside his dreams, time would only tell if peace would greet him when he awakened.

An hour or more went by as the unattended vessel drifted in the near silence of the oceans wakes. Together, he and Randolf drifted alone against the elements above, below, and beyond. Perhaps at the time, it was too early to say, but it seemed like trouble was brewing once again. They say trouble comes in threes, if one believes in superstition. Way out in the lonely sea was where the trio of troubles soon gripped itself hard around the rims of reality.

Within the realms of nature, the third concern began to emerge. It was the weather from the east—or whatever was in it. It swiftly moved in, seemingly as if it wanted to take the place of terrible torpedoes and killer whales, just so it could hand out its own round of havoc too. One could see it off in the distance, looking so calm at the first glimpse. Let it be said that calm sometimes comes before the storm. At least the clouds showed themselves that way. The storm that silently wished to blow in was coming directly for them. The sun had no part of it, for it hid behind the spotty shades of gray and black, taking over the horizon.

THE TIME TO TELL

Not much more than a half hour of daylight was left to go. The brilliant prisms of mostly red color in the sky seemingly offered their sympathies for the death of US-1—but even they looked like they were going away for thoughts of better days. It wasn't long. Within a minute or two, the vibrant colors were gone, succumbing to even more shades of gray and black.

There in the same region of the impending storm, a flicker of lightning appeared. Like the silent deadly whales, it could not be heard or seen, especially from the way US-2 was sleeping. Thunder was nowhere to be found as strange as that may sound.

The likelihood of the storm was fast becoming certainty, but this storm was nothing new. It seemed to be the same hideous storm that was left behind since the dwindling crew set out on their mission. Slowly, it marched westerly, as if it was coming right along with them somehow. Though slow-moving, it looked like it was gathering more size and energy, which, in turn, struck chilling thoughts. So little was known about it, except that it was seemingly within the confines of what was—natural. Hardly a way to escape, it seemed. Like any natural force, it didn't need to rest. It patiently kept coming. No matter how fast the US *Wehrwolf*'s engines could take them, it lagged behind—with its own race in mind. That is, if it had a mind at all.

Indeed, there's always a promise of small but better times when it comes to weather. A promising time was coming just then, when dusk began to set in. Oddly enough, the ocean and rain seemingly knew what was coming. Soft, delicate drops of rain began to follow suit. Along with the ocean's unrest, those subtle speckles of water almost simulated the rhythms of what was approaching. Waves turned more alarming as they crept up and washed over the deck of the sleeping US *Wehrwolf*, giving their own form of incidental warning. The time for *their* telling seemed subtle, but true.

Even if he awoke, the question of what might spur him to continue the journey remained. As he lay there, his head began to rock harder, along with the stronger waves that were well on their way to rising to a more alarming rate than before. He twitched at the sensation of taps of rain hitting his face before he flinched and finally awakened. Another chilly wave crested over the deck and slithered up to him. He dared to study it, as if it looked strange to him. Perhaps it was a crossover from his dreams, but it was as if he was too caught in the sensation that the elements were alive, trying to tell him something. He looked somewhat alarmed, but it was just water, of course. Immediately, he brushed his feelings away. His illusion of minor panic seemed ill-deserved, so he relaxed with a sigh of relief. For a brief time, he seemed quite content to just listen to the rain pattering softly on the deck. He then opened his hands to feel the rain. Another wave lapped up over his hand, offering him a sense of normalcy again. Somewhere in his awakening, he realized that he was alone way out there in the Atlantic without any land to see for perhaps thousands of miles.

He jolted awake fully when he heard the baby whimpering, until eventually the cries soothed him. He brushed off whatever pretense of tension he had and then rolled over on his side to buy another moment of rest and perhaps forget everything once more. He drifted back to sleep, but was awakened all too quickly.

Cra-crack, cra-crack! Rumble rumble!

It was the thunder. This was enough, so he jumped right up to his feet, looking nervous. "Son of a—God, where'd that come from?"

He went on, "Doc? I had this—oh shit. US-1! Where is? Oh no...no, no no, noooo....how could this...how could I? No, I'm on...I'm on a mission...son of a—I'm in this—this mission against—shit, I'm dreaming. Nothing but—hell! Where's my crew-hoo-hoooo?!"

THE TIME TO TELL

Neither of his comrades answered back, of course. He looked out to sea, but nothing was there—just colorless sheets of rain, a nearly all black sky, and a lonesome ocean listening to him with all its undivided attention. The blackest part of the storm was just east of him. Wide awake by then, his expressions faced off with a queer state of fear as he wiped off his face with his shirt.

Suddenly, another crash of thunder rattled him again. He looked up into the blackest part of the storm where the thunder came from and pointlessly rambled, "Did you hear that, you son of a *bitch*? I wanted this mission! Do you hear?! So suck meeeee!" He ditched into the cockpit and closed the hatch in a hurry, mumbling all the way behind himself, "Can't believe I was stupid enough to sign up for suicide… what in living shit was I thinking? Must have been crazy…free America, shit. I'll never see the sand of its beaches. Now I can feel it better than anyone that's already dead."

Through the dim lights of the controls glowing upon his face, fear clearly wrote itself all over his expression. Silence took over again when he stopped talking to himself. The glass in front of him offered little comfort from the rain trickling down, looking as daunting as the veins of mercury sparkling in shadows of black. Eerie was the fact that the storm's approaching wrath couldn't even be heard in the cockpit. The only thing that brought a small sense of complacency for him was the thin layer of glass. He had no idea that beyond that was nothing but a barren, watery hell outside coming to get him.

Just then, he saw the empty chairs next to him. He must have momentarily forgotten he was, once again, alone. Of course, nobody was there, except the strange, innocent, little baby. He saw the baby where he had placed him out of danger an hour or so ago.

Through the glimmer of the control lights the baby, tucked in dry, white linens, smiled, just watching him.

Randolf seemed quite content actually, lying there as snug as a bug in a rug. US-2 watched him as the he tried to grab for anything he could to learn about. Anything he set his eyes on would have been fine: the controls, the leather seat, his blankets, or even the stranger who had just popped in beside him, named US-2, was interesting to him. Nothing was within his reach, but everything must have looked within his grasp the way he moved and tried to touch everything.

US-2 blew off his stress briefly to answer to the baby's calling. Just like a spring, he bounced out of his captain's chair and rushed down below, where the baby's belongings were stored. In no time, he arrived back up on deck with his bubble-like crib in both hands. He then carefully strapped Randolf inside and then strapped the whole crib in the chair as tightly as he could. As a final touch, before closing down his little bonnet, he gave him his bottle and a tucked a few miscellaneous items he thought of as good substitutes for toys. Among a couple items was a pistol magazine stuffed with live nine millimeter bullets and a cigarette lighter.

"There, you happy now? Okay, good."

Through the increasing flickers of lightning shining through the glass of the cockpit, he rubbed his hands as if he was obliviously immune to danger once again. While putting all of his faith on his vessel after that, he reached for the controls and began speaking energetically. "Okay….now, let's reset our course, Randolf…I think I'll call you 'Junior Lieutenant,' okay? Nice to meet you, Junior Lieutenant. Okay, preparing for a stationary dive…establishing stealth propulsion. Speed set to maximum…that's twenty knots. Okay? Okay, let's go. See? Not that bad…that storm's going down…I mean we are going down, Junior Lieutenant."

Gauging by the surprised look of the baby, it was safe to say he hadn't the foggiest idea what US-2 was doing or saying. It wouldn't have mattered, for he became instantly enthralled by the rush of seawater spilling onto and over the glass cockpit. Clearly, he was transfixed by the act of submerging before his eyes.

While US-2 savored every moment of his baby copilot's surprised look, he felt for his pack of cigarettes in his shirt pocket, lit one up, and then relaxed to the sound of utter silence the underwater offered.

He rambled on to the baby in the wisp of his smoky breath, "Wow, that storm was getting pretty rough. I could swear that devil's riding our asses...oh well, we're safe in here. You're in the driver's seat, now, Junior Lieutenant. Fun *huh*? We're going down. Say, what did you say? Where we going? Oh, we're reestablishing our base course—west...should make some time tonight."

He paused for another drag on his smoke. "Yep...before we know it, we'll be at our new home...America...can you say that? Uh-mer-ic-a. Lots a beautiful women, I hear, *huh*? So you're too young to talk? Yes, you're too young...so tell me; you can save this bad world, *huh*? You've got a job to do then. What do they say in America? Get a job?"

He stopped for just a moment, thinking seriously. "*Sheesh*, I'm talking to a baby now...so how's someone like you supposed to save the world, *huh*? That's what I want to know. Okay, don't answer me then...fine...save it yourself then, see what I care."

His junior lieutenant was a good listener—very attentive—until something else more entertaining came along the front of the observation glass. When US-2 turned on the underwater lights, a sudden splash of the ocean's underworld flooded up over the bow and beyond. He wiggled all around from his fingers to his toes, jibber-jabbering with smiles of joy. If he could have talked, he would have said nothing short of "Oh boy!"

Chapter 6

At the dawn of the next morning, the precarious factions within the weather must have given up. On the other hand, a single storm's forlorn warnings could have been nothing more than a passing normality.

Either way, the troubling turbulence had almost blown over completely, lending calmer outlooks than even a fisherman would have liked. It's no secret that fishermen are intrigued by changes in weather. For the anglers of the sea, the sky is a place to look up to, and today it had nothing to hide. The vast openness still handed down clues and residues of dreariness left over from the night before. A sense of calm reigned across the great Atlantic, but the gloominess still hung around—either to sleep or see what might happen next.

Even though the day appeared to be unclear, it did host at least one new boat floating around, likely with the prospect of a decent day's catch. The lone floater seen out there seemed to be trying to take advantage of the calm day break. Measured by common American terms for distance, the vessel's proximity was hundreds of miles westerly from where the US *Wehrwolf* was last seen submerging just yesterday.

Besides this, the vessel's condition showed she had been out there risking her hull at sea quite a few times before. She appeared to be over the hill, to put it nicely. The rundown thing chugged her way westbound, like she might be headed back to a shore that was nowhere in sight at the time, not even through the assistance of a universal set of binoculars.

THE TIME TO TELL

As slowly as she was going, her arrival for land could have been tomorrow, the next day, or whenever. Surely, it was someday.

To describe the risky-looking boat more vividly, one doesn't have to exaggerate. The true question is where to start—with appearance or function? Her blue and white paint was fading and flaking off in big chunks from her bow to her stern. Paint gave color to her looks, but sound gave character to her soul. Her motor puffed of black smoke, like she was burning black rubber inside a furnace instead of the expected diesel fuel. She was running on most of her cylinders, which was a good thing since not all of them were failing just yet. The adage "If it isn't broken, don't fix it" may have been the owner's motto. She kept running and floating on top of the water, and that's all that mattered, apparently.

Wild thinkers had to be aboard this moving mess, since she was way out there in the wide-open sea with no land for hundreds of miles around. Their floating ideas put into effect could have been compared to a bet at a winning crapshoot ten times in a row. Credit should always be given if one can find it when sparring with such odds. One would have to look hard in this case, however. Besides her being deferred from the duties of attention, she must have been someone's pride of the sea at some point. This was a safe bet, in a humorous way. A smidgen of proof backed this up in her name. It was proudly embossed across the stern. She was identified as "*Blessit*," which was nailed up in old, wooden letters—but barely.

Safe to say, the seagoers aboard the *Blessit* were prone to minding their own business. On the flip side, they didn't have much business to get into. They might have been better off minding their own business—whereever they went.

Closer inside the cabin of this poor excuse for a boat, the sound of scratchy radio tunes drifted in and out of an old, partially held-together radio next to two rather grungy-looking fishermen. They matched the boat quite nicely, actually. Their less-than-inspiring attire blended in with the surrounding dirt, filth, and grime, looking more or less like a new form of camouflage. Of course, their silent, lost attitudes had nothing to do with this. Having fun must have been an idea they left on shore a day or so ago.

The two fishermen were aboard. The older, heavy-set fisherman with the worn-out captain's hat held together with fishhooks stood out with an unfashionable, matted beard, among other things. He looked to be the lonely one, pressured into navigating at the helm. The banjo steering wheel he held onto for support originally belonged inside a car. Apparently, the classier, wooden helm had been replaced at some point. Perhaps it was stolen or sold as the only meaningful part left on the boat altogether.

The other fisherman, a younger man, didn't have quite the same burly look, but he desperately needed a shave. He seemed to be looking around for something to do while he sat down with his shoulders hunched. Plenty of fishing line and tackle were there in front of him, but he looked right past them. Fishing wasn't what he wanted to do because fishing poles were nearby with dried bait still on the hooks. Besides him being thin and balding, he was a dead ringer in looks for the heavy-set man at the banjo helm. So much so, that the odds were high they were kin.

Something new came about in the idolizations of boredom between them. It was the radio that faded out of signal. The thin man slowly came around to discovering that playing with the knob on the radio helped to pass the time. His boredom seemed relieved, until his brother looked over to him with a glare for messing with it.

The heavy-set man took his soggy cigar out of his mouth, as if he wanted to say something about the tune of the radio, but he didn't. It had to wait, apparently. He wasn't looking for any trouble, it looked like. Finally, through the twilights of his pause and his partner's static tuning, he mustered up something to say. "*Hmmm*...radio...keep it right there, Jed. Ya ain't gett'n any better, can't ya tell? No foolin' no more now."

Jed left the knob alone just about the time he found a new station. The radio disc jockey came in somewhat clearly, speaking with a happy cheerful tone:

"This is JDVL, J-Devil...jaded by the devil. It's the top of the hour on a gloomy morning for the coastal town of Devil's Gulch, Maine. Enjoy the weather while you can. It looks like another storm is coming in from the Atlantic in a day or so. It'll be hitting the regions all along Devil's coast, the towns of Black Water and Moose Lake farther inland. Stay tuned for more on the weather after this song from Rudy Vallee, "As Time Goes By."

Jed stopped picking his nose briefly. "I *knew* I shouldn'ta listened to ya, Buzz. This is the furthist we ever gone. Now we gotta storm for me to worry 'bout, sheeeit."

Buzz put his cigar back in his mouth then swirled it around. "We'll make it...we'll make it head of th' storm. Hold y'r dick and stop shittin'."

Jed popped up from the bench he sat on and got his pants caught on the rusty fishing hook, so he tried to unhook himself. "Sheeeit...what if I don't believe ya this time? What ya goin' to do 'bout that, *huh*?"

Buzz pulled his cigar out of his mouth again then waited. "*Blessit's* ain't never let us down—so shut up, I said."

Jed got the hook out of his pants, but snagged it in his dirty finger next. He watched to see if it was going to bleed. Of course, it did, so he casually sat back down and sucked on it. "Ya, but—we gots *two* days. With no more diesel it's gonna be th' clos'st one yet...how come you do this all th' time?"

Buzz farted without even breaking a smile. "*Ahhh*, quit y'r complainin'. Now little bro—you said you wanted to catch th' big fish...now, damn it, that's what we're doin'."

Jed started fanning the stench of crap away from his face. Thinking about what his brother said, he looked at his pole, then his bloody finger, and shook his head. Something else came to mind when he caught a whiskey bottle rolling around by his feet. "There you are, mister. You musta been hidin' out under the deck somewhere."

He uncorked it, took a swig, and then shivered. "*Whew*, now that's good, *aaaahhh*. Breakfast whiskey from the mister…want some?"

"Yeah…why not. Little hair-a-th'dog'll suit me good after drinkin' so late last night."

Buzz snapped the bottle from his brother's hand as if he was expecting his brother to change his mind. He then tipped the bottle straight up and watched the bubbles inside. Three big bubbles turned into three big swallows before Jed finally caught on. "Hey, asshole, hey-heyyy. Don't kill 'er. It's all we gots till we go home."

"Okay, I hear ya…*aaaah*, that's good."

Jed went on, "Dirty som-bitch, you do that all th' time too…why you say 'hair the dog,' anyway?"

Buzz looked at his brother with a weird eye that came out of nowhere. "What? Why you say 'mister' all the time then? Shit, don't you remember? Ar' dad used to say it when you were smaller than me…ya…ar' Grandpa said it too. They's from Georgia, don't you know? They said it all th' time."

Jed scratched his head. He either got tired or gave up sucking on his bloody finger, so he picked up a dirty rag off the deck and wrapped his hand up with it. "Oh, tha's right. Think I'd remember…I know why now…never saw 'em. I thought you said theys from Florida last time?"

"Ya well one-a-them states. They all sound the same."

Jed scratched his crotch. "Didn't you say his liver got blown up'r somethin' like that?"

Buzz tipped his bottle then crossed his weird eye. "Shit fire, *whooooweee*…that'll wake y'up, spark-a-fart, wow!

THE TIME TO TELL

Hair-a-th'dawg Rodriquez, *ha haaa*...hey, what you do to y'r finger? You pickin' that nose too hard? *Hu-hu...hu-hu.*"

Jed ignored him at first, but that didn't last long. The only picking on his mind after that was picking a fight with his brother over the whiskey bottle. Before rising to the occasion of an all-out skirmish, they both paused, like statues glaring at each other with fists cranked back. Realizing how ridiculous they must look, they bellowed with laughter. "You can shock a warlock I bet, *ha haaaa.*"

"You think so, *hu hu.*"

Fighting about sharing their bottle quickly ended when Buzz cordially gave up the bottle to his brother. Jed snapped it back then walked around the deck, sipping his short temper away. While he simmered down completely, something out at sea caught his eye. "Hey, look it there!"

Buzz let off the throttle, then squinted with his weird eye. Off at a distance was a fuel pod belonging to the crew of the US *Wehrwolf* floating in the water, with its white flag waving rather noticeably in the wind. Buzz chewed on his cigar before he quickly steered toward the bobbing black tank. "*Ha*! I'm a kid in a candy store...what's it gonna be?"

Jed ran up to the edge of the boat. "Hey, look above it... some flag o' some kind on it."

"Yup, I sees it...just beggin' f'r me to say *hello*, don't y' say?"

Jed suddenly became concerned. "What th' hell is it, y' think? Some underwater volcano rock below?"

"Don't know...we're gonna find out in a Mississupi, *uh*, Mississippi second, I can tell ya' that without scratching my ass."

Jed started jumping side to side. "Don't scratch y'r ass just yet. Wait a sec...no, no—no...sheeit, no. Looks like one-a-them Nazi mines I been hearin' 'bout."

Buzz let off his acceleration. "Nazi mines? How d' you know what a Nazi mine looks like, lizard brain?"

"No look it. I—I mean look at it…it's a cotton pickin' mine."

Buzz took another swig of whiskey to think about it. "Calm down. *Hmmm*, if they wanted us to hit it, they wouldn't be puttin' no flag on it."

"No, I'm tellin' ya, Buzz…saw picture-a-one, a bomb I mean. They're round and black with bolts holdin' it together—just like that one. They been droppin' 'em all over the ocean, no shit!" He went on, "People's legs been blown off…I can feel it already…we best stay away from—"

"*Ah*, chill y'r tongue…I ain't gonna touch it just yet."

Jed ran to the opposite side of the boat, holding his ears. "Watch out! Y'r goin' to hit th' damn thing as fast as we're goin'."

Buzz shook his head as he coasted to a near stop then relit his cigar. "Hold y'r dick. I'm stopped. Just a little tad clos'r ought to be good 'nough." Buzz shut his engine down and waddled over to the side of the boat. With his hands on the rail, he leaned over for a closer look.

Jed leaned over too, showing his teeth with the most dumfounded look. "What you see?"

"It ain't no bomb, asshole, look f'r yourself. It's a damn see-it-all flag on top like I told you. They wantin' you to see it. *Hmmm*, there ain't no ground underneath it…no rock below…*hmmm*. .looks deep down there…not a landmark, idiot…hellfire, y'r wrong again. How many times you goin' be wrong today?"

Jed seemed confused. "I know…if it was a beacon o' some kind, you'd think they'd put a light on it f'r sure."

"What? A beacon now you say? Shut up." Buzz licked his lips and rubbed a little greed between his grungy hands. "Quick…get a rope. See if we can hook it."

"Why do you want-a-hook it? You thinkin' 'bout towin' it?"

"I ain't towin'—now go get a rope."

THE TIME TO TELL

Jed quickly obliged. After a couple of missed throws, Buzz hooked onto its lid then pulled their boat closer yet. Carefully, he began to draw the tank against their vessel, where it softly touched up against the hull.

Jed kept his back turned the entire time, with plugged ears, so Buzz turned him around to face the fuel pod. "See? I said you wouldn't blow up. Now help me get on it."

Jed obliged and offered a hand while Buzz hopelessly hopped and grunted without getting too far. He was just too heavy and awkward to get over the side of their boat. But persistence paid off. With a few more hops, he made it.

After catching his breath, he slowly made his way up to the top of the fuel pod where he found a good place to sit down and rest a little. Awkward admirations got the best of him when he just couldn't take his weird eye off the white flag flying above him on a flexible rod. There wasn't much to see about it, except for perhaps the golden design of the rolling star it displayed. Still, he wasn't satisfied to leave it alone, so he broke the rod down with the weight of his leg and then brought the flag close to his face. He looked it over, smelled it, and even stuck his tongue on it for a surprising taste.

Jed licked his lips from the boat as he looked on. "Well, is it good? What is it, I mean?"

"Don't know....looks like some saw blade picture. Somethin' like that. Gold color...*ah*, it's just a flag...that's all it is—I guess, *hmmph*."

As quickly as he pulled it down, he discarded it into the water and put his ear down on the tank and knocked on it. He looked up and down then knocked again, like he was onto something. "Hey...it's hollow." He knocked again. "Liquid, I think...I bet it's a....it's some kinda fuel." He looked back at Jed. "Hey! I bet this is a—a diesel can. You know—f'r a—a ship 'r somethin'!"

Jed scratched his head, "You mean it's a diesel can? Why so big—out here? Awful big can, don't y'think? Can't pick it up...*hu hu*—"

H.C. WELLS

Buzz then touched around the seam and smelled his fingers. "No, really. Somethin's in there, and it ain't no water—I can tell ya that. I c'n smell it now."

Jed leaped over and picked up a couple of beaten-up buckets, "Hot dawg, we hit th' jackpot. *Ho-ho*, let's, let's—*steal it!* Here, take these."

"What? Put them down. I got bigger plannin' to do."

"Oh, we can tow it! No, not good big bro. They'll catch us! No, we gotta pump it out right now. We're empty too, so it all goes in our tank."

Buzz immediately surveyed the area with his weird eye. "*Shhhhhh!* Quiet, lizard brain…quick, get the eyeglasses. Look around and see if you c'n see anythin'…where there's smoke, there's fire."

Jed jumped to it and skidded to a stop over to the other side of the boat, nearly slipping off his feet. He rummaged around inside a messy chest, throwing things out until saying, "*Ah haaaa!*" He snatched up the dirty, old binoculars on the bottom, tiptoed back, and glanced in all directions with dirt on the lenses. "Nope, don't see nobody. Clear as a bell. No ships. Nobody—nowhere."

Buzz slapped the irritation from his face. "What you whisperin' f'r? No one's out here but us, damn it…do big brother a fav'r. Just, quick, get a hammer. This thing's gotta lock'r somethin' on it. We gotta break'r free before we do anythin'."

Jed ran back over to the same messy chest, got their hammer out, and then looked at it for a moment. Just like before, he tiptoed back and handed it over.

Buzz then straddled the lid and then started hammering the echoes out of it.

Wham! Wham! Wham! "*Whew*, tickles my ass…it's comin'—I see it." **Wham! Wham!**

As Jed looked closer at the fuel pod down by the water, he stepped back. "Hey, stop it a sec…I think maybe I'm seein' somethin'."

THE TIME TO TELL

Wham! "What do y' see?" *Wham! Wham!*
"I think, I think it's sinkin'."
Wham! "Don't be shit f'r brains. Diesel floats." *Wham! Wham!*
"No, I ain't kiddin'. Stop a sec...y'r lower than you were, I might be sayin'."
"Shut up and get me the pump ready. It's comin'..." *Wham!*
Jed shrugged his shoulders. "Okay, then...hey, watch it! I saw sparks comin' from y'r hammer. You'll make'r blow, you will."
"We're not gonna blow up...I'll torch it off if I have to." *Wham!* This stubborn piece a—" *Wham!*
Jed then started flagging his hands. "Stop right there...I—I don't know."
"What?"
"None this looks right, Buzz."
"The hell you say. It's comin'. I can tell." *Wham! Wham!*
"Yeah, the hell I say...I mean all this's too funny...we ain't smart 'nough to do this, Buzz—"

As they kept fussing and working, neither one of them saw the not-so-clean, battle-scarred war machine ascending out of the water at a distance. Ever so quietly, the US *Wehrwolf* slowly broke surface, with US-2 looking quite angry at what he saw. Before his vessel could rise up completely out of the water, he quickly opened his hatch and rolled out onto the main deck, aiming his pistol right at his two suspected fuel pod wreckers pounding away like there was no tomorrow.

A hair must have held his trigger finger back the way he was gritting his teeth, but just then, he loosened up and pulled his pistol back. Sorry disgust quickly laced his face, as if he was ashamed of himself for even thinking about what was on his mind. Gradually, he stood up and lowered his gun all the way down then talked to himself in German "*Pshhhhhh...* civilian bums."

He was faced with a predicament. Time wasn't exactly on his side, so he waved his pistol and spoke out to them in German too. "*Shoo...*go on!"

Buzz and Jed still didn't have a clue he was there, so he yelled a little louder. "Hey, you rats! Go on! Now!"

Jed seemed deaf, and Buzz looked as if he was blind in his weird eye. At least Buzz thought he'd heard something the second time US-2 yelled, causing him to look up and survey the area. He didn't bother to turn around and look behind him where US-2 was, however. Nothing was there within the confines of his neck twisting, so he carried on with his business of blunders rather confidently.

US-2 put his hands on his hips, shaking his head as if he was amazed at how deaf and stiff-necked they were. Catching someone red-handed, stealing or vandalizing his fuel pod way out in the Atlantic was amazing. The odds of bumping into a couple of dumb, deaf, and blind characters in the process seemed remote too.

Thoughts came to his mind immediately as he watched them carry on. He grabbed a cigarette from behind his ear, lit up with a frown, and then took in his first puff of smoke. Patience didn't play out for the short part of his predicament, so he figured on solving it right away by other means.

As a warning, he raised his pistol up and blasted one shot straight up into the air.

Bang!

Buzz leaped back over to his vessel like a big toad on a pole vault. "What the shit?!"

Jed ditched for cover. "*Awww*, look out! Behind us, damn it...it's over there somewhere!"

"Where? The flea-bitten bastards are shootin' at us... can't see 'em where I'm at. Can you?"

THE TIME TO TELL

"What? You want *me* to look?"

"Y'r the youngest. Poke y'r head up and look."

"Okay, then...*ahhh*, I see it. Shit-fire, Buzz! It's some spacey lookin' thing right out 'n the open, 'bout a block away."

As Buzz lay against the wall of his cabin, he stroked his beard thinking. "A block? Must not be here yet, I guess... hold it. I told you to look around f'r ships, didn't I?"

"I did, damn it! It wasn't there a second ago."

"Not true...there ya go figuring wrong again...look again."

"No! I'm tellin' the truth. The—they must a—must of flown down straight from sky. Can't believe my eyes. It's got wings for it."

Buzz opened his weird eye, looking surprised, "The hell you say. Boats don't have wings."

"No? It's a—a *space ship* then, I'm right."

Buzz steadied himself off the deck then poked his head up. "Let me take a look. You're startin' to sound like my ass."

"There, you satisfyin'? What y' think?"

"*Hmmm*, don't look like no boat. *Arrrr*—looks like *uh*. That's a damn—son of a rat's ass, you might be right."

US-2 thought he saw movement aboard their vessel, but didn't quite know for sure. While he became more frustrated than ever, he yelled again, except with a little German slang: "Asshole thief...away with you! Swine! Be gone!"

Buzz ducked back down almost panic-struck: "I can't figure what he's sayin'. Can—can you?"

"Helllll no, bro—*duh*."

"They're speakin' some kind a—*alien tongue*, I think."

Jed backed up closer against the cabin wall. "Alien tongue? It really is a spaceship then. What they look like?"

"What do y' mean what they look like? You saw 'em, didn't ya?"

Jed tried remembering. "No, I was lookin' at a spaceship with wings—that's all."

"You ain't missin' anything then…I can't see that far. Don't look like no alien to me, though. It's got two legs."

Jed squirmed around to face his brother. "Two legs? How do you know how many legs aliens got?"

"Shut up…quick, get me my deer rifle. Be quick—and keep outta sight, y' hear?"

"Gotcha." Jed scrambled over to the corner of the cabin, pulled out a weathered lever-action Winchester from underneath a bunch of rubble and slid the rusty thing across the deck to where his brother sat.

Almost as quick, Buzz jacked a live cartridge into the chamber. "Keep outta sight, little Jed. I'll take care-a-this."

He then peeked his weird eye over the edge of his boat to see US-2, dressed in black and looking might fuzzy.

US-2 stood cut on the top of his deck like nobody's business. He was in the middle of scanning the decrepit vessel with the missing people with his binoculars from top to bottom when he muttered, "Wow, look at that mess…son of a bitch. It can't be. Oh shit!"

US-2 dived into his cockpit for cover just as Buzz opened fire.

Bang! Crash!

It was a direct hit. Cockpit glass on the open hatch of the US *Wehrwolf* fractured in all directions. US-2 couldn't believe it until he threw down his cigarette. "*Awwwh! Arscholoch shysters!* Swines!"

Instantly, he jumped into the center captain's chair and readied his aim with the spin of his brass cranks. He flipped down his optical and jockeyed his crosshairs until he muttered, "There we are." He muttered again, "Have it your way…Zwilling Twins ought to do." With just the click of his switch, a pair of barrels came out from the starboard side, looking like double the trouble. Back and forth they swayed, until US-2 found what he wanted to shoot, which was their entire boat.

THE TIME TO TELL

Before he could pull his trigger, Buzz fired again. ***Peeooowuw!***

US-2 flinched, "Son-of-a...give me a second will you? Okay, bastards, dance. *YAUGHH!*"

Rat-tat-tat-tat-tat-tat...rat-tat-tat-tat-tat-tat!

The blaze of his twin barrels lit up like roman candles, sending a stream of red-hot metal hornets to the *Blessit*. Every round made contact with remarkable destruction. Huge splinters of board and parts of planks shot into the air.

A bit of pity or curiosity caused US-2 to lift his finger off the trigger at that time. Curiosity must have ruled, for he smirked about the smoke he saw rising up from his two barrels and mumbled, "Wow, this thing gets with it." In his recess, he surveyed through his optical, looking at the mess he'd made. As the smoke rose and dust blew away from the *Blessit*'s old hull, she looked even more dilapidated, which was hard to imagine.

US-2 lit another cigarette while he kept his eye in the crosshairs. "*Boo*...did I scare anyone? Come out and play with *der Wolfman, hu hu...der Wehrwolf* is coming to get you, *oww-wwl... hu hu huuu...hmmm*. Where's that fat one? Don't tell me you're dead already."

Fortunately, both brothers were spread flat out on their deck, wide-eyed, alive, and shaking like leaves. Jed sputtered as he shuddered. "You—you—you had to go shoot'em, didn't cha? What we goin' to do now, *huh?*"

Buzz swallowed carefully as he hugged his rifle up close. "I ain't seen fire power like that...gotta get us outta here, that's what." Just then, he made a wild dash for the cabin, bumping into things along his way.

US-2 was already waiting for him with his finger on the trigger. Instantly, Buzz was cut into bits, along with part of his cabin, too. What was left of him got pushed overboard several bullets at a time.

Jed was petrified from the sight of his own flesh and blood disintegrating before his very eyes. He was literally stuck—stuck to the deck, with his sweaty cheek against the crusty, blood-spattered wood, looking like he was staring square into the barrels of US-2's guns already. Slowly, he focused on his fingers gripping the deck beside his eyes. Moving them seemed like a huge problem just then. He seemed insanely happy once he was able to move them. Slowly, he turned to his brother's Winchester lying next to him, but looked away like he wanted no part of the trouble it had caused.

He trembled in despair, listening to what used to sound so sweet and normal—the radio. Miraculously, it was still playing in the decimated cabin. The song called "King Porter Stomp," by Benny Goodman, kept playing like nothing at all had ever happened. Suddenly, he realized what was sitting next to the radio, which sparked a little life back into his water-soaked eyes. It was his shortwave radio he muttered about, ever so quietly. "Cu-call...emergency...I—I gotta call."

Without further ado, he snaked over on his belly, turned it on, and nervously spoke into the partially-damaged microphone as clearly as he could, "Mu-mu...May Day. May Day, do you hear? This 's the *Blessit*, number FV-231...please, anyone? We're bein' shot...May Day, damn it, *ohhh*, woe is me. I'm bein' attacked!'

In no time, a signal scratched back with a woman's voice. "This is the US *Chameleon*, AK 110. We read you. State your location—come in?"

"Fu-for, God, I don't know a location. Days from Maine coast, maybe. I—I can't get up. They come out-a-nowhere. They popped outta nowhere. You gotta get here now. You hear? I'm gonna die. I'm gonna die, I'm tellin'.'

"Calm down. Were you the blue fishing boat passing us eastbound this morning? We're the cargo ship passing through—over?"

"Yes, damn it, now hurry!"

THE TIME TO TELL

"State the vessel attacking you…is it a U-boat? How many—over?"

"What? U-boat? It's a black ship. Ain't nothin' like it—spaceship lookin' thing—with wings, I'm tellin'. It popped outta the sky or nowhere—then landed and started blowin' up the place!"

"Stay put…keep your microphone on. We're headed your way immediately. Over and out."

Jed dropped the microphone and collapsed. "'Stay put,' she says? I'm goin' to hell from here."

All of the sudden, US-2's Zwilling Twins cranked up again, sending a rage of rapid fire right up the *Blessit*'s deck. Ridiculous numbers of rounds sprung up the boards, like giant rat traps snapping up closer to Jed. All he wanted to do was curl up and cover his ears, when the blasting suddenly stopped right below his feet. Warily, he opened his eyes, realizing he was still alive.

While he lay there in the province of fear, he must have felt a most unusual urge to celebrate. Rolling up to his side was the Mister, as he called it. Booze barely oozed from the cork. Urgently, he picked it up, and he tipped it up desperately for a huge swig. Surely, this shouldn't have mattered, but it did for him. Audacity instantly kicked in, with consequences he would never recall again. He swept up his brother's Winchester and stood straight up, as if he had pure metal waiting to be tested all over his frail body. He took his time to aim back at the US *Wehrwolf* for a counterattack, but he didn't take the shot.

US-2 calmly stared through his optical, hardly believing what he saw. It was the black outline of a fearless, skinny man, quivering all over—ready to fire.

US-2 flinched at first, but then he carefully looked through his optics again, as if he was being lured into some kind of trap before muttering, "Look, Junior Lieutenant…. the man's gone crazy." He didn't even have to adjust his aim through those crosshairs of his. Without further hesitation, he lit up his Twins, sending Jed's limbs and body out to sea, piece by piece.

From then on, the *Blessit* floated alone, bludgeoned by gunfire and wet with blood. The only thing left on board that sounded alive was the music of the blood-spattered radio, still playing tunes, without losing a beat.

"This is JDVL radio. I just love Benny Goodman's stomping jazz, don't you? Now for an update on the weather...get ready out there. We are in for a naaasty, and I mean naaaasty, storm front coming in from the east. It's making its way clear over to the coast of Maine soon.

"Sailors out there, beware....you'd better be in because we have a dangerous ship advisory for you right now—"

Subsequently, the shortwave came on by itself next to the radio. "Are those shots—over? Hello? Hello—can you hear me, over? Hello, come in, *Blessit*. This is the US *Chameleon*. We are en route and armed, so please get out of the way if you can. I repeat...we are en route, so, please, get out of the way if you can—over."

In the meantime, US-2 was aboard his own vessel, clueless in more ways than one. While the shocking talk kept signaling away on the shortwave off in the distance and while his fuel pod kept sinking outside of his peripheral view, he seemed quite amused to be out of touch by scanning the damage he'd created to the *Blessit*.

The scene inside his optical was a smoldering mess of fractured boards, broken glass, and a half broken-down cabin splashed over wickedly with the color of blood. While yawning, he turned to the baby. "There now, we are closer to America now, Junior Lieutenant, look. She's now *red*, white, and blue."

After growing bored from looking, he flipped his optical back behind his seat and stretched his arms back, as if he intended on giving himself some slack from a murderous job well done. While doing so, he did stop to interrupt himself like he might have been missing something that he couldn't quite put his finger on. He paused, thinking for a minute while smoke from his twin barrels drifted in front of his face.

Quickly after that, he snapped his fingers and lit another cigarette. As he blew a thin stream of smoke in the soft breeze, he just gazed into nowhere as if wished to forget about the paralyzing predicament he'd fallen into.

After thinking his way into forgetfulness, he grinned and mumbled. "Now I know why they picked me for this job... see me in action, Junior Lieutenant? See that? I bet the bastards don't have the guts to do *that* again...so this is what to look for in America...swines. They're everywhere, eh, Junior Lieutenant? You hear me through that bubble? Here, let me open it up and give you some fresh air."

His junior lieutenant didn't have much to say. From the surprising, round-eyed look he gave, one could only guess what he thought after all the deafening noise of high-flying gunfire, packed in with jolts powerful enough to rattle teeth. His feathers were ruffled, for sure. Maybe he was too shocked to move. Fortunately for him, the power-packed dilemma came to an end through the wonder of time, soothing itself by a little peace and quiet afterward. The fright quickly passed for the young infant. Within a matter of minutes, he soon became oblivious to his surroundings once again. He continued to play with his pistol magazine beside him as if nothing ever happened.

US-2 was as oblivious as the baby was. He still hadn't thought about refueling yet, nor did he see the US *Chameleon* well on her way, filled with an entire crew of warriors he could have only wished to be apprised of.

Seeing such a huge vessel deserved the attention of just about any rival daring to set their unknowing eyes on her.

H.C. WELLS

The US *Chameleon*'s company of sea-goers gave a new meaning to the word "undercover" when it came to brothers of war. They were Maritime US Merchant Marines aboard and representing an auxiliary of the United States Navy.

Interestingly enough, they didn't look like the Navy, for their disguise was cunning. The ship they cruised looked like a cargo ship, but she wasn't a cargo ship at all. She was the equivalent of one of the deadliest vessels in the US Navy's fleet in the Atlantic.

She would have fooled the best of them in warfare at the time. From her slow-moving, single-screw steamer appearance, all the way down to her lengthy, four hundred-foot hull, she had the looks of pure, peaceful deception. Make no mistake—she was the real thing. She was an innocent-looking cargo ship turned into a war enemy's worst nightmare—and bigger than battleships that never hid their guns and cannons.

Her weight seemed to defy gravity the way she floated on top of the water. Apparently, the ocean was heavier by just a few thousand pounds, or she would have sunk straight down in record time. All 6,600 tons of her bashed through whitecaps and wakes as if she was a steamroller crushing on top of everything just to make it flat.

To sum up her dishonesty, she was painted in an even heavier disguise of rusty red and gray, like she was surely not looking for any kind of big fight that day.

One surprise definitely deserved another in this instance, however. Contrary to any belief, she was headed straight to one of the biggest Atlantic battles that World War II's history books never told. What she intended on approaching was a tiny, but mighty contender who was just as secretive as she.

Aboard the US *Chameleon*, the normal day-to-day duties were being carried out, with one exception. Since the *Blessit*'s distress call came in loud and clear, they had inherited the dubious duty of investigating in their very own special way.

THE TIME TO TELL

They had started thinking about their hidden guns and turrets for the first time.

The US Merchant Marine captain making the call for action just happened to be currently involved in a staff training class in the control room, where he was wrapping things up with his private pupils. One of them in the classroom raised his hand and was called upon. "Excuse me, Captain Nelson, if we ever encounter battle, could you go over the German's stratagem again?"

Captain Nelson replied, "Very well, but first, let me finish what I am saying...we're three days out on our third rendezvous mission to seek and destroy enemy U-boats. They can be anywhere along the Eastern seaboard, and they can wreak havoc on the Atlantic supply chain to our allies overseas. So far, we've failed to attract enemy German subs anywhere with our undercover cargo ship. Let me remind you, we are not just going to sit around and fish. If we have to, we will take the offensive to get the message out. We're capable of taking out an entire fleet of subs. Trust me. If we get the chance, German subs will be sunk."

Nelson then pointed to a map on the wall. "Now to answer your question, their stratagem is multilayered above and below water. The Germans' underwater stratagem is to choke off America's lifelines to England and Russia with their elite U-boats. That's where they get the surprise of their lives. Our hidden guns, with special floatation system, can survive almost anything...let me say that we—are—no—pushover. There are only a few other vessels like us. We're going to make a name for ourselves as a bunch of sucker-punching street fighters. Everybody better be with me, because if you aren't, I might have to chain you up in the engine room...we need more workers down there, and that's where the torpedoes wind up first...what do you say? Is everyone with me?"

"Yes, sir! Yes, sir! We're with you, sir! We're with you, sir! Yes, sir!"

H.C. WELLS

Nelson grunted, "Good...before you all go to your standard duties, I must announce a pleasant surprise. I just ordered a formal intercept course, which is prompting our first emergency call. This is no drill." Nelson paused. "We're in for some excitement. The call's not a supply boat, but I don't care. She's a fishing boat with real, live people in distress. The last contact revealed that machine guns may have engaged her. As soon as we determine the target is real, I will be expecting all of you to act. Questions anyone?"

Everyone adamantly replied, "No, sir. No, sir. *No, sir!* No, sir. Yeah, we're ready!"

Captain Nelson adjourned the meeting. "Good, get out of here and get ready...hey, Lieutenant, stay here. I want you by my side... plot a sneak attack on intercept course...oh, you back there... don't sound the general alarm. Just pass it along...one more thing for dispatch...tell them to send a code to land that we're contemplating engagement of an unconfirmed enemy target."

Nelson then spoke more loudly to all his pupils leaving, "*Ha!* At last we get to test our ship and men. I want silence everywhere. Does everyone hear? All lines of communication—radio, speaker, whistles, blinkers, flags—down and out of sight." He turned back to his lieutenant. "Did you get all that, Lieutenant?"

"Yes, sir—right away, sir."

Captain Nelson then moved to the bridge for observation. Along the way, he grabbed his binoculars and spoke indirectly to a growing number of his followers. "This vessel's a Man of War. We're under strict orders from President Franklin D. Roosevelt...did you know that? I love it. Yes, sir. They'll never see us coming, *ha!* Good as a legitimate cargo vessel hull AK-110, *ha!* We'll see what they're made of... quick, did anyone define our target as a U-boat yet?"

The lieutenant stepped up to face him. "No, sir, not yet... but all communications from the civilian distress call indicate that it is."

THE TIME TO TELL

Nelson jolted. "What? How's that? Explain."

"It's hard to explain. The man and his distress call. He said the vessel came from out of nowhere, sir."

"Nowhere? *Hmmm,* sounds interesting. Continue, Lieutenant."

"He said it was some kind of—spaceship, sir. That's why we determined it to be a submarine U-boat…and one more thing, sir. He said it was black."

"Black? Maybe he thought it was gray."

"I know, sir, but maybe it's a new color of U-boat…the Germans have been known to change colors before, sir."

Nelson started surveying across the ocean through his binoculars. "*Hmmm,* good analysis…that's probably what it is, all right…anything else?"

"Yes, sir…what if they already dived and we get struck blindsided with torpedoes?"

Nelson muttered as he looked out through his binoculars. "So. Where were you when I lectured about that?"

The lieutenant looked even more worried. "No, I heard… I mean it's hard to believe, Captain…I'm speaking for the entire crew, sir."

"Oh, you are?"

"Yes, sir…they have a good point, I mean, nobody wants to, I mean, what about our hull? It's chambered below to carry things, not withstand water intrusion, sir."

Captain Nelson took his binoculars down. "That's pure nonsense—tell the crew…the works of Gemini Corporation…built this ship to be impossible to sink with all the floatation material we're carrying. It's better than a battleship…we also have more than enough firepower. Get your head on…we got enough big guns to level Rhode Island."

"I know, sir, but—"

Nelson pulled down his binoculars. "Are you challenging me, Lieutenant? We're as solid as a big, fat, floating cork that's armed—twenty guns—turrets I said. Got four depth-charge projectors. How much more do you want? Feel sorry for the enemy—not us."

"Yes, sir. If we're lucky, they'll surface and come right up to us."

Nelson grinned. "That would be nice. Do me a favor and fetch me a sonar report. Look for more subs. Where there's one, there could be others."

Lieutenant saluted. "Yes, sir!"

Captain Nelson then went back to scanning with his binoculars. "I see them, *ha!* More speed. I want more speed. Tell engineering to give me more speed."

Another subordinate stepped around the corner. "Engineering says we're maximum last checked—twelve knots, sir."

Nelson looked like he just tasted a lemon. "What? For God's sake...our stuffed hull doesn't weigh a thing. It's not like we're carrying iron ore. See what you can do."

"Right away, sir—sending commands to increase speed to more than maximum levels."

Nelson turned to another official standing there. "Did dispatch get any more responses back from this, *uh*, fishing boat called the, *uh, Blessit?*"

"No, sir...she reported only machine gun fire and nothing else."

Nelson resumed. "*Hmmm*, they surfaced on her with fifty calibers...my guess is they didn't want to waste their torpedoes on her." He kept on. "That pisses me off! Poor fishermen...*hmmm*, wonder if anyone's alive still."

The lieutenant pointed. "Getting within range, sir."

Nelson mused, "*Hmmm*, can't quite—there we are. I see two vessels now...targets confirmed. We got them. Prepare for a full starboard attack. Tell our sea scouts on guns and depth charges to be prepared. Stand by to drop concealments—ready to engage on my command."

THE TIME TO TELL

The lieutenant took off again, yelling, "Gun crews...man the turrets! Man the machine guns! Concentrate starboard side! Standby to drop camouflage! No drill! I repeat...no drill!"

Ironic as it was, there was a calm breeze floating in the peace and quiet of the ocean just then. As far as the eye could see, the idle weather seemingly wished to be the only spectator over the vast area that looked like the setting for an impending battle. *"To hell with it"* may have been one primitive way to say what was to come about. The gap of tranquility was nothing but a short promise that couldn't be kept. Peace was but a small faction. All hell was about to be unleashed.

And so it began on that wistful, calm day in the Atlantic in which the weather, for some reason, did not interrupt. At both ends of the tormenting expectation of slaughter were two completely different vessels with completely different missions—to achieve the ultimate goal they shared in common. What remained to be seen would lay itself deep within the pages of blocked-out history—never to be told.

One side had hundreds of combatants scrambling across their decks, aboard "the unsinkable," while the other side contained the far-fetched mechanics of a dream—a dream protected by one lone warrior who was barely motivated, it seemed.

That man named US-2 was the one. A real name might have given him honor, but just two letters and a digit was all they gave him. His fate looked to be tied up blindly with a massive dagger in disguise.

The next series of events would have blown the minds of any—if anyone only had the privilege of knowing, that is.

US-2 was taking his time kicking back and enjoying his cigarette, when a small, shadowy speck of his assailant crested over the seascape directly behind him. Unsurprisingly, the speck didn't stay small for long. For the first time, the US

Chameleon grew into full, naked sight while US-1 was mindlessly carrying on with his carefree attitude.

He didn't notice several things. Something else should have reminded him why he was there and surfaced above the water in the first place. When he nonchalantly glanced down to his fuel level gauge, he quickly awakened to the realization of why he was there.

Suddenly he jarred himself up from his chair and took several glances before he discovered the fuel pod was still barely afloat. Without wasting further time, he floated the vessel over to it for a quick refueling, but as he stood up in his cockpit, he gasped. To his utter shock, the barely-floating fuel pod quickly sank out of sight, leaving only bare bubbles of where it once was.

He mumbled, "What the...? Whu—what happened?"

Immediately, he jumped up on deck to challenge his disbelief. When he found his predicament to be true, he stomped in circles then burst in curses. "Swine-dirty-ass, Doc! I should—I'm dead shit! I'm out! Outta petrol! Son of a *bitch*! So mad I could...I'm sunk! My hatch is broke! The damn thing sunk! Like they said it would! *Son* of a—*shit*! I'm dead. That's it. I'm dead! Should've stayed back home! I—should've stayed—home!"

He yelled up into the sky, "*Raaaah! RAAAAH!*"

Surprisingly, in the midst of his powerful paroxysm, he calmed down. Perhaps a little unintentional stage fright was his dampener. Somehow, he intuitively gathered that someone might have been watching him lose it. He tried to grow eyes in the back of his head. That didn't do any good, so he jerked around and got his eyes full.

Sure enough, he was being watched. The baby he so fondly named "Junior Lieutenant" was locked onto him with shocked eyes that wouldn't blink. Not only that, he looked to be puckering up for a long-lasting cry.

US-2, for the most part, drew a soft concern for his poor, unintended spectator. Quickly, he traded his temper tantrum for a strong, sympathetic mix of wilting guilt. As he looked down and out, thinking in the middle of an unforgiving ocean of pain, he began tapping his foot while the baby kept crying.

Finally, he got a grip on what to do next. Slowly, he opened his arms, while waving nervously to the baby. "No—no, you didn't see that. Don't worry. That's right." He went on, "Don't be like me when you grow up…there's others nicer than me—really. I'm a bad boy, okay? I'll say it first. Good, you understand now. I can figure us out of here. Watch me, okay? I'm figuring it out right now…just give me some time—to figure this out. That's all I need."

On the cusp of his very tiresome explanation, he looked around at the vast areas of the ocean before catching his first sight of what was upon him a mile or two away. Of course it was the US *Chameleon*, steaming along like it was an ordinary business day. At first he was startled, but then he calmed down quickly. Nothing more could really be seen of her, other than she was a massive, domestic cargo ship headed directly for him. To help him further identify her, she was kind enough to turn broadside and show all of her utilitarian shape at the last minute.

US-2 jumped back into his cockpit and then jumped into the center captain's chair, which thoroughly entertained his junior lieutenant enough to stop crying. He then brought his optical over his eye to study his potential visitor. What he saw through his crosshairs caused him to balk. "*Pfffff*, just a cargo ship, Junior Lieutenant." He balked as he looked again. "*Pfffff*…she looks like she's fifteen hundred meters away… *hmmph*. I wonder why the crew's running around on deck so fast?"

He picked his teeth as he kept scoping them out. "Maybe they got to go shit. No, maybe they're hauling shit." Suddenly, he became serious. "*Hmmm*…why did she turn so fast and stop?"

Sightseeing became less entertaining, so he yawned and casually backhanded his optical away from his face. For the moment, scratching his side seemed like the more comfortable thing to do.

Next on his agenda was hardly war-inspiring but productive, nevertheless. He gave his junior lieutenant a change of diaper and a fresh bottle. These priorities alone might have caused anyone to think or practically faint in disbelief.

The eeriness of the irony continued with all the audacity of shock and awe as the two vessels came together for a battle over peace. The so-called cargo ship, without cargo inside, was ready for war, with hundreds of warriors aboard. They pretended to be workers. She was a true "chameleon," all right. At least the members of *their* crew were not changing diapers like the single crewmember aboard the US *Wehrwolf*, which was never made in the United States.

Back on board the *Chameleon*, Captain Nelson looked through his binoculars as steady and still as a statue, locked on the little black figure of the US *Wehrwolf*. His lips grew wide with pleasure. "The poor bastards don't even know who we are." He pulled his binoculars down, grappling for a moment. Then he turned to his lieutenant as if he were befuddled. "I don't know what it is for sure. Looks kind of like a U-boat—I guess. The thing's got *wings* or something. What in the hell can you make of it? Go on, take a look."

The lieutenant took the binoculars from his hands. "It's got to be a new kind of German submarine, sir…it's not from our side. That I know for sure, sir."

Nelson took his binoculars back and tried twisting for more magnification, but his whole picture started to look even fuzzier. "*Hmmm*…looks like new camouflage too. It's beat up…*those damn Germans*. They're always coming up with new crap."

THE TIME TO TELL

He yanked down his binoculars, glaring. "I bet it's a newer version of their Type VII subs. Look at that...they even tried to make it look like a whale with that fin sticking up. *Ah ha*! I can see the barnacles! Jeesuuus Christ, what the hell's next?"

The lieutenant added, "I heard they've come up with Foo Fighters too, sir."

"Foo Fighters? I heard-a-those...thank God they're not for real."

Nelson looked through his binoculars again. "The fishing boat next to them looks lame...they've gotta be dead by now. Wonder why they didn't sink her? They always finish their jobs...you sure this vessel didn't have any communications?"

"Positive, sir."

The chief of guns rushed up to Captain Nelson, gasping, "We're starboard full, sir—and close enough to engage, sir."

Nelson tried rubbing the perplexity away from his lips when he noticed everyone around him was watching him. "*Hmmm...* my ass'll be in the frying pan if the president finds out we sunk that fishing boat. Can you shoot around the civilian craft with your gunnery and not screw up?"

The chief of guns nodded, "Why, yes, sir! They're Navy recruits, sir."

Nelson replied, "What's that got to do with it?"

"They came off USS *Taft* destroyer 'bout a week ago, sir."

Nelson grinned. "Oh, I see, experience. Good, then do it...it'll be them on the line, not us. Drop concealments and commence firing first rounds, but *don't* hit the fishing boat!"

The chief of guns darted down off the bridge, calling out loud, "Sea scouts! Drop concealments! Avoid the friendly! Commence firing first rounds, black watercraft only! Black watercraft only!"

Aboard the US *Wehrwolf*, nothing seemed too exciting still. US-2 tossed a dirty diaper overboard and wiped his hands clean, when suddenly he heard something. The unmistakable whizzing sounds of ammunition flying by overhead. He flinched, "*Ahh*! What?"

Just as he heard big booms of cannon fire a second or two after, he shoved his optical back up to his eye for another quick peek at the unsuspecting ship. "What? Noooo….it's a—it's what? Those *swines!* It's a battleship! Son—of a—lying *hurenshohn!*"

Several more huge rounds whizzed by overhead, clearly missing their mark before blasting the waters nearby.

US-2 reached for his pack of cigarettes, but the pack was empty. "Shit!" On the floor, he found another pack, but it was empty too. "*Hurenshohn!*" Immediately he moved on without them, buckling himself into his chair, when he saw Doc's silver flask lying below his feet. Before one could say "cheers," he grabbed it up and slammed the whole thing down and tossed it out his new convertible-topped vessel. "*Hmmm.* Not bad with the breeze in my face."

Instantly, he cranked the brass cranks until he lined his aim up at his assailant. Close aim got a little closer as he flipped over his crosshairs. What came next should have been to pull the trigger and fire back, but not for US-2. Instead, he clinched his jaw, feeling cruel, and then turned red. Something was about to detonate inside his veins, and it did. He looked to be turning just short of psychotic. The crazy man screamed first—then lay on his trigger.

"*Yaaauugghh!*" **Rat-tat-tat-tat-tat-tat-tat-tat-tat-tat!**

After yanking for all he was worth, a barrage of mettle hornets spewed out the Zwilling Twins, boiling with recoil, pausing only for a second round:

"*YAAAUUGGHH!*" **Rat-tat-tat-tat-tat-tat-tat-tat-tat!**

In the meantime, his band of bullets ruled the roost. Ridiculous numbers of lightning rounds littered the sky, sending the red-hot signal that someone would surely die. The only sign of his despair was the sluggish rocking of recoils in his chair. He kept rocking on the entire time, too.

THE TIME TO TELL

With the kind of delivery he was hooked into, he must have gotten his high from being an all-out manic.

However, the shock of his wartime world came and went when emptiness ratcheted through his finger.

Click, click, click.

His twins were empty. Quickly, he switched his pistol grip, muttering, "It's not over yet, you fake bastards! I'll show you fake…take this!" He yelled into both auto cannons, "*YAAAUUGGHH!*"

Booof, booof, booof, booof, booof, booof, booof, booof!

In the wake of US-2's seemingly endless assaults, the US *Chameleon* received almost all his answers in a very destructive way. Almost everything had met its target on their decks, leaving enough smoke to choke an elephant. Flames quickly burst out in awe, both big and small. Minor vessel damage was what they should have prayed for. What stewed over the decks afterward was pure panic and peril. Those who were sorry enough not to return fire were literally spread out on the deck—or dead.

The US *Chameleon* looked as though she was changing, once again. Guns and munitions were quickly exchanged for water buckets and stretchers, as her mercenaries quickly turned to firemen and nurses.

Captain Nelson was safe behind three plates of solid steel wall, however. He lay face down, feeling just how hard and cold his deck really was against his cheek. He seemed like he was gripping for memories of the last time anything similar had ever happened to him. Somber states of humility could have kissed him good-bye if he didn't move or act. It took a while before he expressly began to change into furious fragments of what didn't seem right. He knew he couldn't just lie there, so he got part way up to his elbows and bellowed, "That's no U-boat! What the hell is it?!"

His lieutenant helped him up. "Sir, do you need damage reports?"

"Hell, no! I can see the damages! Look at all this, damn it!" As he brushed himself off, he looked at part of his remaining crew stuck in their boots. "Well, don't stand there everyone! Get going! They can't sink us. Let them bring on their torpedoes, for all I care. We're just getting started!" He adjusted his collar, took a deep breath, and then stood up straight as he grabbed his binoculars once again. "There... you see? They stopped firing. That's the best they got! They'll never live to see daylight again...commence fire again!"

His lieutenant ran up from behind, tapping his shoulder. "Sir! Some of our crew—our gunners even—they're dead, sir. They're really *dead*."

Nelson turned to face him square in the eye. "Welcome to war, Lieutenant! Wake up...somehow they got lucky!" He then turned back around yelling, "Can't let those peckers get away with this! I want to know what that thing is!" He turned back to his lieutenant. "Lieutenant, you're stalling me. I said commence *firing!*"

The lieutenant jumped up and yelled as he ran off the bridge, "Remaining live stations, commence firing!"

Others echoed down, "Make live stations, commence fire! Make live stations! Commence fire! Move ammo to live stations! Fire!"

Immediately, US-2 was set aback from their return attack. Volleys of rounds from the US *Chameleon*'s monster turrets came crashing down into the ocean. Water continued blasting up closer until one fin at the stern got clipped. Trails of machine gun fire soon followed, inching closer up onto the deck he once stood upon. Suddenly, from out of nowhere, glimmering machine gun holes lit up the cockpit across the control panel as US-2 flinched and danced from one side to the other.

He quickly sat back down next to his junior lieutenant to counter, but his guns just wouldn't fire anymore. "*Aaaaaaah!* We're empty!"

THE TIME TO TELL

Just by chance, he spotted the big brass buttons on his controls. "Yes!" Instantly, he lunged for the one marked "Anachronism Kraft Strahl Kanone," but he stopped within an inch of ramming it with his fist. He then reached for his stealth propulsion controls, but looked through his broken hatch. "Nooooo! I can't dive!"

As the barrage of bullets intensified, he looked over to his junior lieutenant who, at the time, still seemed fine. He closed his eyes and opened them again. "It's the Strong Ray, Junior Lieutenant…it's time. Time to be a man or die, little one. I'm sorry, but we're in this together."

As every cannon fire came in all too close, he went for his big brass at last. Wet and wooly-eyed, the lone blond warrior took a quick glance over to the frail fishing boat and for the first time, saw its beat-up name on her stern sticking out at him. He closed his eyes once more and muttered the frail little boat's wishful name: "Blessit."

Blessings he needed. He was about to embark upon the wildest longshot, which came to him as clear as a bell from then on. Through the hellacious hailstorm of bullets and cannon bombing, he struck the big gun button as hard as he could and waited—then he waited some more. "Come on! Do something!"

For the longest seconds of his life, he waited until finally, something engaged beneath his feet with a mighty thump. Out in back, inside the third bay beside the twin engines, a superficial super sound emerged. Something analogous to perhaps tiny thunderbolts erupting in swirls caused him to look behind in fright. The very essence of it, never before seen of this world, had begun. Terrifyingly so, the sound simulated the reckless spinning faster and faster.

US-2 quickly harnessed himself in the security of his chair and waited a little longer before he had second thoughts. A panicky change of mind crossed his face suddenly as the swirls gained in speed and sound. He reached for his controls, trying to undo what he just engaged, but he barely found the time to whimper, "Oh no...no, I've done something *wrong*. Turn it off...*turn it off!*"

With all that he tried, he just couldn't get the big brass button to come back up. It was too late. Right then and there, he quickly realized there was no turning back. The very weapon that Doc feared the most was about to blow inside the vessel.

CrrrrrrAAAAASH!

A clash of waves quivered through the cockpit. Instantly, the energy gripped ahold of US-2, causing him to jolt. It was as if his very being was slapped into thinking about the boundaries of his consciousness. Reality tested him again with hallucinating distortions everywhere he looked, but there was more. Just when he looked like he couldn't stand its misery, the clash of waves quickly spun into a twirling aura and immediately purged through his entire body, "*Ah!*"

He screamed again, whipsawing in his chair uncontrollably. He seemed potently possessed, except how could that be? The aura somehow seemed to control his very flesh and bones. Somehow, it synched him tight to the makeup of which contained no matter at all. It seemed as though it was his very spirit that it wanted to grab ahold of most of all.

Inside the horrid fixation of such a freak phenomenon, he somehow stayed the course with every gasp of his breath. "I—I have—have a purpose."

From there on, every last second that ticked by seemed like an eternity giving way to his lost self. The only reminder before his incapacitated eyes was his single brass optical, which was begging to be looked through. Amazingly, he saw it. His curious look gave the notion that he was looking at a foreign object. Curiosity was his only savior. Through the trapped isolation of his body and spirit, he looked inquisitively through it. Right there in plain vision was all that he needed to remind him of his mission.

THE TIME TO TELL

Inside his crosshairs and lined up quite well was the US *Chameleon*, blazing away straight at him off the tips of her turrets. However, the force behind him kept feeding upon itself higher and higher, causing him to cringe in convulsions. "*Ahh!*"

He screamed in pain. While he mustered to handle it, he steadied his aim and looked at his red control light slowly switching to green. Right then was undoubtedly the time to pull the trigger, but it didn't work. Just then, a stout, chrome cannon barrel wrapped in coils, flipped out of a hatch directly in front of the ship and locked into place.

Kirthump!

The Strong Ray's gun blocked his view, but he pulled the trigger anyway.

CRACA-POOOOOOWWW!

Its massive kick was so immense that it took every last bit of structural strength the US *Wehrwolf* contained in her hull to survive the recoil. She plunged backward, pounding her stern deep below the surface while her bow sprung up almost vertically into the air. A full, disastrous flip seemed almost eminent, but somehow—she hung in there.

Before Captain Nelson could pull his binoculars down and say "blow-me-down," a shining ray bolted right through the center of his starboard side.

VAAAVOOOOOOMMMM!

The mighty impact cratered the US *Chameleon*'s massive hull and threw her all the way over to the brink of a near capsize. Most of her crew on deck hollered in horror before being catapulted into the ocean. Right behind them, falling on top, were their massive turrets, guns, and debris, which quickly took them to the bottom of the ocean.

While the vessel lay on her side in limbo, none of the survivors still aboard expected horrid after-shocks to come. Unfortunately, they did. Those who clung onto to the rails closest to the point of impact stared down at the brunt of it. Next to them, almost straight up, was a jagged hole big enough to drive a bus through it. They quickly got a good look at her contents, which were never intended to see the light of day. Smoldering next to them and fuming with fuel was whatever they could stuff her hallow chambers with—shredded cork, balsa wood, sawdust, and even trash.

Booom!

Immediately, it burst into a towering inferno, blowing high into the sky. Incredibly, the fire twirled into an unexpected twister of horrid oranges and black.

More crewmembers, scorched from the blaze, fell to their deaths, yet the wounded US *Chameleon* still tried to cling to life. Time was all she needed, apparently. Come hell, fire, or massive impact, she actually looked like she was coming back. Then it happened. Mammoth sounds of creeks and moans sounded off the warning calls that she would soon face her enemy once more—to settle her score.

The remaining crew sensed this too, screaming as they held onto the rails anticipating a monster rock in the other direction. "Nooooo! Noooo! *Aaaaah*! She's coming back! We're going back! Watch out! No! *No!* We're going the other way!"

Screams only imagined in nightmares echoed everywhere as she slowly rocked back from the dead.

KaaaWooooshhhhh!

She returned with a monstrous splash, like an invincible, angry giant stepping back into the ring. Waves of water quickly came to her assistance, caving into her gaping hole, claiming the flames. Clouds of steam and smoke spewed into the air, leaving rotten, hot toxins to cry out, "Beware! I'm upright and ready to fight, once more."

Captain Nelson survived by simply hanging onto the head of his giant cargo of war. He pulled himself back up with the look of sheer astonishment. His observation deck was still in place, even though it took on a new, burned look.

THE TIME TO TELL

His look of astonishment didn't last long, however. He quickly grabbed his emergency megaphone and traded his amazement for spitting rage. "Take whatever guns! Fire at will! I want that thing blown out of the water! Do you hear meeee?!"

As his remaining crew scrambled to the remaining turrets and machine guns, he turned to his subordinates. "Sound the distress call! And you! Go to dispatch and send communications to land for rescue backup, damn it! We've got no choice!"

The US *Chameleon*'s communications scrambled over to the dispatcher, who was inside and on the ball gathering up equipment from the floor. Feverishly, he tapped loads of code for all of America to hear quite clearly.

Tick-tick—tick-tick*…** "S.O.S…S.O.S"…Tick-tick*…** "Unknown alien space water craft"…***Tick-tick*** …"with ray gun attacked US *Chameleon*"…***Tick-tick-tick*…** "S.O.S… S.O.S"… ***Tick-tick—tick*…**"backup vessel needed"… ***Tick-tick*…**"Immediately!"

Winning prematurely *surely* took on a new meaning when US-2 was caught looking through his optical, grinning. Like a true but young champ, he calmly studied his ailing adversary across the flat of the ocean as he whistled a few happy notes. Through the round picture inside his lens, he was quite pleased to see that he might have won the big one.

From his point of view, the US *Chameleon*'s sparse crew was in true chaos, carrying off the dead, tending to the wounded, and putting out fires. As he played with a toothpick he found instead of a cigarette, his chuckles quickly paused, however. In a few more moments, he dropped his grin entirely to mutter, "What in the name of?"

He didn't quite know whether what he was seeing was actually true, so he rubbed his eyes and then peeked through his optical once again, this time with more magnification.

Sure enough, more men showed up on deck and started manning their battle stations with their remaining guns and cannons. He muttered again, "Damn...damn the Hells."

He rocked back in his chair and looked over to the baby in his protective capsule, who was playing with his pistol magazine quite contently. "I give up, Junior Lieutenant...what in the *hell* is that ship made of?" He went on, "Well, Junior Lieutenant...we do or die. We did and now we still might die...it is time to go, *but*—" he raised his finger, "I still have a plan."

He unstrapped the baby with his capsule from his seat and then leaped together with him to the edge of the vessel. For the moment, he looked as though he was taking preparations to a swim toward the beat-up old *Blessit*. As he got his things together on deck, he let Junior Lieutenant know what was inevitably on his ailing mind. "You see that ugly old boat out there, yes? We're going to play boat with this capsule of yours, okay? Don't be scared now, I'll be floating right behind you." Gently, he pushed him out to float in his bubble crib. "There you go. I'll be right back, so don't float too far."

Among other things, US-2 rushed back into the cockpit nervously muttering, "Where is Doc's control box...the black box—where is it? Where is it, damn it?"

Finally, he found it in Doc's satchel. With one swipe, he snatched it up into his hands and read the toggle switches one by one. "Hatch open...gangway ladder...anchor... *hmmm*...engine kill...engine ignition...*ah*, I knew it. There it is—engine ignition."

He then feverishly began throwing things about in the cockpit, as if he was looking for something else too. "Yes, a fire extinguisher! That'll work."

While contorting down below the controls, he wedged the fire extinguisher to his gas pedal, and then ever so carefully started to slow down. Precision mattered, so he took his time aiming his steering controls directly at his fearless

THE TIME TO TELL

foe—"the unsinkable." When everything was just right, he took a piece of rope and tied the steering off exactly the way he wanted it. After that, he stood up, rubbing his hands. "There now. All done."

The biggest upheaval came with such a surprise. He looked as though he was attempting suicide when he leaned over to the big brass buttons and struck the "self-destruct" button with his fist.

Shortly thereafter, his sad, last-ditch effort made a shocking sound that nobody in their right mind would have liked to hear. A small alarm sounded off, signaling with regular ticks that his terrifying plot had begun. Surprisingly, he jumped back like he was tickled. "*Ho-ho*, this is it. Doc says forty-five seconds…let's get outta here."

With newfound vigor, he leaped up onto the main deck with Doc's black box in hand. With some ceremonial wave and kiss good-bye to his assailants, he dived into the sea and caught up with his junior lieutenant floating along. With a few side strokes, he got to a safe distance and then waded back around to watch his crazy idea unfold. Somehow and some way, he looked entertained by his gamble, even though any mishap at all could blow up in his face.

By then, it was quite obvious what he was doing. The crazy man was trying his best to complete an impossible mission. Still, he carried on as if he was just fixing a minor plumbing problem with some crazy-looking electrical switches. He switched the black box engine toggle to "on." Nothing happened immediately, so he waited. Slowly, grief struck his face. He tossed what appeared to be a useless box in the water and cursed as he paddled away as fast as he could with Junior Lieutenant.

Stranger things have happened in their journey. The strangest thing of all happened just then, with a remarkable spark of luck that perhaps even the US *Wehrwolf* herself might have been delighted about. Inside the cockpit of that doomed German girl, an inexplicable thing happened for reasons perhaps only the US *Wehrwolf* could know about. As she pointed hopelessly to her rival across sea, ticking like a time bomb, the rules of engagement had to be broken by her loneliness—alone.

One by one, every one of her set sequences on the controls lit up like a Christmas tree. Somewhere in the midst of all of the control lights flashing, her gloves came off. She kicked her starter lights on. She was just a machine—or was she? The proof ultimately lay in her twin engines, fins, and the spin of whatever lay within her. Like the dragster on race day that she once sounded like, both the Rolls-Royce Merlins started cranking to set them ablaze. Full steam ahead was all she needed to put it all to bed.

US-2 and Junior Lieutenant were but a couple of spectators from there on out. To see the first remote-controlled US *Wehrwolf* must have been relieving and exciting, as US-2 began to swim on his back just to get a better view.

And so it was, as far out in the sea as one could see, their great, dead boat finally woke up to take her bomb elsewhere. Anywhere but there must have felt like a huge favor that could have never been repaid. She said "good-bye" in her own special way when her engines fired up.

BooWAAAAAHHH!

Twin jet blasts of white water shot high into the air, sending the signal that her flag of white spray offered absolutely no surrender. In the blasting takeoff, her stern smashed down onto the sea with a colossal clap, then catapulted forward into a last mad dash. It wasn't just *she* that was going down; she was headed straight for her goliath with a double *coup de grace* grandiose finish.

Onward she sped, faster and faster across the ocean with no one inside her empty cockpit to read the speed. She gained to one hundred knots, and she was far from being done!

THE TIME TO TELL

Captain Nelson, looking straight out with his binoculars, kept focusing on the grave, sinister sight headed straight for them with explosive sounds. As he lengthened his frown, he jumped back and threw his binoculars aside. "My God, look at that thing…it's taking flight…it's coming right at us! Shit, we have a suicide!"

He turned and ran while his lieutenant followed. "Abandon ship!"

"Abandon ship!"

With missile-like speed, the US *Wehrwolf* approached. Anyone would have called it suicide by then. She reached such speeds off her last waking of a jump that her recklessness seemed inevitable. Something else had to intervene for her mindless navigation to succeed, and it did. Just as she glided back down to tap the ocean once again, she leveled off, dipped for more traction, then continuedon.

She seemed like she wanted to go beyond US-2's record of 150 knots. How far she went beyond that, nobody knew. What seemed most important through her ruined hull was that her propellers still churned like a bat out of hell.

No attendance in the cockpit had its consequences, however. The ropes gripping the controls showed signs of letting go. They quickly released the wheel, but it didn't matter. The way this fiendish female kept flying, she seemed destined to get there.

Just up ahead, another ready-made stage of wondering waves offered up a quick blow of the weather. But just when she seemed ready to take it on like the last one, something went terribly wrong. She'd sapped every last drop of that precious fossil fuel from her already-empty tank. Immediately, she spanked herself into a full-fledged lock-up, thanks to nobody except the sinking fuel pod that came back to haunt her.

Kerchuuummk!

Her screaming motors died instantly from the terrible bite of vapor lock. They were done for and froze up for good, but she wasn't done for. Silence traded places with deafening exhaust as she skimmed across the ocean at a wild speed. As she approached the incoming wave, the slashing sound of water came and went too as she launched from it into the air for her last leap of faith.

The black she-tyrant, who once roared across the Atlantic, reduced herself down to nothing more than a terrible time bomb. But her heroism turned into failure when one of her fins caught a surging gust of wind just then.

Crash-skip-skip-tashhh!

Instantly, she flung herself spinning into chaos. The incredible mystery machine made in the name of peace instantly began to shed her existence—piece by piece. First her fins came off. Then out of the cockpit flew everything else, leaving a hopeless shell, ripped of her identity.

Still, she had her complete hull to mull over. Incredibly, at just under one hundred knots, the mindless victory shell kept charging. Maybe it was inertia, but then again maybe it was a mystical push. Nobody really knew how it happened when she collided with the US *Chameleon*, dead center.

Kabooooooom! BOOOOOOOOOOM!

Fire and smoke blistered into a massive, towering torrent as the explosion grew heavy, then finally toppled over.

Down low at the site of the explosion, in the midst of the smoke slowly clearing away, were two torn pieces of what once was the US *Chameleon*, bobbing vertically. She sunk before the smoke had even completely cleared, leaving practically nothing afloat except for cork and balsa wood burning on top of the ocean. There appeared to be no survivors.

Nothing recognizable remained in the area, except for one thing. A single piece of the US *Wehrwolf* began to emerge from among the sinking debris. It was hard to tell what it was until it bobbed up to the surface bearing its mysterious, golden mark. It was the badly scarred mark of the rolling star.

THE TIME TO TELL

The two crewmembers formerly aboard the US *Wehrwolf* were still alive and safe, however. They looked to be the only castaways between the two doomed ships as they swam toward the *Blessit* and climbed aboard.

As the fire and smoke dissipated in the backdrop of the distant sky, US-2 began to explore everything on the old boat. Just like he was a new tenant in possession of a fully furnished apartment, he quickly picked up, opened, and inspected almost everything he encountered along his way while throwing out whatever he had no use for.

The radio was still playing, even though he couldn't understand the language that well. He was quite pleased with the current station, so he dialed it in for a little better reception as he kept rummaging around:

"This is JDVL...J-Devil Maine. We're bringing to you, the most up-to-date, popular songs of yesterday and today. Next is a beautiful song from the Spinners called...guess it for yourself...well okay... It's called 'Comin' in on a Wing and a Prayer.' Hope you like it."

US-2 opened the baby's bonnet to give him a little fresh air, then grinned and said, "That's radio...what's the American saying? What do you say, Junior Lieutenant? Speak up."

The day's recent atrocities seemed like fun-filled excitement to US-2. Close calls, bombs, fire, losing his vessel—none of it seemed to matter. He carried on, swaying and nodding along with the radio's song, as if amnesia was a kind, softhearted friend of his.

On a nearby shelf, he picked up a cache of dirty salmon jerky with blood on it and tried to clean it off with his shirt. His form of dry cleaning didn't work, so he rinsed it in the ocean and took a bite, "*Hmmm*—salty...good taste, Junior Lieutenant. Want some? No? Okay. I eat—you suck bottles, okay? Okay."

He took another big bite. "So...you feel that Strong Ray? What you think about that, Junior Lieutenant? *Ha*, Strong Ray...*eh*, Junior Lieutenant? Didn't think I could pull out of it...felt like *God* or *Satan* or something tugging my ass...wow, never again...glad it's down there under the sea...it's where it belongs, you think? Fine, don't say anything then."

He carried on investigating little things before stopping dead in his tracks. Curiosity caused him to step back to the edge of the boat for a moment to capture the bigger picture of his oh-so-quiet surroundings.

The devastation left behind from his rapid-fire guns was overwhelming. No wonder he stopped to look, but surely he should have seen it earlier. Up close, he examined the huge, fist-sized holes riddled everywhere across the decrepit boat. From there, he traced down the busted, blood-spattered boards at his feet.

Immediately his attitude changed. He seemed so carefree until he walked around nothing but a partially enclosed platform of ruin. Apparently, he'd never before experienced the devastation of his own hands before and was in awe.

Everything he looked at, without exception, was obliterated and sprayed with blood. Larger pools of blood, too thick to dry, still remained on deck. Even the cabin he walked through had been afflicted, all the way up to the red-stained curtains blowing in the breeze in front of the broken window glass. He just kept going from one gory sight to the next, until he stopped to look at what it was he was walking on. Shards of wood and glass mixed in with flesh and blood crumpled beneath his shoes.

He stopped chewing his jerky for the moment and spit it out. What he saw troubled him. He energized his walk as if he wanted to forget, but he continued to make his way through the broken, bloody disarray. At least for the time being, he was marooned aboard the residue of this horrid nightmare, and he knew it.

THE TIME TO TELL

Just then, he looked over to what remained of one cabin wall, which seemed normal enough. His vulnerabilities gathered themselves there too, unfortunately. Staring back at him were old pictures of the two bold, ignorant thieves. He paused to study them, seeking some sort of comfort perhaps, but then his frown dropped even further. The pictures were quite a bit more clear than he wanted them to be. Some of them had frames, but most had none. The frameless ones were simply tacked to the wall, yellowed, and curled around the edges from being hung out in the weather too long. Front and center was a picture of Buzz and his brother Jed, taken in their younger years. Another showed them posing next to a trophy swordfish.

He singled out one picture and stepped over to get a closer look at it. Surprisingly, it was Buzz all cleaned up. He was clean-shaven, posing with a strong arm in swimming trunks. In fact, he looked as young and muscular as US-2 was at that very moment. He comparatively flexed his own bicep like the picture of Buzz for a second and then stared closely at their faces. For a moment, he looked as if he was wondering if they really *were* the same putrid fellows he shot and killed. It was hard to tell, but the picture was of they.

Most all of the pictures of the two brothers shared something else: their blue-and-white boat called the *Blessit* was pictured in most of the backgrounds, except it was almost like new.

US-2 wheezed for a bit and then quickly shook off his drooped face once more. Forgetfulness was his friend once again as he strolled away from the pictures for something else to do. He carried on with his snooping. From one trinket to the next, he picked up each individual piece and either put it back or threw it overboard. Suddenly, he paused, as if he saw something that looked dear to him.

Slowly, he bent down to pick up Buzz's old Winchester rifle, scabbed over with blood. He quickly figured out the gun, cocked its lever, and then aimed out to sea without pulling the trigger. Something shocked him while he glanced through the two sights, however. The front one was broken off.

One didn't have to wonder what was on his mind after that. He looked out to where his ship once was while he sadly shook his head. In all likelihood, he survived Buzz's quick draw by nothing more than poor aim.

As he placed the gun down, he took a knee to pick up a live cartridge on the deck for examination. The cartridge was old and tarnished. Unquestionably, it showed its years of wear from being carried around a lot without ever being used. Somber feelings relentlessly reappeared upon his face. Wisdom's whip must have lashed him again. He hissed, clenching the bullet in his hand before eventually throwing it overboard.

By then, he seemed to have set his mind on trying to forget again. In nervous haste, he looked around for a distraction, so he quickly opened a cabinet next to the captain's chair, but there was nothing but a crammed-up mess of whiskey bottles and nude magazines. He had to think about that one for a minute. While he did, the weather's breezes offered to fan open the well-used, torn-up pages of the magazines. Some of the bottles rolled out onto the deck.

He hissed. Shameful sights of booze and boobs quickly evaporated his remorseful look. That was all he needed. Suddenly, he looked around as if his bloody mess of remorse didn't bother him at all. Somehow, his heart petrified again, right along with the expression of his face. He took another double-take at the mass of liquor they must have consumed. Then he snarled at the magazines stuck wide open. Wishful thinking while drinking was what it looked like. He quickly gathered the items and threw them overboard too.

Immediately after that, he tore through drawers and cabinets, as if he knew exactly what he was looking for.

THE TIME TO TELL

Trash and more trash popped up everywhere. The more he searched, the more desperate he became, until unexpectedly, his eyes locked onto a little brass drawer he must have overlooked below the helm and in front of the captain's chair. Like fire lit his feet, he jumped over to it to yank it open. There it was—or at least it resembled something he was searching for.

"*Tee-he-yeah*! *Ah*, come to Papa."

He ran his fingers through the only thing in there—a nice, wooden box of long, fat cigars. He couldn't figure out which one to grab first—there were so many. Hastily, he picked one out then swept up a nearby matchstick and struck it with his fingernail. He toked on it until a bright cinder glowed from the end. After fanning the smoke away from his face, he dared to breathe freely then whispered, "Marvelous…*ah* yes…marvelous."

"Marvelous" was the word. After he bumped into the captain's chair, he sat down. He didn't notice that it was covered in blood. His rear end squished and slipped around, but he was challenged to notice. What mattered most at that moment was smoking. All he wanted to do was enjoy the calm for a while.

This gave rise to him kicking up his feet in the name of relaxation. Once he positioned himself, he gazed at the old, beaten-down, bloody boat, as if he'd just beautified the whole place by putting on rose-colored glasses.

And so the *Blessit* got what it badly needed. Good housekeeping and smoking must have gone hand in hand too. Most of the trash was already overboard by then, so for the sake of tidying even more, US-2 straightened Buzz and Jed's pictures on the wall. When he was done, he backed into his chair and started to laugh hysterically.

He laughed even more when he spotted Buzz and Jed's half bottle of whiskey rolling around at his feet. With a quick swoop of his hand, he grabbed it up and pulled the cork out with his teeth. As quickly as he could, he guzzled the whole thing down in just a few chugs.

He suddenly became inspired even more. Next, he took a nearby towel out of the blown-up cupboard and cleaned off almost everything with it: the blood from his chair, the battered controls, the broken windshield, and finally the banjo steering wheel. He was productive, only pausing for a break to dial in the radio for a little more fine-tuning. Al Dexter's song called "Pistol-Packin' Mama" had just ended when the disc jockey announced a word from their sponsor.

"Guard your skin the Hollywood way with Lux Toilet Soap. Nine out of ten stars use it. Try Sidney Fox, Kay Francis, and Bette Davis. Whichever star you see tonight—Lux Toilet Soap."

US-2 turned his ear to the radio, as if he suddenly became befuddled. He almost understood the American language. As proof, he took his cigar from his mouth and pieced the advertisement together with a little bit of his own German interpretation,

"Holly who? Toilet? *Ah*, Mr. Holly Hood is on the toilet? American idiots, *pssss*."

Tokes of smoke and German jokes only went so far for so long, however. US-2 quickly came to notice that yet another potential problem had drifted in. Off from the corner of his eye, it caught his attention, so he looked straight at it. Indeed, there it was. Something came creeping up from the unsettled clouds easterly. Eerily, it swooped down as it came together to form jaded shades of grays and black. Somehow, it managed to form itself when he wasn't looking.

It was an approaching storm. Just then, it broke out from its silence and thundered so loudly that it caused US-2 to jump up from his chair. He grabbed the nape of his neck, feeling a tingling sensation.

THE TIME TO TELL

Out of pure curiosity, he carefully stepped out of his frail cabin for a better look, only to get an eyeful. There it was, like a barricade across the ocean as far as the eye could see to the north and south. He seemed puzzled by it. Swiftly, he picked up Junior Lieutenant off the deck and tucked him away. While he was there, he clicked off the radio and walked back outside, daring to watch and listen for lightning and thunder again. He listened and stared at the seemingly idle storm several miles away for the longest time, until it finally happened. Patience gave him what he beckoned for—except worse.

SsssssKAKAkakaka ka kaaah!

A shrilling noise bellowed and echoed across the atlantic. It was more than enough. Enough to send tiny shivers across the surface of the sea.

Rapidly, he grabbed Buzz's pair of binoculars off the deck and looked deep inside the storm. No surprise—he couldn't see a thing except a wicked wall of darkness. He realized the eeriness of its inevitability. He was only looking at a storm, so he put the binoculars back down—carefully.

He tried to forget about the peculiar sound, but it was still fresh in his mind. He was good to have moved-on from just about anything, but this time, he was *really* bothered. Time and again—at least three more times—he turned around to face the storm, but with each glance, he grew more determined that whatever the storm was, it didn't feel right. Before heading back into the cabin, he turned back around for a fourth time and yelled his usual battle cry, "*YAAUUGHH!*"

He stood there, taking a long drag of his cigar. Calmly, he blew his smoke and waited a little longer before huffing. The crazy, young warrior, known for his outbursts, was actually rather controlled and calculated. The supposed believer of revolts and revelations through awe-inspiring anger was simply testing. Whatever it was, he had no idea. Testing didn't work.

Nothing came back to challenge him, so he huffed again and then blew his smoke straight out into the breeze. Perhaps his answer came without him knowing it. He stuck his hand out, feeling how unusually warm it was.

What he witnessed next was nothing new. A few raindrops signaled to him that it was just a persistent weather front, perhaps a storm that was getting a little too close for comfort. He sniffed the air, which smelled of rain. He closed his eyes for a peaceful moment, but then he opened them again. Normalcy seemed to subdue him once again. All he saw that was new in the distance was a curtain of rain, closing in for a downpour about five miles out. It was sure to come soon, so he turned away.

He looked at his watch and swiftly darted to his captain's chair to start the *Blessit*. The boat smoked as much as he did, hurling out black exhaust high into the air. A quick glance down to his fuel gage let him know that there was no room for detours. He had less than a quarter tank to get to shore. Nevertheless, he left the scene with a confident smile and a trail of black behind him.

With a fresh cigar in his mouth, he looked down at the only partner he had. "You ready, Junior Lieutenant? Ready for you to save the world again?"

"I just saved you. Yes, *you*, how about that?"

"You owe me, buddy."

Like the lone martyr he made himself out to be, he hit the throttle, steered away, and never looked back. As he got further and further away from the storm, he kept rambling.

"You want to return me the favor?"

"Tell you what…all you got to do is keep smiling and flashing those baby blues for me."

"When the ladies fall for you, I get to choose the one I want."

"That's how you're going to return my favor."

"Are you listening to me? Can you say, 'momma?' Go ahead, say it…you need to practice that."

THE TIME TO TELL

As for the old turncoat boat called the *Blessit*, she seemed to run just fine. Outside of a few stray boards left in her trail, she moved along as though nothing ever hit her. Perhaps she really was blessed. Another word was born as she slowly floated away with her new claim to fame. The letter *I* dropped off her name and floated away. Six letters remained with a gap, leaving her with the new name *Bless_t*.

Chapter 7

Just one more evening had passed. US-2 with his single crew of a baby was barely ahead of the storm off the coast of the northeastern United States. Coincidentally, the storm following along was one of the first in the United States to ever get a name.

The new agency, or Weather Bureau of America, officially called her "Hurricane Victoria." Not that it mattered, really. She could have been called something else. It was just odd how nothing lined up too truthfully. Some storms were bad, and some were worse. Hurricane Victoria seemed a little more controlled than most in recent memory. The *Bless_t* vessel she seemed to be following was interesting enough, but where they both were going was what nobody fully understood. It was an ancient place that had been troubled since the beginning of Earth's time, a place riddled in eerie history.

The little coastal town that sat upon this ancient place was called Devil's Gulch. Sadly, it was a town that caught more than its share of gale-force winds and sideways rains. Waves beat down and ravaged the town's once long, beautiful, sandy beaches, taking megatons of rocks and sand away. It was like some hideous work of art in progress. The coast looked as if it was a storm's favorite landing spot. The forces worked so slowly that hardly anyone noticed.

Plausible causes would be worth mentioning—if there were any. All that was known was that age-old storms seemingly had some grand, master plan to eliminate the ancient land there altogether. The patience of nature works within the centuries, while human beings work only within their lifetimes.

The people in the small town of Devil's Gulch, or plain, old "Devil's," as they called it, felt quite safe within the milieus of their own lives. This particular time with Hurricane Vicky was just another wicked night. The town was modestly safe. The people seemed to be prepared for Hurricane Vicky, for hurricanes had happened before.

The resident ancestors were adept at surviving Devil's young history in America. Locals evolved and learned how to survive there. For almost two centuries, they did so and did it very well. Other than an occasional demonic storm passing by, life seemed to carry on.

There was more of a dark side for those locals who were critically in touch with this ancient place, unfortunately. To some, life at Devil's might have been called—barely adequate. The cute, quaint, little town, known for its historical storms, was, in fact, charmingly peaceful. One might say it was a place of beauty within the beast. Honestly, it would be an understatement to say the village looked anything less than a living dream—at certain times. Discounting this freakish fact, Devil's had it all. The sleepy community could have been characterized as inviting.

There were no secrets about its weather. As a reminder, the nasty nor'easter storms slammed down their sledgehammers just to let residents know not to be too comfortable there.

The warning words *caveat emptor* were even placed on an occasional real estate sign here and there for anyone considering this land of the brave. Why this particular, almost free land, had to be slammed so wickedly so often and for so long, no one knew. Indeed, this was the true nucleus of what was so profound. Few newcomers and outsiders knew about the storms. But who cared? To most, that's just the way it was—as long as the confines of its problems stayed there.

Maybe it was the Gulch area? Maybe it was geography's angle on the equator, just right for perfect storms? Of course, maybe nobody was willing to believe that Devil's was like sleeping on a bed of nails. Worse yet, maybe it was the dawn of a nightmare. Maybe the place got ripped away from the pages of history, where no one could tell of this. Maybe it started before anything else.

Old-timers dating back to the early 1800s grew weary and wise of the periodic assaults staged by the Atlantic. This wariness led the villagers to shelter themselves with bricks as the building material of choice.

The other building material of choice was one that was abundantly affordable from nearby local mines—solid granite. Thankfully, this was a natural defense against the elements. As a result, comfort slipped in through the bricks and mortar and life seemed to change over time. Every so often, the hazardous weather was overlooked because of it. Rightfully so, the beauty of the brick soon overcame the secret about the nor'easter storms and their seeming destiny. Only the very few never forgot, and these few never forgot what their parents told them. Those who lived there for generations were instinctively reminded. Those who knew, didn't speak of the storms much. When or if they did, they talked as if a coming storm was just another storm.

So it was that most of the stores, shops, and service buildings were all well-prepared for the nor'easter's occasional blows. The local courthouse, post office, gas station, craft stores, barber, bank, food stores, physicians, and even the children's schoolhouse were crafted by the manly hands of masons. Some even used granite bases to give their faces the strongest messages of all. All of the main buildings followed along this way, except for one type of building, however. Incidental perhaps, but for some reason, the most faithful of them all did not build their masterful buildings of brick. These were the churches.

THE TIME TO TELL

Devil's Gulch had closed down early in anticipation of the storm. The streets were dark and desolate. Afterward, the storm swept into town to pay one of its regular visits, though it had a brand-new she-name this time around.

A small piece of downtown still showed some signs of life moving about through the hurling gusts. Up a block from the shorelines being ravaged, a couple of brave business owners were hurrying themselves along, locking up their establishments in the squeeze-packed rack of long, tall, brick buildings.

One fellow standing out in front of his business with a flickering light over his sign, "Port Rock Lobster Restaurant," was just about ready to leave, while the other businessman across the street at the "Bell Light Bar" establishment was having some trouble fumbling with his keys through the punishing rain. Their intentions were simply to go home to safety like the rest of the merchants already had.

The restaurant owner yelled out across the street to the bartender as he opened the door to his sporty-looking, early forties Hudson Commodore, "Hey, Otter! This one's a doozy!"

The oddly-named bartender found the right key finally. "What?! I couldn't even get my regulars down here tonight!"

"What? Speak louder!"

"Never mind! What brought this in, you think?!"

The restaurateur cupped his ear. "What?! Yeah, that's right! Good thing we got brick walls!"

Otter dropped his keys, then fumbled for them again. "Whaaaaat?!"

The restaurateur didn't feel like sticking around, for the wind's howl was simply getting too loud. He just nodded as he stepped over to his coupe. Unexpectedly, he lost his fedora to a strong gust. Just like that, his hat was too far gone down the street for him to even think about chasing after it. He just hopped in his car and drove off in a hurry.

By then, Otter was well on his way too. He ran for the door to his late thirties, shark-nose Graham sedan, jumped in, then sped away.

Right after their departures, their buildings, along with the others connected to them, were left in the dark to fend for themselves. Hardly a single light was left in sight. What little bit of light that was left only showed the lonely, wet sidewalks. Nearby, storm drains took in all they could handle from the curbs. Above them was more of the same. Small creeks were running down the streets to meet them.

A short time later, the outer rims of Hurricane Vicky came ashore, offering more than a casual visit. By looking hard through the sporadic spectacles of lightning at the street corner, her spotty, twisted shape was easily seen. Indeed, she looked mean, hovering out there a mile or so. She was a terrible tempest, all right, breathing heavy with the invisible touch of her twisted winds.

She wasn't the newcomer into the eastern United States like the brand-new name *Victoria* suggested, however. The storm had started off in Europe and made its way halfway across the world, as a matter of fact. Now it seemed like *it* was crashing down without invitation on one of its favorite places—downtown Devil's.

Not too far from where the storm barged in, maybe a mile or so, sat a quaint, white farmhouse on a four-acre clearing surrounded by a fortress of sturdy evergreens. Swinging in the wind at the edge of the farmhouse's wraparound porch was a cute, wooden nameplate, which could hardly be seen through the rain. The porch light helped out, however. When the name plate swung just right, it proudly showed off the residents' name: "The Coolidges."

Around to the side of the Coolidges' farmhouse, facing north through the window, was a young, blonde woman, easily seen under her kitchen light. At the time, she seemed warm and cozy inside while she did her dishes in the midst of the storm. Every so often she'd glance out the window, even though she couldn't see much. It was too black out there. She looked like she was staying nervously busy while the whistling winds and crashing of thunder outside gave off signs of disturbance yonder.

Suddenly, before she could even look outside her window twice, an eerie sound echoed up all the way from town, then made its way right through the screen of her partially open window.

SssssKAKakakaka ka kaaah!

She jumped and dropped a dinner plate, sending it crashing into pieces all over her floor. Immediately, she slammed the window shut. She thought nothing of tending to her broken mess, but rather stood nervously staring out her window. With just the thin plate of glass protecting her from the unknown sounds, she kept glancing through it, but still couldn't see much. What was in front of her was nothing more than a wet pane of glass that looked black inside a window frame, nothing more. When she looked again a little harder, she noticed only her own reflection looking back at her. Her familiar face gave her some comfort, so she went about her business of cleaning up the broken dish on the floor.

Sharing the kitchen with her was a handsome, young man who looked about the same age as she. He was sitting at the kitchen table, listening to a small, wooden radio while he fixed a toaster. He kept working, hardly disturbed by the breaking dish, which had landed near his feet a few seconds ago.

He tested the toaster to see if it worked, then glanced down at the broken mess on the floor. "There…toaster's fixed…that's the second dish this month. I can't fix that, Chantain."

Chantain patted her chest. "Oh dear…almost lost my breath. Eddie, listen….did you hear that? Your friend's not pulling pranks again, is he?"

"Hear what? Pranks? Oh, you mean Al? He hasn't pulled anything since our wedding night a year ago. *Naaaaa*, it's just another storm. Why do you leave the window cracked anyway?"

"So I can hear anyone sneaking up….oh, never mind… you men can't understand. It sounded like—like…I don't know what it sounded like."

"I know what it sounded like, dear. It's Hurricane Vicky breaking up on land. Radio said so. Suppose to clear up tomorrow, I hear…ought to be a good time to go treasure-hunting on the beach. Good time to check it out."

Chantain looked at Eddie as she threw her last piece of broken dish into the trash. "Oh, Eddie…sometimes I think that war injury of yours affected your hearing too. You really didn't hear that? Sounded like some—I don't know."

Eddie put the toaster aside. "What? Speak up…you're speaking too quiet."

"Oh, never mind. It wasn't important anyway…I don't know why you keep fixing that toaster. I should just throw it away."

"Why? If you'd quit pulling the plug out by the cord like I told you, it wouldn't need fixing all the time." Eddie quickly leaned over to tune in the radio on the buffet next to him. "*Shhhhh*, be quiet a sec. Here's what I've been waiting for."

"*—now for the latest news and weather updates on JDVL—J-Devil radio for Moss Lake, Black Water, and Devil's Gulch, Maine… Hurricane Vicky is breaking onto land at this very moment. She's a good one, but she's not going to be as bad as she appears. Just a lot—and I mean a lot—of wind, lightning, and rain as far as we can tell—*"

Chantain suddenly grew annoyed. "That's a new thing, isn't it—naming storms? How come they've got to name storms after women now? Don't we get enough?"

Eddie paused. "That's because ships are ladies…oh, I know what you're thinking, *pssss*. You women…you all think you're getting played with—shorted all the time...for crying out loud."

Chantain carried on, drying dishes. "How can we ever get ahead if we're always getting blamed for all that goes bad?"

"Women have got nothing to do with the weather, Chantain."

She threw her towel down then picked it back up. "I'm going to call that Weather Bureau, or...or...whatever it's called...then I'll see if I can change it."

Eddie shook his head while he continued with what he was doing. "Give it time...women'll change it all...give it time."

JDVL radio continued:

"—and if you're a resident in the areas of Black Water, Devil's Gulch, or Moss Lake, take precautions. Even though the storm's weakening, the coastline will still be receiving the brunt of the storm. Heavy rains with wind gusts expected in excess of eighty-five miles per hour at some point this evening. Good news in tomorrow's forecast, though. We're expecting relief by morning and—"

Eddie lit up with a smile then pointed to the radio. "See...I told you. It's supposed to clear up. You want to go down to Port Rock Beach? Look around with me tomorrow? I bet I find something. It'll be fun."

Chantain rolled her eyes. "No. That was luck, you finding that ship's bell. None of the stuff's worth anything you find."

"Sure it is...it is lost history."

"No, sorry. I've got better things to do."

"Okay, then, suit yourself." He paused to scratch a minor itch of annoyance from his ear. "Say, how come you say I can't hear? I can hear fine."

"No, you can't."

He leaned back in his chair then crossed his arms, puffing himself up then let go of his long-held breath. "How many times do I have to remind you? I got shot in the war. It wasn't a grenade blasting in my eardrums. What's that got to do with anything?"

Chantain confidently stuck her nose up in the air. "Because you say 'what' too much."

"I say 'what' because you speak too quiet all the time... *sheesh,* sounds like you're whispering...are you sure you want me to hear half the stuff you say?"

"That's not it, Eddie."

"Sure it is...like you're paranoid or something. Now you're hearing things out the window."

Just as Chantain finished drying her last dish, she threw her towel at the sink and put her hands on her hips. "I'm not paranoid, so stop calling me that. Something was out there—I could hear it."

Eddie reached over to the radio, tuning it in again. "Hold on...*ah,* good. Hey, this is what I've been waiting for. I can't believe this happened. Listen, will you?"

Chantain reached for the coffee pot on the stove with her empty cup in hand. "It's about that war, isn't it. That's all you men ever think about. Why anybody would listen to you shooting each other up is beyond—"

"*Shhhhh...*hush up...here it comes."

"*—and now for a strange, new local report from our special news edition called—'Wars of the World'. The unsinkable warship, the US* Chameleon, *which vanished in the Atlantic just a day or so ago, may not—I repeat—may not have been a victim of Hurricane Vicky way off the eastern coast—*"

Eddie slapped his knee. "*Ha*! I knew it. There, you see? I told you that they got it all wrong."

"*—we now have unconfirmed reports from private sources that the ship's distress calls had leaked out about the discovery of an alien space-watercraft attacking a fishing boat...you heard it, a space* *watercraft...it only gets better, folks...they say a ray of light that came from the alien vessel was the cause of capsizing her."*

Eddie squinted. "What?"

"—more controversy arose when their last signal code stated that the water-spacecraft had, in fact, taken flight while heading straight for them at the last second. All communications were confirmed to have ended with the warship after that. All the two hundred crewmembers aboard President Roosevelt's secret ship may be missing too. As the investigation continues, more sides to the story have been—"

Eddie went on, "What in God's name? Some kind a spaceship, they say? *Ahhh,* I can't believe this."

Chantain's high heels clacked right up to the radio to turn it up. "Hush. I want to hear the rest of it...it's interesting, for once."

"—the auxiliary of the US Navy, known as the Merchant Marines, have denied the presence of any such alien spacecrafts, however...they said and I quote, 'It's preposterous propaganda.' Quote, 'This will be thoroughly investigated to determine the source of such rumors in our country's trying times of disaster.'

"Still, the surviving family members of the lost crewmembers have been calling the telephone lines for more explanations since all the mission supposedly entailed was the protection against German submarines along the Atlantic's cargo lifeline to Allied countries. The US Navy has taken over now. They are determined to investigate further into the location to see if any wreckage can be found, but so far, they expect absolutely nothing—"

Chantain covered her mouth, gasping, "Oh my God... it's like they vanished clear off the face of the earth. That's terrible."

H.C. WELLS

"—*rescue efforts of the missing crew have been aborted until the storm passes. Government officials involved say that the chances of finding any live crewmembers are slim. They will not give up anytime soon, though, they said—*"

Eddie, much more timid now, pointed to the radio while he took a sip of coffee. "You see? I think I told you it was some...some German U-subs blasting cargo ships off the coast. Their enemies need supplies, and the Germans know it."

Chantain swiftly turned away and stomped her heels back over to wipe the countertops. "I know that space stuff exists... it's people like you who just don't believe in flying saucers."

Eddie kept listening to the radio, looking sad. "Space saucers, *huh?* So you believe that part—instead of me?"

"—*and now for the regular news from 'Wars of the World.' We have an update on Europe. In a surprise move, England has begun to rethink its strategy to bomb Berlin's key civilian populations in retaliation against the huge German blitz. Winston Churchill made a public announcement regarding confirmations as such. He now believes the only way to force Germany to surrender is to attack the heart of those German civilian populations now.*

"*Parts of Germany reacted. They intercepted Churchill's comments because allied intelligence just discovered that German elites commenced an emergency plan called 'ODESSA' to evacuate certain privileged civilians and children into remote places outside of Germany to spare their lives.*

"*Little is known about their escapes, other than their ties with the Vatican Catholic Church. As a result, Catholic leaders in America were put in the hot seat. They had no comment, other than denying any involvement and those were European Catholics—'it wasn't us,' they say.*

"*The US government knows there's more to the story, however. Currently, military actions are trying to crack down on a whole consortium of other countries assisting in the secret underground*

THE TIME TO TELL

ODESSA operations. That's all we know, and that's it for our update edition on—'Wars of the World.'"

Eddie turned the radio off then sat there playing with his coffee cup. "*Hmmm,* never heard that before…*uh,* good coffee. Is it new coffee?"

Chantain didn't answer so he went on, "Those Nazis are done for, you know…watch, it'll happen. They're as good as gone."

Chantain cocked her head and rolled her eyes. She'd heard his war rhetoric too many times, apparently. As a way of expressing herself, she fussed with wiping off her countertops a little harder. "Soooo, after you go down to the beach tomorrow, can you drive by the new church like you said you would?"

"Yes, I said I would, didn't I? What's the preacher's name?"

"Oh, I don't know…some preacher."

Eddie paused to rub his neck as if some sudden strain of vibes strongly interfered with their conversation. "No name, *huh?* Well, it's…maybe it's a better place than the last church you found us…remember that? Everyone swore they saw God…then they pointed up at the stained glass with the sun shining through it. What was that preacher's name?"

"His name was Father Baxter."

"Yeah, well he had God on backs'ter his stained glass, according to everyone on the church benches."

Chantain didn't see any humor in that. She leaned against the kitchen counter and lit a cigarette, blowing her smoke into a quick daydream. As she gazed out the dark window in front of the sink, she tended to her hair in the reflection. "I thought he was a nice man. He looked good too."

Eddie paused then abruptly said, "What's his looks got to do with anything?"

"Who? Excuse me, what?"

"I said what does *looks* got to do with it?"

"Oh, I don't know, seeing someone that looks good while hearing about the gospel is nice is all. Don't get so hot about it."

Eddie didn't seem hot at all. In fact, he was quite poised and soft-spoken. He looked the other way. What caught his eye, quite by accident, was the small portrait painting of an immaculately handsome example of Jesus Christ hanging on the wall by the clock. It was a copy of an original, meticulously framed in glass and oak, with decorative gold edges. The artwork was done so nicely that not even the subject's golden hair or beard was out of place. Jesus definitely glowed with the original artist's dazzling perception of how the Son of a God ought to look.

As Eddie stared at the almost-perfect picture with every pastel color in the right place, his face stilled. "That picture up there. Did you buy that or did someone give it to you?"

Chantain looked at it for herself. "What? Oh, that? I bought it."

"Tell me about it."

"Well, practically fought some lady over it down at the store. *Sheesh*, it was embarrassing. Why do you ask?"

"Jesus sure was a knockout, wasn't he? Even though nobody knew what he looked like."

"Where do you come up with this stuff? What do you expect Jesus to look like, anyway? Some hobo with one leg or something?"

Eddie dropped his expression all the way down to his lap. "I never thought he was like that picture. I mean—"

"You should hush up sometimes, really."

Eddie took her advice, softening his cynicism for the moment. He sat comfortably in his chair, playing with his wedding ring. He wanted to make up for his words, so he turned to his loving side instead. For him, it seemed easy enough to do.

THE TIME TO TELL

Right before him was an amazingly attractive wife in a flattering dress beneath the cutest little apron. Her hourglass figure clothed in white cotton, pink silk, and lace, created shock and awe. Not to mention her cleavage. This was not in short supply.

Eddie ran his eyes down her long, wavy blonde hair as she whirled it about in the kitchen. He then tried to look into her deep, brown eyes, noticing her flawless, smooth skin, but she kept moving about too much. He swallowed before coughing. "You know...you almost match that picture there. I mean, you're perfect to me—do you know that?"

Chantain quickly took her apron off, stuffing it in the drawer next to her. Awkwardly, she looked from side to side, practically everywhere except at Eddie. "What? *Um*, why are you staring at me that way?"

Eddie stood his solid frame up from his chair. He pulled out his walking cane from beneath the kitchen table where he had kept it hidden the whole time. For a moment, he rolled his fingers over the brass dragon-head handle, as if he needed to think more carefully. In time, he gestured a step forward toward her, but hesitated. A few more seconds dragged on, until he swallowed softly again. Finally, he remained where he was, back where he started. Still, he made the best of an awkward situation by standing up straight, as if wishing to present himself in a more formidable manner. He paused, brushing his fine, dark hair back with his fingers. Courage seemed to be what he was working on, but courage must have had its boundaries. He was giving up more by the second. Ultimately, he sat himself back down, withdrawing. That was when a final piece of sorrow fell into place. He looked down at his cane in a swarm of complexities.

He mustered words of praise. "You look pretty tonight. I may not have much, but I love you more than all the men and money in the world and—"

"*Ah*, Eddie. We've been through this before."

"I know…I know you've heard me before…I can't say it enough…it's just that I don't want to lose you. I'd not only be embarrassed around town, but—"

Chantain crossed her arms, squeezing herself. "You're pulling that jack-of-hearts again, aren't you?"

"No! I mean—no…look at me, will you? I'm as honest as you are beautiful. You got me wrong.

I'm straightforward, I admit, but it's for the best. I can't hide my feelings. I just can't."

Chantain desperately wanted to find something to do, so she opened the drawer next to her just to poke around in it. "Well, I'm not falling for it again if that's what you think."

Eddie gestured with an open hand. "Okay, maybe you're strong…you want me to say that? I will…I'll do anything. I keep handing you my heart, and you keep…I mean—you keep getting stronger while I—I—oh, never mind."

Chantain stopped what she was doing. "You—you—what? Might as well finish what you're saying."

"Okay, I will…you keep getting stronger while I wither away…I—I mean, look at you, Chantain."

Suddenly she found a fingernail file in the drawer, so she picked it up and began filing her nails with great interest. "*Huh?* Look at me. What?"

"You've changed."

She carried on. "Now it sounds like you're picking on me. I think *you're* the paranoid one—not me."

"Paranoid? Oh my God, Chantain."

"Look, your cane doesn't bother me…get it out of your mind if that's what you're thinking."

Eddie looked at his cane as if it was the farthest thing from his mind. He dropped it to the floor. "Okay, it's gone… there…I don't care about it, can't you see?"

"*Hmmmph,* that didn't do any good. You should pick it up—really. Go around and hurt yourself is what you're going to do."

THE TIME TO TELL

Eddie strained. "Look...you said you wanted to have a child, I remember. You know—the children we talked about? Do you remember any of that anymore?"

Chantain sighed briefly, then switched to work the fingernails on her other hand. "Yes, of course...you're the one who should be reminded. You got shot down there. You know, injured?"

Eddie bent down to pick up his cane. As he slowly stood up again, he looked as if he couldn't believe what he was hearing. Carefully, he sat back down at the table. "There are other ways, sweetheart...come on. Where do we go from here?"

"Nowhere—I guess."

"Look, Chantain, honey...we can't...can we at least talk about it? I mean—"

"I think you've said enough. As far as I'm concerned, this conversation's over. I can't really hear about your and my problems anymore tonight." Chantain then turned her attention somewhere else. She darted around the kitchen as if Eddie wasn't even there.

All the while, Eddie tried to gaze into her eyes, but soon gave up. Looking straight at the wall seemed to do after that. He took her silence as a sign to leave. After a couple of ill attempts at getting up from the table, he finally succeeded. Slowly, he hobbled into the hallway, but before he left her sight completely, he stopped. "Are you sure you don't want to go with me tomorrow? We can pack a lunch. A mile hike's all it is."

Chantain quickly replied, "No, I said...besides, it's foolish on that leg of yours. I've got things to do."

Eddie turned to face the dark side of the hallway. "Oh? What things?"

"I'm going to town—to meet some members of our new church." She paused a moment before speaking quickly.

"Thanks for reminding me...I need the keys to the Pribil.[29] May I have them?"

Eddie hobbled up close to her, taking his time reaching into his pocket. He then handed them over carefully, but before he gave them up, he held them away from her grasp. "I know it's foolish on my leg. I thought if I worked—or hiked around, things'd get better."

"Keys please?"

"You know what I mean? Things can—or might heal."

"That's ridiculous, Eddie." Chantain quickly took the keys from his hand. "Oh, may I have ten dollars for gas and groceries? We have to eat."

Eddie reached into his other pocket, pulling out a small fold of bills. As he pulled out a ten, he tried to get closer to her. "I got my disability check cashed a day early. How'd you know?"

She took his ten but kept looking at his small fold of bills. "While we're at it, you may as well give me forty-five more. I'll pay the landlord while I'm in town."

Eddie slowly counted it out. "There now...you think if we had a kid, do you think things would be different?"

Chantain licked her thumb, double counting the money herself as fast as a bank teller. When she was done, she backed away, stuffing the money in her purse "I don't know. I—I can't think right now, all right?"

Suddenly the storm's lightning outside intruded through the windows, interrupting Eddie. "Wow, it's really getting with it out there." He took a deep breath and then sat down at the table instead of heading off to bed as he'd planned to do. With a seemingly new perspective, he carefully positioned himself as he watched Chantain scuttling back and forth from counter to counter, putting things away.

---

29 The Pribil was a single prototype, designed by businessman, Alexius R. Pribil of the Pribil Aircar Co. Mr. Pribil sought the assistance of Ray Harroun, an eight-time winner and record holder of the Indianapolis 500. Its powertrain was a four-cylinder Continental engine with thirty horsepower. The motorhome concept quickly ended when Mr. Pribil died in 1938.

THE TIME TO TELL

His suspicions got the best of him, and he said flat out, "Are you trying to stay busy? Is that what it is?"

"No, I'm just...working...that's all."

Chantain suddenly changed her tune. "Okay, let's talk about it then. I'm no different than you are, except you don't have to think about children—I do."

"Chantain, you don't have to go getting mad about—"

She went on, "You wouldn't know about birthing a child. You'd fall over and die if that happened."

Eddie let out a hard long breath, "I'd die? *Whew*, you know—one of these days."

"What's that supposed to mean?"

"You women...one of these days, you're gonna figure out how to stick the plug on babies."

"What did you say?"

"You watch...you heard me. It'll happen."

"Well, I never...*hmmmph*, since you brought it up so crudely, it sounds good to me. By the way that's *pulling* the plug. Not *sticking* in the plug. Only a man would say that."

Eddie started fiddling with his wedding ring again. "Sticking—pulling—what difference does it make? That'll be the day we all change...the men too. All hell's going to break loose."

"Good, because men don't want to be responsible—why should we?"

"You didn't hear me. That's exactly what I mean!"

"I don't have to hear, Eddie. You're coming in loud and clear...we'd have the same things you men have. Of course, you men wouldn't want that now, would you?"

Eddie frowned. "It works both ways, dear."

"No, it doesn't. What's your idea? Lock us up in the home while you men run free? That's slavery, if you ask me."

"So that's what you think. We're the masters, and you're the slaves?" He then muttered to himself, "Can't believe I'm hearing this."

"Look, Eddie, why don't you go to bed like you were going to do; quit your nonsense. If I didn't know any better, I'd swear I'd heard this shit from you before."

Eddie bounced up from the table. "There you go saying 'shit' again—like some rotten guy. So you want to become part of the irresponsible, nasty clan of men? Get on with it then. I'm done after saying what I said...see what I care."

"You called your own kind that, not me."

He went on, getting angrier. "Hell, if you can't beat 'em, join 'em, right? You heard this same shit? What the *shit*? Pardon me while I go take me a *shit* before I go to bed...goooood night!"

Chantain stood there, waiting for him to come back around the corner, and sure enough, he did.

He pointed straight at her face. "Think what you want...you women won't need us men someday."

Chantain shrugged her shoulders sarcastically. "Why would you think we need men in the first place?"

He glared, slowing down his conversation. "You watch...you'll be nothing but a bunch of black widows."

"Good God...that sounds real romantic."

Eddie kept glaring "No, you watch...mark my word, mark—my—word."

Chantain abruptly turned around and stomped her heel. "Shut up! Men can go out and *screw* anyone they want while all we do is stay stuck at home...youuuu, you have—no—idea."

Eddie hardly blinked. "Oh, yes I do. Women are all that's left to control what's good in this world...terrible to think about, isn't it?"

THE TIME TO TELL

Chantain started getting busy again. "That's not what the Bible says…I'm ignoring you now. Do us both a favor and go to bed."

"Who cares if it's in the Bible or not? That's what I think."

He stepped back into the light of the kitchen. "You don't believe me, do you? I can tell. I can tell by the way you prance around…women have *all* the power they need—right in the palm of their hand. They couldn't see it if they tried."

Chantain whipped around, glaring at him. "Go ahead. Stare at me. I see what you're thinking."

He went on, "Hungry blaaack widowwws…that's all we have to look forward to."

Quickly, Chantain reached for her pack of cigarettes. "Yeah, well, men run around being a bunch of sex gods while we stay at home watching it all happen."

She began shutting him down, switching the rest of the kitchen lights off one by one. When she finally reached for the last, low-hung lamp above the kitchen table, Eddie jumped from across the other side, blocking her arm before she could yank the chain.

The old, dim paper-stained lampshade barely swung between them. Above the low-hung light was the darkened ceiling; the only thing that could have disconnected their glares. When the light shade finally settled down, the two of them slowly stood up straight into the shadows above the light.

Obviously, they were livid with one another. Their standoff kept on silently, even though thunder and lightning continued outside uncontrollably. Eddie was the one to give in first, letting his glare fall to the floor. Quite honestly, he looked like he wilted from guilt. He backed away from the table and then kept backing out of the kitchen until he backed completely into the hallway against the wall.

As lightning kept flickering through the windows, he slowly looked back up at the picture of Jesus hanging by the clock, ticking away. "Sex gods? You think a man dreamt up that painting? A woman painted that sexy Christ picture, I kid you not...sex gods, my ass."

Chantain drew a wretched smile as she slowly followed his eyes over to the picture too. "*Hu*...I always did have a problem with that picture. They're all over, everywhere. You want to hear how pathetic you are?" Lightning struck, lighting up the kitchen as she continued. "Why was Jesus a *man* in the first place? *Hmmmm*? Tell me that."

Eddie stepped back into the shadows of the hallway, looking to the floor. After that, he silently hobbled out of her sight.

Chantain kept watching for him to return to the kitchen for a third time, but he didn't.

Just then, the weather outside seemed to have its way. The only light left on in the house at the kitchen table flickered for a while before going out entirely. Chantain didn't care about the power outage. She sat down in the dark, with little intention of leaving the kitchen. She lit a stubby, white candle she'd found in a drawer, placed it on a saucer, then sat it down in front of herself on the table to watch it burn. Through its dim flicker, with the sound of pelting rain outside, she slowly broke down in tears.

For some inexplicable reason in the seconds that followed, she abruptly replaced her sorrow with anger as she wiped her last tear away. Something inside of her was definitely turning her thoughts around. Immediately, she got up, retrieving her pack of cigarettes, along with her rather odd-looking ashtray. It was a cute, brass ashtray with a tiny statue of a Scotty dog sitting just on its edge. She sat back down, lit up her smoke and gently brushed the little doggy's head with her thumb. It took a little dexterity, for the little dog was only a few inches tall, with a head barely the size of a thimble.

She was thinking way too deeply and probably more than she should have. Peace of mind was what she was looking for. All of it was there—warmth, her cigarette, even the artwork of her ashtray—playing their part to help her wind down from her trials.

She kept petting the little Scotty dog as if it were her real, loving pet, even though it represented the ever-popular, nationwide symbol of President Roosevelt's own loving dog. Unfortunately, even the little statue itself served to sooth her only temporarily.

Soon, her other moods revealed themselves through the candlelight shining up on her beautiful face. She may have moved her anger aside, but she showed a callused grin. Silent thoughts circulated through her mind, causing her to huff a time or two, but then she swiftly drew down on the candle with a stone-cold look. She blinked over and over again, staring into the candle, even though it didn't do her much good anymore. Her cigarette had burned almost completely down without her smoking it, so she took a last drag and then smashed it on top of the little Scotty dog's head. She then picked up her candle to guide herself to the living room sofa. Earlier, she'd set a tidy set of blankets and pillow where she intended to sleep. After softly laying herself down without undressing, she blew her candle out and went to sleep.

Chapter 8

Early the next morning, the sun, in all its life-giving glory, tried to peep through the clouds above the town of Devil's, except it just couldn't quite make it. The clouds didn't seem to want to go away anytime soon. The sporadic gleams offered by the sunshine and the still, quiet morning after the storm marked the time for the majority of living things to get an early-morning start.

In front of the quiet Coolidge house, a single eastern kingbird sang a lonesome song just outside the gravel parking area. The old pine tree where the bird sat had fallen victim to Hurricane Vicky's wrath.

Another eastern kingbird soon flew into the fallen tree to accompany the lonesome singer. Soon after, both birds sang together to a different tune, sounding a little sweeter than before. The little two-bird band kept it up until their cheerful song brought the first early promise of day to the entire forest nearby.

Other animals quickly came out of the dense forest, walking into the meadow with no real cause for alarm. Harmony was stepping in stride with wild majesty, it seemed—until they all heard something terribly intrusive. From the front of the Coolidge's driveway, an abnormal sound echoed through the forest.

Kirpop!

It was a backfire from a car hardly in tune with itself, let alone anything surrounding it. The intrusive sound made its way through the cracks of the Coolidge house and right into Eddie's sleeping ears buried beneath his covers. Instantly, he sprang up in bed. The sound didn't come back, so he scratched his head wondering if it was perhaps a nightmare. While still dazed with confusion, he glanced over at Chantain's empty bed, which probably looked confusing to him too. It hadn't been slept in.

Then it happened again: ***KirPop! Chug-chug-chug-chug***.

Eddie exhaled, mumbling, "Oh…it's just my car…*whew*…thought it was the war, son of a…I gotta fix it one of these days."

It was the Coolidge's Pribil camper car, all right, or whatever else it was laughingly called. Describing the vehicle was a bit of a "pribiling" problem in its own right. She was spacey-looking, fastened together with pop rivets over a balloon-like shape of aluminum skin. She should have been shiny, but she wasn't anymore. The blemishes she incurred were a standing testament of time or wear and tear; a far cry from the heyday of her glorious design.

While she sat motionless in her driveway, she chattered and backfired, as if not really wanting to drive away. Even though the inventor designed her to be much better, Eddie's worn-out version left little more than a mechanic's money dream of endless repairs now.

Her tired exhaust sounded like it was riddled with holes, or maybe even falling off. It let out all different kinds of noises only a muffler shop could decipher. Next to, or blended in with, her exhaust noise was the hint of an off-timed cylinder fire. It didn't matter anyway since the exhaust made sure to cover all other noises. Surely, she was ready for a complete overhaul from the looks of her smoke out the back, which made one wonder where the fire was. Eventually, it cleared away when the motor found its groove of idling more smoothly.

Amazingly, she was roadworthy—well almost. She was still right out in front of the house, opposite the fallen tree, but the old half-breed-looking camper car was actually able to move. In a way, it was moving, but not ready for transport. The sorry, silvery-looking thing rocked back and forth on her unusual trio of wheels, hoping that any minute, she would get going or her driver would figure her out, whichever came first.

Clearly, the automobile was under some kind of stress, as worn out as she was. However, her problem was compounded with conflicts involving her operator inside, who was obscured by the fogged-up windows. Gears ground as the motor revved and the exhaust bellowed. She simply couldn't do anything except sway forward and backward.

The driver of this spacey bubble car, or co-conspirator of problems, joined in with the camper car's noises in no time. The vehicle wasn't doing so well, of course, but the driver's mouth was working just fine. The fair opinion by then was that the vehicle didn't share her problems; she was creating them all by herself. The question that had become so maddening was, "Who in the world was behind the wheel, making more fuss than the sick car?"

An unladylike temper flared up with the engine, as if their throttles were connected together. After catching a glimpse of some blonde hair swirling, trying to clear the fog off the windows, one might make at least some positive identification after that. The fanciful figure moving about through the fogged-up glass in the driver's seat was indeed Chantain Coolidge. She rolled her window down to keep from further fogging the windows and shouted discontentedly and loudly out the window.

As one of her final acts, she hit the steering wheel twice, with double the anger. "*Grrrrrr-squeeeel!*" She threw a gruesome glare out the window that could kill a bear. In fact, her invisible vision trail of fire went straight up to the front porch of her house as she spat, "Where is that loser? Can't he hear that I'm having trouble?"

THE TIME TO TELL

She turned to look forward through the smudgy, finger-printed windshield. "*Grrruff...* Eddie's fault—can't believe I'm even *in* this—this—God-awful—this—this—rolled up little—blimp!" She went on ranting, "I should club some sense into that man. What a stupid love affair with this thing!"

She snatched up had her cigarettes and flipped open the nickel lid of her lighter, stroking up a flame with hardly any effort. Her cigarette was between her lips before the flame. She took a deep puff and spoke through her smoke, "At least my cigarette works."

Calm is the bomb that blows away madness. Chantain was no different. Suddenly, a stark reminder out of nowhere caused her to lift her hand back up off the top of the gearshift knob to take a look at what was underneath it. Low and behold, it was the Pribil's funny gear-shift pattern, showing her how to put it in gear.

She nearly burned herself with her cigarette after that. "Oh shit."

Suddenly, with a whole new approach, she softly ground it into gear. With her and the Pribil working together, they took off. While the Pribil did her part, driving on command, Chantain steered clear of all obstacles. Confidence works in covert ways, and she showed this as she drove. She flicked her ashes out the window. "I knew I'd figured it out without him."

Pleasant self-assurance took her all the way to the end of the driveway before dumping her off right at the edge of the street where she had to stop for passing traffic. That's when her problems took over again. She looked both ways before muttering, "God, where'd all these people come from? Who lives out here anyway? Let me out, you jerks."

Beauty and the beast were on the move. Unfortunately for Chantain, people noticed only the beast. Her gold wristwatch reminded her that she was late and needed to make up some time. Through her flurry of hurry, she drove down to the first corner, nearly overshooting it. Just then, a couple of cars traveling the other way honked, getting her back on the right side of the road. Her brakes didn't quite work as well as they should have, but she had an answer for that. She shook her fist out the window.

Their closest neighbors, a middle-aged couple, heard at least some of the commotion from next door. They were several hundred feet down the road and received ample notice of Chantain's ridiculous rendezvous. They were clearing their driveway from debris left by last night's storm when here she came, delivering backfires for free.

They kept waving to her as she passed them by, but she never waved back. All she wanted to do was hide her face and mumble as she drove by. "Oh God, it's Al and Julie Johnson… what kind of timing is that?"

Once she had the chance to get up and go into the next gear, she floored the gas to head down the first big straight stretch, but nothing really happened. All the poor old Pribil had in place of speed was a powerful hoax of smoke.

Back at the last corner, Al shook away his disbelief. Most assuredly, he'd seen the Coolidges with their Pribil exit the neighborhood many times before. Having said that, he still took a break from his branch raking to walk out into the middle of the street and watch the oddball car disappear.

While pushing up his thick, black-framed glasses up in front of his eyes, he sniffed and wiped his nose. "Well, Julie, looks like Chantain's off to 'n early start, ain't she…wonder why Eddie's not drivin'?"

Julie wasn't too far away from him. She waddled her heavy, short frame over to her wheelbarrow, dropping an arm full of branches in. "Why don't you go over and have a talk…you ain't seen him in a while, you know…see if they're gonna make it."

"Make it? You mean their marriage?"

THE TIME TO TELL

"Yeah, I—I doubt if they are."

Al started raking again. "Yeah, maybe. I guess so...they ain't bad neighbors, 'cept that car-a-theirs."

Moments later, Eddie hobbled out of his house to stand beneath the covered porch. He stretched his back as he looked around. All he could see was debris and damage from last night's storm. Most noticeable was the big pine tree. He was reminded about Devil's as he looked up into the sky just above the surrounding trees. He held up his hand, noticing that the breeze seemed a little warmer than usual, while the sky was looking gray and cold.

Despite chores needing to be done and the unsettledness of the weather, he hobbled further from his house. He soon took himself and his dog to a well-traveled trail, which looked to be nothing more than a hollowed-out passageway in the foliage at the edge of the meadow. Without even hesitating, he plunged into it, calling his dog: "Come on, Major. We're going to the beach alone again, I guess."

The day seemed right enough, and the walk didn't appear to be too strenuously far. It was mostly level ground and scenic too with a few millponds along the way. As they picked their paths through the more dense part of the trail, one could hear the motion of the ocean getting closer, without really seeing it.

Surprisingly, the waves didn't sound like any kind of sandy beach for treasure-hunting as one might have expected. Quite the contrary, they sounded terribly destructive, like megatons of water clashing into massive walls of rock and tall cliffs.

The closer they got to the treacherous sounds, Eddie and his dog seemed to settle into a routine of their own. Eddie spoke out to his dog, "Listen, Major...the weather's at it again, sounds like!"

Neither Eddie nor his dog saw the trail quite the way it actually was, however. Rightfully so, they seemed quite unaware as they poked along through the residual leftovers of the storm blocking their path. Havoc was hiding well beneath their high steps. Massive, broken-off limbs and uproots of the forest stared straight up at them, like dead militias in some natural warzone. This was no neighborhood where neighbors picked up their spoils, like back in town.

A few animals were even caught by surprise by last night's assault. Pieces of their fur and feet barely stuck out among the twisted sticks. Adding to the eeriness were the stacks of older piles left from previous seasons—perhaps more than just previous years.

Eddie wasn't unusual for not seeing the destruction. If anyone ever did, it was likely someone just like Eddie—scavenging for some little trinket of opportunity.

And so, with invisible blinders on, he trekked right on through the storm's devastation until they were finally close to where he wanted to go. Soon his destination was within sight through the spotty, blue-gray of sky peeking out past the last few trees.

Port Rock Beach contained some pretty hefty cliffs filled with massive rocks that had been tumbling to their surrender for eons.

The striking impression it shoved into one's face was not to go there. Nobody did, from the looks of it. It was uninhabited as far as the eye could see. Overall, it was a remote wilderness in which they stood at the northern tip, where the beach didn't get much better further along. This was where Eddie wanted to go. For the time being, he decided to give his leg injury a break. From his vantage point, he looked down the rocky edges, getting mildly dizzy for a spell.

Just as he began to settle down in the peace and solitude, something caught his eye. Nearly straight down below, about one hundred feet, was a dilapidated fishing boat caught up in the waves and rock. She was wedged there between the rocks quite helplessly, soon to break up or even disappear completely.

The ocean always did have a habit of dismembering and carrying away the dead before consuming things entirely. Just like the wounded lands and forest behind him, it was another work in progress, except this boat's life was completely gone, and Eddie was there to witness the final disintegration of her existence. He paid attention this time, unlike in the forest he had passed through.

In a nutshell, her cabin roof was completely gone, and her fractured hull was hanging on by a thread. She was going to break in half. It was just a matter of when. Other parts of her were already scattered about. Some pieces were even tangled in patches of seaweed where a few crabs were looking over them. In fact, the poor, old vessel was ravaged so badly that her color was almost completely stripped away. She looked like the beginnings of driftwood, with faint colors still clinging to blue and white.

Eddie stared intensely at the wreckage as he stepped as close to the edge of the cliff as he could, trying to get a better look. Without too much hesitation, he began to negotiate his way down the most sensible way he could. There were places to step, but his bum leg began to feel the risk. Slightly down a ways, he stood. As he studied the boat for more details, a little piece of ground suddenly slipped away, causing him almost to fall. He began to rethink his predicament a little more cautiously after that. The mild-mannered man was apprised of his situation once more when he looked at his cane and the hand holding it. His grasp had turned tense, showing the white of his knuckles beneath his skin.

He knew he had to do something, so he closed his eyes, summoning a whisper. "Calm down…you can do this."

It worked. In time, the tension in his hand began to relax. Unfortunately, when he opened his eyes again, he realized the gravity of the situation he'd gotten himself into.

H.C. WELLS

Impulsive carelessness was biting him, sinking its strain deep down into the nape of his neck.

His dog barked from above, reminding him of the way back. The only thing the dog could do after that was dart back and forth while wagging his tail. This offered absolutely no assistance, except perhaps to turn Eddie's frown into an abstract smile.

Eddie carefully waved. "No—no, don't come down, Major. *Stay!*"

Major seemed to be a problem at the moment, but he decided to mind. Instead, he hung out his tongue and wagged his tail as wildly as ever.

Eddie continued to study the boat, not wanting to give it up. He tried, but he couldn't quite make out the name on her stern. All of the wooden letters were missing, except one. It was the first letter—*B*. That much he could see.

He chuckled half-heartedly. "Can you make out the name, Major boy? Had seven letters I think." He went on, "No signs of anybody from what I can tell, *eh*, old dog? You see or smell anything?"

Nothing seemed too pressing, so he took a little balance check with his feet then simply took in the scenery for a little while. A minute or two drifted by when he caught himself watching the huge waves gaining size, launching up, and then landing with seemingly pinpoint accuracy right on top of the boat's already-dilapidated hull.

He took out a scrap piece of paper and pencil he was carrying and jotted down the letter *B*. With that single clue, he wrote down a few seven letter words, trying to guess the name of the boat. The three words he wrote, he muttered, "Believe—beloved—bequest." He snickered, not believing any of them.

Deciding next to be slightly spiritual about it, he closed his eyes and got his pencil ready. He was trying to rely on telekinetic forces, by which his pencil alone would move.

THE TIME TO TELL

Shockingly enough—*it happened.*

Either he pushed the pencil or the pencil pushed itself, plain and simple. The pencil took off nervously across the piece of paper, like a needle of an Ouija board, except it left some form of odd handwriting.

His pencil kept going until it poked through to the palm of his hand, causing him to cry out, "*Aaaah!*" His hand began bleeding, so he quickly put his paper and pencil away. As he tended to his minor wound, a strange look suddenly came over him. Quickly, he took his paper back out to discover something shocking. "What? It's words? Where'd that come from?"

He read the words, "Begone—battle—beyond?"

He then quickly counted the letters. "*Hmmph*, that's stupid. Six letters each—that's not right." He carried on, "Come on, Eddie…you're slipping." He then reread the first words he wrote, circling the first one before yelling up at his dog, "Maybe she's called *Believe*. I believe, Major…you think? Ha…*Believe?*"

He turned to the wreckage when somberness struck him square between the eyes. "No…I don't believe it…*hmmm*, whatever…too bad." He quickly cast his guessing games aside and sank into a mood of indifference. He looked as though he had forgotten about the name altogether as the minutes slugged by. For the moment, he seemed caught up with watching the old, broken vessel continuing to crumble. Waves pummeled and gouged her flimsy boards, spitting fragments too small to identify out all sides. Piece by piece, she was slowly being dismantled.

At least from Eddie's angle, by looking through the boards and into the *Bless_t*'s cabin, nothing appeared to be worth saving. The baby in his capsule and the man named US-2 seemed long gone. From the looks of the sorry wreckage, he was right to mutter, "Nothing could've lived through that."

Slowly, he turned his somber stare in another direction, as if wanting to carry on with something else. He smelled the air, pausing for a brief moment. The sounds of the broken hull cracking, mixed with the sounds of sea kept intruding his thoughts, however. In that brief moment, his tranquility caused him to wonder, "*Hmmm*, something happened."

He shook his head as if denying those thoughts repeatedly, "*Hmmm*...so—so violent." He rubbed his arms, feeling the goosebumps beneath his clothing.

Suddenly, for no apparent reason, he looked up above into the spotty sky, which, again, gave him pause to think about his peculiar, ongoing feelings. Nothing was up there, except for shady clouds. They were circling high above, as if watching him. Through this mild distraction, he fluttered his eyes, turning away from the sight of them. "Sky—feels so—evil. I got—I gotta get outta here."

By this time, something had also come over Major, for he immediately stepped forward and began barreling down toward Eddie, without speaking a single bark.

Eddie shouted, "No, Major! Go back!"

He kept coming.

Before Eddie knew what to do, his dog was already there by his side, crowding him on his tiny plateau. He quickly made up his mind to return to safety with his dog. Little by little, he began making his way up when he heard a tremendous crackle from down below.

Finally, it happened. The rough waters had broken the boat into several pieces, dislodging her remains and sending them out to sea. Eddie's curiosity arose once again as he witnessed new contents of the boat he hadn't seen before, drifting in all directions.

In the midst of the mess, there were no signs of the baby. All traces of his unique crib and his last protector, US-2, were nowhere to be seen. Then unexpectedly, from out of the deep, the ocean churned up a limp, partially-clothed body to

THE TIME TO TELL

the foamy surface between the seaweed. As the body swirled about, face down, Eddie cried, "Oh God! Noooo!"

Immediately, he began the unthinkable. With his bum leg and all, he scaled down the treacherous outcroppings of rocks. He slipped a time or two, but caught himself along the way. When he got close to the bottom, he slipped and fell the rest of the way, hitting a small patch of sand. As he staggered up to his feet, the sea threw him down to his knees again where it seemingly wanted to keep him. He fought back by leaping onto higher rocks, only to lose his bearings and whimper wildly, "*Awh-ah-awh.* Where do I go? Where?! Oh God!"

Major was the only one to hear. Loyal to his calling, he bolted down and around the steep terrain, whimpering and barking. He had fallen victim to the same circumstance that Eddie had. By the time he got out of his predicament, Eddie had managed to scale over the rocks and tide pools, looking for the man he had caught a glimpse of.

As Major came up right behind, Eddie commanded, "Major...git 'em...git 'em...git 'em, Major!" In no time, the dog jumped over a few boulders and found the floating man. Together, they both pulled him to the safety of a nearby stretch of beach. Eddie moved the victim over onto his side.

"*Ahhhhh!*"

Staring right back at him was the putrid white face of US-2, wide-eyed and gashed almost beyond recognition. Eddie looked away, but looked back just as a black crab expelled itself from his slashed-up mouth of broken teeth. He then fell backward, backpedaling as fast as he could across the sand until he hit a wall of rocks.

Nausea slithered up through his gut until, "*Bluuuuuaaaaah!*" The sudden spills of illness lasted for a good while, until Major yanked his attention away. Off at a short distance, the dog barked relentlessly at something else behind a pillar of rocks.

Eddie collected himself and jumped to his feet, hobbling closer. "Major's got something. He's barking...there's more. Stop, Major! *Stop!*"

Just as he rounded the huge pillar of rocks, he saw only a portion of the dog, snapping in and out of a long, deep crevasse about twenty feet wide. The fur on his back stood up high, and his tail signaled that he was onto perhaps a challenging intruder.

GRRrrrrRRrr. Snap-snap. Bark-bark! GrrrrrrrRrrrrr.

As quick as Eddie could handle his cane, he hobbled into the mouth of the crevasse, only to be in for yet another rude awakening. Nothing was there, except for a rock-solid dead end and a bunch of great black-back seagulls standing on a mound of seaweed.

Eddie nearly dropped his cane. "What? You're crazy, Major! Good gosh, they're gulls."

The gulls stood their ground against the rage of Major as Eddie quickly hobbled up from behind. "Hush, Major...it's just a bunch of big black-backs. *Shhhhhh*, hush now."

Major obeyed and quickly backed out, where he took a spectator's seat on the soft sand. When he did this, the birds blossomed into a bunch of raging, beaked brutes, raising their feathers, hissing, and lunging.

Eddie was caught up in amazement, and for good reason. The fiendish seabirds weren't acting like peaceful scavengers at all. They were downright fearless. Intimidated by their intensity, Eddie hesitated to go any further. He dared to stick around, wanting to see what they were up to, but he hadn't the slightest urge to turn his back on them. Nobody would have.

The longer Eddie stayed there, the more agitated the birds became. Eventually, Eddie backed away to get some distance, which calmed them down. At least for the moment, time was on his side. Soon, his patience paid off. He watched as they carried on with their business before they were abruptly interrupted. Two of the gulls systematically started pulling the heavy seaweed away from the huge mound they were all perched upon, while four others stood on guard.

Eddie drew his eyes in closer to the pile. "What in—this is wild." The huge pile looked like nothing but a solid clump of impenetrable seaweed. Nothing else revealed itself, except tubes of green, several feet long.

Inquisitively, he muttered, "Waaaait...there's something there, underneath that seaweed. Hey, Major, I wonder what it is?" He commanded his dog to stay, as he quickly decided to get up the courage to approach the birds once again. And so he did—ever so slowly. A sea snail might have been faster.

Halfway there, he questioned what he was doing. Straightaway, the gulls had enough gall to fly into action, dashing toward Eddie, seeking a piece of his head. Eddie had no time to run, so he quickly ducked and swung his cane furiously until the ornery bunch of birds got wise. His weapon was effective, but they didn't chicken out. They simply rerouted to the safety of higher ground directly above the clump of seaweed. One might say they made a strategic move. Now they had higher ground for a vertical dive-bomb campaign, together or separately, whichever they chose.

Slowly the tables turned, however. Eddie took his time getting to the seaweed pile, as if he meant no harm. "It's okay... easy now...I just want to see what you have under there... it's okay now...easy, easy." He kept up, "There now...I'm not so bad...easy, easy...I just want a peek...good, good...that's it, you big ugly things...nasty things, aren't you...hissing like that...come on, I'm almost there."

With one hand on his cane, ready to swing, and his other hand digging through the seaweed, he felt something down about a foot deep. "*Huh?*" To Eddie's dull surprise, he revealed a clear capsule container with a bunch of dry-looking, white linen inside.

Still, he hadn't fully trusted the great black-backs above, as they were more fidgety than ever. "Easy...easy, you tough guys...I just want to take a peek...see what this is...okay?" As he twisted the latch, the bonnet discharged with a tiny hiss, startling him. "*Ho*, did you hear that, Major? It's sealed. I like that...must be something good."

While he kept a close eye on the birds, he ever so gently fingered through the soft linens until he poked something. "*Huh?*" As he pushed the linens aside, the face of a cute, little blue-eyed baby looked right back at him with the most surprising grin.

Eddie gasped, "Oh, my, it's a—it's a baby." He turned to Major. "Major, it's okay. It's a real live—baby." He then looked up to the band of battling birds watching over him. "Oh my God, it's a baby."

The great black-backs seemed to have a silent answer for him. Without further ado, they simply flapped their wings and took off, high into the sky. Eddie stood up to watch them as they flew around in a circle before leaving entirely.

Eddie hollered, "Wait! How'd you...? Where you...? Wait a minute! Where you going? Waaaait! Come back here!"

Major casually walked over to see what the inexplicable nonsense was all about. He stuck his nose inside the capsule to take a sniff then abruptly pulled back as if he just smelled a quandary of stench, trapped in quarantine.

Eddie flinched too. "I know, I know...he's ripe. I'll do something about that...later, though."

He cautiously looked around. "Not here, though...not the right place." He picked up the baby out of the crib very gingerly. "Boy, they bundled you up good-n-tight didn't they...wonder what your name is."

As they left the beach together, Eddie suddenly became overly cautious. He glanced all around, almost too much. He left no rock unspotted, as if anticipating someone's approach at any time. When he felt the time was right, he

THE TIME TO TELL

dashed out into the open toward the same rocky cliff he came from. Just as he began to climb, something caught his attention. Something peculiar poked him from the bottom of the baby's bundle, so he quickly felt it. "*Hmmph*, that's odd."

He opened the covers, and there it was. "Holy sh—gold? No, it can't be…" He looked again, "Oh my—it is." Gleaming in his hand was a golden medallion chained around the baby's ankle. With his thumb, he caressed the embossed design, polished to the highest degree. As quickly as he could, he covered it up along with the baby before the light of day could take another glimpse.

Without delay, he placed the baby safely on the sand and made a hobbling dash back with the prospect of picking through the tragedy for more clues. He sloshed through the rising tide, shoving away boards and debris, but nothing came up even remotely as nice as what he'd just found.

The very next thing he did was glance feverishly over at US-2's dead body, but, unfortunately, it was floating away. Eddie caught him with his cane just in time and pulled him back to land for a quick search. Nothing was in his pockets, nor were there any golden lockets on his ankles either.

He realized he didn't have much time so he began to leave, but then stopped, gasping in remembrance: "The crib." Off into the crevasse, he hobbled to look further. The inside of the crib revealed little else, though he noticed something beside a baby shoe that instilled fear into him. It was the pistol magazine, still filled with bullets. He dropped it back into the crib quickly muttering, "What? German military."

An even greater state of alert crashed his nerves. He dashed glances all around, as if he was right, square in the middle of something he feared terribly. It was as if illusions of a combat scene were growing more realistic by the second. Paranoia quickly invited itself inside his mind, slapping him coldly across the face,."*Awh!*"

Alarming alacrity flooded his senses. All too quickly, he dropped his posture and began to bury the crib in the sand, right where he found it. To hide things better on the top, he took handfuls of seaweed and strung them all over, then backed his way out of the crevasse. Indeed, the scene of the hidden crib looked convincing. He looked around again, as if he was being watched by a whole platoon of rivals hiding behind all corners of the cliffs and in the water too.

Painstakingly, he continued on. With every chance he could, he darted from rock to rock for cover until he picked up the baby again. On his way up the treacherous climb, he whispered to his newfound cache, "Let's go home…little tinker. You just never know what's after the storm here at Port Rock, do ya? What goes with those German bullets in your blankets? Wish you could talk…I was military once, little soldier, yes…don't want no big, bad Germans coming to get you, do we? No, no, no…you're safe with me, that's right, Mr. Military. Got shot once, but took five of them down, yeah…. you should've seen me, *ha*…I was the Big Daddy…my ol' gun was firing until my barrel melted down…took care of those bad guys…yes, I did."

When he reached the top, his paranoia seemed to stay on the beach. After that, he was riding high as the tide with cheerfulness. He turned around to look at Port Rock Beach one last time before heading back into the forest. As he glanced down at the disappearing wreckage, he saw that it was almost entirely gone.

US-2's body had departed so far out to sea, he could barely be seen.

Ceremoniously, Eddie blew him a departing kiss goodbye. "God be with you, my pal…whoever you are."

Major had no idea what his master was doing, or why, but he did keep a close eye on the incoming weather from the East. He froze up his four-legged stance as if he were seriously troubled.

THE TIME TO TELL

Eddie looked down, then nudged him to move. "Come on, Major, what's wrong? You can't see the dead man anymore, can you? We're doing the right thing...come on, let's go."

As he hobbled off, he turned back around. "Come on, boy. What's keeping you? We haven't got all day now...chip-chip, let's go."

Finally Major picked up his paws and tagged right along behind.

As they made their way back into the forest, Eddie continued muttering nothings every step of the way. "Wait 'til we show you to Chantain! Boy, oh, boy, you's a game-changer... wait 'til you see your new mommy, eh? Oh, goodness, how this is going to change things. We have this house. I have this car that pops...yeah.....oh, boy...a popping car...hey, do you like the name "Coolidge?" That's my name. You get to have it too, if everything goes right...you see Major here? He's my dog...no, I mean he's *our* dog, yes...you know where we live? Oh, you don't? We live here at Devil's. Yes, we do...Devil's. That's where we live."

Chapter 9

Eddie seemed to have a whole new start on life. With his newly discovered baby in hand, he broke from the tree line and back into his property next to his house. Proudly, he marched right up to the front steps as if he hadn't a care in the world.

Suddenly, something out of place jarred his smile as he reached for the front door. He couldn't quite figure it out until he looked to where his Pribil was usually parked. "*Hmmph*, your mom's not here yet. I know, we get to surprise her now…sound like fun?"

He opened the door to his house, letting his dog go in first while he flanked off into the living room. Though he was momentarily out of sight, he made a lot of racket to make up for it. In fact, he made so much noise that Major stopped eating to come out of the kitchen just to see what Eddie was up to. From the dog's view, he saw nothing but his rear end wiggling as he rummaged around part way inside the hallway closet.

Eddie yelped, as the dog did too, "Yes!"

Ruff!

Apparently, he hit the jackpot inside his closet. Out he came, tugging on a crib that was stuck in the clutter. It wasn't the technologically advanced capsule the baby was found in, but it was quite functional, nonetheless.

His next task was getting it out of his jam-packed closet. He pulled and tugged, until the crib and a whole slew of other items came falling out with it. Eddie didn't care—not even the spilled jar of pennies could bother him.

THE TIME TO TELL

After he sat the crib down in the living room, he hobbled back to the closet area to rake all of his articles, including the coins, back into the closet. He quickly shut the door so they could repeat their fallout the next time the door opened.

The next task on his agenda involved setting up the crib close to the sofa. It was right next to the front door, too. First impressions must have meant everything to him because that was the first thing Chantain was going to see when she walked through the door. To give the impression even more impact, he washed the baby. After a thorough cleaning, he placed the baby in the crib with fresh, new linens and then decorated his pen with a broad array of little toys he'd dragged out of unexpected places.

Finally, his little baby stage was set. He stepped back to see his results and at last breathed a sigh of relief. He looked around, wanting to speak, but Major was the only one available to listen. "There...it all looks like part of the house. Wouldn't you say, Major?"

His fast work took its toll, for resting never sounded so good for that leg of his. He plopped himself down on the sofa and waited, but the waiting lasted only a few seconds. Quickly, he jumped up as if he'd forgotten the most important detail of all. He barreled out his front door and turned around quickly, just to pause and face nothing but an empty porch.

His neighbor, Al Johnson, way down the road, heard the slamming of Eddie's door clear over from his house. The surprising sound caused him to stand up from his chair at his own porch to catch a distant glimpse of Eddie involved with what looked like some unusual behavior. His thick glasses only compounded the problem, so he tried correcting what he just saw. He adjusted his glasses and then squinted while muttering, "What in th' world?"

Al may not have known what Eddie was up to, but in all seriousness, it looked like he was catching his neighbor rehearsing some sort of walk similar to Chantain's. He did it quit convincingly, too. Right there before Al's nearsightedness, Eddie gathered up himself around his busts, which clearly wouldn't have looked right at whatever distance. Eddie's feminine walk started up his steps and continued to the front door. It didn't sit well with Al at all. He quickly called his wife, who was minding her own business inside the living room. "Hey, Julie, dear...come see this...I think Eddie's turning fairy 'r somethin'."

Eddie did a fantastic job of acting, by the way. He wanted to perfect it, so he did it again. With all his embellishments of what he thought Chantain should do, he casually opened the front door and swaggered with his hips into his own living room. If that wasn't bad enough, he preposterously grabbed his mouth, as if expecting Chantain might be shocked and delighted by such a surprise. His final act ended with a staggering walk as he fell back onto the sofa. As he lay there, sprawled out in a daydream, he just smiled up at the ceiling.

Meanwhile, Julie, who was next to Al on their porch, was watching the whole thing without the assistance of her husband's dirty glasses. She shriveled her lips and scratched her big curlers in her hair. "That's bad. No wonder their marriage is fallin' apart...what's gettin' into that man, you think?"

Al shook his head. "Don't know. Thought I saw him carryin' some kind a' baby earlier...Maybe he was pretending that too. Sure confusin' me now. It was a real baby or he's gone fruit—I know that."

"*Nah*, it can't be that bad. Maybe I should have a talk with Chantain 'r somethin'."

Al guided Julie back inside their house. "No, no...don't do that, we ain't got all th' facts yet. He ain't turnin' fairy on me yet. I'm supposed to go over there, remember? I'll talk to him then."

THE TIME TO TELL

Meanwhile, back at Eddie's house, Chantain was definitely headed for a big surprise. It was just a matter of when. What he didn't calculate too accurately was the length of time before she arrived. In the process of his waiting, he slipped into a light sleep on the sofa.

The little infant, who kept watching Eddie from the comfort of his crib, did some serious acting of his own. He warmed up with a whimper and blasted out, bawling as loud as he could.

Eddie jumped off the sofa like his house was on fire. "What? *Oh-ho-ho*, you must be hungry."

He rushed into the kitchen with his cane clacking alongside of him. All sorts of other things clacked and clanged too: bottles, tin cans, pots, pans, and more. Finally, he returned to the living room with nothing but a single baby bottle of warm milk in hand to show for all the racket.

The poor child must have missed a few meals, for he took to it in a hurry. A minute or two was all it took before he almost fell asleep with the bottle at his side.

KirPop!

Eddie thought he heard a familiar backfire from outside. Quickly, he glanced out the living room window, seeing exactly what he'd been waiting for. Chantain had just pulled into the driveway and was driving around the fallen tree. She parked, kicked open the car door, and shut the motor off all at the same time. She walked toward the house with an armload of grocery bags blocking her view to make matters more interesting. This gave her about as much grace in finding her way as being blindfolded on high heels. Through some memorization, she managed to get up to the porch in one piece.

The screen door was a bit of a delay, but nothing the pointed front of her delicate shoe couldn't handle. With a poke and a blind nudge, she found her way inside as she'd done many times before. While she barely looked over her handfuls of bags, she meandered right past Eddie and the crib and into the kitchen. She quickly involved herself with putting away her groceries.

Eddie scratched his head, wondering where he went wrong as she spoke from the kitchen. "I noticed you haven't started the tree-cutting outside yet…I almost ran into it with that ugly car of yours."

Eddie perked up. "What tree? Oh yes, it fell I guess…it fell from the storm last night."

Silence broke out in the kitchen when she suddenly stopped in the middle of what she was doing. "No kidding, Eddie. I thought it fell on its own…"

"Don't worry, honey. I'll get to it right away." Eddie, wishing to buy a little more time, picked up his newspaper and ruffled the pages, figuring that sooner or later his busy wife might come around, and she did.

Chantain stopped again in the kitchen, pausing in silence before speaking. "Are you babysitting Arlis for the Johnsons next door again?"

Eddie almost busted up laughing before he calmly answered, "No, what gave you that idea?"

Chantain's high heels came knocking up to the entryway of the living room before she stopped to glance at Eddie with his face in the newspaper. She then glanced over to the crib before huffing her way back into the kitchen. As she took her time pouring herself a cup of coffee off the stove, she leaned back against the counter and stared at the refrigerator like something was wrong. "I seeeee…well if it's not Arlis, then who is it?"

Eddie turned another page of his paper. "I don't know the baby's name yet. Why don't you come out and have a seat."

"I'm fine right here where I am. Just answer…kids just don't pop out of the sky, you know. Who is he—or *she*? Is it a boy or girl?"

Eddie put his paper down and stared at the floor, as if thinking things might not be going the way he'd planned.

THE TIME TO TELL

Sadly, the excitement from his cute little surprise soon drained all the way down from his face. All too quickly, he rubbed the nape of his neck and blew through his cheeks. "*Whew*...he's ours?"

"Ours? Don't be funny. So he's a boy, is he?"

Eddie used all of his cane to stand up. He then put one hand in his pocket and rocked back and forth, figuring out what to else to say. "No, really...I found him while treasure hunting."

For a long five seconds, silence ruled inside the Coolidge house. That is, until Chantain dropped a single spoon inside the kitchen sink. She rushed out of the kitchen and then rushed straight over to the crib. "*Ah*, you're right. It isn't Arlis."

She seemed bewildered all right, but not in the way Eddie had hoped. Still, he came over to her side and tried to put his arm around her. "It's true. I was walking along the cliffs at Port Rock when I saw a wrecked boat. You know, below. Someone wrecked out at sea or in the rocks. I couldn't figure which."

Chantain backed away from the crib. "What about his parents...what—what...was anybody there?"

Without hesitation, she ran for the phone in the kitchen. "We have to call the constable right away. The poor mother must be sick, for heaven's sake."

Eddie was behind her every step of the way. Gently, he reached over her shoulder and took the phone out of her hand to hang it back up and then softly said, "They're gone."

"You mean—you mean you saw them? They're gone? We still have to call the constable right away."

Eddie leaned back against the wall. "It's no use. They must have passed away in the storm. I saw one of the dead bodies float away...it was a man."

"What about the mother? Did you see a woman?"

"There were no others."

"People don't just vanish like that. What about footprints? Maybe she went for help. I mean—I mean…did you see any footprints? Footprints don't lie. Well, did you?"

"No, I thought about that right away. My footprints were the only ones."

Chantain blinked before blindly backing against the counter, where she stopped to support herself. She grabbed her coffee cup insecurely with both hands and held it against her chest. Without saying another word, she put her coffee cup down and walked unsteadily back into the living room, ever so cautiously. If one didn't know any differently, she looked as though she expected to see varmints lurking underneath the furniture.

The baby lay at the end of her path. As she slowly approached the crib, she ratcheted her empty eyes down and looked at him, frowning.

The baby, on the other hand, couldn't have been brighter. He was lying there, blanketed in the purest sense of bliss imaginable, just begging with his arms to be picked up and loved.

Chantain flipped around so fast that even Eddie seemed to question the authenticity of her smile. It came from nowhere as she quickly asked, "Is it okay to pick him up? Is he okay, I mean?"

"Sure, go ahead."

Chantain ever so carefully picked him up. "Oh, he's a boy all right. I knew it, I could tell."

"Oh? How could you tell?"

"We just know these kinds of things. We're supposed to be moms, you know."

Eddie let out a huge gasp of relief as he fell back onto the sofa.

Chantain came around to sitting down next to him with the baby. She rocked and cuddled him, talking sweet nothings into his ear. Suddenly, without much warning, she looked mildly bothered. "It's a miracle he's alive, I guess."

THE TIME TO TELL

Eddie seemed anxious to explain his heart out. "Oh, you'll never know. It was awful. The boat...there was nothing left. I mean it was *gone*. The place was crazy dangerous too. Me and Major almost never got down there to save him. You wouldn't believe what happened next. There was this dreadful dead man...*uh,* then I got sick! I hadn't got that sick in a long time...oh and *uh*—and *uh*—then there was the *um*—"

Chantain inched closer. "Yes, go on. I'm listening. What happened next?"

He went on, "Then—something strange happened...yes, I remember...something strange."

"What was that? It can't be any stranger than finding a baby alive on a shipwreck."

Eddie stared out the living room windows in a mystifying daze. "Oh, the baby? He was safely wrapped in this like—crate thing."

"Crate thing? Oh, you mean a *crib*. What's so strange about that? They really make them good these days."

"Good these days? Oh yes, good these days...it was a real good crib...made of Lucite or something—I think. *He*—*he*, yeah, it protected him good."

"Really? Maybe we can go back and fetch it then."

Eddie flinched. "No! We can't go back. I mean, the tide came in. It's all under at least ten feet of water now."

"Really? Are you sure, Eddie? Because—"

"Yeah...there was this deep crevasse. I barely got out in time with the baby. It must have floated away. Yeah, it floated away—never to return. I—I mean it sunk, maybe under the sand and seaweed or *uh*..."

Chantain calmed him down, "Okay—okay, I get the picture. Don't worry about it. It's just a crib...I didn't want to walk that far anyway. Whoever heard of Lucite? The wooden ones are the best."

Eddie fell back onto the sofa. "*Whew*, good because it was terrible. We almost didn't get out of there alive."

"*Hmmm...*that bad, *huh?*"

"Yeah, all kinds of things: crabs, the smell, the weird weather...attacking animals. Really, ask Major. He was there, weren't you, Major?"

Chantain looked at the dog lying over in the corner, content as could be, without a care in the world. She expressed her disbelief with a quirky look. "Attacking animals? You've got to be kidding, right?"

Eddie shook his head, then nodded nervously. "Great black-backs! A whole flock of 'em."

"What? Oh, I see...seagulls were attacking the dog...and then you."

"Yes. Did I tell that part already? No I didn't—but that's almost the way it happened. That's what they were too—seagulls. They *um*—attacked—only me, I guess...they left the dog alone."

"Why would they leave Major alone? He's always got his nose in those kinds of things."

Eddie glanced over to Major. "They didn't do anything to him. He was—lying down....hey, *uh*, listen I don't mean to change the subject, but...I was a little bit of a jerk last night. What I'd like to say is...I'm really sorry for saying what I said."

Just about then, she rotated the child to her other leg and something poked her. She looked funny, then immediately opened up the baby's linen and caught the golden gleam of the medallion. Almost immediately, she gasped. Without thinking, she swiftly tried to tug it off the baby's ankle, but it wouldn't come out of the linens. As the baby cried in pain, Chantain exclaimed, "It's gold! How come it won't come out of there?"

"Hey, easy with his leg, Chantain. It's attached. I forgot to tell you that. Hey—hey, knock it off. You'll pull his leg off."

Chantain regretfully let go. "You forgot about *this?* Why—why, it's gold! It weighs a ton too, I can feel it. This is a lot of gold!"

THE TIME TO TELL

Eddie looked disappointed. "Well, I actually wanted to show you the baby first before I—"

"Quick, take it off...I wanna hold it in my hands."

Eddie held her hand back. "Not now, the thing's secured real good. Really, I checked. Someone didn't want it to get lost, I think."

She really got excited then. "*Tahhh*, do you know how much this could be worth? Oh my God, look at it."

Eddie sagged before thinking of something. "Well, *hmmm*, maybe it's not solid gold. No, I'm serious...go ahead. Look at the color. It's slightly off—darker. Can you see?"

Chantain immediately put her wedding ring up against it. "*Hmmm*, well, *hmmph*. You're right...it is a little darker." She quickly pulled her ring hand away. "I don't care—it's still gold. I can tell gold when I see it...you can't fool me."

Immediately, she placed the baby on the sofa between them, examining the medallion more closely. She rubbed it and felt around the sides. Her fingernails navigated the lines of the rolling star symbol when her impromptu detective work spotted a hairline flaw in the seamless design. "*Ah-ha*, it's a locket."

She figured out how to open it. "Oh, look...something's inside of it."

Before Chantain could grab it, Eddie already had it in his fingers, opening it up. "It's a note, I think...*hmmm*, how about that, I never would've thought...it looks like it's...it's written in German."

Chantain fluttered her hand. "You picked up some German words from the war, didn't you? What's it say? Maybe it's something good. Hey, I know. Maybe it's a *treasure*. What's it say? Hurry!"

"Hold on—I'm not that good. I have to go to the table and flatten it out. I need more light too." Eddie kept his eyes glued to the wrinkled paper all the way through the living room and into the kitchen. As he felt for the back of the chair to sit down, Chantain yelled from the living room, "Well? What's it say? Do we have anything?"

"Hold on, I said...the writing's sloppy. It's hard to make out...it's from his father, it looks like...*hmmm*, says his name is...*hmmm*, looks like his name is—Randolf?"

Chantain cried out, "Randolf? That's all? That's terrible. We can't name him that."

Eddie was still having difficulty. "It says here...it says the *uh*—ku-ku-keep-su-sake belongs to Randolf, along with this note...yeah, I think that's what it says. I-I can't quite figure out the rest...oh, I know what it says...it says that the keepsake and lu-letter will help my son find who his pu-pu-parents, I mean *father*, is. It looks like it says where they're buried, if I'm reading it right. Yes, I think that's what it is."

Chantain shouted, "Who cares where his father's body is? What kind of monkey Dad is that?"

Eddie coughed as he went on. "Hush, be quiet a minute, I'm reading some more. Where was I? Oh yes, here we go... says some, *uh*, their grave at—oh, damn...never have been good at names.'

"How did you get Randolf then?"

"It says so. I can read that...this is a place with a bunch of writing and directions, I guess."

Chantain walked into the kitchen to pick up her coffee cup. She then leaned against the counter, staring out the window looking thwarted. "That's silly Why would we want the kid to know about his parents if we can't get him back to them? They're dead." She turned to Eddie as if she had an idea. "So you can't read where they're buried? Nothing important, is it?"

"No, it doesn't look too important. Things that stand out or are well known I can read easier. I can't decipher the rest...it's smeared like he wrote it in the rain or something. The writing's kind of sloppy too, like someone was in a hurry, or they didn't care."

THE TIME TO TELL

She sipped her coffee then rubbed her lipstick off the rim. "Sounds like a disrespectful, deadhead father to me...oh well, it doesn't matter. I'd never tell him about the gold thing *or* the letter. Nobody would want to go see their dead parents. That's stupid." She then brushed by Eddie, leaving the strong scent of her perfume behind. He got up to follow her as she made her way back into the living room, but before she could touch the child again, Eddie stepped in front of her to reach down first.

"What are you doing, Eddie?"

"This is Randolf's letter, and I'm putting it back where it belongs...in his locket, which you were kind enough to discover. There, it's back inside, snapped shut, for safekeeping. I feel better now."

"Boy, aren't we tough, bullying your way around me like that? Maybe you didn't hear me. I said he's never going to want to know who or where his dead parents are. Anyway, stop calling him Randolf."

Chantain then felt his bottom, quickly realizing his change was way overdue. "I suppose you want me to change him too?"

"Would you mind? I changed him before you got here, didn't I? Oh, come on now...let's not keep track of things."

"*Hmmph*, maybe I *will* keep track."

Eddie quickly moved for the front door. "Tell you what. I've got to clean up that tree outside and I won't keep track of that, okay? I'll let you two get more acquainted while Major and I make some sawdust and firewood. Come on, Major, let's go outside."

Major darted out the door with him, but before he closed the door, he poked back inside smiling. "*Um*, Chantain...do you think this could change things?"

"What? Change what?"

"You know, between you and I...I mean the baby and all."

Chantain lifted Randolf's dirty diaper up in the air, looking like she was disgusted already. "I don't know, Eddie...do you know what it's like to change a diaper for someone else's child? Yeah, I guess you do...*hmmm*, too bad."

Eddie went on, "I said I was sorry about last night. I mean it—and I'll make it up to you, I promise. I mean, you know, the Jesus picture in the kitchen? All that stuff. It must have been the storm; that's all."

"Okay then...I said I heard something last night."

"I believe you now, really. He's cute, isn't he?"

Chantain smirked. "So, you think a child can change things in a relationship?"

"Well, yeah. You even said if I could only *uh*—if I didn't have this injury of mine, you—"

"I know what I said. Don't go repeating it all the time, please."

"Okay, I won't...I know he's not ours, but—what do you think?"

Chantain turned her back to him, fondling the medallion. "I need to think about it, all right?"

Eddie leaned against the doorway, hanging his head before slowly picking up his chin. "I'll take it as a 'yes' for now...look, I don't want be the only guy around town with a rocky marriage, do you? You think everyone's catching on about us? You think?"

Chantain raised her eyebrow. "Think what? Everyone's more married than ever around here, looks like to me."

"Yes, that's what keeps a guy like me—"

Chantain glared. "Straight. Is that what you think you are? A Mr. Nice Guy?"

"Yes, I try to be. As long as someone's around. I suppose you wouldn't understand. Anyway, could you give the kid a chance? What if I said please...I mean I'll do anything to please you and—"

"Okay, okay, stop it. Let's not get into this too quickly. We'll talk about it later, okay?"

Eddie stood up at the doorway and then stood up even straighter while he tapped away the nerves down through his cane. "Yes, okay…oh, are you sleeping in our bedroom tonight? I-I mean, your bed of course. Not-not mine, I mean…I wouldn't want you to be uncomfortable on the couch for too long."

Chantain looked as if a migraine was coming on. "Yes, I am. Whatever gave you the idea I wasn't?"

"Nothing, I guess."

Eddie had very little more to say as he stepped out of the house. While slowly closing the door behind him, residues of doubt crossed his mind. He lingered on the porch, thinking, as he watched Chantain through the window tending to his newfound baby. While he limped down the steps, he looked like he was hanging on a thread of hope. Again, he looked back again through the window of his home to watch the promising picture. Portrayed there behind the glass windowpane was Chantain, looking like she had started to come around to caring for the child without him. From the outside looking in, she appeared as though she was talking to him, rocking him, dancing, and even playing with him.

However, the inside walls of their home told another story. One could listen in on the deception that went way beyond those homey-looking, curtain-laced windows. There was nothing for her to hide behind in there. As she carried on, playing with the baby, she played along, singing loving songs of the thorn. "*La-di-da, la-di-da.* This is fun dancing around, no? You bet, little cutie…does Eddie *really* think that I could ever love someone *else's* baby? No, no, nooo, you're not mine, you cute little thing, you."

She carried on, "*Goochie-goo*, I'm smarter than Eddie. You know why? I know what you will do when you grow up, yes. You're going to hate Stepmommy. Then you know what? Oh, my gosh, tickle-tickle....you're going to become an even bigger problem, until you find out who or where your real mommy and daddy are...*goochie-goo*...good luck, little cutie. How do I know? I was one of those little stinkers myself, *goochie-goo*...yes, we got something in common, yes...except I had only one parent gone...you have two, so there. What do you think about that, you poor little cutie?"

Eddie seemed so excited with what he saw through the windows, he just had to rush back up onto the porch and poke inside the door once more. "What, honey? I thought I heard you talking. I mean, you look like you're having fun."

Chantain jumped up, patting her chest. "You scared me...don't do that."

"You know, I was outside...I can see you two having fun through the windows."

"Oh yes, the blinds are open, aren't they." She went on, "Say, while you're there...don't get this wrong but—we still need to call an authority. I mean, we have to make it right so...so nobody can take him away from us."

"Do you really think so? I mean, we can do it if you think it's—you know, right. I mean, nobody'll give us trouble, I'm sure of that."

Chantain nodded, straining to smile.

Eddie gave in. "Okay, I'll call the constable as soon as I finish up out here."

As Eddie closed his front door and stood on the porch, his neighbor, Al, was watching him from his living room window. He pulled his face away from between the curtains and put on his jacket. As he headed for the front door, he spoke over his shoulder. "Julie, dear. Eddie's out gettin' ready to clean up that tree-a-theirs...I'm goin' over."

Julie peeked out from the kitchen. "Don't forget about that bundle-a-rags you thought was a baby."

THE TIME TO TELL

He muttered as he closed the door behind him. "Holy cow...how could I forget that?"

Eddie was well into the job of cutting and piling up limbs when he thought he heard someone panting in a full sprint behind him. He turned around just in time to see Al practically falling down to a calm stroll with his hands in his pockets.

Eddie shook his head and continued to chop limbs. *Chop.* Wonder what— *Chop.* —the nosey neighbor wants this time.

Seconds later Al came from behind. "Hello, neighb'r. Was that storming a wild one last night 'r what?"

Eddie kept chopping. "Oh, hi, Al. I thought that was you running—or walking—" *Chop.* "—whichever." *Chop.* "Yes, it was a bad one. Haven't had a storm like that in quite awhile. Blew my favorite tree down here." *Chop.* "Nearly hit my Pribil."

Al adjusted his glasses as he looked through two dirty lenses at Eddie's silvery-looking car a few feet over. "Too bad."

"What? What do you mean, 'too bad'?"

Al just shrugged one shoulder, then put his hands in his pockets. "Oh, nothin'...too bad you lost your tree. Sure was a nice one. I got up early this morn and cleaned my mess up, before ya. Took me time. Saw Chantain runnin' the dickens off 'n your Pr-uh, Pri-uh...car. Do y' need some help?"

Eddie paused right in the middle of his axe swing. "Sure, Al, I could use some help...here, take this axe, I've got another one right over here...I was expecting you, maybe."

And so, the two teamed up with axes and handsaws like busy beavers, until Al started in again between his chops. "This morn when y'r wife rounded th' corner, I thought she was goin' to rollover with 'at three-wheel bus-a-your's."

"It's not a three-wheel bus, Al, how many times do I have to tell you?" Eddie seemed to be running thin on patience, so he put down his axe and hobbled over to his Pribil to take a break. He tapped the insides of both rear tires with his cane. "See here? Two tires in the rear, about fourteen inches apart. It's designed this way for more efficiency...precludes the necessity of having a differential. No differential means less weight; less material weight means less waste; less waste means more cost savings."

Al kept on chopping. "More cost savings and all, I know. Heard y' before, but she corners like hell."

Eddie picked up his axe and started chopping again. "I told you this before. I know I did. The cornering comes from the front wheels, not the rear ones. Maybe you need your ears cleaned."

Al paused to adjust his glasses. "I know th' first time you said was, *uh*, 'bout a year ago, I think. But you can't travel fast with a design like 'at. Not safe. Maybe that's why the Pribil comp'ny went outta business. You ever applied thinkin' into that?"

Eddie stopped for a second to feel the cutting edge of his axe. More perturbed, he started chopping a little harder. "No, Al, guess not. Here's one for you I bet you don't know. Mr. Ray Harroun was one of the main partners of Alexius R. Pribil."

"What? Ray Hurray? Who's 'at?"

"They worked together inventing the Pribil camper car. So you don't know who Ray Harroun is?"

"Nope, can't say I do...he the inventor of the squirrel cage wheel 'r somethin'? You know, them squirrels get rollin' pretty good on'em don't you think? *Hu hu*."

Eddie looked at Al in the most peculiar way, "*Ha ha*, very funny...he was the winner of the Indianapolis Five Hundred—eight times. I think he was the very first winner of the Indianaoplis too. That's who he was...don't talk about how fast it goes because it's not meant for speed like you think."

THE TIME TO TELL

Al looked genuinely sad. "Well, *uh*, sorry...didn't mean to offend your Prickle, or whatever it's called. Still unsafe, though, you have to admit that right here."

Eddie just kept working. "They didn't call it the 'Pribil Safety Aircar Company' for nothing, you know. It's safe for cornering. The triangular frame is made of vanadium; it doesn't bend."

Al puckered his lips into an *O*, "Oh? Vanadium? There y' go with your fancy words again...why'd they call it an aircar company anyway? It's not like it flies or anythin' like 'at."

"Because it's crafted from aircraft-quality design, you bozo. Look at it. Those narrow wheels in the rear are not only efficient, light, and safe—they go along with the looks. You see anything about that teardrop that's different?"

"Now that you mention it, it does look like a—fat, short, aero-plane without wings, doesn't it?"

Eddie threw his axe aside, then picked up his saw. "That does it...one more smart-ass remark and I'll talk about something of yours."

Al dropped his axe. "No-no-noooo...you got me wrong. I'm jokin' with ya. I was just—"

Eddie began sawing, "Hell, Al, I know how smart you are. I didn't think you knew about this teardrop design, though. The body slopes back to the rear wheels. This completes the look of the only true teardrop design to this day. It's a real teardrop, not just some partial, flat teardrop that most trailers have."

Al perched his hand beneath his chin, thinking with that oh-so-unflattering expression of his. "Oh? There's a difference?"

"Yes, I'm telling you...it's a three-dimensional teardrop."

Al suddenly looked like he had lost interest. He couldn't remember where he dropped his axe until he stepped on it. He then picked it up and continued, "I didn't know that. Well, still, you should know that Chantain was tryin' like hell to speed in it this morn and it was swayin'. Teardrop, wingless, aero-dynamic, three-wheeler 'r not. I saw it, and I don't wanna see one-a-you wreck 'n get hurt. That's the truth... take it 'r leave it."

Eddie calmed right down. He picked up his cut limbs and began to throw them into a pile not far away. As he walked back and forth, he said, "Yeah well, that's life... that's Chantain. I can't teach her nothing. I told her that the instructions said not to drive the damn thing over forty-five."

Al rubbed his nose and finger-wiped his glasses. "I didn't mean to pop off so much. Ain't nobody never heard of a home with a motor before. That's really what it's about. I c'n see that. Maybe they should've called it the motorized home or somethin' like 'at?"

"That's ridiculous...call it a what? A *motorhome*? It's a camper car, for Christ sake. You *camp* with it. You don't see motors sitting around in your living room do you? Sounds like you're stepping in grease everywhere, *sheesh*."

"I do like teardrop trailers, y' know. Been thinkin' about buying one f'r myself to tow behind my car."

Eddie grinned. "What? You mean that hot, stinkin' heifer of yours?"

"You aren't talkin' about my wife, are ya?"

"Noooo, I'm talking about the stupid car you drive."

Al looked behind him, then all around before shaking a finger. "Oh...my Lincoln Zephyr...well, well...it is hot, isn't it? With twelve cylinders 'n all. How many cylinders yours got?"

"*Four*, damn it! It's efficient. Don't need anymore."

"Oh, that's a third the car mine is...three times four makes twelve."

Eddie started throwing the branches on his pile a little harder. "Let's talk about something else, can we? This is getting on my nerves."

THE TIME TO TELL

Al seemed genuinely cooperative. "Oh, well, okay...my baby, Arlis...yeah he's doing fine, growin' like a weed."

"Yeah, well, how's Julie been with her knitting? I don't care about your kid right now."

"Boy, that Arlis...he sure is a bundle."

Eddie wiped the sweat off his forehead, looking just a tiny bit on the nervous side. "*Ahem*...I wonder what the weather'll be like tomorrow. What do you think?"

Al started pitching in with piling up the branches. "I think Arlis is goin' to be a big kid...say...my wife and me, well, *uh*...we saw you carryin' a clean, white bundle...looked like a baby's head stickin' out of it. You came from right over there yonder I think—today. What's with 'at?"

Eddie glared at his axe, then reached for it and started swinging again. "You sure do have a knack, I'll tell you what."

Al stepped away from the flying wood chips and smiled. "I'll take that as a compl'munt. So where's he from?"

"He's not from anywhere. He's mine."

Al dropped his bundle of limbs, squinting preposterously. "*Your* baby? I thought you couldn't have kids. You're shot up down there, right?"

"That's right—I can't. I found him."

"You found him? Where? *Ha*, nooo. In the storm? Lay it on me, 'cause that's goin' to be hard to—"

"*Ah*, knock it off, Al. I was down at the cliffs at the head of Port Rock. Major and I. We found us a wrecked, abandoned boat. I found him there."

"You're really—you're not kidding, are you? Were there any others? You know, surviv'rs? Women or somethin' like 'at?"

"Nope. Just the baby."

"Well, why would you want a baby? You got it made. I mean—you 'n Chantain can jump around like rabbits 'til y'r hearts' content and not worry 'bout a thing."

"That part's nice. You already have kids, though. If I could have just one, I might be able to keep Chantain around. I wouldn't go to pot then."

"I didn't quite catch all 'at."

Eddie stopped what he was doing. "Hell, you know it's true, Al…you're not letting me in on one of the biggest secrets in all the town of Devil's. A kid might save my marriage, marriages save people, people save towns."

Al looked off into the nearby tree line, as if he were bothered. "You didn't get that from me. Why didn't I come up with 'at? Come at me again? Did I hear you say kids 'n marriages, people and what? Saving towns?"

"Something like that, Al."

"Y'r pretty good for not havin' any-a-those little shits in y'r house."

Eddie kept working. "It's true, damn it…I know that you know it…give it up."

Al faced Eddie while he scratched himself. "Devil's gotta keep quiet somewhere, I guess. I admit it's hard work. Well… y'r right on one thing. Julie never worries 'bout me runnin' around anymore. I ain't as good lookin' as you, but—I sure had my share of wild women, I tell ya."

"Oh yeah? Al the Great Woman Slayer with four eyes."

"Yeah, man. I tell ya…just put a bag over their head…I didn't care. My wife knew it too. That's why she nailed me to the cross 'n got pregnant."

Eddie stopped in the middle of his swinging. "So *she* wanted to get pregnant and *you* didn't?"

"That's right…a lotta men are like 'at I thought. It was all three pregnancies, in fact. I was a wild mess half th' time and couldn't get her fat ass off'en me. I have to say though, if it weren't for her, I'd probably be dead. I had to give up a lotta shit when the little farts came around. I'm a new man now…guess you can call me 'accoouuntable.' Dependable as the—day is long. *ha*. Who woulda thought."

THE TIME TO TELL

Eddie started chopping again. "See, for me it's just the opposite."

"Opposite? How's 'at?"

"Chantain doesn't want kids, I don't think. I do. I'll know for sure if she wants one pretty soon, though."

"*Hmmm*, you two would be up a creek without a paddle if neither-a-you want kids...*hmmm*, kids save towns, marriages, and...what else you say?"

"Never mind what I said. We'd both be maniacs—burning down villages—blowing up everyone if I can't get this going."

Al bent down, picking up sticks. "There you go again... do us a favor...take out a knife 'n stab yourself 'cause you won't be saving the town, I tell ya that, *ha ha*....kids work all right, so there y' go...I know about it. I'm surprised y'found out."

"Yes, that's what I thought...one of those secrets nobody wants to share...this kid I found might work."

Al started walking in a circle, thinking with his hands clasped. Then he came back around to face Eddie shaking his head, looking half-worried. "*Hmmm*, I don't know....th' kid's not hers...no, won't work."

"What?"

"I said I don't think it'll work...she's as good as not having a kid. Maybe worse—he'll be some kinda stepchild now with her."

"Al, you were just talking straight for once. What the hell?"

"No, let me tell ya...my wife and I? We think the same. There ain't-a-whole—I mean there's not a lotta breakups goin' 'round...I hate to say but—if there *was* any, I'd lay th' odds on you 'n Chantain."

Eddie stepped back. "What? *Ah* shit, Al, what kinda crap's that? Thanks for nothing."

"Sorry, but it's true. I'm talkin' straight...I didn't know you before you got injured. You might-a-been different back then; I don't know. You two just seem like you're headed there, that's all. The little snots 'n runny noses helped me but—a strange kid ain't gonna help you. I gotta give y' credit for thinkin' that way, though."

"We're not headed for divorce. This'll work—you watch. I think it's time I go get cleaned up. Thanks for helping me out or whatever. Talk to you later."

"*Huh*? Oh, that quick? Here, just a few more sticks on the pile...sure thing. Guess I gotta go too, I suppose...*hmmm*, I wish y' luck. I'm done from here. Let me know how it goes."

Eddie's cutting job seemed done too. Just as he began hobbling away with an armful of axes and saws, he looked back at Al squinting up into the gray clouds.

Al turned around to say, "Hey, Eddie, y' better get that big burn pile-a-yours lit up. Look up...we ain't seen the last-a-the weather yet, I'm afraid."

When Al made it back to his home down the road, he casually stepped up to the porch and then looked back to see if Eddie was watching him. He wasn't, so he barged through his front door like a fireman entering a house burning to the ground. "Julie! Where are you? Julie! Where you at? I can't find ya!"

"I'm out in back!"

He darted through the kitchen, nearly slipping off his feet, then blasted through the back screen door of his porch, nearly scaring his wife half out of her wits, "You're not going to believe this, Julie!"

Julie dropped her dirty clothes by the wringer washing machine and backed up against the wall. As she stood there shivering from fright in her thin nightie, she barely sputtered, "Wha-wha-what's the matter? You scared the tar outta me, damn it. You all right?"

"Yes, 'course I am. Eddie 'n the baby I thought I saw? Excuse me, gotta catch my breath...okay, this morn? It *was* a baby. Get this. It's *his*."

Julie gasped, "What do you mean it's his? What the hell did he do? Go out and find it under a rock 'r somethin'?"

"Yu-yeah. How'd y' guess? Port Rock to be exact! Did y' call Chantain about it?"

"No. You were supposed to snoop, not me."

Al nodded. "I did…he found th' baby inside a wrecked boat by Port Rock. There was nobody there, and that's why it's all *his*."

"Well, I never heard such a…" Julie piled up Al's arms with clothes all the way over his head until he couldn't see anymore.

Al let out a muffled protest, "Hey-hey-heyyy!"

"Do the wash. Straighten up your back, will you? You're hunching again."

"Where y' goin'?"

"I've got to take off the supper so it won't burn. Then I'm gonna find my sweater and march right over to hear Chantain's side-a-this."

"Better change outta those nighties 'n slippers. You're showin'."

Julie hurried inside. "I'll put a sweater on…where's my sweater?"

"I don't know. Look upstairs."

Julie spoke from inside the house. "Oh, Al…wring the clothes all out too, will you? I can't find my sweater…oh, dear…don't wanna dress."

Al stood there like a clothes basket with two legs before he finally dropped them back to the floor. More pressing issues came to him, like listening to Julie opening and closing doors and bickering with herself as she moved throughout the house. "Why, I never. They ain't good enough… that child belongs to somebody…don't they know that? Chantain's no mother. She's a bitch…Eddie's goin' to kidnap the poor thing."

Back over at the Coolidge house, things seemed to be quite calm. Eddie had hobbled down the hallway and into the bathroom, where he was actively cleaning himself up. He splashed water on his face then hung his head low in the sink to think. Something was weighing on his mind, and it showed. Still, he carried on with what he was doing. He stood up straight to take his shirt off and started mixing some shaving cream.

While the water filled the sink, he looked at himself in the mirror, feeling both sides of his face. Then he let go and grabbed both sides of the sink, letting thoughts invade his mind again. He whispered, "The constable." At that moment, he left the bathroom. He almost picked up the phone, but stopped. Instead, he went back to the bathroom to finish cleaning up. Without delay, he picked up his mug of lather and brush. Before he could say, "Holzsager Antiseptic Shaving Cup," the writing on the face of the mug, he had a white beard of cream painted on.

Next, he reached for his old single-edged razor knife, but saw a new and different looking one next to it. He picked it up for a quick examination, but quickly found himself confused. He twirled it back and forth, noticing it had two cutting edges on each side, instead of one. After playing with it for a while, he decided to try it out. His first three strokes were so smooth he had to look closer into the mirror just to make sure it was working. It certainly was, but when he tried to finish up, the new thing wouldn't work anymore. He shook it, dunked it under water a time or two, but ultimately gave up.

He poked his partly-shaven face out the bathroom door, yelling down the hallway, "Chantain, this new razor you bought...did they tell you how to use it at Gloria's Market?"

Chantain yelled back from somewhere in the house, "Yes, you have to rinse it out after every stroke they told me—or it won't work!"

Eddie suddenly looked relieved and finished up with success. He then wiped himself with a towel when suddenly, from out of the blue, he heard Chantain scream at the top of her lungs.

Eddie rushed out into the living room, where he saw her teetering on the edge of being traumatized. He looked around for perhaps a rodent in the room, but all he could see was her, by herself, with a comb in her hand, staring at the back of the baby's head.

Quickly, he asked, "What's wrong?"

Chantain could hardly talk. "I—I was cu-combing his hair when I-I discovered this ugly black mark on the baby. Look at it. It-it-it looks like a-a spider or something—look!"

Eddie fanned the baby's hair back to take a look for himself. In an instant, he recognized it. The little dime-sized mark was the same symbol embossed on the golden medallion attached to his ankle. To make sure, Eddie quickly compared the two. "It's okay. It's the same thing that's on his medallion, see? Look, look up close."

Chantain dropped the comb and bent down to take a closer look. Still, she wasn't satisfied so she swept his hair aside for an even closer look. Suddenly, she stood straight back up with sharp accusations. "It's not the same. It's got something different about it, like initials or something. That's a grubby tattoo. What kind of animals would tattoo their child?"

Eddie looked a little more closely to see what else he could make of it. That's when he spotted the same thing Chantain did. Six very tiny initials were tattooed below the circle of the mark, "Wait. You're right. It isn't the same. There's—there's tiny letters underneath it. I see them too, *hmmm.*"

Chantain grabbed ahold of her head as if she had an instant migraine. "What's it say, quick? Something evil, isn't it? I just know it is. Well? Six letters, that's not good...that means it's—"

"Hush up, will you? I'm busy...*hmmm.* It looks like the initials say..."

Eddie pulled his head back. "Hey…wait a minute. I know what it is." Carefully, he sat down on the sofa, in a whirl of bewilderment. He gazed back at the baby in his crib, whispering in a daze, "Odessa. My God…he *is* German."

"What did you say?"

Eddie blinked and babbled. "Excuse me? Oh, wow. The beach where I found him…it was a soldier."

Chantain stomped over closer. "I hate it when you whisper. Tell me…what is it?"

Eddie clutched his cane. "Calm down. Stop hovering over me like that."

"Tell me—I mean it."

"Okay, do you remember what they said on the radio last night?"

Chantain paused, then gasped. "Yeah, some flying saucers stole one of our battleships. He's no alien. Anyone can tell that. He-he's some devil cult thing, isn't he? I just know it, and you can't say it, can you?"

Eddie got up, his face plastered with disgust. "No, no, no…you listen to all the wrong stuff, for Christ's sake, now listen to me. The radio said spies reported that the churches aided and abetted certain people. You remember now?"

Chantain kept quiet, so he went on, "You know…. civilians? Children even—out of Germany—to spare their lives from Churchill's bomb threats and everything. You've got to remember that."

Chantain seemed thoroughly confused. "Y-yeah, I think so…but-but-but—what's that got to do with his God-awful tattoo? It's dreadful—six letters. Like the '666' mark of the devil or something."

"Shush, Chantain, calm down—"

"I mean look at it…it-it-it's *BLACK*, with this—demon head in a circle—with four horns! It's like this—*eye* with spikes staring *back* at me."

THE TIME TO TELL

"*Shhhhhh*, calm down and get ahold-a-yourself, will you? I—"

"It's staring right at me—from the back of his head, too. He's like a Cyclops or something!"

Just as she started losing control, Eddie shook her. "Stop it now! Enough-a-your superstitions…I hear it all the time." He waited while she calmed down. "Okay, that's better…it says 'ODESSA,' now. That's the name of their escape route or something. The kid's from Germany, honey, not-not some-some devil's cult. He's nothing more than a poor, innocent child. I read the note to you—or can't you remember?"

Chantain wiped her eyes then bit her fingernail. "It's just scary. I can feel it."

"You're getting worked up for nothing."

Chantain crossed her arms, pouting. "Okay, ODESSA, I'll buy that…what in *hell* does the symbol mean then?"

Eddie leaned back into the sofa, looking puzzled. He grabbed his chin and tapped his cane. Even *he* looked concerned. "*Whew*, I don't know…the note mentioned something about the symbol being on the tombstone of his real parents. Maybe it's their family symbol? Like *uh*, cattle ranchers or something. We have that here in America too, you know. *Ah*, you confused me all up, Chantain…I know it can't be anything worse than that."

Chantain blossomed like a flower in the morning sun, turning on a dime. "Why, of course. Why didn't I think of that? Is that sort of thing common in Germany? Maybe they even branded their livestock with it. Do they have cows or goats over there?"

Eddie downplayed his concern. "There…you satisfied now? Because I'd really like to go get washed up. Sometime, I want to get that medal off the poor kid's ankle before it hurts him."

Chantain quickly smiled. "*Ah!* You mean you're taking it off? I mean, like you said—it's probably not gold, I mean… okay, I'm satisfied. He's such a doll. How could I ever think such awful things anyway, right?"

Eddie stood back up, patting Chantain on the shoulder as he hobbled by. Just as he turned the corner into the hallway, Chantain's voice came from behind. "Eddie? Did you call the constable? I mean just to be safe?"

Eddie paused in his tracks, holding his head low. As he began to walk again, he slipped back into the bathroom without saying anything.

Chantain kept staring at the hallway, waiting for him to say something, but all she heard was the bathroom faucet turning on.

Nervously, she pretended to play with the baby while speaking overly loudly. "*Ahem*, why yes! Yes, sir, big guy, you're such a doll. Your daddy owned some rich ranch, that's what. You're going to grow up and become a big ranchman someday, aren't you? That's right…come to Mommy and get a sweet hug. There, all better now…all betterrrrr."

After a short while, Eddie stepped out of the bathroom looking quite sharp. Amazing what a little hair oil, a clean shave and a fresh set of clothes did for him. The man was handsome when he wanted to be.

He stopped partway down the hall where the full-length mirror was to appraise his looks. He liked the reflection looking back at him—well, almost. To perfect it, he stuck out his chest, though he really didn't need to. He was naturally muscular. He then sucked in his stomach, which wasn't necessary either. It was as flat as a board already.

In a few simple words, he was about as presentable as they came, standing there in a red plaid, wool, button-up shirt. He noticed his shiny nickel belt buckle was a little off center just above his long-legged Levi jeans, so he fixed it. After that, he had the confidence to strike a slight pose in both directions before nodding.

All he needed was to be a little happier, so he began to look around for Chantain. His supposed partner in life was somewhere about in the house. He poked his head around

THE TIME TO TELL

the corner, looking into the kitchen first, but she wasn't there. He quietly tiptoed his cowboy boots further down the hall, sneaking a peek into the living room, where he saw a sight he'd only dreamed of before: Chantain playing games and chitchatting to the new child.

Eddie gently fell against the edge of the doorway in awe, as he took in the sight of an oh-so-sweet, tender, loving mother. Pleasant thoughts ran through his mind, so he shared them. "It's happening so quickly...you know other parents have to wait months—years sometimes—to have a kid."

Chantain listened from behind. She didn't turn around, but she did grin about it. "Yes, I know...he is kind of cute, isn't he?" She went on, "You know, it must've been hard for the real parents to give him up."

Eddie's posture melted. "You know, I guess some mothers risk their lives to have a child...it's true, isn't it?" Chantain nodded as he carried on, "Think about it...we could be lucky. You're still as healthy as ever. No medications, no surgery, no complications at all." He walked up from behind, touching her shoulders. "How is he?"

Chantain turned around and looked Eddie over with a rare gleam in her eye. She quickly stood up, freshening up her hair as if desiring to compare with his fresh look. "He's fine...he's a lot of fun...smart too...sooo, how are you? You look—good."

"Who, me? I feel pretty good. Say...it'll be dark before too long. I'm going outside to light the branches. Should be a nice fire."

Chantain seemed challenged not too fall into his arms. "Oh, I hadn't looked outside all day. You finished the tree already then?"

"Yes, I did and I raked up too. Al came over and helped. My leg didn't even bother me. Anyway, you know where I'll be in case you need me."

"Okay. You know, I haven't had a cigarette all day. Surprising how a kid can affect someone. I think I'll have one now—but not by the baby, of course."

Eddie nodded with a smile and stepped outside, softly closing the door behind him. With pleasure, he hobbled over to the burn pile and lit it up with a bit of paper and a match. After that, he stood back to let the pine needles catch on and do the rest. They quickly did, engulfing the pile into one great, bright, orange feeling of warmth. From the look on his smiling face, he was feeling warm as well.

Blissfully, he watched as the embers danced freely up and away. Higher and higher they went into the sky, just to spite the night. He turned around to warm his back as he looked across his humble home with all its surroundings. He saved his best and longest glance for last. Chantain passed the living room window with the baby in her arms. Just before she closed the blinds, she saw him at the last second and paused to give him an enthusiastic wave.

He sent a sexy grin, waving back in return, then whispered, "*Ahhhh*, so far so good...what a way to close the day."

The surroundings of his house gave him cause to look around with some new ideas. More dreams came flooding into his mind as he selectively explored the scenery. The silhouettes of treetops stood high through the fire's flickering glow in the shadowy distance. He took in a deep breath, smelling the simple, sweet fragrances of the forest and the fire behind him. After summing up all his simple pleasures, he whispered, "Maybe I'll buy this beautiful place someday—spend the rest of my life—just the three of us...*ah*, smells good."

By then, the burning pile had turned into crackles and pops of dancing, hot flames. He rotated around to watch the fire for a while, letting his hands get warm. When he felt a little too warm, he merrily stepped back a couple steps away from the flames. Just as he found his ideal temperature once again, seemingly without a thing to bother him, he heard something he must have recognized as not so peaceful. It was the sound of quick footsteps, followed by impatient mutters of the feminine kind.

Out in the dark toward the roadway somewhere was someone fast approaching. She was mumbling to herself and that *someone* was getting closer. When he heard her footsteps making their way onto the gravel of his driveway, he turned around and muttered, "Oh, it's Julie...wonder what *she* wants."

The light given off from the fire made her look even bigger than she was. It was her shadow cast up onto the wall of the toolshed that made her look so big. It must have been at least ten feet tall and ten feet wide. He muttered again, "Thank God Halloween only comes once a year."

With her shadow of the dark giant behind her, she scuffled into a short-stepping hurry, heading directly for the door to his house. Somewhere in between, she finally spotted Eddie beside the fire, but didn't have much to say to him. She didn't have to. If looks could talk, she looked about as angry as a puffed-up old hen missing her chicks.

Eddie turned away as if he wished to ignore her. In a worn-out fashion, he blew through his cheeks and shivered. "Wow, haven't seen a look like that since my mother gave me a whipping." He paused, "Wait a minute...Al, that rat... *hmmph*, he probably said I sunk a ship, killed a crew, then stole all the women's babies...*hmmm*, I'm a pirate....yeah... Eddie the pirate."

As Julie kept walking, she never took her eyes from him for one second. She held her sweater up tight around her neck with one hand, while she carried her baby, Arlis, in the other. Eddie looked back again just as she opened the front door to his house. Then without knocking, she stormed inside the front door. The porch light even flickered as the screen door slammed behind her.

While Eddie stayed next to the fire, he shook his head and tapped the angst down through his cane. He appeared as though he was going to let the chips fall where they may. One thing seemed to be going his way, however. He didn't have to go inside because he could hear Julie from outside fairly well.

Julie started in immediately, barking out, "Al told me you're taking a child. Is that true?"

Her grand entry without a knock caught Chantain by total surprise. Quickly, she covered up the baby and his gleaming medallion just in time before Julie could see it. Before Chantain could turn around to say hello, Julie was already there, looking over her shoulder. "What's that? Did you take a child or not?"

Chantain patted her chest. "No! Why, no, I didn't take a child. Why didn't you knock? Criminy, you scared me."

Julie stepped back, giving herself space as she started bouncing her baby nervously. She then looked at the crib of blankets again. "If you didn't take him, then who did?"

"Slow down. Wait right there, my lady...Eddie found him in an abandoned boat this morning at Port Rock."

Julie pointed with her nose. "Well? You goin' to show him or not?"

Chantain hesitated. "Why, sure. You can't hold him, though...let me see here...there's his face."

"That's all?"

"Yes, that's all you get for now...isn't he cute?"

Julie studied Chantain with a queer eye, then studied the baby over-bundled in blankets in the same queer way. To her, the child looked as if he was cocooned in a suspicious manner.

As for the newfound baby in the crib sticking his head out, he had something to say without even saying it. The cute little guy looked up at Julie with such a smile that Julie's iron-clad look was immediately erased. She stumbled back, losing her breath. "*Hooooph,* Al never said he was...he was *this* cute. Come to think of it, he didn't see him, did he? *Hmmm,* what's his name?"

Chantain sat down beside the crib and folded her fingers together over her knee, looking too pinned-up to tell. "Well—"

"Oh, come on, Chantain. Tell me, for Pete's sake...what's his name?"

Chantain quickly sat on her hands. "Why...it's, *uh*...Ru-Rand—"

"Oh, come on, spit it out. What you say 'Rand'? Rand what?"

"No! It's not 'Rand'...Rand, dol—"

"What? Oh my God. 'Doll'?"

Just like that, Chantain smiled and fluttered her eyes as if she knew what his name was all along. With a new, wholesome expression painted across her face, she proudly said with complete and utter confidence, "Yes, that's right."

"What's right? What I do?"

"That's his name. How'd you guess? His name's 'Doll.'"

Julie looked at her as if she were seeing double, "Doll? *Ubb-dubb uh—Doll?* What kind-a-name's that? Wait a minute...how did you know his name's Doll?"

Chantain scuttled her butt backward in her chair. "Well, Eddie found a letter from his dead parents along with him. They said that's what his name was...cute, isn't it? I mean, look at him. He's such a doll. Don't you think?"

"Yes, he is...*hmmm,* so I mean—wow. You got a letter from the dead parents? That's spooky...oh my God, wait a minute...they really dead?"

Chantain didn't say. She just kept shifting in her chair, trying to tie her fingers into knots. Eventually, she got around to some fearful act of painfully nodding "yes."

Julie was no pushover. She seemed to smell that perhaps Chantain's story might be phony, but just as she began to grill her some more, Arlis started crying.

"Oh, now-now-now...oh, you been such a good boy, Arlis...*goochie-goo*. What's wrong?" Unexpectedly, she changed her tune. "Oh, I'm sorry about this...it's my whine bag, Arlis here...give me a sec...there-there now, what's wrong?"

Embarrassed, she looked to Chantain. "You see? You see what you have to look forward to, Chantain? There-there now, Arlis, my boy...*sh*, Mommy's right here, *shhhhh*...oh God, I ran out th' door without a bottle...oh no...you wouldn't have a bottle-a-milk, would you, dear? I really hate to say this, but he really lets go until I poke a bottle in his mouth."

Chantain aberrantly offered. "Oh, I suppose. I mean, I guess so. You just stay *right* there and don't touch anything. We don't need both the babies crying. I'll be right back."

She skipped off in a hurry, making a bunch of noise in the kitchen before coming back to the living room with a fresh bottle of warm milk to hand to Julie.

Julie looked at the bottle, then looked up to Chantain with a look of surprise. While she tended to Arlis, she kindly said, "I never thought I'd see the day that Chantain would have a bottle in her hand...the bottle feels warm too...is the nipple sterilized? Where'd you get it?"

"Oh yes...sterilized it five minutes ago. Eddie had the stuff in a drawer from when he babysat Arlis a while back."

Julie blushed, "Oh, that's right, I remember...me and Al had to leave town. Why, thank you, Chantain, for being so thoughtful."

"No problem."

Julie went on, "Wow, can someone really change that fast? You used to tell me to leave when Arlis got this way. You even told me to get my milk at home once. Remember?"

Chantain seemed distracted. She quickly sat down and leaned over Doll's crib with a smile and a hand tucked under her chin.

Julie asked again, "Hello? I'm still here...remember?"

"Who? What? Oh, yeah, I remember, Julie."

"So his name's Doll, *huh*? I can tell you like him."

"Me? Like him? *Hmmm*, I don't know. He's not mine really, but he's hard to ignore."

Julie continued as she rocked Arlis in her arms. "He's hard to ignore because that's the mom side of you cryin' out. Maybe you could be a real mom—who knows?"

"What do you mean by that?"

"Oh, I guess I could say now since you're thinkin' of bein' a mom. Ever since you two moved next door, you were always this beauty queen with fangs, *ha!* I guess this'll take care-a-that right away."

Chantain sneered. "Thanks a lot…so the truth comes out just because I have one of these in my house?"

Julie suddenly looked around as if she were searching for a place to backpedal. Nervously, she looked for something else to look at, but she seemed marooned right there in her chair. Finally, she looked back at Chantain with no resolve. Her splendid looks offered no resolve either. She was plastered in a silk dress with a figure to die for and her attire wasn't even stained.

Julie muttered, "Hardly fair too. You got a ready-made baby overnight."

Chantain didn't say or do anything except look Julie over from head to toe. What she saw was a woman, well-entrenched in the life of a seasoned mother who didn't have a smidgen of makeup on.

The sorry silence seemed to press on.

The more Julie glanced around, the more estranged she became. She started to chew her jaw, stewing up another rash of feelings. She took a look at herself briefly by glancing down at the top of her breasts. Describing her as unfashionable was an understatement, based on what she was wearing—or not wearing. Besides the fact that her thin nighty had been worn too many times, she was blatantly geared more toward the serious work of feeding babies than amusing men with fancy brassieres. She didn't have one on, or she couldn't find one to fit. She'd let herself go more than she might care to let anyone see. The truth of the matter was that she was still in the doldrums of not fully recovering from the long, hard several months of carrying and birthing her own son.

Immediately, she shook off her shackles of self-pity, trading them in for thorns. She stuck her nose up in the air. "It's a shame he's not yours and Eddie's. I mean, for real."

Chantain dropped her smile like a lead anchor. "What did you say?"

Julie still carried on, steadying herself as she gripped onto one side of the little wooden chair she was sitting on. "I-I-I mean, if only you and Eddie *could* have a child—of your own. I mean, you wouldn't have to settle for *someone else's*. That's like raising some child of your lover's former lover. How awful...don't you think?"

Chantain briefly appeared as though she just took a walloping blow between the eyes, but she recovered like a champ. She stretched and yawned with her arms from end to end and arched her back. To show the best of her, she stuck out her glamorous chest too. Quite hard to miss was her shape behind her tight, white silk dress. Under all that was her brand-new bullet brassiere, showing no fear of sagging whatsoever. "Well, yes, of course...my baby would be the most beautiful and charming of all....*hmmm*, I thought you knew that." She then dropped her charm, like a box of rocks. "I mean, look at you and Arlis...I mean, *um*."

"What about Arlis?"

"Well, anyone can see the resemblance of you two in my old chair. Speaking of which, I've got to get a new one—one of these days—soon I guess."

Julie tried to look at the chair she was sitting on, but her body wouldn't let her. Not that she wanted to see her chair. She must have seen it many times before—empty. The invisible chair was there, unfortunately, beneath hips and thighs the size of a tree trunk.

Realizing all this, Julie wiped her stubby nose then sheepishly adjusted Arlis back into her lap, which could have been anywhere. Still, she sat tough. "We look just fine—isn't that right, Arlis? Yeah, you're cute...Mommy likes your little nose and wooly red hair, doesn't she?"

Chantain grinned. "At least that's all you see."

Just as Julie began to say something, thunder came rattling through the windows with a massive clap.

Both of them jumped.

Chantain quickly closed all of the windows then headed for the front door. "That didn't sound too good...I think I'll call Eddie inside before he gets rained on. Maybe you should go before it starts raining too. I hate to see you and Arlis catch a *cold* or something."

Julie cordially got up to head outside. "Yes, I best be going. It's pretty dark out there too...here's your bottle. Thanks for our little visit anyway."

Julie stepped out into the yard before turning around. "Oh, Chantain, honey?"

"Yes?"

"I never expected you to be a mother. Hope, *uh*, Dolly works out."

She then turned and walked away, taking a good dose of sorrow with her. As she passed Eddie and disappeared out into the street, Eddie turned back to the fire, warming and rubbing his hands, muttering to himself, "Who woulda believed. *Hmmph*, didn't think I'd see her leaving like that."

He then offered a glance up to Chantain, who was still under the light of the porch, glaring at him. "Everything go okay?"

Chantain didn't answer, nor did she call him inside. She just turned around and closed the door behind her. Shortly thereafter, the porch light went out.

Eddie rubbed his hands whispering, "Al...that rat-fink... wonder what he's doing right now."

Al was trying to relax in his living room chair with his feet kicked up on his padded stool. Apparently, he was waiting for Julie to return. Periodically, he glanced at his small cuckoo clock ticking on the wall. Next to him was his low-boy cabinet radio, playing a rather scratchy signal of the news. Every so often he looked up to the ceiling where he heard his older two children upstairs making noise.

They were making a little too much noise actually, so he folded his newspaper down and grabbed a broom next to his chair and thumped on the ceiling with it. "Quiet down up there!"

After they quieted down, he took a drag from his dirty, worn-out tobacco pipe and tuned in his radio a little better.

"—and now more news from inside the station here at JDVL. The famous author, Vera Connolly, who wrote the highly controversial articles for Better Housekeeping Magazine in February 1933, is back in the news again. Her laughable stories titled 'Is Your Man Worth Fighting For?' and 'Thousands Of Women Go to War against Divorce' look like they're starting to come true nearly a decade later.

"The little-known female writer claimed America was going to become the land of divorce. You heard me right. Her credibility was under attack when she exaggerated the her numbers that nearly two hundred thousand divorces were granted in the United States in just one year.

"Well, when it comes to fussing over facts, it makes little difference a decade later. The joke is on us. America is well on its way to Connelly's outrageous predictions made back then. The divorce rate has nearly doubled to four hundred thousand nationwide.

"Who's laughing now? The divorce numbers have started to climb so high that some US government officials answered. They say there's no cause for alarm. Their reasons given were, in part, due to

THE TIME TO TELL

war. Whether their reasons for blaming the war are plausible, only time will tell—"

Al yelled to his kids upstairs, "Shut up the noise! I'll get the belt out! Holy cow! Trying to get some peace and quiet here!" He paused for a sound check. All was quiet, so he hurled his pipe back in his mouth and puffed as the radio kept playing.

"—tonight's news is brought to you by Fels-Naptha...smell the clean Naptha odor for the difference. Remember, everybody loves a gentle giant. Don't forget Crisco...Crisco—instead of bacon grease. Also brought to you by Mersman Tables from the Mersman Brothers Corporation...some know more than others."

Al had no more than quieted down his children when a noise from a slamming front door shuddered throughout the house. Julie barged into the living room with Arlis. Without saying a word, she made a beeline right past Al and directly on into the kitchen, where she grabbed the telephone. She frantically dialed the rotor as fast as it would go.

Al stretched his concerned neck out to look into the kitchen. "Who you calling at this hour, woman? Nothin's open."

Julie blindly waved him away. "Never mind. Don't bother me right now. Can't you see? I'm trying to dial. See? You made me mess up. Now I gotta dial all over again."

Al grumbled then sat back down to bury his face back in his newspaper as the radio continued.

"—and now an update on the war locally along the Eastern seaboard. Our special edition of Wars of the World. The two hundred-member lost crew of the US Chameleon *is now officially considered one hundred percent unaccounted for. From the way it looks, the mystery behind the vanishing battleship continues.*

"No evidence was found at the scene except a floating piece of material which was said to have come from an unidentified, flying spacecraft with unusual, never-seen-before markings. The discovery further raises the question, 'Did President Roosevelt's unsinkable warship actually have an alien encounter?' Fact or fiction, so far the US government refuses to release any further details or pictures of the strange material found floating, thereby confirming the possibility of at least some support to the story they deny—"

Julie's face lit up after waiting on the phone. "*Ah*, finally you picked up, hello? Is this the constable? I'd like to report a lost baby at a shipwreck at Port Rock Beach. Yes, that's right…no, it's true…*uh huh*…yes…right. I'll hold, but you better hurry before I change my mind."

Al put his paper down and set his pipe in the Folgers can he used as an ashtray, then glared into the kitchen. "What you doin'? Hang up that phone—now."

"Shut up, Al. I know what I'm doing."

He went on. "When you goin' to stop pokin' y'r nose in other people's business?"

The radio kept playing.

"*—we'll end the evening with a song called 'Stormy Weather,' by Lena Horne. An appropriate song for tonight's weather. Stay dry and stay tuned to J-Devil.*"

Julie kept talking on the phone. "Hello? Yes, he was found by Mr. Coolidge sometime this morning….what? Excuse me? You already have a report of a shipwreck…what? You have no record of a baby lost? Of course, you don't, because he was gone before y' got there. That's ridiculous. Yes, I'm telling the truth! Okay, then, what about surviv'rs? Yes…no, that's wrong….*uh-huh*, there *was* a baby, I'm tellin'—who am I? Well, never you mind. The baby's located at Eddie and Chantain's place just outside-a-town if you don't believe me…their last name? I told you, it's Coolidge, like 'cool—idge.' Yes, like the old president. Good, you know where they are then. No, that's all the information I have. You do th' rest. When you goin' out to see 'em? Okay, bye then."

Julie hung up the phone and looked back at Al, who was frozen stiff in his chair with a stone, cold glare. The only thing moving was the smoke rising from his pipe. She insecurely asked, "What are you staring at? Stop smoking that way. You know how I hate that."

Al threw his newspaper aside and tapped his ashes out into his can. He had a good grip on himself, but patience let him down. He swatted the radio knob, nearly busting it off. After that, he defiantly stomped out of the living room while Julie tried to follow. "Wait…where you goin'? Wait, you know it's not right f'r them to have that baby…you know it, Al…Al, honey? Can you hear me, dear?"

Chapter 10

The next morning rolled around with hardly a sound except for the weather's early morning rain. It came and went. In all reality, the Coolidge home was still dripping from its eaves as if the sobs from the sky had only just begun. Their home seemed as though it were being lightly tested, as strange as that may have sounded. The roof shingles were starting to form the warning signs of failing. Moss and mold started to gather in clumps, ever so slowly.

Inside the aging Coolidge home was a warm and cozy feeling, however. The comfortable setting was just like most Sunday mornings in Devil's Gulch. Eddie and Chantain were really no different from most others in the surrounding community. They, as well as others in the town, cherished the ritual of serving their respects each Sunday.

Yes, indeed, it was a dear time for the loving veneration of Earth's creator. Eddie and Chantain, being a part of this everlasting tradition, were proudly dressed and ready to go to church. They were well-prepared for the weekly occasion, outfitted in what they believed to be their best example of divine clothing. One could say they looked and acted typical for the Sabbath. The two of them seemed well on their way, having just finished their breakfast before taking off to explore a new church they had previously discussed.

Chantain excused herself from the table and began to put the dishes away while Eddie finished his last bit of coffee. While he did, he looked at his newfound baby lying in a padded basket, smiling. Right along with his cute little smile, the gold medallion sparkled out in the open, begging for attention too.

On a whim, Eddie popped out of his chair as if he had just retrieved an idea out of thin air. Chantain stopped what she was doing, curiously watching him as he rummaged through a kitchen drawer, looking for tools.

It didn't take long for her to notice that with Eddie's newly-gathered tools, he was well on his way to performing surgical maneuvers on their baby right then and there on the table. In fact, he'd already laid Doll flat out on the hard, cold surface and he was getting ready to grip down with a huge pair of ranch fence cutters next to the baby's delicate little ankle.

She quickly ran over. "Wait! That looks dangerous to do around Doll, don't you think?"

Eddie stopped while looking irritated. "What did I hear? Since when did you come up with the name 'Doll?'?"

Chantain started going about her business without saying. She nonchalantly put her remaining dishes in the sink, turned on the water, and felt the flow until it started getting hot.

Eddie patiently waited. "Well? Since when have you stopped talking?"

Chantain looked out the kitchen window, showing little concern. "Very well then, I'll say. Since last night when Julie was here."

"Why in the world would you call the boy a lousy doll?"

"I don't know—he's kind of cute like a doll. Besides, you can't go around calling him 'Randolf'...it's worse. That's German, silly."

"German? Who cares if—"

"Look, the name is German, you idiot. You know, the war? Besides...sounds like some Reindeer without a twisted nose that never existed."

"Reindeer? For God's sakes...Oh, I get it. Well who cares if it's German or not. His dad named him that. Owe some respect to the guy...why I, *aaah sheesh*, never mind."

"Too late…I already told Julie anyway."
"What? You're already telling people?"
"It's just the way it is—so get over it."

Eddie's mind went blank as he looked at the blank wall. After being thoroughly sidetracked, he remembered what it was he was doing—removing the medallion from Doll's ankle. With his huge set of fence cutters, he latched onto one of the golden chain links and squeezed down with all his might. It didn't break, so he tried harder until he began to quiver and shake. He even held his breath. Still, nothing seemed to give, so he let go with a gasp. "*Tah*, what's this made of?"

He must have been prepared for the unexpected, for he quickly placed the cutters down and grabbed another pair of tools—his trusty chisel and hammer.

Chantain gasped and got in the way "Eddie, what are you doing now?"

"This ain't no gold. It's as hard as hell."

"I'm not letting you hurt him. Put those down."

"Don't worry; I won't hurt him. The stuff's got to be mixed with something to be *this* hard."

Chantain put her hand in the way. "What about this? It's my table too. You'll break it."

"Oh, so that's what you're worried about? *Hmmm*, bring that cutting board over here then. Probably better anyway."

Chantain seemed cooperative enough, even though it was a wild expansion of Eddie's idea. She fetched the cutting board, but before she delivered it up, she pulled the meat cleaver out of it. She then looked at the meat cleaver and thought twice about what Eddie was doing. "No, you're going to butcher him. I can feel it."

Eddie wheezed, "Come on. I'm not that clumsy—just hand it over."

He then placed the cutting board under Doll's foot and paused in careful thought.

THE TIME TO TELL

Meanwhile, Chantain came up from behind to hand him a surprise. "Here, might as well use it then. It's sharper than that awful chisel of yours, don't you think?"

Eddie shook his head again. "The meat cleaver? Sometimes you amaze me, Chantain. Put it down." As she did, he instructed, "Thank you...okay now. I've got to strike the chisel real hard. Hold the baby's leg still while I hit the chain away, okay?"

Chantain nervously nodded while she held Doll's leg with closed eyes. Eddie placed the chisel on one link and then let go with a busting blow.

Crack-Chink!

It was a success. Doll wasn't even scathed, but before the medallion got a chance to lie by itself on the table, Chantain snatched it up and began fondling it.

Eddie saw this as he gathered up his tools and put them away. He tended to Doll, massaging the red ring around his ankle, when Doll started to whimper and pout. Eddie brought his eyes in closer, out of concern. "That's funny. He's okay... I didn't even touch him, and he's crying."

He turned to Chantain, who by then was ignoring the both of them. In fact, she'd scuttled off with the medallion to another corner of the kitchen with her back turned.

Eddie couldn't help but notice how engrossed she was, so he walked up from behind and snatched the medallion out of her hands. "I'm going to put this in a safe place, where it belongs."

He left the kitchen with Chantain following close behind. "Wait...where are you going? Where are you going with that?"

By then, Eddie had already made his way down the hall and inside their bedroom, where he began unlocking the door to a very old, black safe. "Right here in my antique safe where I keep all my personal things. Where else?"

After she watched him stash the medallion inside and close the big, thick door, she frowned and leaned against the wall with crossed arms. "When am I going to get the combination to that? *Hmmm*? Don't you trust me?"

Eddie double-checked the handle, making sure it was locked tight, and it was. He then slid past her at the bedroom doorway. "When you stop looking at valuables the way you do…that's when."

Chantain looked up to the tall ceiling of her bedroom, rolling her eyes before following Eddie back into the kitchen in a huff. "Well aren't we picky today. How about you? Aren't you even going to ask about the new preacher we're going to see this morning?"

As Eddie tended to Doll, he smirked. "Oh, what's this one about? Hard to keep track of them all."

"I heard about him at Gloria's Market when I bought some milk and bread the other day."

Eddie stopped what he was doing. "You heard about him at the ding-dong grocery store? That's as bad as the one on the bulletin board out in front of Gloria's two months ago."

"What's wrong with Gloria's? Besides, Julie and Al go to church over there. They really like the man, I guess."

"Oh? This ought to be good. What'd they say?"

"He's good because they feel the hell being scared right out of them when they go."

Eddie smirked as he carefully handed Doll over to her. "Sounds about right for Al, with his past…what's he preach?"

Chantain looked as if she hadn't yet settled on who was to walk with the baby. Begrudgingly, she took him. "He preaches nothing but Old Testament. You know—the ugly part of the Bible."

Eddie walked around her and into the living room. "So what's this church called? The *Old* Fellows or something?"

"Real funny, Eddie. It's called the 'Church of the *Original* Testament'…their scriptures came first, you know."

Eddie mumbled to himself, "*Sheesh*, of course. I might have guessed."

THE TIME TO TELL

Chantain then came into the living room with him. "Excuse me? I didn't hear. You keep walking away."

"Oh, nothing, we have to get going. Look at the clock. The preacher's probably fine."

Chantain sauntered over to the nearest window, looking out. While pausing there, she asked, "What's the matter?"

As Eddie put on his shoes, he watched her looking outside at nothing. "Oh, me? I'm, *uh*...I'm just trying to hatch out all these churches everywhere. Just when I thought I heard it all, something else comes along...nothing against you or anything."

Chantain turned back around, looking coy. "I know...when it comes to Devil's, we need a lot of churches around here, I guess."

Eddie smiled. "*Ha*...do you realize what you just said?"

Chantain didn't see the humor. "What's that? Well, it's true...think about it. Devil's Gulch has a lotta churches."

Eddie paused. "Not just here, I'm talking about everywhere...there's too many everywhere, my dear. They're multiplying like-like, who knows what it's going to be like in fifty years. Sometimes, I wonder what the future of our whole country's going to be like."

Chantain sourly cross her arms. "*Hmmph*, well you'd multiply too if the government gave you a free ride and something to hide behind."

"Oh God...sure I'd like to multiply, but that's a whole different story, if you know what I mean."

"Sorry I said anything. Please don't get started on that again." She went on, "Can you do me a favor and open the blinds before we go. This place is too dark. We need to get some light in here."

Eddie went from room to room, opening them all, gazing outside toward the scenery while talking to himself. "There we go...now out there's a church where a man could easily find God...yes, right out there...look at that."

Residues of last night's rainfall still lingered. He glanced over to the burn pile he had stood beside last night. It was still smoldering and almost completely gone.

The next thing that caught his attention was the dead stump left over from the fallen tree he and Al had cut off. Half of its jagged roots were still sticking straight up in the air, while the other half still remained underground. As he gathered more of the serene sights outside, he softly muttered. "At least I have something to work for now."

Just then he spotted the same pair of eastern kingbirds perched on the top of the tree roots next to the burn pile, looking as if they had nowhere to go. Still, they were making do with what was there.

Something happened just then as he gazed beyond the birds. He quickly spotted an accumulating number of unusual occurrences. A raccoon stood off at a distance in the grass in the broad light of day, looking right back at him through his window. A pair of rabbits seemed to be gazing at him and the house the same way.

He muttered, "*Hmmm*, coons and rabbits—together?" He spoke over his shoulder, "Hey, Chantain. Raccoons—they come out at night, I thought. Don't they?"

Chantain spoke out from the kitchen. "Yes, all the 'coons I know about, anyway."

Eddie stepped closer up to the window, looking even more puzzled. He gazed more broadly around his entire wild landscape. He saw even more animals coming out, seeming to congregate as well. At first, he spotted two deer, but soon, more came out just behind them, looking straight at him before he whispered, "*Nah*."

He then hobbled over to another window, glancing in the other direction, just in time to see a bobcat emerging from the dense tree line. Like the other animals, the cat seemed to be looking directly at him. He muttered again, "*Hmmm*, that's funny...maybe my house...squirrels pole dancing on my roof or what."

He spoke over his shoulder again. "Hey, Chantain...did you put out those salt licks like I asked?"

"No, I couldn't find them. Where'd you put them? You know I hate that nasty barn. You didn't put them there did you?"

"Yeah. They're in the barn. Sorry, I forgot. No problem, I'll do it when we get back." Almost immediately, he turned away from the windows, dismissing the animals as nothing but a wild set of coincidences.

An automobile pulled into his driveway just then, quickly chasing away the curious stands of animals. The hard-driven, overworked-looking automobile was a far cry from the typical kind. It was a former military surplus car, better known as one of those "black-out" cars, mandated by the US Department of War. It was stripped of its glamour for preservation of raw materials—a far cry from flashy since much of the car's excess body parts were donated to the cause of making more guns, bullets, and bombs. Besides looking stripped, it was dull and gray as the day was long. Below, on the driver's side door, was a hand-painted sign that identified the driver as "Constable Torrance Holt, District 1." The "1" could have meant most anything, except for its rank in good looks. Unquestionably, it was the law car called upon to go out and investigate the Coolidge house for the baffling idea of mysterious shipwrecked babies.

Past its foggy glass and behind the wheel appeared a tall, heavy-built younger man, presumably Torrance Holt himself. He looked around curiously, considering the right place to park within the Coolidge premises. The place most interesting to him was right beside Eddie's Pribil car, which wasn't too far their front door. The Pribil offered a little entertainment for the constable. He was so consumed by looking at the silvery camper car, he almost bumped into it. His fixation was far from over. After bailing out his door, he walked backward

H.C. WELLS

to the Coolidge porch as he kept looking at it. Awkwardly, he stumbled on the row of steps that led to the covered porch. Matters of business soon overcame him after that. Quickly, he turned around and started organizing his clipboard as he stepped up the stairs more forwardly. With plenty of loud footsteps in his hard, cold boots, he paused before using his clipboard to tap the wall by the front door.

Knock, knock—knock.

Eddie had just finished adjusting his tie, while Chantain was readying herself to head out the door with Doll when they heard the knocking at the door. Both of them froze right where they were, looking at each other.

Their dog, Major, quickly did the talking for them by growling and barking at the front door as Eddie whispered, "You expecting someone?"

Chantain backed away from him, whispering, "No. Why would someone be out here? It's Sunday."

Eddie stepped back into the living room where he instantly spotted the strange, government-issued car through the front windows.

Suddenly, a deep voice spoke came from outside: "Constable Torrance Holt. Answer the door, please."

Eddie immediately turned around, stumbling over Chantain. "Why did you call? I said *I* would."

Chantain scuttled passed him to put Doll back into his crib then shrugged her shoulders as if denying his accusation.

Eddie continued, "Well, if you didn't call, who did?"

Torrance Holt spoke up. "Open up, please. I can hear you. Please, it's the law."

Time was of the essence. Eddie quickly gathered himself before opening the front door very slowly, part way. "Excuse me, sorry it took so long. You know dogs. We were just leaving for church."

Eddie opened the screen door then poked his head out. "Something wrong Mr. Constable?"

THE TIME TO TELL

"Not quite yet, I hope."

First impressions must have meant everything. The constable glanced up and down at Eddie, with his nice necktie, dark blue jeans, shiny cowboy boots, and clean tan shirt. Then he glanced down at the old dog at his feet, wagging his tail and refusing to leave. Whatever disposition Major had a minute ago, he had gotten over it quickly.

Torrance breathed normally, let go of the gun on his holster, and relaxed his stance. As quickly as that, he tipped his ranger's hat. "Sorry for the intrusion this morning, but, *uh*, we received an unusual call. May I please come in to explain?"

Eddie looked back to Chantain, then back to Torrance. "Why, sure...this won't take much time, will it? We really do have to go. It's a new church. You know, we don't want to *uh*, be late."

"No I wouldn't want that either, sir. Just a routine visit is all."

Eddie opened the screen door a little further and invited Torrance inside. Quickly, he offered the constable a cup of coffee, which he graciously accepted. He showed him to a seat in the living room to sit down.

Right from the beginning, seat selection might have been the first tip-off. The chair Eddie directed him to was the smallest, most uncomfortable-looking wooden chair, farthest from Doll's crib. Incidentally, the crib was standing out like a beacon around the bigger, more inviting three-piece sofa set.

Torrance got comfortable, nevertheless, but he looked a little suspicious already. As he took a couple notes on his clipboard, he noticed that Eddie was growing nervous about where he should sit in his own home. Finally, he settled on the sofa where he started tapping his cane.

Chantain wasn't much better. Her feet had grown tree roots in the center of the floor, so Eddie tapped her with his cane. "Excuse me, *uh*, Chantain? The man said he wanted coffee. Can you get Mr. *uh*—what was your name?"

"That's Holt....Torrance Holt. I don't care how you serve it, ma'am. I'll take it any way you give it."

Eddie nodded back and forth to both of them. "That's great. Thank you Mr. Holt...can you please now get Mr. Holt whatever he wants? It'll warm him up to what he's thinking about—I think."

Chantain strolled into the kitchen. "Oh, sure, right away. It's still hot from breakfast... I think...of course, it's hot. What am I saying? Coffee, I like coffee...do you like coffee, Mr. Holt?"

Torrance took off his hat. "Why, yes, I do—a little too much." He then continued with Eddie. "Excuse me, but did you just buy that sofa?"

Eddie felt its material before answering. "No, it's been around for a long time. Why do you ask?"

Torrance raised his eyebrows and tried rubbing the strain from his eyes that had suddenly popped up again. "Oh, I see. You folks must have moved around your furniture. That's why you couldn't...oh, forget it."

Just as the visit looked like it might smooth out, silence began to build throughout the room all too soon. Chantain still hadn't come out from her quiet hiding place in the kitchen, so the two men began looking around at anything but each other while the grandfather clock ticked.

Then suddenly, from the dead quiet, Doll decided to break the silence with a puckering cry. Multiple things happened. Chantain dropped a spoon in the kitchen and Eddie jumped straight up and then stood there like he'd just sat on something extremely hot. The only one who didn't seem bothered was Torrance. He didn't know where or who to look at first; toward the kitchen noise or at Eddie rubbing his rear. When Eddie and Chantain finally calmed down, he immediately jotted down another note on his clipboard. When he was finished, he pushed his utensils aside on his lap and turned all business. "So you have a baby. What's its name?"

Eddie quieted Doll down with a quick bottle of milk but didn't answer him. Instead, he quickly sat down, just as Chantain came back out with Torrence's cup of coffee. As she handed it over to him, she looked across the room as if Eddie was the one responsible for their predicament. Not only did her glare say this, but it also said he'd better fix it too.

Eddie haphazardly read her face, stuttering, "Oh, h-his name is—well, Chantain named him. It's Doll."

Chantain glared at him harder and then went back into the kitchen. By this time, Torrence's eyes were wide open, shifting back and forth like ping-pong balls. Somewhere within the last few feet of Chantain's walk, he must have uncovered a mile of information. Nevertheless, he had to get on with the rest of the formalities to complete his investigation. His coffee was too hot to touch anyway, so he carried on without so much as a sip. "I've got to get on with this...we had an anonymous call that you found a baby at a shipwreck down at Port Rock Beach. Is that the baby, Mr. Coolidge?"

Eddie's still face looked about as fragile as a house of cards. "Yes...oh, *uh,* yes. That's him. He struggled on as his voice slowly went hoarse. "I can't pretend to be a father. The baby's fine, really he's fine...not hurt...nothing like that."

Just then, Chantain came out to the doorway of the kitchen, leaning on it while watching her husband flounder entirely on his own. Pity might have been the most appropriate feeling, but not with Chantain. She looked as though she saw all of Eddie's shortcomings simultaneously, right there before her very eyes. Through her indignant expressions, one could only guess with all of the shortcomings she was thinking about.

Eddie just had to look up to his wife, standing there with her arms crossed and giving him the look that he was headed for a grueling argument sometime later. Oddly enough, he appeared as though he wanted some sort of time-out to talk with her. But, somehow, he knew he was on his own by the way she glared at him. Disgrace was all that she offered silently, among other things.

Eddie withered, only to face yet another unsuspecting sight across the room, sitting there in the name of the law. He glared too, but in a different way.

Chantain traced the problems through the path of each of their eyes. She walked back into the kitchen to let the two of them do the rest. As she walked over to the kitchen sink to think, she suddenly became intrigued. While she gazed out of her window, her eyes shifted back and forth, as if she was reaching for something to say. "Say, Mr. Holt...you found out about it so quick!"

Torrance pulled out a different kind of paperwork from underneath his clipboard. "Yes, I did...when it comes to Devil's, news travels pretty fast."

Practically with the snap of her fingers, she lit a cigarette and then bit her lip, grinning, "So...how did you find out?"

Torrance didn't look up as he continued filling out his paperwork. "Well, I can't really say...all I can say is someone seen you folks and knew about the wrecked vessel too. You know somebody like that?"

Chantain whispered through the smoke of her breath, so quiet that only her kitchen window could hear. "*Ah*, Julie, my dear...she's a better bitch than I thought."

Torrance seemed to do his job well. However, he was a little behind when it came to the mechanics of the warm, clean-looking home he was invited into. He had to stop to look up. For the moment, all he could see was the extreme sadness that he had somehow bestowed upon Eddie. The constable looked as though he could almost feel Eddie's pain, but business was business. He gathered up his clipboard once again, and then tested his coffee before taking a sip.

THE TIME TO TELL

He spoke up while still reading over his paperwork. "This is the best I can do, Mr. Coolidge. Since you've given me no trouble...says here we had an abandoned boat wreck... *ahem*...says here too...*hmmm*, that there was no record of a crime—or survivors—at the site."

His hand reached for his handcuffs to reposition them beneath his seat as he went on. "The thing I'm having trouble with here is that the two brothers, by the names of Jed and Buzz, who owned boat, died in the storm miles out at sea...they had no baby, nor was there any mention of a baby."

He paused to loosen his collar before continuing. "I checked with their nearest relatives even...so *uh*—where did the baby come from?"

Eddie looked down at the constable's handcuffs and pistol and swallowed. As quick as the sweat came off his forehead, he must have thought he was as good as dead.

Torrance couldn't take his eyes off Eddie, not even for a second. Softly, he said, "Don't get me wrong, Mr. Coolidge. I believe you—but I gotta problem. Somehow, I believe this other person's story too."

Torrance adjusted his gear in his chair once more. He then looked past Eddie as he pulled a toothpick from his shirt pocket to place in his mouth. He accidentally bit down on it too hard when he asked, "This is much stranger than what I just saw here in your living room...so help me out, for the sake of the child. The boat was lost way out at sea...what happened when you arrived at the scene?"

Eddie suddenly opened his eyes wide. "*Ah*, I'll do anything to help him. Me and Major, my dog...we were walking when we saw this boat wrecked beyond recognizable—below the cliffs—in the rocks."

"Go on."

"Okay...we went down to see if we could identify the boat—but we couldn't. All I could make out was the letter

B on the stern. We made it down close—to see more. That's when we found the baby. Really, that's my story."

Torrance leaned to the edge of his chair, studying Eddie's every move. "Did you find either Buzz's or Jed's bodies? They were described with dark or black hair, one fat and one real skinny. They were brothers in their late fifties and early sixties."

Eddie suddenly looked puzzled. "*Hmmm* I-I *um*...I just *uh. Hmmm.*"

Torrance seemed to be applying the pressure where it counted. "Well? Please, Mr. Coolidge...you're taking too much time here. How can I believe in this if you don't—"

"Yes! There was a dead man there, but he—but he looked—so much—so much younger."

"Very well, we'll get back to that...continue."

"No, don't take me wrong, Mr. Holt. It was awful."

"Awful you say?"

"Yes, awful.. well, the boat kept breaking up. Me and Major—well we pulled the man out of the water, but high tides came in too fast and took him out to sea...we had to save ourselves because the beach was getting flooded out—really. All I could think about was the baby...that's all I ever thought about. I know it sounds strange, but it was the—baby I wanted to save I needed to bring him back—here—to my home."

Torrance relaxed a little. "This dead man. Did he match the description of one of the two men I just described?"

"I-I don't know...he was so-so torn up from rocks, and-and bloated too ..all I can see in my head is the solid whites of his eyes...that was all. He was long gone."

Torrance rocked back and took a few more notes. "*Hmmm,* so you don't know their eye color either...their eyes were brown—both of them. Cases like these...salt water can destroy a human body quick. This much I know. What about the hair?"

THE TIME TO TELL

Eddie swallowed hard. "The hair? His hair was—I don't know. It was darker?"

"Yes, but not necessarily the hair on his head…sometimes the sea just pulls people's hair completely off…so if any of it was left, what color was—"

"Gone! The hair was *gone*…I'm sorry I can't be of much help…I was so caught up saving the baby that—"

Torrance interrupted. "Wait a sec. You mentioned the boat. Maybe we have another boat. What color was the boat?"

"Oh, it was blue and white—I think."

Torrance took a double take through his notes. "Well you're not sure about anything, but you're making good now. The boat was indeed, blue and white." He then looked at the name of the vessel in his notes. "The letter *B* you saw, stood for the name of the boat."

Eddie sat up at the edge of his seat. "So you know the name? I tried to guess what it was. All that came to my mind was 'Battle, Beyond—Begone."

Torrance chuckled, "It certainly wasn't any of those, I can tell you that. She was called the *Blessit*. Wasn't blessed this time, I guess. Her owners, Buzz and Jed Newman; they were out of New Hampshire. It's a crying shame."

Eddie looked shocked. Without thinking, he murmured, "That's funny…they were Americans…"

The constable put another toothpick in his mouth. "Excuse me, Mr. Coolidge?"

"Oh, what? Oh, America…that's funny they drifted so far—away from shore—from America I guess."

"America? You didn't think they'd be from somewhere else did you?"

"No…guess not…sorry I said that. I don't know what's gotten—I'm nervous right now, I guess. Where else would they be from, right?"

Torrance then grabbed his coffee and drank down his last drop. He looked at his notes again before finally putting himself at ease entirely.

But just when Eddie thought Torrance was done questioning, Torrance put his coffee cup on the little brass stand next to him and began to look around at their home.

Curiously, Eddie started looking at his home too, as if he was trying to figure out what it was that intrigued the constable so. In all truthfulness, the home, with its contents, was very safe-looking, clean, and pleasant. It looked built for children too, with the crib in the warmest spot next to the fireplace. More nice contributions included the baby bottle, clean diapers, selections of toys, and a married couple working together to keep it all up. Their dog even communicated a pleasant message. He was nothing but a wagging bluff.

The more Torrance looked around, the more open-minded he became, so he got up and walked over to see inside the crib. He even reached down to uncover Doll's face so he could see him a little better.

Eddie looked down at his cane between his legs. "So this is it, I guess?"

After Torrance got a good look at Doll, he sat down beside him on the sofa. "Who's crib do we have here? You have other children, do you?"

Eddie seemed ashamed, "No, I can't have children. This cane...it's a war injury I have where I can't have any. As for the crib? Well...it was just hopeful thinking. We use it once in a while to babysit for a neighbor."

"A neighbor you say...is that the only neighbor you have? I don't see any more along the street."

"Yes, the Johnsons? They're down the road about a block maybe."

Torrance huffed as if he were irritated before Eddie grew more concerned. "Look, I didn't do anything wrong. Please

THE TIME TO TELL

don't take me in...you got to believe me. I was going to call, but nobody was alive."

Torrance looked directly into Eddie's eyes. "Why didn't you call? That's the first thing you should've done."

"I was hoping that maybe if I waited, I could keep him—stupid. *huh?*"

Torrance paused as he rubbed the nape of his neck, thinking. "You know, everything matches—except for the baby. Tell you what...I don't have the facilities to take care of the child, nor do I know of anyone else here in Devil's, so—"

Eddie stood up. "I have the best home for him right here, I swear. He can stay here as long as he wants. I mean, look... he's a cute little bugger, look at him. He's as safe as can be right here—and-and you can come by anytime to check up on him—really."

Torrance scribbled down some more notes as he tried not to show his smile, "Yes, you are correct again...he's a bugger, I have to say. I'm not supposed to do this, but I'm going to leave the baby with you until we can gather more information. Here, please take my pencil, and I'll tell you what to do...put all your information that you said on this form for now....I'll see what I can do with this."

"Of course! You bet."

As Eddie filled out the form, Torrance seemed somewhat relieved. "Glad you could help, Mr. Coolidge. It's not often I get calls like this—and someone being a volunteer like yourself." He spoke out loud toward the kitchen, "And thank you too, Mrs. Coolidge, for your understanding—and the coffee too. He then looked back to Eddie "The last thing I need is extra paperwork, if you know what I mean...this one's a mess, I can tell."

Shortly afterward, Torrance gathered up his belongings and politely made his way to the door, while saying "goodbye" and "thank you."

Eddie seemed so happy he could hardly say a word as he watched the constable leave.

Chantain peeked out into the living room. "I never heard such a thing. What got into that man? You got his name I hope."

"Yes, I did—I've got it right here on his sheet of paper... oh, *whew*...wow."

Chantain moved to the middle of the living room then pointed urgently. "Go out and see if he's leaving. He's testing us or something."

"I don't think so, but I will anyway." Eddie grabbed up his cane and bolted out the door, just in time to usher the constable to his car. Before they got too far, Torrance stopped in front of Eddie's Pribil with the oddest look on his face. "Oh, glad you came outside, say, *uh*—"

"No problem, I just wanted to thank you for your—"

"What is this thing? I'm just dying to know what it is."

Eddie looked at his car then looked at Torrance. "Oh, that? Yes, that...that's a Pribil, a 1937. It's a camper car—supposed to put covered wagons and camping trailers out of business."

Torrance looked at it a little more closely. "*Hmmph*, you don't say...I thought that's what it was...so you don't have to pull it? It drives—on its own?"

"Yes, it does...all by its lonesome...on gasoline. It's efficient too."

"A camper car, you say? Don't think I've ever heard of one."

Eddie stepped in front, "Oh yeah, they really exist. It's got sleeping accommodations on the davenport in back."

Torrance walked right up from behind and tried staring in the windows. "Does it have an icebox, cookstove, picnic table, and all that?"

"Oh yes, of course it does."

"*Hmmm*...where can I find one of these?"

Eddie then started to walk toward Torrance's car while he explained. "That's just it. They went out of business the same year they made them I think. Or at least that's what I was told."

"You're not selling it are you? What's it worth? Fifty bucks?"

"What, this? Selling? *Hu hu*...oh nooo. They claim only one other's ever been made. I found mine at an equipment salvage auction down at Portsmouth."

Torrance opened the door to his car. "I never would've known...so this one makes two out there?"

"Well, yes...there's got to be more out there, though. I just know it."

"*Hmmph*, so ugly I like it. Keep your eyes out for me one, will you?"

Torrance then dropped into his car, closed his door, and started up his ignition. Just before he took off, Eddie motioned for him to roll his window down. "So what kind of car's this? Did someone steal stuff off it? If they did, I'll keep my eyes out for you."

"Oh no. It's one of them stripped-down military surplus vehicles left over from the war. Beats driving my own. So anyway, I'll talk to you later."

"Wait...I know you won't say, but you think there's a chance we can keep him? The baby? I mean, I don't want to get my hopes up or anything, but it sure would be nice."

Torrance smiled. "No-no...I don't want him. Got two of my own. Keep your hopes up—you never know."

"So that's it for now? I can just keep carrying on? You know, driving my car—with him inside around town and all."

As Torrance drove away, he yelled out his window. "I'll drag my feet on this one. How's that sound?"

"Sounds good, Mr. Constable! I mean Mr. Torrance—I mean Holt...*he-he*, yeah, I guess...don't mind me...'bye!"

Just as Eddie stopped waving good-bye, he turned around, almost stepping over Chantain who was right behind him. "Excuse me...I didn't see you."

With Doll hanging awkwardly off her arms, she blurted, "How in God's name did you pull that off is what I want to know."

Eddie walked around her without answering, so she stomped her heel. "Walk away from me, will you?!"

"I'm not walking away...we have to go, remember? Come on."

She quickly caught up from behind, talking to his back. "You didn't find the baby at that shipwreck, did you? Admit it." She stopped as he kept hobbling. "You're a liar...what other crazy things you come up with while I was in the kitchen, *huh*? Anything else I don't know, *huh*? Spit it out now or there'll be hell to pay."

Without him saying a word, he opened the passenger door and regally invited her to climb inside with the rolling of his hand, which she did. When he hopped in the other side, he spoke above the baby crying, "I don't care what you say, I found him there...I'm not talking about it anymore. We're late for church. What do you have to say about that?"

Chantain looked like she was suffering another one of her migraines. "Church comes once a week. Lost babies don't. Why didn't you tell him about the father's note? Tell me that one, *huh*? That would've been the right thing to do, Mr. Smooth."

Eddie cranked the key. ***Kirpop, vroom vroom!***

"Because I'd have to give up the only thing that belongs to the poor kid, that's why. He'd walk away with the baby for sure then. Anyone would pocket that thing the first time they got their hands on it."

Chantain stared out the window hard. "Not the *gold* thing...I'm talking about the *note*."

Eddie lunged for his shift knob. "You don't want the child? Is that what all this means? Because if it is—"

"I never said that...I'm talking about the right thing to do. Don't get mad about it."

THE TIME TO TELL

Eddie turned his car around. "In case you're wondering, dear, that note and the *gold thing* weren't supposed to be separated...anyone can see that. Why can't you?"

Chantain kept looking out the window as they drove off in a big hurry. "Why can't I tell? It probably used to be a useless pocket watch...yeah, that's probably what it was. Someone took the innards out of a broken watch so they could put a cute little note in it to make it look special—good God, Eddie. That's how people are."

Suddenly Eddie hit the brakes at the edge of his driveway. "You know that's all you think about, isn't it? Money... and now it's that gold thing. I bet that little wedding band I gave you on your finger doesn't mean a thing 'cause it's not big enough, is it? Tell me! You want to know what I think about? All I think about is how to save our marriage with a kid, while you're throwing the baby out with the bath water. When he came along, it spoiled things didn't it? *Didn't it?*"

Chantain rolled her eyes. "That's real flattering. Tell me some more. Real men don't care about a baby, so why should you?"

Eddie looked both ways. "I'll tell you some more...it's a good thing he *did* come along because I'm starting to think you *never* wanted kids. Now you blame *me* for something you never wanted."

Chantain stomped the floorboard. "Shut up! You're getting ridiculous. Damn you! You're such a headache sometimes. Babies have got nothing to do with it...I'm caring for him right now, aren't I? He's someone else's fun, mind you."

Eddie drove out of his driveway and continued down the street. "Okay then, I'm laying this on the line. Do you want to be the only couple we know in Devil's who winds up in divorce? *Huh?* Take your time answering then. I don't care."

"No..."

"Okay, then, neither do I...I don't want to go through life in a black hole—by myself—living the courtship thing, woman after woman, acting like I'm twenty. If we can't make it work, you might find us living like there's no tomorrow, then what?"

"Just drive, okay? I had enough. We'll be going through town...I don't want everyone to see us this way so calm down. It's a day of worship, remember?"

"Yes, good idea. I'll drive...that's what I'll do—drive... I'm driving...need some fresh air. I think I'll roll my window down...there, that's better. I'm driving on a Sunday, to church, like everyone else...it's a good day—for church."

Eventually they both simmered down. However, Eddie was left in the driver's seat, feeling around his steering wheel like it was a big circle of ready-made remorse. In fact, he began to look like he was feeling guiltier the longer he drove along. Chantain, on the other hand, hopelessly gazed out her window as if she didn't even want to be in the same car with him or the baby.

As they drove past the trees along the little paved road, more houses began to appear. The outskirts of Devil's soon succumbed to the busier side of their little town. Eddie lured himself to the passing landscape outside his window, for more austere reasons than simply driving or sightseeing. His periodic glances of interest were nothing new or exciting really, just accumulating the number of residences as they got closer to the residential district by the ocean.

In this section of town, one could see the homes adhering more to the bricks and mortar of the little community they belonged to. The occupants slowly revealed more about themselves. They were families mixed with the elderly, mostly, dressed very nicely and on a clear time schedule. Some loaded into their cars, while others simply walked down the clean, well-kept sidewalks. Their most outspoken silent unity about themselves too was that they were all headed in the same general direction, which was downtown Devil's to church.

THE TIME TO TELL

Eddie periodically glanced at the growing numbers walking along the sidewalk, which seemed to help him gather peace for the moment after arguing with Chantain. Breaking the silence was on his mind, so he glanced across to her, noticing she hadn't moved a muscle while driving the whole time. She wasn't doing anything to give herself away, so he began with a cough. "*Ahem*...looks like we're just about into town...I don't want to carry an argument into a new church, soooo...we okay—with each other?"

Chantain didn't answer, so he awkwardly continued. "Excuse me...you never told me where we're going...where do I go?"

"Oh, I didn't tell you? Just look outside and follow the people."

"No, sweetheart, there's a little more to that. Can you please tell me before we get into town?"

Chantain dropped her arm off her door rest like it weighed as much as a spade full of dirt. "Nine Ninety-Five Church Street...with all the rest of 'em...where else you think it was?"

Eddie juggled his eyes back and forth between her and his driving "Nine Ninety-Five Church? That's all the way down church row—at the end. There's no parking there."

Chantain kept looking out the window, nibbling her nail. "And what's wrong with that?"

Eddie glanced back and forth preposterously. "You don't see? You don't see the hang-up? We have to park on Main. Then we have to walk past everyone to get there. You ask what's wrong with *that*?"

Chantain laid a lazy-looking set of eyes on him for the first time since they left. "You wanted to know, didn't you? Besides, it'll do you some good. You said you wanted to walk on that leg of yours—make it better."

Eddie almost spat over his steering wheel. "*Psssss*...if one more thing goes wrong, I hope this isn't it. Christ sake, you can sure pick'em."

Eddie funneled with the traffic, turning right down a sharp, down-sloping street, smack-dab into Main Street of downtown Devil's.

Luckily, he found a parking spot near the head of Main Street where no other vehicle could park—except a Pribil perhaps. The triangular, down-sloped space looked a little chancy since it was right next to a fire hydrant.

Eddie turned off his key, resting his arms on top of his steering wheel as if he were extremely disappointed. "Look at everyone. It's too busy…thank God we left late."

"Don't be smart, Eddie…let's just get going before all the church bells ring."

Busy it was. Downtown Devil's on a Sunday seemed like the place to be. Church Row's attraction seemed so invisible, yet it had always been there. If someone didn't know exactly what the area was famous for, he or she might say all of the people were going to a carnival, a show or a big event where most everyone in town attended. It was captivating to see such a unity of great interest, but there were no great carnival flags or music, nor were there balloons to inspire their path along the way.

The only sign that led the entire parade funneling in from all directions was a street sign on the corner next to Main. It had been there a while, rusting away from the ever-persistent work of the weather, no doubt. It sat on bolts on top of an old, galvanized pole with eerie red streaks of more rust, streaming all the way down to its base where the streaks spilled onto the sidewalk.

The rusted street sign contained the fading words "Church Street"—for the time being at least. Its letters used to be clean, crisp, and white. Now, they were weathering away, hardly readable.

Church Row was so crowded that driving in there with an automobile was not only impractical, it was almost impossible. People crowded in no more than three feet apart. No

THE TIME TO TELL

problems surfaced in this business of overcrowding, however. People were tolerant of one another. They stepped and skipped along peacefully next to one another at arm's length, in harmony.

As Mr. and Mrs. Coolidge walked with the baby into the stream of people, they gazed down the row of churches so beautifully lined up. The churches themselves were decoratively constructed in different fashions, mostly of finely crafted wood. All of them had beautiful, high steeples, which came in different colors and shapes, ranging from short and stout, to high in the sky.

All of these establishments shared a similar camaraderie. Most obvious were their small gathering lawns, of which their members quickly took advantage. They were pristinely kept and indulged with tasteful varieties of plants and rocks, giving the people even more of that *something* they longed for.

The town's small, close-knit population had a long-standing tradition of good showings every Sunday. Church Street's sidewalks were the most worn-out in town. Heavy-laden trails wearing into the sidewalks to this area established the fact that people loved to congregate there. Church Row's road and sidewalks were not short, however. The row seemed to grow and grow the further the Coolidges walked.

Attractive churches were popping up about as quickly as the pace of their walk. Quite admittedly, the first church at the entryway to Church Row was the most beautiful establishment in the district. It sat on the biggest property on the corner and was called the Second District Church of My Christ. From the way the Second District Church looked, one might wonder what the First District looks like.

The Second District Church of My Christ's name was proudly engraved on a monument of granite out front, riling up one's curiosity of exactly how something so big actually got there. Perhaps slaves had rolled it up there, back when slaves were legal in America.

Behind this behemoth monument on the elevated lawn stood the town's most prominent residents. They talked discreetly among themselves. Their conversations, just loud enough for others who were walking by to hear, were telling. They felt no compunctions about their church membership being the most exclusive in town. It was they who gained the most interest from the flow of other churchgoers who had to pass by their church on the way to their own.

The most elite members among them were the best positioned on the lawn. Quite obviously, they were the men who took their status more seriously than others when it came to praising the Lord. They held their heads up the highest, showing off the most elaborate pipes and fattest cigars. Their apparel sparked the idea that their expenditures were nothing short of astronomic. All of it was there on display, from pinstriped suits and fine fedoras to shiny, gold watch fobs. No gravitating trends were left out.

The women standing next to the men were largely the same, on display in more flamboyant apparel, like dazzling peacocks. Some actually wore peacock feathers, which happened to be in style at the time. Other women were dressed with the rest of the top styles: angora wool frocks, tweed swagger coats, elegant fur, wedge-heeled shoes, gypsy brown head scarves, and lettuce-green cloches. The riskiest showstoppers dared dressing in black felt toppers.

As if that wasn't enough, this entire stronghold on the best corner lot was looking down from their elevated lawn, straight down at the Coolidges walking by just then.

Eddie subtly waved up to the crowd, of whom he knew little about. None of them even acknowledged him, but they did keep staring and talking as if they had important things to say while they looked on. Eddie slowly lowered his hand and kept hobbling, whereas Chantain looked back longingly, as if wanting to be part of their world.

THE TIME TO TELL

Eddie whispered out the corner of his mouth, "*Ah* yes, just what I like to see and do...walk by the biggest snobs in town every Sunday. Welcome to Church Row."

Chantain pulled on his shirtsleeve, whispering, "*Shhhh*, quiet...they might hear you."

As they continued, quickly coming upon them next was another popular church, with a heavy, stout sign of bronze letters that said "1st Fatherhood Mission of Original Baptist." It too had an elevated lawn and large numbers of people, who were dressed more similarly to Eddie and Chantain. Being moderate and mainstream made this church a popular choice, it looked like.

As Eddie hobbled on by, he discreetly elbowed Chantain. "Oh no, here we go...wasn't too long ago we went there."

Chantain whispered back, "Until we had a falling-out with their beliefs...they're too blasé if you ask me...worked out for the better I have to say...just wasn't me."

Eddie tilted his look the opposite way as various members of this former church were watching him like hawks and glaring. Finally, a couple of them vaguely waved. Eddie went on, "Great...real great. We get to walk past this every Sunday too, just to get the cold shoulder...all because we joined forces with a new church we know nothing about."

Chantain whispered, "So...they're a bunch of dominoes anyway. Why do you care?"

"Because you dragged me away from the only friends I had in town...they're all there. You see 'em? That's why."

Before they got too far down the sidewalk, Eddie kindly waved back at them. For a moment, he almost said something, but Chantain pulled him away. "*Shhhh*, don't say it, whatever it is...they'll just talk about us."

And so they continued further down the long, busy row of religion. After they had passed a few more churches with similar difficulties, they seemed to be almost home free.

More importantly, the traffic was beginning to taper off the further they walked down the street.

They passed an older couple who were complete strangers. Eddie tipped a good day to them with his cane, but the old couple didn't acknowledge them whatsoever.

After the old couple passed them by, they looked back, speaking to one another rather loudly. "See that man? Why'd he wave?"

"That's strange. He's not from our church."

Eddie heard the insolent little comments. Without even thinking, he looked back as he kept hobbling along, compelling himself to speak aloud. "A good day to you too! May we all praise the Lord and love thy neighbor!"

A few others who were walking along the sidewalks suddenly heard him. All of them, without question, scowled their disapproval, which, quite frankly, spoke louder than Eddie's words.

Chantain yanked his arm again, whispering, "Shut up, Eddie. That was *rude*. These are good people around here... what's getting into you?"

Eddie turned back around and started hobbling normally again, except this time, he looked fed up. "You can let go of my shirt now. They're gone...thank you."

He adjusted his sleeve then smirked. "Good people? I was no ruder than they were...you hear what that lady said, or do you need hearing aids like they do?" Quickly, he turned back to yell at them again. "Hey, old man...we're Old Testament down here. An eye for an eye!"

Surrounding couples walking by, gasped as if they couldn't believe what was happening on Church Row. They looked ahead at the old couple, who by then had jumped onto the lawn of their church.

Eddie turned back around. "Did you see that? Those old folks jumped onto their church lawn like it was some kind of safety barrier. Now look at them. Now they're brave enough to glare back at us."

THE TIME TO TELL

The old couple back on the lawn kept glaring as they grumbled, "Why, I never. Did you hear that?"

"What church he go to? I wanna know right now. Speak to their preacher's what I outta do."

Chantain whispered for Eddie to turn back and walk forward, so he did.

He then adjusted his tie as if getting prepared for some other mordant gesture. "This walk's getting to me...three or four more churches and a block to go. *Ah* yes, smell the air, Chantain. Isn't today just a fabulous day?"

"Why you do things like that is what I want to know."

"Do what? Oh. Well, we go to the Church of the Old Testament...might as well start preaching it."

"Oh, Eddie...just because they call it that doesn't mean you have to go out and shout about it."

"Shout? I wasn't shouting...I can hardly wait to see what it's about. I'll make a guess...it'll be just as crazy as the rest of these places. They all tag themselves with who they are. It's idiotic."

Chantain huffed, "Calm down. You'll see...it's not what you think it is. I can tell you that right now."

Suddenly, another family was about to cross their path. Having witnessed Eddie's comments already from a half a block away, they crossed the street as quickly as they could to avoid them entirely.

As Eddie watched them make their escape, he tipped a "good day" to them with his hat, without saying a word.

However, the crossers had plenty to say behind his back. "Why'd he wave, Mom?"

"Quiet, son...just be glad they're not 'n our church."

"Yeah, sinner's what he is."

"But, Dad..."

"Hush up son...just keep walkin'."

Just about then Eddie looked at the next address coming up, which was a "925" hanging up on a wrought-iron post.

"So, uh...Chantain. Have you been this far down Church Row before?"

"No. They said it was the *last* church at the end of the row. That's all I know."

Eddie calmed down as he glanced ahead to another gang of church members huddled quite close together. They were hanging out at the edge of their lawn, waiting for Eddie and Chantain's arrival, which was going to happen at any moment. There were a good number of them, perhaps ten or twelve. Unlike the other church dress codes, this group was dressed uniformly, in mainly black. Additionally, they did themselves well to stand at attention with papers and Bibles over their hearts. Even the children beside them looked that way.

Eddie suddenly became serious. "Haven't seen these people before. Who are they?"

Chantain moved Doll to her other hip as they kept walking. "They're new around here...growing fast, I know that. They call themselves the 'Prophet of the Witness,' I think."

"Prophet of the—what?"

"Yeah, they steal members away from Julie's church all the time, she said. She told me not to listen to them when we walk by."

Eddie covered his smile. "How do you steal members?"

"No, it's not funny...it's easy. The most convincing ones win...the way it should be, I guess."

Eddie smirked. "The way it should be, my butt....Julie hates you. She's got to be the one who called the constable about me finding the baby even. Why did you listen to her about her church?"

"I don't listen to her. It's hard to explain. Guess we have this love–hate thing goin' on...besides, I can't think bad of her for calling anyway."

Eddie looked the other way, muttering, "*Pshhh*, black widows again. Love and kill."

"What did you say? I didn't hear."

THE TIME TO TELL

"Oh, nothing. Do you love to hate Julie? Is that what you're saying?"

"Something like that...not really, why do you care anyway? Friends are just friends."

"Oh, just trying to understand you better, that's all."

Just as Eddie and Chantain stepped within range of the Prophet of the Witness members, they jumped out onto the sidewalk, stopping the Coolidges in their tracks. Eddie cordially stepped up closer to them, tapping off the seconds with his cane, waiting for them to move, but they didn't.

The tentative group quickly came closer in a silent, eerie fashion, until they were almost within arm's reach. Two members up front, including the tallest one of the group, committed a faux pas by rushing into Eddie's face as the rest of them quickly encircled Chantain and Doll.

The tallest man started with the delivery of their emphatic claims, as the others next to him eagerly followed up.

"Our church is the *true* church," the tall man touted as he raised one of two different Bibles.

"You must not look any further," the older lady pleaded as she waved her hands.

"Please take one of our pamphlets," the young lady said, as she shoved papers under their arms.

"The end is coming. Save your soul!" the shorter man predicted while shaking a Bible.

Chantain quickly became overwhelmed. No surprise that the other Witness members saw their best chance in her first. Weakness sprouted from her face and body like fast-moving vines, strapping her up.

Eddie was much less receptive to the tall man staring him down. They stared eye to eye at each other, as if they were being introduced in a boxing match. The gloves were nowhere to be found. The tall man put on a fraught face and then grabbed Eddie's arm. He pulled Eddie even closer to look into his eyes. He was shocking and believable too—even before he said a thing with his shaky voice. "*Ho ho* the end is nearrrr. Our church witnessed it. Do you know what that means? You know what it meeeeans?"

As unwelcome as the solicitation was, the tall man, along with the rest, seemed to be within the virtuous bounds of their beholder. They continued with more or less the same recurring words, until Eddie abruptly fizzled to the end of his patience. He threw their literature to the ground, and grabbed Chantain out of the crowd by her arm with him. As he kept tugging on her arm, he looked like he was pulling a stuck body out of a haystack. "Come on, let's go!"

Finally, the upheaval stopped once he had gotten her and Doll loose. As quickly as the charade had started, it quit, but their next ploy seemed almost as well-rehearsed as the first. Immediately, they silenced their rhetoric, only to throw out appalling looks.

Eddie backed off cautiously from the synchronized scorn. All the while, he kept Chantain and Doll close behind him, guarding them with his arms. Once he distanced himself, he caught his breath and announced back to them. "We're going down there—to *that* church. We'll be going now. Thank you very much."

As they both stepped up their pace, Chantain patted her cleavage. "*Whew*, that was a little claustrophobic back there."

"Just keep walking. We're almost there."

After the hullabaloo they just witnessed, Chantain managed to look at the literature she held onto. "I didn't know what to do when they circled us like that." She turned the pages. "Julie—she never—she never told me they were—they were *that* way."

Eddie looked over his shoulder, only to find that they were still being watched. Even though they were much further away, the small crowd appeared to be as sour as they ever were.

THE TIME TO TELL

Quickly, the Witness members got back on the lawn of their church, falling into the position of holding their literature and Bibles over their hearts again, as if nothing had happened. Waving good-bye or any other farewell gesture seemed to be out of the question among them.

Eddie twisted his face into a bizarre frown. "Good gosh, look at them. They look at us like we're the enemy now... don't wanna be witnessing any more of that."

Chantain, on the other hand, seemed to recover all too quickly. She was already in the stages of being bemused as she continued looking through the literature they gave her. "I don't know, I kind of like how they do it. Sure could make a believer out of me; that was strong. Did you see how hooked they were on this stuff?"

Eddie balked at the sight of her looking at their literature. "What? You mean you liked it? You know, it disappoints me that you drift from one idea to the next so quickly, Chantain."

She yawned, walking and reading at the same time. "That's how easy it is to make up your mind, Eddie...try it sometime."

Eddie hissed, "*Sssss*, do you even remember which church we were going to this morning, or does it matter?"

"Yes, silly...those people back there were good...I must say."

"I can't believe it."

Chantain kept turning the pages. "Believe what?"

"It's like you got this—floating mentality."

"What's wrong with that...there's a lot of people like that...prevents boredom."

Eddie snatched the literature from her hands and flung it high into the air over his shoulder before Chantain could even blink. It's not like she wanted to blink either. She pretended to read more of what wasn't in her hands anymore. "Wow, big boy, what a shotgun move that was."

Nonchalantly, she noticed herself gazing at her beautiful hands. As they kept walking, she turned them over to look at her manicured nails.

Eddie huffed, "I bet you feel like scratching me with those fingernails of yours. If that's the only way I can get my back scratched, then do it—please." Sarcastically, he pointed to the back of his shoulder. "Here, over to my left a little bit...scratch there for once."

Chantain licked her lips and rolled her eyes. "You wish, dreamer...why did you throw my stuff away?"

"*Hmmm*, let me see now. We're going to your new church? *Hmmm*, let's see what this one's about before you take us on another wild-goose chase."

Chantain seemed to do well to forget and move on. When they got closer to the end of the row, Chantain quickly saw a pair of recognizable faces in a welcoming crowd of smiles, straight ahead on the lawn of the Church of the Old Testament.

She smiled and waved. "Here we are...hi! I can see Al and Julie out front waving at us right now."

Eddie soon joined in with a halfhearted smile and wave.

Quickly, they left their experience behind them—almost. The Prophet of the Witness members kept watching their every move from afar, including their happy waves to friends of another church. All of them looked sour, for they had just seen Eddie litter the sidewalk with their literature moments ago. Reckless abandon seemed to be running through their veins.

The tall man, for one, gritted his jaw, not making a sound and unwilling to turn the other cheek. His snarling glare was worse than that of the others, looking as if he wished to strike Eddie down. Without hesitation, he nudged his little son, nearly knocking him off his feet. "Well, boy? You witnessed it...what you waiting for? Go get it."

The obedient boy busted from their crowd as he had done many times before. When he got to Chantain's papers

THE TIME TO TELL

Eddie had tossed, he skidded to a stop and plucked the colorful pieces up.

The way back from his speedy fetch was different, however. The little lad decided to take his time. He walked back, while looking at the front picture on the main flyer. Child amazement struck his face; his little observance was marked all over with innocence as he continued walking. He stroked the pretty, colorful picture gently with his tiny fingertips, which brought much attention to what was pictured.

Admittedly, the picture was quite nice. Perhaps it was too nice. He wanted to feel what was in the picture, but the paper was smooth to his touch. The artwork did work in its own magical, cogent way. It was fascinating to look through the eyes of that particular boy. The picture meant a thousand words to him, even though it was a simple picture created by just one artist.

The pseudohistorical scene depicted Jesus Christ hovering high off the ground, with golden-yellow rays of light beaming from behind the gifted one's golden-brown hair. Below Jesus were dozens of men and women, clearly in agony, dressed in rags, pleading for their lives and begging mercy with their hands together. The words *"He's coming!"* were arched above the wonderful artwork, which seemed to be the theme or title of the print.

While the boy slowly strolled back to his group in a blissful daydream, he was startled by his father's impatient yell. "Get back here, boy!"

Instantly, the boy shook himself from his daze, realizing once again his diminutive subservience under a watchful eye. Quickly, he brought back the discarded literature and carefully handed it up to the tall man as he was trained to do.

Swat!

With one big, unthankful swipe of the tall man's huge hand, he took it away then slapped it back into his satchel.

As he looked at the clock on the steeple of his church, he grinned and muttered, "It is time."

Just about then, the Prophet of the Witness church bell rang, echoing down Church Row. Not even a second later, all of the church bells began to ring. A bonging orchestra of bells of all shapes and sizes sounded off all the way down Church Row, from end to end. Rings of offbeat rhythms reverberated through the streets and all the way downtown with a kind of hair-raising splendor unmatched anywhere else.

Those few who were tardy on the sidewalks and streets quivered in the midst of the raid of bells gonging from everywhere around them.

As far as Chantain and Eddie were concerned, they were among the last ones filtering into the majestic-looking house of worship at 995 Church Street. It was a fancy, old building dressed up in gingerbread woodwork and wooden, Old English letters painted in gold over the entryway that said "Church of the Original Testament."

The flamboyant facility inside was well-appointed, big and crowded, with an open-style cathedral that created the feeling of greatness. It housed about two hundred members and their guests each Sunday. This complimented the open-door policy the church had.

Everything inside seemed to be underway. Voices vigorously chattered throughout, as the organist played the familiar church song "All People That on Earth Do Dwell." Everyone attending seemed vibrant, paying veneration to God as they waited. Most of them were talking about the weather. Rightly so, considering its turbulence from the days before had kept them practically locked-up inside their homes.

While the small talk went on, none of them forgot why they were there, however. Every last one of them kept a vague eye out for their man of God to arrive. The word "priest" was used here and there among them. He was due to pop in soon, and he did so—inaudibly. Without much detection, a mordant-looking, gray-haired man with a bushy beard appeared from a very small door congruently cut into the lines of the highly decorative wooden trim in the wall behind the sanctuary, high up on stage.

The servant of God was intricately clothed and wrapped in a colorful, full-length robe of gold, red, brown, black, and even a touch of white.

Just after he appeared, he paused to see if any of his audience had noticed his presence. So far the majority, if not all, hadn't. They seemed too busy standing and socializing. It went without saying, but this man of God wanted it that way. By no means did he disturb his followers verbally divulging their affairs.

Finally, he brought himself out into the open, but with a new set of gracious eyes and posture. Patience was part of the picture he wished to portray, so he slowly made his way to center stage, walking like an ancient, decrepit man, though he wasn't nearly as old as he looked.

Little doubt remained. The man of God was in a wild, preplanned approach he could call his own. His last stretch of walk confirmed this as he strolled with his head down. Every so often, he would look up to the tall ceiling as if he wished to see through it. Then gracefully, he shut his eyes. All the while, he slowly slid his moccasin shoes across the beautiful, deep red mahogany hardwood floor, which was much nicer than the floor below where his audience was.

The huge, weathered book held tightly to his chest with crossed arms was indeed dear to him. Unmistakably, this was his personal Bible, which looked to be in terrible condition. The idea of separating him from it was most certainly out of the question. He was protecting it too well.

Time had to be brought into perspective too, in order to give a full understanding of the priest's presentation, which began before anyone knew. His dramatic, detailed, introduction was expressed in minutes—not seconds.

There were new steps, which he dealt with in the time it took for him to reach the pivotal point before the podium. He had to go to one more level, which was hard to detect until he got there. One step at a time, he gracefully climbed almost two feet higher behind his tall, ornate podium that hid almost half his already-tall body. At this level, he exhaled a noteworthy breath of peaceful air, as if he was done—but he wasn't.

With more calculated grace and peacefulness, he carefully laid his Bible down to rest, and for good reason. One could see the whole book by then, barely tethered together. It would have fallen apart had he not been careful.

The time had come for the Priest to gaze around at the wonderfully packed church before him. It was safe to say that by then, he was ready to begin his Sabbath day sermon.

The lady below on the organ was the only person who seemed to know what was about to happen. She appeared to be growing a hair of distress. For the first time that morning, she missed a key on the organ as she kept a close eye on the priest. She became the one to watch after that. "Nervous" was the word, as she waited for a cue to stop playing.

The priest raised his hand as if he were the conductor of her symphony, ready to silence her. His hand was shaking, which actually drew minor concern among a few. Something was coming. Many sensed his beginning was not going to be all that ordinary.

Just then, the poor organ player gawked with tiny moans of fear as she yanked her hands back from the keyboard to cover her face.

Suddenly, from out of the blue, **WHAM!**

The priest slammed his fist down on top of his badly beaten Bible. Before his audience could react, the priest began brutally shouting, "Burn in *Hellll!*"

The cathedral that everyone sat in had been well-designed for voice amplification. It sounded like an echo chamber

THE TIME TO TELL

specially rigged to pierce the ears with satanic condemnations, or whatever else he cared to yell about. With such a surprising entry, there was no wonder that he literally electrified the crowd. In fact, he'd sent them reeling with echoes of shock and awe before they even sat down.

All at once, everyone dropped to the pews, as if wishing to duck for cover. High-pitched gasps and small, shuddering cries bounced from all sides of the great room. One could not imagine what it sounded like in such a long room of hardwood walls towering at least twenty feet high. There wasn't so much as a piece of carpet to help muffle the sound. The sound waves brought the sinners out to holding their ears even.

A pudgy woman with hair that was curled in the front, but flat in the back, seemed to be the most affected by the hellacious echo of his shout. She let out a whimpering bawl, telling it all, "I lied! I stole it! *I stole it!*" After her shocking confession, she almost fainted. Luckily, her husband caught her or she would have fallen backward.

At the same time, a skinny man with sunken eyes and bony cheeks hysterically lunged out into the aisle as if he had just encountered a parade of paranoid ants in the middle of his back that he couldn't reach. "*Waaawaaahaa*—help me, help me, preacher! They got me!"

And so the priest did help him—in his own fashion, that is. Immediately after he stared the skinny man down, he slammed his hand on his Bible, roaring, "*Fire* burns your flesh in the bottomless pits of eternity, with Satan!"

He slammed again. "Evil does what it wants toooooo!"

Then, like a frog vexed in hot water, he whipped his audience limp and ferretted out whatever place they tried to hide. There was no place for anyone to go, except to perhaps hide in their mind. Somehow, he broke them out of hiding there too.

Again with his fist, he pounded his broken Bible, delivering another bitter blow so hard, dust blew from the pages. "I said—*to Hell with you!*"

His audience spun into yet another chorus of gasps, wishing to escape. This time it was the woes, shaking out a couple more into the aisles hollering repentances. Others, who were still holding on, either grabbed their handkerchiefs to doctor their noses or simply to hide their faces in fear.

Just as the audience began to settle down, the priest paused. When he did, he stood up straight, sniffed, and then gazed around for a long minute. Cordially, he went about his business, acting as if nothing ever happened. "Ladies and gentlemen—infants and offspring. It is time for prayer. Let us pray for the sinners who come before us today. Bow your heads now, before our all-powerful God. It is my prayer, which we all giveth together:

> "Dear God in the greatest kingdom of all.
> I seen beforeth me.
> Some of us in my holy house hath sinned.
> I ask you. Have mercy on their souls to do with as you wish.
> God—grant me as holy a servant, the power to teacheth.
> I wish to teach the difference of Christians and—Christians of War.
> Bring me the holy weapons through your teachings to defend you, oh Lord.
> I wish to teacheth about war.
> I say these blessed forthcomings to be righteous, first in the name of Gauwd,
> And then our brother above us, Jesus Christ.
> Amen."

Everyone answered, "AMEN, amen-amen, amen-amen. AMEN...Aaaamen."

He graciously continued, "Thank you all. The Lord now has giveth me the power today to teach about Christianity and war. Before I provide for our dear Lord, I wish to see a show of hands with the heavenly father's questions. How many today—consider thyselves Christians? Show the hands… come on, come on. I wish to see them."

The entire room eagerly raised their hands without delay.

Apparently, this wasn't what the priest wanted to see. Agitation strapped him up tight on stage, tying him in a quagmire. From the constant changes in his looks, one might have guessed that he was headed for a hard, strenuous lecture. He shifted his eyes back and forth through the crowd, rolling his fingers across the top of his podium.

Suspicion seemed to be lurking in his mind too when he asked an almost identical question: "How many consider thyselves—Christians of War?"

The crowd came alive, buzzing with whispers, as they looked at one another across the aisles. Apparently they were discussing what his point was. The vote seemed muted since everyone had already raised his or her hand on the first choice. Soon, all of them became starkly quiet, compelling themselves to sit on their hands. Miraculously enough, the result was 100 percent unanimous, with nobody showing a single hand.

The priest, once again, rolled his fingers then shifted his eyes, except now he appeared upset. His awful glare conveyed the thought that he believed his audience was nothing but a bunch of scoundrels. While he wiped his face, he gracefully stood up tall, looking at his Bible. He might have been thinking of what bodily gesture he needed to use next. As he carried on, this became obvious. He shifted his body to one side, trying to decide, but couldn't quite make up his mind.

Indecisiveness finally gave way to what looked like the pure play of anger again. Self-control had never looked so painful. Whatever little bit of control he had gathered from before must have been hanging by a thread, so he surprised everyone by growling, "*Grrrrrr*, that's what I thought your answers would beeee."

Very clearly, he wasn't happy with his audience's unanimous, lop-sided show of hands between Christians and

Christians of War. As a consequence, some of the people sitting in the pews, not wishing to anger him, begged to change their minds. Oh, but no. The stage for bias was already settled as far as their priest was concerned. It showed when he let go with a massive blow to his Bible. **WHAM!** "You're *not* real Christians!"

His accusations, mixed with antagonism, seemed almost too much for his audience. They quickly sank down to a new level. Some slouched, while others sank down lower than the backs of the pews themselves.

Peacefulness seemed to be where the priest wanted to return, time and time again, however. And so he did—along with a few other emotions. He turned back to his podium, rolling his fingers, but this time he dramatized yet another surprise. Pain and anguish came raining down upon him. His audience started to feel it too. Before they could get comfortable, he switched to a bizarre act of deep meditation. Hardly anyone could figure that one out. Perhaps he hadn't used it for a while. Ultimately, his audience changed right along with him, showing grave concern.

Then, unexpectedly, one frightened gentleman in the back spoke his piece regarding his vote. "But the war. I'm no Christian of War…Germany's doin'—ju-ju-genocide!"

Pretty soon, four of his neighbors squirmed around before gathering up enough courage to speak out also. "Yeah, that's right—"

"That's right, Preacher…first it's Jews, then it'll be—then it'll be us Americans!"

"That's not what God wants…German Satanism is what they are!"

"Yeah, that's right!"

The priest stroked his beard, looking as if he were deeply entertained. "So now some of you…you thinketh real Christians don't kill, maybe. And me…I think *none* of you are real Christians of War. *Hmmm*, I seeeeeeeee. We have much work to do this morning."

THE TIME TO TELL

He cleared his throat, opened his Bible to where his bookmark was, and pulled up his reading glasses that hung from his neck on a chain sturdy enough to leash a dog with. "Nobody here is a real Christian just yet. For it is I—with the power. It is I with the power of Gauwad'ehh—to teach you real, true Christian faith in my house."

He continued. "Christians of the New Testament like to teacheth peace and looove'hh. They say that the Bible was the greatest—the greatest book ever written'ehh. Yet we have a problem and God sees you right here now. Either you are ignorant—or you deny the word of Gauwad'ehh! This is your problem! Christians of the New Testament embrace the Old Testament. Yes, that's right. All of us, everyone, embraces the Old Testament one way or another. Instances lay before you."

He opened his hands. "Look at the Ten Commandments. That's Old Testament. Did you hear? Ten Commandments were written—in the Ooooold—Testament'ehh!"

He adjusted his reading glasses and rearranged his papers while shaking his head in total denial.

"Genocieede'hh! That's right, genocide. The Germans are doing it, and so are weeeeeeee!" Right here—America. We are at war! We are a founding nation of—slauuughter. We're cleansing the evil as we speak. It may get worse—and, oh yes, it *will* get worse…we're killing for what is right'ehh. It is genocide, and it is God's will. It's good triumphant—over evil….*hmmm* yesss…holy warrrrr."

He took a break to drink from his shiny, ornate brass cup as he kept one eye on the crowd.

Everyone, even the children, were glued to their chairs in shock, stiff as mannequins. Then, with a somber sense of gratitude, he held his cup up, giving them all a silent toast, sort of relaxing his crowd.

Surprise seemed to be his disguise, as he set the stage for a chilling surprise once again. Before his audience could relax too much, he hit his Bible, yelling, "The Bible teaches *genocide!*"

Then calmly, he went on, "It's the greatest book ever written, they sayyyy. Christians taketh out what they want from the great book. Call it evilll. It's—selective reeeeading of holy words, I verily say...those down the street'ehh. Those here on Church Street'ehh...those preaching right now say that certain things in the great book do not apply to their teachings'ehh."

He burst out, slamming his Bible repeatedly. "Real Christians would never do that! God is perfect. God is forever with all the wisdom of perfection! God and his people tell us right here in these scriptures." He went on, clenching his fist. "God doesn't change his mind thousands of years later—and say—'Oh, forget what I said.' Poppycock! It's here—in this book now! Bible's Old Testament scriptures aren't out of print. It does not amuse, no? Is that the kind of God you want?" He continued, "Are you *real* Christians or not?!"

He calmly pulled out a piece of paper with quotes, but before he read them off, he looked at his shaken-up audience. "Old Testament, brothers and sisters...these are words from Gauwad'ehh: Book of Exodus, chapter 34, verses 11 through 14; Book of Leviticus, chapter 26, verses seven through nine—"

He then stopped in the middle of his quotes, feeling interrupted by the hundreds of shuffling pages in every corner of his church. Pages flapped and fanned out loudly, as if he were giving a sermon in the middle of a paper factory.

"This is *Gauwd's* time, not yours! Look up chapters 'n verses later—on your own time!"

Everyone, including the Coolidges and Johnsons, quickly took his advice by closing their Bibles immediately.

Eddie, being the last person to close his Bible, glared at Chantain, as if feeling the whole sermon was preposterous.

Chantain moved her lips silently: "Give—it—more—time."

THE TIME TO TELL

The priest moved on, "The Bible details the fury of God's genocidal wrath'ehh! Massacres after massacres—multiple prophets—under the direction of Gauwad'ehh. Even in the words of—God himself."

He slapped his Bible repeatedly. "All you—" *Whack!* "—have to do—" *Whack!* "—is open your eyes—" *Whack!* "—and read it!"

He then raised his hands. "It is I! I—have the power of Gauwad'ehh—to help you understand that you are not real Christians until you embrace *all* of God's word. God's words are not fruit that you pick and choose. It's a sin to take from this book what you want. Praise the Lord and have mercy on your souls for not following all of God's word."

He continued, sipping from his cup in between sentences. "Look at Noah." *Sip.* "God cleansed the earth with the flood of water." *Sip.* "Hu! Noah's Ark—his survivors?" *Sip.* "That is all that was left of them." *Sip.* "That was genocide—don't you think?" *Sip.* "You know that one, so we will move on.

"Moses! Look at our beloved Moses'ehh! Book of Numbers 31:7; Numbers 31:15. They killed the kings of Midian...and the people of Israel took captive the women of Midian and their little ones; and they took as *booty* all their cattle, their flocks, and all their goods. All their cities in the places where they dwelt'ehh—and all their encampments, they burned with fire.

"Moses was enraged with the officers of the army...so you spared the women! Kill every male among the little ones, and kill every woman who has had sexual intercourse with a man, but keep the virgins for yourselves...divide them up evenlyyyyy. Numbers 31:15. Moses defeated the leaders of Midian. Joshua 13:21."

He huffed before continuing, "Moses, ladies and gentlemen, was on the ballll...here we are. Taketh more holy accounts I want you to read: the books of Judges, Joshua, and

Numbers too...amen, praise the Lord...look at our beloved Joshua! Book of Judges 6:1; Exodus 17:13...Deuteronomy. Be sure to read Deuteronomy 25:17! Don't forget Samuel...1 Samuel 15:2, 1 Samuel 27:8, 1 Samuel 30:1...all these! Genocide is hiding in the cracks of time. Time never changes; only sinners do!'

Just as the priest was working his mysterious ways, so was another within the silent crowd. This little person was Doll, and he was about to be silent no more. He warmed up with a sputter; then he puckered until finally he hummed along with a nice, constant whimper.

Of course, this didn't help to soothe the priest up on the podium. Quite the contrary, his reaction was like splashing cold water on his face without knowing who did it. Immediately, he scanned the crowd, trying to pinpoint the epicenter of his newfound nuisance. The source was not easy for him to find because the echo bellowed back and forth from everywhere. Eventually, he found him to be in Chantain's arms, behind several pews of taller people, well positioned out of sight.

By then it was too late. Doll's contagion of crying had spread to yet another baby not far away—Julie's baby. Within seconds, Julie gave Arlis a bottle, quickly shutting him up. After that, she glared at Chantain, suggesting she do the same. When Chantain did, she whispered, "There now...watch the wild man up there with the big voice...that's it, good boy."

The priest continued, "Praise the Lord for quiet...thank you mothers out there. Now brothers and sisters, genocide cannot be right and wrong. The truth holdeth the staff which bears all. Christians aren't the judges of God's word in his Bible. They cannot condemn or excuse the brutal conduct of prophets. Christians say genocide never took place to cover it up...that is—hog wash!"

He went on, "The Bible must be a lie then, if true. Do real Christians conceallll? No! Some say God or prophets in scriptures *dreamed* that it happened because they *wished* it to happen. To hell with that...interpret, my people...the Bible cannot lie. May they burn in Hell! To all the wishful thinkers outside this church...*to Hell with you!*"

He stopped for another sip of water. "This is what I sayyy... bloodshed and genocide is forestalled until the great Joshua returns'ehh! The World War may never be over brothers and sisters. The scriptures in the Bible were holy wars, and we have a God of war. We will have a peaceful God only when the wars are gone. Take my word, which is the old word'ehh! Become believers in scriptures. Original Testament of God. Our—Gauwad'ehh."

Just then, a brief time elapsed while the priest gave a subtle hand signal to two young boys hiding behind the sanctuary, holding beautiful, ornate, gold-plated platters. Immediately, they stumbled to the front of the audience into the center aisle. As the priest motioned for them to carry on, they slowly moved on down the center aisle and passed their platters in opposite directions in hopes of receiving generosity.

Generosity they received. Coins clattered, metal to metal, onto the golden platters as they slowly circulated hand to hand. Plenty of money was there to give away as it turned out. Adult and children hands reached out to drop in their share. Some were dumping handfuls of coins, while others delicately placed silver dollars and half dollars. Even paper dollars were showing up.

As the tithing continued, the priest signaled to the organist to play along with the chiming of coins. Money was gladly exchanged to the tune of some odd configuration of the organ's sporadic harmony, which imitated the sounds of falling coins.

The priest carried on, humming in monotone, "*Hummm, hummm*...there sayeth more books, chapters, and verses to taketh to your homes. America, *hummm*, on the path of righteousness. War is righteous...*hummm*, we here called upon by our Heavenly Father in this world war. *Hummm,* let there be genocide against evil until we have the holy goodness of peace on earth. *Hummm,* forever and—ever.

The organist hardly paused as she stopped to turn the pages to the beginning of a brand-new song announced by the priest. "Sing along please...everyone, the Christian battle hymn, 'A Mighty Fortress Is My God,' page 44."

He carried on. "*Humm,* Micah 3:1; Micah 6:16; Habakkuk 2:8,12–17; and lengthy literature from the book of Isaiah; Isaiah 4:3, 5:7–18, 26:21, 33:15, 34:2...*hummm,* read it all when you go home...read, read, reeeead brothers and sisters, read'ehh."

He went on, "Now we sing...sing along...join the fight... 'A Fortress Is My God'...Praise the Lord for the War of Righteousness."

Chapter 11

Time kept stepping along, turning the pages of life for Doll and the Coolidges. Doll alone seemed to stay within arm's reach with that which was hidden behind the impenetrable gates of history's long forgotten secrets.

None of history's hidden ways would have mentioned this time without tethering in the weather. Time was largely unrecorded. As remembered, storms were intermittent, appearing then disappearing, leaving forgotten thorns in beds of forlorn warnings. Of course, storms faded away, to no one's dismay.

Looking back in weather's time frame, nothing came blowing in by way of Devil's, except Doll. He had drifted in almost a year ago. Seasons passed as expected, feeling like new seasons filled with a little more of the weather's surprises.

Weather is often associated with legendry, but then again, maybe not. One ancient ruler, "Augustus," Latin for "majestic," is one of a few. Maybe he didn't seem threatening enough in the spheres beyond. He was just a natural-born man with a Roman name who later become more popular. Some of the trivial truths he left behind seemed as interesting as his name, however. He was adopted posthumously. Later he was renamed "Gaius Julius Caesar Augustus," or "Octavius," as he was called later.

Augustus went on to become Rome's first great emperor in 27 BC, without really changing Rome's gross worldly approach. He died quite normally too—except he died in the forever memory of his name. In other words, he checked out with his ticket to death in the month of August, leaving the world behind—wholly in the same condition that it was.

Of course, the weather never tried to take the blame for destroying him or his empire's fame. Rome, along with its many leaders before and after Augustus, fell through societal failures. Rome's demise came through long-ailing tortures of political, economic, religious, military, and foreign invasions, as well as menacing traitors from within the great empire itself. Rome wept, and then was pushed out where it fell from its towering nest onto the rocks where it lay to die. It didn't matter whether the weather was sunny or not as its eerie super-era came to pass. The weather hardly had a care in the world.

Eons later, sunny, calm days occurred quite often in the small town of Devil's. Plenty of glorious, sunny afternoons shone down on the region's calendar. Usually, it was in the summertime when it happened, and this particular summer was 1945. More specifically, it was the sixth day, and the month was August.

Down through the town and up its quaint streets was that same, inviting farmhouse belonging to the Coolidges, showing off its white-painted appearance, even though signs of age were imminent. Small insidious marks of weathering had begun to show upon the walls. Time would tell if it would get worse and how quickly. Beginnings of cracks ran along the lap siding and chimney stacks.

Despite the ever-persistent conditions, the good day gave at least one cause for celebrating. A celebration worth mentioning was a grand, little celebration in which the date was picked out by Chantain, coincidentally—or not. As ill-omened as she was, she was brave enough to pick the name of Doll—all by herself. Just as she picked out Doll's name, she was kind enough to pick his birthday too.

And so it was. An official birthday came to be. Cars were parked close and far, all around the Coolidge parking lot in

THE TIME TO TELL

front of their house. To emphasize the importance of Doll's first-time occasion even more, a chorus of what sounded like mainly women could easily be heard from outside the open windows of the family home.

A beautiful, high-pitched harmony of soprano carried on and swept along with that old, familiar tune known to practically everyone: "*Happy birthday to you! Happy birthday to you! Happy birthdaayy dear Doll-aaaall. Happy birthday tooo youuuu!*"

The happy song could be heard out in the forest, attracting yet another odd group. Rabbits, raccoons, squirrels, deer, quail, and a few birds appeared all at once from the outer rims of the meadow and along the dense tree line. They kept their distance from the Coolidge home as they always had.

Inside, where the singing party was, a head count of seven women and five tiny boys huddled together. At the center, by the coffee table next to the birthday cake, little Doll was standing. The table height seemed just right for him. He wiggled his hands, giggling with laughter at the sight of the stubby, non-birthday-like candle burning on top of a sweet, homemade cake of chocolate.

After his birthday song ended, everyone clapped, suggesting to Doll that he think of a wish before blowing out his ceremonious candle. Doll really didn't know what to think, so Chantain got his attention by popping up with a crazy, blowfish face and putting on a good show of pretending just how to blow the candle out. "Okay, Doll, you see here? You get one chance at this, so make it right. Make a wish and blow out the candle. It'll come true."

Things weren't happening as planned, so Chantain lifted him up and held him across the table as close to the candle as she could. Doll was so close his face glowed.

The women standing around with their children gathered closer all speaking together. "Come on, blow!"

"Wish for something, big guy."

"Come on, big boy. Blow it out!"

"Make a wish come true!"

"Blow like this."

Doll suddenly understood as he glanced at everyone's cheeks round as billiard balls. He gave the candle a strong, blowing whirl, which looked like it was good enough for the job—except it wasn't. Strangely enough, the flame refused to leave, so a second try was called for. He reared back and blew again with all the breath he had. For a moment, the stubborn flame looked as if it were done for, except it bounced right back onto the wick like it wanted to stick around.

Awkward surprise plastered everyone's faces. Oddly, no one said a thing about it until Chantain looked at the candle a little more closely. "*Hmmph*, wonder what the candle's made of?"

Everyone else seemed to be wondering the same thing, so they all inquisitively leaned over to take a closer look, but before they got too close, the tiny flame mysteriously vanished before their very eyes.

Chantain flinched. "*Aw*...oh my. I didn't see that. *Hmmph*...oh well...you did it, Doll! How about that?"

Almost everyone laughed it off, except for Julie. She was seated behind the rest of them without the benefit of seeing what had just happened. Still, she reacted to their cheers by putting on a strained smile. She stewed there for a while until her little smile went away. Nevertheless, the party quickly moved along, leaving her sour attitude behind.

Up next came the presents. Without delay, the women quickly shuffled in their bags, popping up with Doll's little surprises wrapped up with their own personal touches.

Julie didn't quite follow or fit in with the dazzling gift wraps; she was the first to pull out a box wrapped in a wrinkly, brown paper bag. At least the bag was cut up to resemble wrapping paper. She placed it in Arlis's chubby little hands so that he could mimic giving it to Doll. He did so with a fumbling hand-off, and Doll got a hold of it before it hit the floor.

Julie grinned. "This present here's from Arlis. Ain't that right, Arlis?"

Arlis hadn't anything to say since he was barely aware of what was going on. Some good came of Arlis's gesture, however. The other three mothers thought the idea was great, so they quickly caught on, doing the same playful hand-off game with their own children. One by one, they coaxed their toddlers into holding their gifts and giving them away.

The second mother kneeled down with her son, smiling from ear to ear. "This nice one has a pretty, gold bow. It's from your friend *Landon*."

She got back up as the next mother kneeled down, her eyes twinkling. "This one with the cute teddy bear wrapping is from your buddy *Dwight*."

The last mother did the same. "And this one's from *Glenn*...say happy birthday, Glenn, honey."

The other two women had no children, so they both kneeled down and simply gave the gifts to Doll while praising him for how cute he was. After Chantain heard their cute comments, her smile loomed a little to the gloomy side before she expressed her gratitude. "*Ah*, you ladies didn't have to say that...he is sort of darling. I wish he wasn't."

The two ladies were surprised as they spoke together. "What am I missing?"

"What? You wish he wasn't?"

"Come on now."

Chantain came back, looking disinterested. "If he wasn't so cute it would be easier on me...haven't heard a thing... Eddie's still hoping to keep him."

Julie perked up. "Oh? You still—haven't? You still haven't heard anything about keeping him yet?"

Chantain went on. "No. Eddie's been calling Mr. Holt once a month...no word still."

Then all the ladies joined in. "No, that's terrible...wow."
"What? I don't believe it."
"That's torture."
"When do you think you'll have an answer, Chantain?"
Chantain appeared so artificially sad, looking to the floor when she sniffled. "Oh, I don't know. I think he said he should have an answer pretty soon."

Julie looked confused, shuffling her eyes back and forth. "Pretty soon? When did our constable say that one?"

As Chantain tore into Doll's gift wrap for him, she didn't bother looking up. Finally, she got around to answering Julie's question, which everyone else seemed to want to hear too. "*Huh?* Oh, I don't remember when Eddie said that. It's dragging on forever, it feels like."

Julie quickly moved on to things that were more interesting to her. In the midst of everyone's small talk, she kept looking at Doll's birthday cake, which was left unattended and untouched. Quickly, she obliged herself to step forward and be the first one to cut the cake. As she picked up the knife next to it, her tongue became part of her tool selection as well. It moved along her lips, in tandem with her careful knife-slicing. When she was done cutting it all up, she looked relieved. "*Ahhh*...there now, that's better."

She then handed servings to everyone, saving the biggest piece for herself. After stuffing her mouth with a forkful of cake, she began talking. "If there was a problem, they couldn't let y' know anyway. I bet they take Doll away."

The other ladies in the room paused, exchanging uncertain expressions. Between the gift wrap that had just vanished from Chantain's hands and Julie looking mighty hungry, they really didn't have much of an appetite for cake.

Landon's mother compelled herself to speak. "Well, I think different. The longer you wait, Chantain, the better it is. They just have to see if anyone's going to come claim him is all."

THE TIME TO TELL

Dwight's mother took a bite of cake, making a point with her fork. "Yeah, that's right. Doll's as good as yours. They just have to give it at least a year, so they protect themselves."

Landon's mother chuckled. "Well, if Doll was—you know—Vietnamese like my son, Chantain would already have him by now."

Everyone laughed, but Julie seemed to be one step behind. "Landon's Vietnamese? I thought you folks were Mexican or Filipino or somethin' like that."

The women drew silent for a moment as Landon's mother struggled for words.

Dwight's mother quickly said, "*Uh*, the cake—*um*. It's really good. Who made it?"

Chantain wadded most all of the wrapping paper under the coffee table for the meantime then brushed her hands of her job well done. "Oh, I did. I just threw it together. The candle is one I use for emergency when the power goes out. It's been hanging around the kitchen for a while now... comes in handy, actually."

She stepped around the children playing on the floor to refill everyone's coffee cups. The infants quickly became a central source of entertainment. Unavoidably, they attracted comparisons. Slowly but surely, everyone's attention focused on the mystery of Doll. He wasn't too different. Boys were boys. Laughs were exchanged, and small pats and gestures were made, but they continued to watch more seriously at the way Doll warmed up to his lineup of new toys.

Quickly, they realized that he had begun to plan something for the other four children who, quite frankly, didn't know what to do with themselves on the floor. Doll was the host. He broke into the toys, which were still in their boxes. Then he sorted them outside their boxes in a line, as if he were deciding something in an orderly fashion. He then looked at each of his friends.

The first gift he picked up was a spinning top with ten little Indians colorfully decorating it. He walked over and gave that one to Arlis. The second toy he juggled was a windup Teddy Roosevelt Bear, which he quickly gave to Landon. The third toy, a metal truck, he was very decisive about; he gave it to Dwight. Last, but not least, he picked up the little ball, before passing it to Glenn.

His actions charmed all the women. One of the childless ladies soon spoke up. "I thought they were all the same age. Didn't somebody say that?"

Chantain nodded. "Oh yes, they *are* the same age. They're about fourteen to sixteen months, except for Arlis...he'll be two."

Julie, who was in the process of having seconds on the cake, quickly put her saucer and fork down. "He's eighteen months. A long way to go before two, Chantain—gosh."

Landon's mother never took her eye off Doll while the others were talking and carrying on. Without saying much, she slowly put her plate of cake down in the midst of her intense observation. "*Um*, Doll's walking good. I mean *really* walking good."

Dwight's mother caught on quickly, then nodded. "I'm noticing...he even handed out one toy for everyone, like he knew where they should go. Did anyone see that? Are you sure he's not a year and a half, Chantain?"

"Sure I'm sure...well, if he is, it's not by much. Eddie took him to the doctor the first chance he got after he found him, and the doctor said he couldn't be more than three or four months back then."

Glenn's mother seemed to be counting up the months in her head. She then pulled her portable calendar out of her purse. "I see—back then? *Hmmm*, let me see....*hmmm*, why did you pick August for his birthdate? That would make him, *uh*—"

Chantain quickly placed her plate of cake to the side, tending her lips with a napkin. "I know, I know...that would make him one year and two or three months. I just figured his birthdate didn't matter—so I picked the month of August."

Real quietly, the rest of the women idled themselves in different postures, waiting for Chantain to explain further, but she wasn't inclined to do so. Resisting still, she looked away, touching the nape of her neck. To kick a few more seconds through the space of their stares, she watched the children play as if letting it go would help, but it didn't. Silence among them awkwardly closed in on her, causing her to peek back at everyone watching her for a better explanation.

Glenn's mother sat up to the edge of her seat. "Well? Are you going to tell us about the month of August?"

Chantain bashfully patted her big, blonde curls. "What? Oh—August…I guess everyone wants to know why I picked August then."

All of them stared right at her, replying all at once. "Yes!"

"Oh, it's nothing. It's stupid. Nobody wants to know."

Julie blurted, "Chantain. Come on. Cough it up. I'm your cotton pickin' neighbor, and I hadn't heard that one yet."

Chantain slapped her thigh, huffing, "All right already… you know…don't tell me nobody knows—Leo? Leo the Lion? If I had one of these kids of my own, I think I'd have to have some important guy, I guess. Like a king."

Suddenly the women softened up as they spoke to each other. "Oh yes, of course."

"A leader…a lion, *grrrrrr, ha ha ha*…so cute."

"My son's Pisces, the smelly ol' fish. Wish I could've chosen his sign."

"Oh, and the weather's so nice in August too."

"Oh my gosh, Landon got Cancer."

Everyone exclaimed, "Cancer? What?"

Landon's mother chuckled. "No, I mean his sign is Cancer. You know, the crab?"

Julie didn't soften up at all, nor did she chuckle through any of their small jokes. She sat there like an iron bulldog.

"Wait a minute, hush up everyone. Chantain, *um* Leo? King? So lions are kings, you think? *Ha!* They're kings of beasts maybe."

Landon's mother wittingly smiled. "King of beasts? Oh, Doll isn't that; look at him, Julie. Give the birthday guy a break. I mean he's just a cute little boy."

Julie picked up another serving of cake. "No...my grandpa n' dad was Leos. They were th' most arrogant, hot-headed, bad-tempered men I ever saw. No, no, no, Leo's r' monsters."

Someone else asked, "Whatever happened to your dad anyway, Julie?"

Julie looked at everyone one at a time. "I thought everyone knew. He passed away. Both of 'em—my grandpa too. Don't get me wrong, may they rest in peace, God bless their souls." She then quickly pointed. "You know, Chantain, you shouldn't go 'round hexing Doll with signs that way. Somethin' terrible wrong could happen."

The rest of the women jumped in. "Oh, lighten up, Julie."

"Yeah, at least your son has real parents, Julie."

"The poor kid's gotta go through life wondering where he came from, Julie."

"Yes, Chantain can do whatever she wants. Isn't that right, Chantain?"

Chantain brushed her off. "I'm okay about it, really, everyone."

Then she glared down at Julie. "It's just a month, Julie. You're just jealous 'cause I picked it, and Arlis will probably be a Virgo his whole life. Get over it, sweetie."

Everyone blushed and covered their mouths, chuckling. "Virgo? You mean the virgin? *Ha ha.*"

"Arlis, a permanent virgin? Oh my, *ha ha.*"

"That's so funny. *Ha ha.*"

Julie scowled. "*Ah ha haaaa*, I guess that's funny to you... He won't be no fruit, sweethearts. I can tell y' that...okay then Doll's a year and a couple or so. Get on with it. That would make him June maybe. What's that sign? *Huh?*"

Landon's mother quickly answered, "I just love the study of zodiac. June, I like to think of as the amazing Gemini. The twin. The great achiever of change."

Julie huffed, "Twins? Well, last I checked, Doll was by himself. Can't change that."

Landon's mother chuckled. "No, Julie. Gemini has the power to change things. He can even pledge his own allegiance if he sees it fit."

Julie kept up. "Pledge his own allegiance? Sounds like someone disturbin' our country or something? Maybe *he's* the one that's gonna be the fruitcake instead-a-my son. You know, one-a-those who tries climbing in bed with my son with weird ideas. *Ha haaaa,* the laugh's on someone else now."

Chantain quietly got annoyed. To cool herself down, she stood up to gather the empty dishes around the table slowly, but her backlash couldn't wait. "Those kind of weirdos died off with the Roman Empire dear. Everyone knows they are no more. We all know what happened to those idiots, right ladies? It's the forties now, so get with the times, Julie. Doll's going to be a *real* man, not a fake."

Dwight's mother asked, "Oh wow…pardon me for changing the subject because I need to…Getting back to Doll normally, please. If the constable says it's okay to keep him, are you going to adopt him then?"

Chantain seemed perplexed. "I just don't know. Eddie's making that call. Not me."

Glenn's mother asked, "You don't sound so good. Eddie doesn't have a problem with him, does he, Chantain?"

Chantain bobbed her eyelids in a quirky way. "I really can't say…he'll be coming home in an hour. If anyone's still around, they can ask him on their own when he comes through the door."

Glenn and Dwight's mothers backed down. "Oh no, that's all right."

"Me too, that's okay. I wouldn't want to interfere with anything."

Chantain then scanned over everyone. "Anyone here thinking of having another son? Maybe Landon wishes he could have a brother?"

Landon's mother quickly looked down to the floor. "No, I-I I'm sorry I—"

Chantain continued, "What's wrong?"

"Nothing's wrong...I mean, you know. Doll might be hurt to *um*—to be living with me and my real son...you seem like a better fit to me, no?"

Chantain delivered the dirty dishes into the kitchen then walked back out. She sat down, crossing her legs, looking at everyone in a huff. "That's just it... I'm not his real mom. Nobody here can tell me a kid's not going to have problems with that."

Julie seemed out of touch with their conversation again. She was too busy growing green-eyed as she watched Doll gaining the other children's following. By this time, he not only had shown them how to use their toys, he now seemed to be in the process of figuring out how to spin the top for her son.

The youngest woman, who hadn't said a thing during the whole party, observed Arlis faltering on his feet more than the others, so she timidly asked, "*Um*, Julie, is Arlis, *uh*, walking yet?"

Julie snapped out of her obsession with Doll. "Why, of course he is. Look, I'll show you."

She picked herself up and marched right over to Arlis, just as Doll let go the spinning top for everyone to see. What a show it made. For at least a second or two, the women were mesmerized. The other toddlers got an eyeful of the crazy contraption that seemed to be defying gravity.

THE TIME TO TELL

Everyone laughed hysterically as the top changed directions around Julie's feet, who was in the middle of trying to steady Arlis for a test walk. "Stop laughing everyone. I'm tryin' to help out Arlis...oh, darn that spinning thing is in m' way." She kicked the top away, but that didn't help matters one bit. Doll trotted to rescue the fallen top, giving it another quick spin to start it all over again.

Arlis saw the top take off, except this time, he wanted to chase it. Julie let go his arms just in time to see him take off, then immediately fall face down.

Crash!

"*Puh-puh...boo-hoo! Boo-hoo-hooo!*"

Julie quickly snatched him up. "That's all right, sweetheart. You're not supposed to run; you're supposed to walk. There, there, we know you can walk. It's okay. Mommy makes it feel better."

Landon's mother felt the immediate aura of discomfort growing, so she scooped up the spinning top before it could do any further damage. When she looked at the top, she saw the cute little Indians painted on it. "Oh, how cute. Hey look, everyone! It has ten little Indians on it, like the song. Did anyone see that?"

Dwight's mother quickly took credit. "I fell in love with it when I bought it. It looks like a flying saucer moving around on the floor, doesn't it?"

Through Arlis's cries getting louder, Landon's mother quickly tried to help out by singing the "Ten Little Indians" song. In no time, the rest of the women caught on, impulsively singing, "*One little, two little, three little Indians! Four little, five little, six little Indians! Seven little, eight little, nine little Indians—ten little Indian booyyys!*"

Arlis quickly quieted down, watching the grown-ups sing, when yet another noise came in to raid their party from outside.

Chug-chug-kirpop! Chug-chug-kirpop!

The irritating sound rattled through the windows and screen door as one of the quiet ladies blinked toward the driveway. "Oh my—what was *that?*"

Chantain started to explain when Julie beat her to it. "Oh, that's Eddie coming home. Don't bother. We live down the road and have to hear that thing-a-theirs, backfire all the time. You need to get it fixed, Chantain."

Chantain rose up quickly from her chair, stepping into a morose manner of cleaning things up that didn't really need cleaning. Her subtle message was well received. Doll's little birthday party was abruptly over.

After everyone's long faces looked as if they didn't want to go, they gathered their purses and children and quietly invited themselves to the door anyway. Their timing couldn't have been better either. Eddie came walking inside, intercepting them at the door. All of the women were standing with their sons, when each of them turned back to thank Chantain for having them over.

The good-bye gestures should have given Eddie enough time to get out of the way of the door, but he didn't. He was too preoccupied watching everyone, while holding onto some books under his arm. Julie wiggled her way up front, through the others, to face Eddie. She then glanced down at the books he was carrying as if they looked strange. "My, my...since when 've you gotten interested n' books? What you readin'? How to fix noisy cars?"

Everyone lightheartedly rolled with the joke, until Eddie's smile dropped. Quickly, he focused on his books, which he had forgotten he was carrying. He awkwardly moved aside, preventing Julie from seeing their covers. "Yes...so how is everyone?" Nobody bothered to answer, since they had been through his greeting when he came through the door.

Minor worries seemed to be bothering him. He swallowed down a faint sense of anxiety as he glanced over to the grandfather clock, watching it tick.

THE TIME TO TELL

Chantain seemed to know her husband all too well. She gave him only so much time before crossing her arms and glaring a daunting signal of her discontent. "You're early, Eddie. The least you could do is answer Julie's question."

"Oh no...I'm early? I mean—I-I'm sorry. Oh, these books? They're nothing really, just history books. Books of—historical symbols and things."

Landon's mother seemed genuinely interested. "Oh, that sounds interesting. Can I see what they are?"

"*No.* I mean, no...you know, it's just guy stuff. I don't know why anyone would be interested in this stuff—"

Chantain rolled her eyes. "Oh God, that's Eddie's hobby. He can never get enough of that World War. He's always listening, reading, or doing *something* about it."

Eddie seemed grateful. "Yes, that's right...I mean Chantain and I go 'round and 'round about it. Ever since I was discharged, I've become more critical. I mean of the war, not of Chantain."

Everyone paused in the face of his conversation as if they were sorely confused. War seemed like a sour subject from the looks of them. Their words dried up once again. Tongue-tied silence filtered throughout the living room, except for the children who had started to get fidgety.

As the clock's seconds moved along with sporadic interjections by the children, Eddie stayed anchored there, nervously tapping his cane. "Hmmm, yes good day, isn't it? *Um,* sorry but—it's never been my thing to talk to a house of women—to, *um,* talk about the war? Not good maybe... hey, I've got some things to do outside until the party's really over. I'll just—"

Glenn's mother stepped closer to the door. "No, no, Mr. Coolidge, you're not breaking up the hen house. We've been here quite some time, actually. Everyone was just about to leave anyway, right ladies?"

Landon's mother nodded. "Yes, that's right. We were just singing songs for Doll and the kids to break up the monotony."

Everyone agreed as they shuffled their purses onto their other shoulders.

Eddie suddenly relaxed. "You really had a good time? Wow, that's great. There's nothing better than seeing a bunch of Doll's friends here. My gosh, there's Landon, Dwight, Glenn...I see Arlis next door all the time. All the kids—they're growing up so fast, aren't they?"

Chantain started tapping her foot. "Yes, but not fast enough, Eddie—if you know what I mean."

Eddie hobbled aside, clearing the way for them to leave. "Maybe next time the husbands will throw a birthday party or something."

As the women exited in single file, each of them thanked Chantain and Eddie for having them over.

Landon's mother, however, stopped on her way out. "So, Eddie...what do you think about having a Leo on your hands?"

Eddie watched Chantain go to the kitchen, leaving the two of them alone. "Whatever Chantain says goes, I guess. He's supposed to be a Gemini, did anyone mention that?"

Landon's mother seemed bothered. "He might wind up with two signs. They're not meant to be together—I mean in one person."

Eddie chuckled. "Yes...a Gemini-Leo, I guess. That's right, you like astrology, don't you? Not possible, right?"

She scowled toward the kitchen, watching out for Chantain. "*Hmmph*...Leos are kept away by more than a month for a reason. I don't know what could happen...it could be dangerous."

Eddie smiled, holding the screen door open for her. "Dangerous? Oh, come on...it's not possible anyway, right?"

THE TIME TO TELL

Landon's mother hesitated before stepping out. "You never know...there's always a first time. I know how Chantain is, though."

Eddie smiled. "Yeah, well, she's quite the devil's advocate—I-I mean for Devil's Gulch—isn't she?"

"*Hmmm*...maybe she was tricked into giving the poor kid what he needs for some reason."

Chantain strolled up from behind. "I heard that. I knew I was important for something...did you hear that, Eddie? I gave Doll just what he needs."

Eddie said his good-byes to the company and then spoke to Chantain as he left the doorway. "Yeah? Who *or what* sent you down here to do your thing is what I would like to know?"

Chantain shut the door then laughingly said, "*Ha!* Very funny. You want to know who? It was a team of angels...that's who...I could just feel them tickling me all over today."

By then, Eddie had already hobbled into his office just off the side of their living room. "Angels, she says. No kidding."

Without further ado, he eagerly opened his rolltop desk, clearing his sloppy mess aside and placed his books down. While doing so, he hissed to himself, "*Sssss*, angels, she says." He pulled up his chair to look at the first book. It was thick, with a lot of text and not a lot of pictures, so he quickly set it aside, moving on to the next.

In the midst of his hurried research, he became mildly interrupted by the sound of music coming from the living room. He paused to glance from his chair, noticing that Doll was the one who had turned the radio on. For the moment, Eddie looked as if he was getting ready to go out there to tune it in better, but Doll already beat him to it. He whispered as he sat back down thumbing through another book, "That kid sometimes...where was I? *Hmmm*, let me see now."

He fanned through the pages until he got to a spot that revealed various generic illustrations of symbols. Suddenly, he became intrigued enough to whisper as he slowed down through some very intriguing pages. "*Ahhh...yes...*this is more like it...symbols, symbols...*hmmm.* Stars, right here, *yesss.*"

He knew he was on to something, so he reached into his drawer, pulling out a rough pencil tracing he had made of Doll's medallion. Then he flipped through more pages while comparing his tracing to the pictures until he ran out of symbols. "*Hmmm...*nothing."

Without successfully matching Doll's symbol, he turned to his last book. Quickly, he turned to a chapter discussing and displaying more groups of symbols that didn't relate to stars at all. This group of designs mainly ran vertically and horizontally. He muttered, "Crosses maybe."

He flipped through those pages too, concluding once again that nothing resembled Doll's rolling star there either. Disappointment glued a blank page on his face, so he shoved the books aside and rocked back in his chair, tapping his temple with a pencil. In the face of his dim lamp, his little bit of homework seemed to be at its end. Shadows of doubt cast down upon his hard-thinking glare. He just didn't want to give up that easily.

Just then, Chantain peeked through the French doors with a piece of cake and a cup of coffee in hand. "I have some leftover cake Doll didn't eat. Do you want it?"

Eddie nearly jumped off his chair. At the same time, he awkwardly slid a newspaper over his books, trying to hide them. "Oh! You scared me. Thank you for thinking about me...did everything go all right before I came home?"

"Yes. About as fine as expected—until Doll started showing up Arlis and them."

"I would've guessed that. What happened?"

Chantain handed his cake and coffee over, then walked over to the window to stare outside. "Oh, you know. He's walking around like he's been doing. Some of the other kids aren't walking all that good. This time—this time something else happened."

THE TIME TO TELL

"Oh? What's that?"

"Doll figured out the new toys that he got for his birthday."

Eddie took a big bite of cake. "What's wrong with that?"

"Well, after that, he shared them." Chantain quickly whipped her hair around, facing him. "Then—he showed them how to use them."

Eddie stopped chewing. "What did they say? Anything?"

"Nothing really...they probably thought Doll had the toys already. That's what I would've thought."

"Do we? What are they?"

Chantain didn't bother answering at first. She glanced at her pretty, red fingernails as she wandered back over to Eddie. Then she surveyed his desk to see what it was he was so involved with before casually saying, "He doesn't have any spinning tops. He figured out how to push down the spinner thing that makes it work. You ever see one of those before?"

Eddie stopped to think. "*Hmmm*, no...can't say I have. Well at least he didn't play with the radio like he's been doing."

"Oh God, no. I'll never tell that one." She went on, "I thought Julie was going to come out of her skin when Doll and Arlis got together with the stupid top, my gosh. She tried to make her kid walk in front of everybody while she almost tripped over the top. It was spinning all around. Pretty funny, really."

Chantain then leaned over Eddie's desk. One of his books wasn't hidden quite well enough beneath the newspaper. Immediately, she saw part of the page, revealing black and white diagrams of crosses. "That's not war stuff. Looks like religion to me."

"What? Oh, *crosses*...yes, well—it's nothing. They relate to war one way or another."

Chantain abruptly snatched up the book, flipping through a couple of the pages. After suspecting she might have been on to something, she forged a big, fake yawn as if she hadn't a care in the world. "You're not telling me the truth. Who do you think I am?"

"Okay...why can't I get some privacy around here? I told you before, and I'll tell you again. That symbol of Doll's is probably some kinfolk mark—from his dad—or maybe his mother. I don't know."

She wasn't buying it, so Eddie showed her the rest of the books. "Look for yourself. Here you go. You won't find it anywhere in these books."

She suspiciously opened one of the books to the page he'd creased. "*Hmmm* interesting war stuff you got...says here, 'The cross is one of the most ancient human symbols, dating back thousands of years.' *Ha*, look here—it says 'before Christ' even."

Chantain then buried her nose into it. "*Hmmm*...this is as good as my science-fiction crap. Maybe I should read this tonight before bed." She flipped the page. "Listen to this...it says, 'The four sides of a cross, or the cardinal points, often give meaning to the representation of the world into four classical elements: Earth, Water, Air, and Fire—"

Eddie put his cake and coffee aside. "Oh, come on, Chantain. I was just looking at some pictures, really."

Chantain marked the spot with her finger, glaring back at him. "I want to continue if you don't mind...it says 'Some ancient cultures of Japan, China, India, and Greece and their philosophers have added an additional element, which is sometimes not visible on the cross's four points. The works of Aristotle, Plato, Hinduism, Buddhism, and others have added such an element, which is called various other names and has different meanings ranging from aether, quintessence, stars, void, and even the Universe. Some of the concepts defined in the additional element, range from corruptible, heavenly, or things not of our—natural lives.'"

Suddenly Eddie became interested. "Wow, it says all that?"

THE TIME TO TELL

"Hush up. I'm reading...it says, 'It is not known exactly when the first cross was made, but predominant theories indicate just after the time of the circle...older circle symbols were made during the Stone Age. These were diagonal crosses or Xs, technically termed as a—saltire.'"

"*Hmmm*, let me take a look at that."

Chantain handed his book over. "Doesn't sound much like your typical war stuff to me."

Eddie turned the pages back and forth. "Sure it is...let me show you...*ah ha*, yes, here we go...look, there are all kinds of military iron crosses here...says so right here. Oh, look here. Here's the Egyptian Cross, the Greek Cross, Saint Andrew's Cross, Celtic Cross, Swastika...Christian Crosses are military too...they're all war...yup, all about war—pages of them... Doll's mark isn't there anywhere. Go on, look."

Chantain snatched the book back. "Okay then, I will... *hmmm*, hope you don't mind if I read more...*hmmm*... the Coptic Crosses of different ages in Egypt. *Hmmm*, the Sunwheel Cross used throughout Native American culture. The High Cross of Ireland...*hmmm*...the Canterbury Cross dating back to 850 AD. The Crucifix Cross? Oh, look...the Crucifix Cross is all about Jesus. Is that about war? Look here, the Lorraine Cross of Joan of Arc. Jerusalem Cross."

As she kept reading and looking, her eyes and mouth suddenly opened wide. "Oh my God, look at this."

"What did you find now? *Sheesh*."

"Here are crosses with daggers and upside-down swords... crosses with shields...*hmmm*, I never would've thought these church crosses would—oh, this is interesting."

Eddie looked like he threw in the towel. "No, just keep looking until you're satisfied. There's stars too...here look in *this* book. Five and six-sided ones, even."

As she kept looking, she somehow slowly swayed herself out of suspicion. At some point, she became satisfied. Without further hesitation, she closed up the last of his books, leaving them on the desk. Strangely enough, she even covered them back up with Eddie's newspaper. "Okay."

Eddie coyly picked up his cake and began to eat again, just as Chantain blurted, "I know you're hiding something… okay, I admit…I'd like to believe that terrible tattoo of Doll's is just something simple like—something like—"

"Look…it's probably what I said, honey, some family symbol. What else *can* it be?"

Chantain pointed to one of the books. "That book there, they even covered one of those crosses with a *skull* and-and *cross bones*."

Eddie took another bite of cake, speaking with his mouth full: "Well, I *did* say I was looking at ugly war stuff, didn't I?"

"Oh, I know. I just wish I knew if he meant something bad."

To appease her mind, Eddie cordially opened up one of the books and turned to the page of another cross called the Saint Peter's Cross, which he pointed to with his fork. "This'll help you out…look here…if Doll's mark was evil, it would be an inverted Christian cross, like this one. Now *that's* evil, my darling…don't worry about it."

Chantain gasped, "Why, why that's…that's the-the Jesus Christ cross—except upside down. I didn't see that one…you mean all you got to do is turn it upside down? That's stupid. The one on my necklace turns upside down all the time."

"I know honey, that's what I'm saying. It turns upside down on your neck because you move around…they're called accidents."

Almost instantly, she let down her guard, relaxing. "Well, how do you like the cake?"

Eddie almost missed his mouth with his next bite. "Oh, the cake? It's good. Real good…don't throw any away. I want it all."

Just then, a song came on the radio that Eddie liked, so he yelled out to Doll in the living room. "Hey, Doll, turn it up a little, will you?"

Chantain shook her head. "He's not that good."

"Oh, wanna bet? You're out of the house a lot. You miss what that cute little kid is really about."

As Doll turned the radio's volume up a little bit more, Chantain frowned, then swiftly headed out of the office while talking over her shoulder. "You just taught him that—like you taught him how to turn it on. You can't fool me."

Eddie carefully watched her leave before letting out a huge sigh of relief. Quickly, he picked up the book Chantain was reading and thumbed over to that particular section until he whispered, "It looks like a star…it's a cross—a saltire cross."

He continued, "*Hmmm*, a rolling star with four legs—it has to be."

As he anxiously flipped the pages back and forth time and again, he just knew it had to be there, but it wasn't. Soon enough, he began to frown and mutter, "Why isn't it here? Got to be somewhere…where the hell is it?"

Among the many pages of diagrams, photos, and colored drawings he looked over, including several varieties of four-sided crosses, he read carefully into the text. "The family of equilateral crosses with arms bent at right or left facing angles…some were saltire."

He paused to mutter, "*Hmmm*…interesting." He then picked up the pencil tracing to look at it again, before nodding. Indeed, Doll's symbol had right-facing star tips, like it was in motion. They were tilted in the fashion of an "X" as well. He softly whispered as he kept reading, "These types of crosses are—some of the oldest archaeological human symbols ever found. They date—what?"

Eddie looked up blindly at the wall, softly repeating the text: "Ninety-five hundred years BC…the Neolithic Period? What in the hell is that?"

With a whole new rush of fervor, he quickly thumbed to equilateral crosses and saltires to see if Doll's symbol could be stuffed somewhere in the corners of those pages. It wasn't, however. There were all sorts of ancient symbols from Sanskrit, with the right and left geometry.

The photographs revealed more pictures and descriptions, which tantalized him. Some artifacts were pictured there too: the Indus Valley Civilization, Iran in the first millennium BC, India, Buddhism, Jainism, Hinduism, the Samurai Hasekura Tsunengaga, Ancient Greek, Bronze Age, Baltic, Celtic, Finnish, Slavic, Sami, and even—ancient Germanic. He looked closely at all of the pictures with their symbols, and there they all were staring back at him. All of the symbols shared a similar equilateral design.

He whispered, "*Hmmm*, nothing stands out...nothing like Doll's." After staring at them a minute or two longer, he rubbed his eyes. "Nothing...wasting time maybe."

Inexplicably, Eddie soon lost what little bit of enthusiasm he had struggled to keep. After a while, all he looked to be doing was fanning the pages into some other daydream of his. After that, he simply closed the books up without further interest.

As he got up from the desk, he yawned and stretched. His pencil tracing caught his eye in the middle of his stretch, so he stopped to look at it one last time before wadding it up. Clear across the floor was his trash basket, so he zeroed in on it and gave it a lucky toss. Closure to Doll's mysterious, emblematic folly came to an end all too quickly it seemed. He rubbed the boredom from his face, murmuring, "That's the end-a-that."

Shortly thereafter, nothing seemed to amuse him, except for perhaps the song he liked on the radio in the background, which was now ending. He lazily gazed up at the ceiling, doing nothing in particular, just as the radio started in with a special broadcast.

"This is not a test...I repeat...this is not a test. JDVL radio is interrupting this program with a special emergency announcement from the President of the United States of America. Please stand by."

THE TIME TO TELL

Chantain rushed over to peek through the office door. "Come out, Eddie. Truman's going to talk on the radio it sounds like. I wonder what it's about."

Eddie walked out, shrugging away his pent-up aggravations. He stepped back into the living room of noise. Doll's spinning top contributed its share of noise, while Major barked at it flying around on the floor by itself.

Eddie pointed to the radio blaring away. "Do you know what Truman said when he first ran for office? It's the only thing I agree with him on."

Chantain sat down to get ready for the emergency announcement, which hadn't yet come on. "No. Why would I remember what he said? I hardly remember what *you* say half the time."

He went on, "The damn goofball said that his choice early in life was either to become a piano player in a whorehouse or a politician...then he said there was hardly any difference between the two...can you believe that? That's what he said."

Chantain quickly lit a cigarette. "Oh, come on, Eddie. He wouldn't say that. Why are you so down on everybody?"

"He did too say that. That's no lie...the dirty rotten Democrat. That's the only good thing he ever said."

"Now, Eddie. You voted for Roosevelt, didn't you? He was Democrat. You liked him."

"That doesn't mean a thing. Truman's a *scoundrel.* That's all I got to say."

After prancing in a circle, he finally sat down next to the radio, with Doll and Major at his side. This didn't stop Doll and Major from making more racket, however. Eddie had enough, so he took the dog outside to the porch and then hobbled back in to sit down again. Chantain picked up the other half of the noise, who was Doll, and sat him on her lap just as the emergency broadcast hit the airwaves nationwide:

"*—now for our President of the United States...Harry S. Truman.*"

H.C. WELLS

"Sixteen hours ago an American airplane dropped one bomb on Hiroshima, an important Japanese Army base. That bomb had more power than twenty thousand tons of TNT. It had more than two thousand times the blast power of the British 'Grand Slam,' which is the largest bomb ever yet used in the history of warfare.

"The Japanese began the war from the air at Pearl Harbor. They have been repaid many-fold. And the end is not yet. With this bomb, we have now added a new and revolutionary increase in destruction to supplement the growing power of our armed forces. In their present form, these bombs are now in production and even more powerful forms are in development—"

Chantain became disinterested right away. Immediately, she put Doll back down on the floor then clacked her heels back to the kitchen in a huff. "Oh, thank God we're bombing them... for a minute, I thought *we* were the ones getting bombed."

Eddie lifted his cane in the seat of his chair. "Wait. Where you goin'? This is big. Some bomb with twenty thousand tons of TNT, did you hear? That's revolutionary technology."

Chantain was in the kitchen by then, clanging dishes. "I don't care. As long as we're not getting bombed, that's all I want to hear."

President Truman continued:

"—It is an atomic bomb. It is a harnessing of the basic power of the universe. The force from which the sun draws its power has been loosed against those who brought war to the Far East."

Eddie yelled toward the kitchen, "They call it an atomic bomb...it harnesses the powers of the universe, he said!"

Chantain yelled back, "Did they get rid of all the Japs, or just some of them?"

Eddie glanced over to the noisy kitchen, shaking his head as if he didn't even want to answer that question. He muttered his answer to Doll instead. "Christ sakes...can't believe her sometimes, Doll."

President Truman went on:

"Before 1939, it was the accepted belief of scientists that it was theoretically possible to release atomic energy. But no one knew any practical method of doing it. By 1942, however, we knew that the Germans were working feverishly to find a way to add atomic energy to the other engines of war with which they hoped to enslave the world, but they failed. We may be grateful to Providence that the Germans got the V-1s and V-2s late and in limited quantities and even more grateful that they did not get the atomic bomb at all.

"The battle of the laboratories held fateful risks for us, as well as the battles of the air, land, and sea, and we have now won the battle of the laboratories, as we have won the other battles.

"Beginning in 1940, before Pearl Harbor, scientific knowledge useful in war was pooled between the United States and Great Britain, and many priceless helps to our victories have come from that arrangement. Under that general policy, the research on the atomic bomb was begun. With American and British scientists working together, we entered the race of discovery against the Germans.

"The United States had available the large number of scientists of distinction in the many needed areas of knowledge. It had the tremendous industrial and financial resources necessary for the project, and they could be devoted to it without undue impairment of other vital war work. In the United States the laboratory work and the production plants, on which a substantial start had already been made, would be out of reach of enemy bombing, while at that time Britain was exposed to constant air attack and was still threatened with the possibility of invasion. For these reasons, Prime Minister Churchill and President Roosevelt agreed that it was wise to carry on the project here.

"We now have two great plants and many lesser works devoted to the production of atomic power. Employment during peak construction numbered one hundred twenty-five thousand, and over

sixty thousand individuals are even now engaged in operating the plants. Many have worked there for two and a half years. Few know what they have been producing. They see great quantities of material going in, and they see nothing coming out of these plants, for the physical size of the explosive charge is exceedingly small. We have spent two billion dollars on the greatest scientific gamble in history—and won."

Eddie shouted in the direction of the kitchen. "Hey, they're making new plants for these bombs and employing one hundred twenty-five thousand people. I'm gonna to have to tell my dad about this. Maybe he can get a job in his backyard!"

President Truman continued:

"—but the greatest marvel is not the size of the enterprise, its secrecy, nor its cost, but the achievement of scientific brains in putting together infinitely complex pieces of knowledge held by many men in different fields of science into a workable plan. And hardly less marvelous has been the capacity of industry to design, and of labor to operate, the machines and methods to do things never done before so that the brainchild of many minds came forth in physical shape and performed as it was supposed to do.

"Both science and industry worked under the direction of the United States Army, which achieved a unique success in managing so diverse a problem in the advancement of knowledge in an amazingly short time. It is doubtful if such another combination could be got together in the world. What has been done is the greatest achievement of organized science in history. It was done under high pressure and without failure.

"We are now prepared to obliterate more rapidly and completely every productive enterprise the Japanese have above ground in any city. We shall destroy their docks, their factories, and their communications. Let there be no mistake; we shall completely destroy Japan's power to make war.

THE TIME TO TELL

"It was to spare the Japanese people from utter destruction that the ultimatum of July twenty-sixth was issued at Potsdam. Their leaders promptly rejected that ultimatum. If they do not now accept our terms, they may expect a rain of ruin from the air, the like of which has never been seen on this earth. Behind this air attack will follow sea and land forces in such numbers and power as they have not yet seen and with the fighting skill of which they are already well aware.

"The Secretary of War, who has kept in personal touch with all phases of the project, will immediately make public a statement giving further details. His statement will give facts concerning the sites at Oak Ridge near Knoxville, Tennessee, and at Richland near Pasco, Washington, and an installation near Santa Fe, New Mexico. Although the workers at the sites have been making materials to be used in producing the greatest destructive force in history, they have not themselves been in danger beyond that of many other occupations, for the utmost care has been taken of their safety.

"The fact that we can release atomic energy ushers in a new era in man's understanding of nature's forces. Atomic energy may in the future supplement the power that now comes from coal, oil, and falling water, but at present it cannot be produced on a basis to compete with them commercially. Before that comes there must be a long period of intensive research.

"It has never been the habit of the scientists of this country or the policy of this government to withhold from the world scientific knowledge. Normally, therefore, everything about the work with atomic energy would be made public."

Eddie leaned over his foot stool, blatantly speaking into the radio's speaker: "What? You're making secret bombs to blow half the world up and you're going to make it *public*? For God's sake...what kind-a-shit's that? *Aaaaah shhhh*—that's Truman for you."

Chantain poked her head back into the living room while wiping off a dish. "This is supposed to be stuff you like... you're angry. What's wrong?"

Eddie didn't say a thing. He just glared at the radio as it continued with the broadcast.

"—but under present circumstances it is not intended to divulge the technical processes of production of all the military applications, pending further examination of possible methods of protecting us and the rest of the world from the danger of sudden destruction.

"I shall recommend that the Congress of the United States consider promptly the establishment of an appropriate commission to control the production and use of atomic power within the United States. I shall give further consideration and make further recommendations to the Congress as to how atomic power can become a powerful and forceful influence toward the maintenance of world peace. This is Harry S. Truman—"

Eddie went from being angry to being shocked. He carefully lifted himself from his chair to reach over and turn off the radio. He then carefully sat back down while holding his cane with both hands. "There it goes...that is going change history for a loooong time."

Doll somehow felt Eddie's sadness. While wearing almost the same lonesome face as he, Doll got up off the floor to offer him his brand-new spinning top. Eddie gently took it from his little fingers and looked at it for a sincere moment. He shook his head, then kindly handed it back. "Thanks, Doll, but you better hang on to this yourself. Go play, okay?"

Chantain spoke out from the kitchen, "Why'd you turn the radio off?"

Eddie didn't answer. He just kept staring at the radio.

Chantain came into the room, wiping another dish. "What's wrong? Is the speech over? Dinner's ready in five minutes...better clean up."

"Yeah, I guess you could say it's over. We just unleashed some secret bomb that unlocks the universe...now the

THE TIME TO TELL

President says he wants to make all of the secret work *public*—in the name of *peace*."

"Oh? That doesn't sound right...what's he thinking?"

Eddie got up out of his chair and began pacing the room while stroking his hair. To kill more time, he looked at Doll playing with his toy, then stared straight into Chantain's eyes with the sorriest of looks. "This war's not ending."

"But didn't the radio say it would keep the Japanese and others from making more war, or something like that? I heard it."

"No, no, no...you watch. If anything, wars are going to continue...how long, I don't know...forever's my guess... only time will tell."

"Time will tell? What do you mean *time will tell*. Sure it's over, Eddie. Open your ears. Truman said so. Germany already announced their surrender a while ago. It's over for good."

Eddie stood in the middle of the living room, tapping his cane nervously. "No...you don't get it, Chantain. I've been there. I know what war is."

Chantain dropped back into the kitchen clanging dishes. "There you go again, thinking you know everything just because you've been there."

Eddie kept staring toward the kitchen with a wretched look. "Can't you see? No, you don't see it, do you? All we do in this country is go out and kick ass." He went on, "Then we dust off their clothes, supply them with Band-Aids...get this, Chantain...we give them back their country after that too... brilliant—real brilliant!"

"Well that's the right thing to do."

Eddie rubbed his hair. "*Sheesh*, what? I've got news for you. I bet we give Japan back their country after this is over. Tell you what...Germany gets to keep theirs too. All these little peon countries do is stir up trouble—can't you see? We need to control the wackos."

"*Ha ha*, very funny, Eddie. You sound like a dictator."

"Who said I was trying to be funny?" He pointed to the kitchen with his cane. "What do you think is going to happen when we go blowing up every country in the world then let 'em go? Shit, that's worse than being a dictator. That's insane."

Chantain walked into the living room, wiping her hands with a dish towel. "No, it's not...it shows compassion, Eddie. Something you clearly don't have."

"Oh yeah? The next time an ax murderer comes into our home, remind me to kick his ass, give him back his ax, and send him out the door with an icepack on his head and of cup 'o warm milk."

Chantain busted up laughing. "You're funny sometimes. Don't be ridiculous. You didn't even hear what I said."

As she walked back to put the rest of her dishes away, she yelled, "I don't know about you, Eddie...sometimes I think that war injury of yours affected you in more ways than one. Why don't you become one of those new pranksters I heard about. An *activist*, I think they call it."

"An activist? They're just fly-by-nighters starting a new thing. But holy bajeez, somebody's got to get it right around here, and it won't be me...I can tell you that right now. Don't worry—an *activist*, she says."

"What do you think America should do, Eddie? Take over the world?"

Eddie sat back down and grabbed up his newspaper. He looked like he wanted to read, but put the newspaper down instead. "We took over the Native Indians, didn't we? Nobody had a problem with that. You don't see us signing our country back over to them do you?"

"That's different, stupid."

"Stupid? You mean like your activists becoming popular? Where you coming from? Wait a minute...can you imagine that? We kicked the Indians' asses, and then set them free on reservations smaller than their tee-pees. There's another problem we have. They're still scalping us with all their bullshit even now—and you call it stupid? I don't think so! They're separate countries now—right here in the middle of the country we took! *Sheesh*, for Christ sake...bad enough...if you're going to start something, by God, I say *finish it*."

Chantain yelled back, "You're getting a little too hot under the collar again, so you should really stop it or—"

"We screwed up. That's what we did...we're still screwing up."

"Very well, then, be stupid...Indians are nice people now...we helped them, and you can't say different."

"We helped them, all right. We gave them blankets with diseases inside and told them to go home to their reservations and be warm, shit...wait a minute...after the massacres, only the angriest, toughest ones survived. Then we put them on little pieces of land and said, 'Be good now.' *Ha*!"

Eddie ruffled up his paper in front of his face, carrying on, "Now we got President hair-trigger Truman saying we got king bombs, and we're goin' to make the energy *public* for Christ sakes—in the name of peace?! Smoke a peace pipe on that one, my dear."

Chantain stopped what she was doing. "*Hmmm*, now that you mention it, maybe that wouldn't be a good idea."

"Thank you...none of it's a good idea. Truman should've kept his mouth shut...kept it secret or something. This way he could've at least spared us—our children." He paused, but then he started up again. "You know what else Truman said not long ago?"

Chantain paused in the kitchen looking sarcastic. "Let me see now...that he was a Democrat, and you hate his guts... am I right? Food's on the table."

"No, no, no...he sounds so right about what he said now...the loon said he never gave anybody *hell* and that he just told the truth. They just thought it was hell. He really said that. I heard him."

Chantain rolled her eyes. "We're the ones with the bomb, silly, not them. Nothing's better than that. What could possibly go wrong? Now come on and eat."

"Didn't you hear? He's taking it pub—*ahhh* forget it. I'm done talking. Throw in ten or twenty years—then talk to me about it."

The telephone rang in the kitchen just then. Chantain picked it up then put her hand over the receiver and yelled toward the living room, "It's Torrance Holt. You want me to take care of it?"

Eddie hobbled quickly to the kitchen. "No...I'll take it. Hand it over...thank you."

He went on. "Yes, Mr. Holt...yes, we heard about the bomb. Just listened to it on the radio...I'm glad you're glad....what's the news? You got any? Yes, I know...no...nooo. I can't believe it."

Chantain walked away, smiling behind his back as Eddie kept his ear tightly against the receiver. "Noooo, wait, you mean...oh my God, you're kidding me...yes, I know...I know it's hard for me—that's it, I guess, then...okay then.. all right. I'll keep it to myself...I have to hang up now so I can tell Chantain."

Eddie quickly hung up when Chantain touched him on back of the shoulder. "Oh, Eddie, I'm so sorry. It's too bad that—"

Eddie turned around, grinning from ear to ear. "Sorry? What? We get to keep him, *ha haaa*! Can you believe it? *Ha haaa. Woooohoooo*! I just can't believe it, *ha haaaa*."

Chantain sat down at the table and then quickly dished out the fried chicken, potatoes, and gravy. "Calm down...sit down, will you? I guess I'll get our you-know-who from the living room."

She stomped off. "Doll, get your butt in gear now. You've got food on the table! I'm not picking you up this time, so march in here on your own."

Just as Doll came around the corner, Chantain grabbed him by the arm and stuffed him into his high chair.

THE TIME TO TELL

Eddie suddenly stopped eating. "Hey, easy there. You'll dislocate the little guy's shoulder." He quickly got up. "Here, let me help you, Doll. Looks like your foot's caught in the seat...there, that's better...have some potatoes, big guy. Here you go."

He continued as he sat back down, eating. "Hey, guess what, little feller? You're a Coolidge kid now. An official member, *ha*! We're your family. Ha! A real family!"

Chantain kept playing with her food as if she'd lost her appetite, while Eddie wasn't quite so finicky with his plate. He got a hold of a big spoonful of potatoes and kept eating. However, somewhere between his appetite and manners, he noticed Chantain being silent.

He grabbed his napkin, clearing his voice. "*Um*...sorry for getting too excited. Did you hear everything on the phone?"

"Part of it...we get to keep him so... that's great. So *um*—how long?"

"How long? Oh, Mr. Holt said *um*, all we have to do is sign some papers and Doll is—he's ours—for good. I can't believe it. He's finally—he's finally ours."

He paused for a reaction. "Something wrong? *Ahem*... Chantain...say something because—"

"Oh no. It's just going to take me a while for it to sink in. That's all—really."

"You don't look too happy. You're—you're happy, aren't you?"

"Yes, of course I am. It's just that we had a big day with the birthday...I mean, the president's announcement with the big bomb and all too. I mean, wow." She then started cutting up her chicken. "Now I hear we get to keep Doll...it's just a little overwhelming...don't you think? I mean, think about it."

Eddie began eating again. "Of course. Never thought of it that way. You know that bomb's going to get us in trouble. You know that, don't you?"

"Yes, I guess. I mean *um*...it sounds like it."

Eddie suddenly became all smiles. "Hey, *um*, I've got some more good news I haven't told you about. Want to hear?"

"Yes, of course...what is it?"

He took a big bite of chicken. "Yeah, well...do you remember our old pastor? I mean, our first one, from a while back... Pastor Johnathon McKoowey—from about three years ago?"

Chantain was so surprised, she coughed. "Oh, *ahem*, excuse me, the gravy's hot...*yes!* I mean yes. How did you find him?"

"I found him."

"Are you sure you got the right John I'm thinking of? Pass me the buns, please."

"Sure, here you go...he's the right John...the young guy. Well, you know what I mean...close to our age. You liked his preaching I recall."

"Yes, of course. Go on—what about him?"

Eddie dived into his plate again. With a full mouth of food, he waved his fork, saying, "Well, it was serendipity. Here I was—at the library—checking out those books you saw...that's when I ran into him." He then continued with second helpings of potatoes and gravy. "Funny thing, he asked about you."

"Oh my. You told him I was fine, I hope...does he still have his Church of the Baptismal Mission?"

Eddie grabbed another chicken leg, then talked with it in his hand. "Yes, the one you were baptized at. Now let me finish, all right? Well, his church, he said, is booming. He now has *three* churches...can you believe that? Yeah, *three* churches...a brand new one here in town, one in Black Water, and the one in Moss Lake. The one we used to go to way back when."

Chantain picked up her fork, thinking. "But I didn't see him anywhere on Church Row. How come I couldn't spot him?"

"I know. He's outside of town somewhere. I have to go check."

THE TIME TO TELL

Chantain then picked up her butter knife, thinking once again. She gingerly sliced into her chicken, as she stared right past Eddie. "*Hmmm*, I bet he's bringing in a lot of money, *um*—I mean charity now."

Eddie kept his eyes on his plate, not really paying attention to anything else except keeping his mouth full. "Oh, you bet...sure is good chicken."

"He was single, wasn't he? Does he still look the same?"

Eddie grabbed his glass of milk, then downed it. "*Ahhhh*, that was good food...of course he looks the same. You expecting him to pick up a gun and go get shot during the war or something? Heck no, those preachers—they take care of themselves. Sort of makes me mad."

He carried on, "Look, I've been thinking...you know we've tried a few churches over the last couple years. I don't know about you, but—I don't think the Church of the Original Testament is right for us. I mean, the preacher is good, except he's—well, it's just that he's sort of—"

Chantain dropped her knife. "*Uh*, radical! I know. He's no good...so when do we go see Pastor McKoowey? He's really more like—well—what we're looking for, right?"

"Wow, that was easy. So how can you give up Julie and Al's church that fast? Wait, never mind. I think I know."

"Well, for the same reasons as you. After listening to what you said, I just hate walking up and down Church Row all the time, bumping heads with others. You know, everyone's just—and he yells too much while he beats his Bible to death...I'm sure you know what I mean."

"*Hmmm*, well...boy, do I. You're right. *Hmmm*, so it's okay? I mean, I feel like I'm up to my neck in alligators with some of these churches. I really don't want to make the Witness crowd either if you know what I mean. The crap's so political down in town that, well...so you really think it's bad too?"

"Sure I do—like President Truman...it's all too political. Soooo next Sunday, I get to—I mean we get to go to his church in town? I mean, out of town. That's where he's at, right?"

"Of course. Good...our old pastor guy must be doing something right or he wouldn't be growing so fast. I mean, how does the guy do it? Three churches—that's something."

"He must be energetic...maybe he needs help or something. I like a preacher that's energetic, don't you?"

"Well, I guess, if that's what it takes."

Chantain drifted in thought as she carefully picked up her glass. Her eyes browsed around her old kitchen. She felt around the edges of her plate, then felt around the edges of her old, nicked-up dinner table. She even drew her wandering eyes over to Doll, sitting there next to Eddie, hardly looking cute with that mess of mashed potatoes on his cheek.

Abruptly, she put down her glass, observing Eddie with his cane leaning against the wall, before licking her lips. "'Course, you know...I picked him before you. Do you remember?"

"What? Oh, Pastor McKoowey's church you mean? I know you did. I didn't think much of him before. After seeing these other churches, he doesn't seem half bad now."

She then gazed out the kitchen window as she twirled her hair in her fingers. "So you really don't think he's—a little young for being a pastor?"

"Not really. He got in on the ground floor, that's all. At least we're familiar with him, right?"

"Yes, I know...this'll be the last one. We could even go to all three of his churches sometime. That would be fun, checking out what he's got. So how do you think he does it? Did you ask?"

Eddie was finished with dinner by then. He pushed his plate away, looking almost too satisfied. "Oh yeah, he told me. He preaches three times every Sunday—morning, noon, and night. His nighttime session's the one here in Devil's. We should stick with that one to save on gas."

Chapter 12

Eddie and Chantain's plans for the coming Sunday were not led astray. That very Sunday evening, Eddie's little camper car was seen chugging north along the little, two-lane highway headed for their new/old church. Eddie, behind the wheel, turned a quick, smiling glance over to Chantain on the passenger side, holding Doll in her lap. He wasn't the only one happy, for she returned his smile with one of her own. Whatever hidden frustrations they may have felt a week ago were surely gone. For now, anticipation glowed on their faces when they saw their church just ahead.

Eddie put on his blinker, letting off his gas for the next turn when all of the sudden his Pribil turned on its notice to turn too.

Kirpop!

Eddie looked the other way. "Oh, didn't mean to do that. I got the parts…I'm fixing it, I promise."

Chantain didn't say much. She kept smiling directly at the sight of the church, a plain, white building layered in weathered burlap siding just ahead on the left. "That's it, I bet…yeah. There it is. I see a cross."

"Yes, that's the place—I guess…*hmmm*, didn't expect it to look like that…oh well. Welcome back to our new church. Nice to be back."

The building left little to the imagination. It was an oversized shoe box that looked like it belonged in the generic domains of plain-sided bureaucracy. The only things new about the building were the flimsy, hand-painted sign out front, marking the establishment's name and the cross nailed up on the side of the wall, which was built out of recycled boards.

Eddie pulled into the overly-spacious, flat parking lot, but to his surprise, he immediately encountered a maze of potholes, which he wasn't too successful navigating around. After holding on to his steering wheel, he asked "*Hmmm*, you remember this place from before?"

"Not really...you've been here in town longer than I have. What was it?"

"It's the old Devil's Gulch Grange. Pastor McKoowey didn't change much, from what I can tell."

Chantain never looked away. "He didn't have to. Why should he? Kinda looks like a church to me."

Eddie inaudibly replied, "I suppose."

Just as he turned to park, a startling honk heckled him from behind, causing him to look into his rearview mirror. "What the—? It's Al behind us and that stinkin' heifer of his...did you invite them along or something?"

"No. I told Julie all about my ex-pastor—that's all."

"Did you talk about how good he was or something? That's weird."

"Oh, that's right. I did...she mentioned something about wanting to see him for herself sometime."

Eddie blew through his cheeks. "Oh? Well, looks like she's seeing right now...glad they warned us way ahead of time—with their horn."

Chantain twirled a small strand of her hair between her fingers while she looked up to the roof of the car. "That's not nice for you to be calling Julie a heifer. Anyone can see that without saying it, you know."

"What? *Ah* no, I'm talking about Al's car. His Lincoln Zephyr."

"Oh God, are you serious?"

Eddie squinted. "Of course I'm serious."

THE TIME TO TELL

Chantain went on, "All this time, I thought you were talking about Julie when you said that."

Without incident, he parked on the far side of the lot while looking over his shoulder at the same time. "Great, now they want to park by us. I can tell by looking."

Everyone bailed out of their car doors with their children and Bibles in hand.

Eddie quickly hobbled out in front, trying to distance himself, while Al anxiously rushed up from behind.

"Hey, Eddie, wait up...slow down. Hey, you like hearin' stuff 'bout the war, don't ya?"

"How'd you guess? Come on, we're almost late."

"Well, here's a tasty piece-a-gov gossip for ya...heard it on the radio while I was comin' over here."

Eddie stopped to wait for him. "What? Bigger atom bombs being dropped? As if one-a-those wasn't enough."

Al adjusted his black glasses, which now had a piece of white tape holding them together. "No, not at all. You're talkin' old news there. I'm caught up to you now. We can go."

"So, Al, what you hear?"

"After Germany surrendered? The United States recovered flyin' saucer technology from the Nazis."

"Oh, come on, Al. Not on Sunday, okay? By the way, what happened to your glasses? That tape between your eyes bothers me."

"Oh, *uh*, I broke 'em. No, no...this is big news. Just give me a chance to explain."

"Explain what? Your glasses or your crazy story?"

"No, *ho*...no story, we're talkin' facts. I'm layin' it on ya right now...we transported German saucer technology back over here—and get this—they said that soon we'd be able to fly to the *moon* because of it."

Eddie looked straight ahead at the door to the church. "*Psss*—you know, you don't have to make up a bunch of excitement just because I never invited you here this evening."

Al stepped ahead, blocking him from walking into the door of the church, so Eddie stopped. "Now what, Al? Go on inside. I'm barely on time for once."

"I'm serious. You gotta radio 'n that car-a-yours, right? Just turn it on when you get outta church. They'll still be talkin' about it, I'm sure."

"Okay, I'll do it if you go on inside."

Al apparently didn't realize what he was doing, so he stepped aside then funneled in close behind Eddie. As he looked around, he puckered his lips like he was surprised. "Hey, this is the old grange, isn't it?"

"Yes, Al…of course, it is."

Al went on, "Hey, *uh,* Eddie…you're not upset with us comin' to church with you three are ya?"

"What gave you that idea?"

"Oh, I don't know."

Eddie softened up a bit. "I'm not upset…just don't let other people's bull-crap stories pull you around by your ear all the time."

Al chuckled. "Oh, you mean Julie? I thought it be fun to go to another church…especially after hearin' you two were comin' here."

Eddie muttered, "I give up."

All of them walked together down the center aisle before quickly realizing they'd just stepped into a crowded, popular place. The Church of the Baptismal Mission that evening was a full house with just a few seats left.

Eddie was leading the way so he pleasantly suggested with his cane for Al and his family to take a seat ahead of him. As Al and Julie funneled down a row of pews, Eddie asked, "How did you break your glasses, Al? Julie hit you or something?"

"What? Oh, I sat on th' dang things when I got outta th' tub."

Eddie then waited for Chantain to come along, but she was lagging behind with her eyes glued to the front of the church.

THE TIME TO TELL

Eddie traced her view. Her eyes burned a line straight up to the stage and sanctuary where Pastor McKoowey was standing. He wasn't doing anything special at the time except adjusting his tie. Eddie quietly waited for Chantain to step closer so he could invite her down the row, but she kept strolling right past him as if he wasn't there.

Before she got too far, he touched her shoulder. "Something got your attention, dear? We're all sitting back here—in this row." Chantain tried fanning off her unadulterated blush. "Oh, sorry. I wasn't looking where I was going." She then fumbled to sit down as fast as she could beside Julie, who seemed to be caught up looking at Pastor McKoowey in the same mesmerizing way.

Eddie quickly forgot about her petty distractions. He gazed with a little amazement himself—except not at the pastor. He was mesmerized with the warm feelings he saw with all the pleasant people around him. Rightly so, the little house of the holy was packed, wall to wall, with perhaps seventy people or more.

He quickly sat down, where his gaze of praise continued on down to the fine-looking details directly in front of him. On the backs of the pews were small, homemade bulletins, which he and the rest of the parishioners quickly helped themselves to. Eddie muttered to Chantain while looking inside of the flyer. "Well organized. Nice schedule of events this evening, it looks like."

Pastor McKoowey, standing on stage behind his modest podium, looked nothing like his building. He was very attractive, well-mannered, and pleasantly-dressed in a sharp suit of peaceful earth tone colors and a formal tie. His golden-blond hair was a little longer than most.

He looked to be organized above all else. In the last seconds of his preparation, he adjusted his necktie again, then took a sip of water from his glass, sitting on a fold-up tray next to his podium.

He also seemed caring enough to politely wait for the talking to subside from the room before he began to speak. It didn't, however. The clock on the wall that he glanced at, suggested that they were ten minutes past the hour. Still, he stood there blooming like a flower without much intent to interrupt.

His show had to go on, however, so he timidly began to speak with a few patient false starts through the chattering crowd. "Excuse me...excuse me...excuse me...thank you... excuse me...thanks everyone for your wonderful expressions. It's so nice to see such an enthusiastic group mingling in my new church...what am I saying? I mean to say *our* new church."

He continued a little more loudly: "So let us get a move on...*ahem*. Sister Thelma will lead us with our first song in the Filmore's Gospel Songbook, page eighty-eight, titled, 'Onward Christian Soldiers.' We'll sing three verses of the song in remembrance of the World War, which is mostly behind us now. It is time to move on, isn't it? Hopefully we can forget about it now. Wouldn't you all agree?"

Everyone enthusiastically agreed, so he went on, "What a war it was, yes...going on six years...too long...okay now, please welcome Thelma."

A presentable older lady in the front aisle gingerly picked up her songbook. Silently, she thumbed to the proper page then, full of vibrancy, she stood up only to give everyone a mildly surprised show of static electricity on her pink frock and raglan sleeves. A neighboring woman sitting in the pews, apprised her of her problem, so she quickly brushed it down then sashayed to the center front where everyone could see her. As a token of more reverence, she graciously nodded to everyone then tenderly raised her hand to start the song without a piano or organ to accompany her. Everyone joined in, right on time.

THE TIME TO TELL

"Onward, Christian soldiers!
Marching as to war, with the cross of Jesus going on before.
Christ, the royal Master, leads against the foe.
Forward into battle see his banners go.
Onward, Christian soldiers!
Marching as to war, with the cross of Jesus going on before.
Like a mighty army, moves the church of God.
Brothers, we are treading where the saints have trod.
We are not divided, all one body we.
One in hope and doctrine, one in char –i –ty.
Onward, Christian soldiers!
Marching as to war, with the cross of Jesus going on before.
Crowns and thrones may perish, Kingdoms rise and wane,
But the church of Jesus constant will remain.
Gates of hell can never 'gainst that Church prevail.
We have Christ's own promise, and that cannot fail.
Onward, Christian soldiers!
Marching as to war, with the cross of Jesus going on befooooore.

The hymn ended well-timed. Once silence fell, Pastor McKoowey quietly took over. He took a moment to look into his mirror hidden below his podium to check his hair while his audience shuffled around, putting away their hymnals. His fingers seemed to do for a quick, impromptu comb while he waited for everyone's undivided attention. A minor problem quickly arose that he seemed to be expecting. To his minor aggravation, his cowlick at the top of his bangs didn't want to cooperate with the way he wanted to look. He decided to leave it when he noticed two younger ladies up front, sitting together, catching on to his little, inconspicuous problem with flirtatious, covered smiles.

Pleasingly relaxed with himself, he announced, "Onward, Christian soldiers! I like that. Don't you? This can be a part of our topic of discussion tonight. It fits so well with the war."

Almost everyone interacted positively as the pastor paused for a few seconds to let the topic sink in. He then emoted in a convincing way, "I'd like to open the evening with a prayer first...please stand up with me, won't you?"

When everyone did, he stood his six-foot frame up straight and then closed his eyes and bowed his head.

> *"Dear Father, our Lord in heaven. Please hear our prayer.*
> *We all wish to reach out to bring your presence into this holy Church of the Baptismal Mission.*
> *Let all of us here tonight thank you for bringing this World War against evil to its conclusion."*

He paused then continued,

> *"Bring peace and prosperity here across these great lands now that the war is over.*
> *Now I must ask of you, our great Lord, to let us look into the future of our nation.*
> *Let us lead the world into peace. Let us lead by example of goodness.*
> *May every other nation look up to us to seek guidance,*
> *And when—the time to tell has come, we will be ready.*
> *Please embrace this nation with all of its bountiful people—unspoiled.*
> *Amen."*

Everyone replied, "Amen."

He moved on, "Okay, I have two new families—well, let me correct myself...I mean one family has returned to the church, and one family called and told me they were coming for the first time. They are the Coolidge and Johnson families...please stand up so everyone can see you."

The Coolidges and Johnsons nervously stood up, nodded once or twice, and then quickly sat back down. Pastor

THE TIME TO TELL

McKoowey extended his hand out to them with a proud smile. "I have something special to say...Eddie and Chantain Coolidge are blessed from the heavens. Eddie there, well he was kind enough to tell me a little more about themselves before coming back. You see, he and his wife are unable to have a child. From the grace of God, Eddie found the beautiful one you see right there in Chantain's arms. How about that?"

Everyone looked at the child as Pastor McKoowey continued, "Amazing...the child was left for them to take care of. My, my, the Lord works in mysterious ways, doesn't he? Just think everyone, God himself delivered a baby just for them."

The crowd praised in *oohs* and *ahs*, smiling as he continued, "So now I hear they just got word from the authorities that *uh*—excuse me, what's the child's name?"

Eddie spoke up. "Doll's his name."

"Thank you...Doll is now legally theirs everyone...praise the Lord, hallelujah!"

Just then, two ornery-looking young brothers in the far back of the church squirmed and ducked behind the pews giggling. "A dolly boy."

"A Doll—what a name, *hu hu.*"

Nobody looked around, nor could they put their finger on where the subtle comments were coming from. Pastor McKoowey discovered the impertinent behavior rather quickly, so he talked a little more loudly: "The Coolidge family left; now they're back. Why? They saw the light of our true church. They brought someone else with them too."

He went on, "The Johnsons are neighbors of the Coolidges. Bless their hearts for coming along and giving us a try too... we're glad to have you as well." He paused then continued, "Today's been a long day starting this morning. I've been on the run with three churches now. Isn't it great I can serve? The Lord works too hard. Apparently, he wants me to work harder."

He went on, "Getting back to our guests. I hope to have something pleasing for our guests tonight because they recently came from the Church of the Original Testament last week...I'd like to make them feel at home right here with the Bible's *New* Testament that we all share and speak about so much here."

He coughed, then continued, "My topic tonight isn't one I normally talk about, so I don't know how all of you will react. It came from one of my thesis reports in advanced religious studies back in church seminary. Personally, I like it very much—but my professor didn't. I didn't get a good grade on it...anyway, so it goes."

He cleared his voice. "Before I get on with it, please remember...the Bible was written by over two hundred authors on three different continents. It took over fifteen hundred years to write...so if you were waiting for the first copy back then, you'd die waiting for it *hu hu... hu hu.*"

The crowd chuckled as he carried on, "Thanks, I need that...it was one of the hardest, most controversial things I put together in my religious career...I even thought about burning it, if you can imagine. Soooooo..." He pulled his handkerchief out and placed it on his podium. "Like the Old Testament, we have our share of violence and symbolism in the New Testament too. We just don't like to talk about it too much. Maybe a few of you think otherwise."

He breathed deeply while leaning way over onto his podium. While gathering himself up in a lazy look, he carefully put both hands together, resting his fingers over the edge.

Procrastination must have been his partner in speech, for he held himself there with an open mouth, not saying a thing for more than just moments. Unknowingly, he set the stage for his listeners to grow concerned. Most of them even looked as if his lecture might not be a good one.

When he woke up to realize their concerns, he faltered, then grinned and moved on. "It's about the Bible's last book...the book of Revelations."

THE TIME TO TELL

Some of those in his audience snickered very quietly while others shuddered in their shoes without saying anything at all.

At some point, Pastor McKoowey found a way to keep moving on. "The current events apply, even though I wrote it four years ago. The war today—and our great nation. Thank God it's over, no? I'd like to believe the war stamped out evil. The evil tyrant of Germany is finally done. Praise the Lord."

He picked up his pace. "So...it is time for us to move on...are we the chosen nation to do this? Is our nation good or righteous enough to carry on leading the world? I'd like to quote a few words from a simple, wise man looking in on America for this very answer. When he came to our country, he was touched deeply inside. Really, it makes no difference if he was religious or not. It's what he said that counts.

"His name was Alexis de Tocqueville, a French philosopher back in the eighteen hundreds. He once said, and I quote, 'America is *great* because America is *good!* If she ever ceases to be good, she will cease to be great.' This goes along with my talk, which also happens to be the timing of the rapture. Notice how Alexis compares America to a woman and not a man. I know exactly why. So what part does America play in it? When is the rapture coming? I'm sure you all would like to know...well, wouldn't you?"

Everyone in the audience either nodded or muttered, "Yes," so he went on. "Right now, today. America is good as far as I can see—at least for now. I'm not talking about the future yet. We are blessed. Most all nations, with the exception of our enemies of the war, look up to us. We set the example. Are we the richest country too? I say 'yes.'"

He paused, then carried on, "Our money says, 'In God We Trust.' Our song says, 'God Bless America,' doesn't it? We're even thinking about putting the words 'One nation under God' in our Pledge of Allegiance in maybe a year or two. But does all this really make us the chosen country of

God? It helps, but let me explain...these things with 'God' spelled out in them can come back to haunt us. *Why* is very simple. If we don't live up to it now that we've said it, we'll hit the ground hard...we may never get up either...excuse me, I *uh*—"

He felt his temple sweating, so he grabbed his handkerchief and carried on, "Let's look at the people, and let's look at the Bible. The Bible, with all its faults and the faults of the prophets who wrote it, strengthens and reinforces goodness in people. It's the highest degree of moral backbone that any church delivers, is what I'm getting at. I see a lot of it right now—right here in America today. Don't you?"

A few in the audience nodded as he sipped water, carrying on, "Something else...America even has this certain attraction that every other country wants to be a part of. So going back to what Alexis de Tocqueville said, it was good. Remember what he said, 'so long as we stay—good.'

He went on, "Liberty—freedom hasn't condemned us yet. I haven't seen our free market built on greed yet. What about our political system? President Roosevelt? He will be remembered. Our own people have not taken sides against us yet. Well, my good people? What about tomorrow...I mean next year, or next decade, or a half a century from now?"

Nerves suddenly crept up on his neck, daring him to continue. "Okay, here we go...what about the smaller things? Things like sexual promiscuity—divorce is not rampant. What's that mean? It's good. We have to be pressured as people to do good. We still tie ourselves down to higher morals... is there more freedom there? No, not really...is it good?"

His audience nodded while others muttered, "Yes." Some even sat up at the edges of their pews, showing even more interest than before.

Pastor McKoowey mustered a bit of courage to move on. "Yes, I think so...granted, we still smoke cigarettes...the

THE TIME TO TELL

Prohibition of alcohol has ended...what could be worse? I mean, come on....are we the real chosen nation?"

Nobody felt compelled to answer, so he kept his head glued to the cover of his Bible. He looked up and down, feathering the pages as if he were indecisive suddenly.

In the midst of another one of his delays, he looked like he was headed for a train wreck. Wildly so, he looked as though he were ready to turn his own lecture upside down before he'd even got started. He quickly let go a gasp of air, frowning. "*Tah*, I admit...this goes against popular belief, but I-I...I don't know. I wish I could tell if we were...I don't know...I've studied the Bible backward and forward. Maybe someone will know more later."

He then leaned all of his weight up against the podium while tapping his fingers, not wishing to look at anyone. "Telling you otherwise would be a lie...I'll just continue with it...I just want to say that much, okay?"

He then stood up, quickly flipping through his Bible until he pulled out a shoddy piece of paper that appeared to be old and wrinkled. As everyone looked on warily, he laid the wrinkled paper by his Bible on the podium and then proceeded to read it out loud as if he were still at some church school class. "There are no scriptures that actually talk about the word 'America' as God's chosen nation, and I know why. Most of us agree that America plays a significant role in the world. The Bible talks about such a city, which can be implied as a nation. This city, or nation as it implies, is the significant place."

He then stopped reading to interrupt himself. "Some of these things I put together are not the mainstream, okay? So where is the significant place the Bible talks about? Nobody knows?"

He continued off the cuff. "Okay, then, nobody wants to answer. Here's one. I can point to a location in the Bible known as Babylon...the mystery of Babylon. Where is it? Many people associate Babylon as the great place that people look up to. This is all great—big deal right? Babylon is America they're talking about—so what? Maybe it's somewhere else, right?"

Everyone seemed silently glued to the chairs by this time. He looked everyone over nervously and then carried on, "Wrong...this is where it gets bad...this significant place eventually gives itself to crime, filth, lust, greed...many more things I hate to talk about. This significant place falls to its final destruction by God's wrath. This here Bible I have supports this, how?"

He swallowed then wiped his temple with his handkerchief. "God does it through the seven angels, it says...it's right here in the scriptures. This is how it starts, believe it or not. They say that fornication by women will be widespread, as written in the scriptures, and will be the first calling for God's rapture...at least we have a clue. We know the rapture can't happen too quickly. Fornication isn't happening on every street corner, right?"

Some of his audience looked puzzled, so he tried clarifying. "Forni—*uh*—fornication? You understand? That's, you know, *uh* sex between singles, *um*...well, look it up. I need to move on.....*um*, so this is it...the answer...women have to be careful, unlike their boyfriends having fun. Does anyone understand? You know, women make men righteous."

Eddie stood up, waving his cane, shouting, "*He he* yeah! Halleluiah! *Yahahaa*, amen!"

Everyone around him glared as if he smelled. Suddenly Eddie realized he was the one they were looking at, so he sat back down softly. "Oh, sorry...excuse me...excuse me...just getting into it...sorry."

Pastor McKoowey offered him a subtle glare too. "Thank you for your support, Mr. Coolidge, but that won't be necessary...everyone, please turn to Revelation thirteen, seven through ten."

THE TIME TO TELL

Everyone fanned their pages as he started to read: "One of the angels said, 'Saying with a loud voice, Fear God, and give glory to him; for the hour of his judgment is come: and worship him that made heaven, and earth, and the sea, and the fountains of waters. And there followed another angel, saying, Babylon is fallen, that great city, because she made all nations drink of the wine of the wrath of her fornication. And the third angel followed them, saying with a loud voice, If any man worship the beast and his image, and received his mark in his forehead, or in his hand. The same shall drink of the wine of the wrath of God, which is poured out without mixture into the cup of his indignation; and he shall be tormented with fire and brimstone in the presence of the holy angels, and in the presence of the Lamb.'"

He then put his finger on his place before glancing up to continue, "Then the seven angels with their seven plagues poured them down on earth...*ahem*...excuse me...we're going to skip around...go to Revelation sixteen, sixteen through twenty-one, and I quote, 'Then they gathered the kings together to the place that in Hebrew is called Armageddon.'"

He continued reading, "And the seventh angel poured out his vial into the air; and there came a great voice out of the temple of heaven, from the throne, saying, it is done. And there were voices, and thunders, and lightnings; and there was a great earthquake, such as was not since men were upon the earth, so mighty an earthquake, and so great. And the great city was divided into three parts, and the cities of the nation fell and great Babylon came in remembrance before God, to give unto her the cup of the wine of the fierceness of his wrath. And every island fled away, and the mountains were not found. And there fell upon men a great hail out of heaven, every stone about the weight of a talent and men blasphemed God because of the plague of the hail; for the plague thereof was exceeding great.'"

He then glanced up, checking his audience. Even though they showed signs of boredom, he still went on, "Now this is the part that grabs me…it's the women. Women cast away their righteousness of conception—then traded it for pleasure…do you see this sudden change taking place? Do you see it? Yes…it's true…fornication starts this whole mess…you know, sexual consent—with anyone—for fun? Says here…it starts the clock ticking to the end of the world as we know it."

Before he knew it, a number of women in the audience scowled, glanced at eatch other, and then glared back at him.

Pastor McKoowey nervously muttered, "Not good."

He grabbed up his handkerchief, tending to a trickle of sweat that now seemed to be falling from more sides than just his temple. "I know what you're thinking, ladies, don't…it's not that…men are always ready since the dawn of time. It's the women's decision that tips the scales. It-it-it's devastating. It-it eventually brings—a chain reaction of other evils which go along with it…then, you know—it's time to kiss the world good-bye."

Nerves seemed to get the best of him. When he took another sip from his glass, he couldn't stop shaking. Quickly, he put it down so no one would notice. "I…I started this, so I'd like to finish… let's skip forward again to Revelation seventeen, one through five. It says, 'And there came one of the seven angels which had the seven vials, and talked with me, saying unto me, Come hither; I will—shew—unto thee the judgment of the great whore that sitteth upon many waters. With whom the kings of the earth have committed fornication, and the inhabitants of the earth have been made drunk with the wine of her fornication. So he carried me away in the spirit into the wilderness and I saw a *woman* sit upon a scarlet coloured *beast*, full of names of blasphemy, having *seven heads and ten horns.* And the woman was arrayed in purple and scarlet colour, and decked with gold and precious stones and pearls, having a golden cup in her hand full of abominations and filthiness of her fornication. And upon her forehead was a name written, Mystery, Babylon the Great, the Mother of Harlots and Abominations of the Earth."

He paused with his finger in the Bible as he divided up his audience. Disaster had begun to unfold before his very eyes in two ways. The men notably yawned, while the women had become restless. Some of the women were whispering to one another across the aisles, looking more irritated than ever.

Still, he dared to continue. "Y-y-you see? The whore we are talking about? It's symbolism. Symbolism…that's right… the whore is—two things at once: she's the representation of all women literally and she is the mystery nation too. Sorry, but—she is where the hellish beast resides. It resides, waiting to unleash itself in the women's decision and her nation to *conquer everything*."

He clamored for support from his audience, but it didn't happen. If there was any support, nobody smiled to show it. If anything, most of them swayed away as he dragged on. "Please, don't do this to me, ladies. Just calm down—hear me out. I know this sounds like—*uh*. Listen…we're not just talking about a *prostitute*. The lady I'm speaking of is the symbol of the women as a majority. It's about gifting sex without thinking of children. That starts greed, lies, intoxication, thievery, fraud, and indulgence…all of it. Look, I know, men are already there—waiting anxiously. Imagine us both, thinking the same thing. What can this do to all of us? *Poof*—just like that—we're all gone."

Julie Johnson, along with quite a few other ladies, looked downright infuriated. Chantain, however, wasn't affected by the pastor's comments whatsoever. The way she gazed at him up at the podium was the reason. Her eyes must have deafened her ears clear down to the center of her brain. In short, she looked as if she had just been struck in love by the mythological Cupid.

Seemingly, nothing was left of her except for a frozen body, stuck in place on the pews, smiling up a bunch of dreams. She put all of her smiling attention directly toward the man up on the podium, Pastor McKoowey, preaching about women starting a catastrophe to end all else.

Nevertheless, other women made up for her. In growing numbers, they became appalled by his words. Eventually, a good half of all the women had become upset. Wildly, the half who didn't grow upset became upset at those who *did*.

Above the argument of the crowd, Pastor McKoowey's speech looked as if it were going to come to a screeching halt. If he didn't do something quickly, something was going to happen.

Boldly so, he continued where no man should go. "Look here...the purple and scarlet colors decked in gold and precious stones and pearls could be our greed. And the golden cup she holds...that's gold because it's precious what she's drinking. She's drinking the filth of abominations and the filth that later comes along with-with—"

One lady in the far back of the rows tugged on her husband's arm, suggesting she wanted to leave and another woman did the same.

Pastor McKoowey saw them. "Hey, don't go, please...sit down. Come back. At least let me continue."

He continuedYou need to hear this, I think. Oh, the beast? The beast the woman is sitting on? That's consensual without...that's the kings! Thousands—no wait...*millions*... great men following right along like idiots. Why tie the knot? Why settle down? It's free love. Why is this? Because we don't think about children!"

Instantly the crowd drew silent, so Pastor McKoowey slowed down. "Yeah, us men...We don't have the burden of children." His audience resumed its restlessness as he continued again. "No, hear me out. The women become beasts, like

THE TIME TO TELL

the men already are. Women's guidance isn't there anymore. Their partners who—who are—it's all a lopsided mess!"

Two more women dived out the door as he continued, "What about the seven heads? The mystery place of Babylon has mastered the art of lies through her not telling about all these-these *partners*. They never tell...you kidding me? The men don't tell either...*nobody tells*. They all say they they're good as gold! We're all two-faced, but when *she* frees herself, she grows seven heads—meaning—she's ready to do it sevenfold, over and over again. That's why the ancient prophet guys say what they say!"

Another wave of women grabbed their purses and took off out the door. Still, he refused to stop his lecture. "Thu-there's the ten horns...they represent her very defiance. She *horns*, all ten of the commandments back into men's face in defiance...multiple heads, multiple horns, multiple stories, and lies, deceit, greed, and openly doing it too!"

He paused, watching a few more members leave. "That's when the clock starts ticking—to end everything. There it is, folks...staring at us—right between the eyes."

Julie leaned across Al's lap, glaring at Chantain. "Don't ever say anything about our church *again*. You and Eddie can *have* this place." She went on, yanking Al's arm. "Come on. Get up, Al. We're outta here."

Chantain still seemed to be caught up with Pastor McKoowey. In a belated fashion, she shrugged her shoulders, letting Julie and Al step by. "Well, at least he's not some ugly, hairy guy like at some churches I know."

Just then, Julie triggered a huge wave of walkouts. Others gathered their belongings, pulling their spouses out the door.

Pastor McKoowey stopped again. "Please...everyone... stay put. I have just a few more verses. I have to read—"

Quickly, he closed his Bible as he watched another wave of people leaving. Sadness molded the sag of his expression, but by then the damage was done. He folded his handkerchief neatly then wiped the sweat from his face and neck. As he did, he slowed way down, gazing across the pews of his half empty church. "I guess this wasn't the greatest subject to talk about...don't hate me for saying, but let's just say for a moment that Babylon *is* America. There could be good news. The end isn't happening anytime soon, I think. You want to know why? Maybe it doesn't matter."

Nobody answered, so he answered for them. "Because we haven't figured out a good way to stop having kids."

He saw two more couples sneaking toward the exit doors, so he stretched over his podium to speak out to them: "There's more! Revelation seventeen, five...the Prophet John spoke out and said the location of Babylon is a mystery!"

Just as they left, he humbled himself, "Really...it could be any country. If God named a specific place, we would fix it immediately, wouldn't we? That would change prophecy, which would render this here Bible—false."

He lowered his face down in disgrace, continuing, "It's ridiculous to think that a country kill itself off this way. So why didn't the rest of you leave?"

The sparse numbers between the empty pews didn't answer, so he hesitated to ask, "Nobody wants to talk? Well, I'll just finish up by disagreeing with my talk then. Sounds like I should after tonight."

Suddenly, he tried to get the attention of two others ducking out the doors. "I know you can hear me out there! Revelation twenty-two, eighteen through twenty-one...God warns me that if I add or take away anything in Revelation, God will strike me down."

He went on yelling toward the doors, "Hey! I'm still here, aren't I? Where you going? I could've said the whore was sitting on top of the beast—or another woman! I didn't!"

One old woman still seated was hunching over in the pews. Several seconds later, she woke up to a gasp, "Oh my

THE TIME TO TELL

God....Preacher! Cryin' out loud! That'd be worse! What if *that* came true?"

Pastor McKoowey half-heartedly snickered. "Oh, don't believe me. It's just a wild comment...just letting my anger do the talking, that's all."

The old lady whistled in relief. "Holy be-crickets...thank God you made that one up. Never heard of that one before."

Pastor McKoowey slowly grabbed his old, wrinkled paper off the top of his Bible and then wadded it up and threw it in the garbage basket nearby. "No more, never again...I go and lose my attendance with one speech...I knew it...never should've talked about it."

He looked back at his remaining audience, realizing they were looking back at him in stark silence. He straightened up then carefully placed his hands back on his podium. "I-I guess I should be pleased with the few of you. What am I trying to say? I don't know what I'm saying...oh well, that's it for the evening."

Quickly, he turned to the side of his podium. "Excuse me, Sister Thelma? There won't be a closing hymn tonight. I've done enough damage. I'll say the closing prayer, and we can just let everyone go."

Sister Thelma jumped up. "Wait...I'm sure the rest of us would like to sing. What do you say, everyone?"

A very old man with suspenders and a belt buckled just below his chest stood up the best he could. As he gained his balance with his handmade cane, he raised his hand as high as he could, which was barely above his shoulders.

Pastor McKoowey pointed to him. "Yes, Clarence? You can put your hand down."

"Wait a second...I want to hear more about the men going to pot because-a-women! What's 'n your hymn f'r that?"

Clarence's wife bickered while tugging on his arm. "Sit down, honey. There's been enough commotion f'r one night. Y'r makin' it worse."

Pastor McKoowey sent a sorry smile of regret to everyone, then thought a while before finally saying, "Sure…why not… Sister Thelma, please lead the rest of us with the hymn 'Hear Your Country's Call.' It's on page one ninety-one."

He then looked at the Clarence still wobbling in his stance. "Sorry, Clarence…my talk wasn't about any of this happening here or now. It was about the future. You don't have to worry about a thing."

Clarence looked disappointed. He caught his balance as he sat back down. "What about the hymn? Is it about women going to pot in th' future then?"

Everyone chuckled, as did Pastor McKoowey. "I'm amazed at just how old you are, and you're still going…how long you two been together if you don't mind me asking?"

Clarence looked down, scratching his cheek pondering, while his wife answered, "It'll be seventy years in a couple months."

Pastor McKoowey raised an eyebrow. "Wow…aw, well, I'm sorry to let you down on the hymn, Clarence. It's not what you're thinking. It's just a patriotic song because we won the war, that's all. We'll make it short and sing one verse. Okay…shall we, everybody?"

Pastor McKoowey stepped back over to his podium. "I'll make it a short prayer, and then you can all go home and have a good evening."

Everyone bowed their heads as he prayed:

> "Dear Heavenly Father. Please forgive all those who have left us tonight.
> Amen."

Everyone gathered their belongings and headed for the door when Pastor McKoowey spoke above the noise of footsteps and mutters: "Eddie…Chantain…don't forget to see me before you leave."

THE TIME TO TELL

Chantain whipped her hair around, facing Eddie. "What's this about?"

"*Um*...I have a feeling it's about those donations we still owe."

As Pastor McKoowey stepped down from his podium and onto the floor, Eddie came up to him, shaking his hand. "You haven't lost it. That was one of the best speeches I heard you do."

Pastor McKoowey looked around, making sure nobody heard. "You think so? Oh, by the way, about you standing up and yelling 'amen'...thanks for the support, but don't speak out in our church that way. Pretty soon, everyone will do it if I don't say something."

Eddie apologized as Chantain strolled up from behind, holding Doll and looking the pastor over. "Hello, remember me?"

Pastor McKoowey nodded and guided them both to a door just to the side of the room. "Please come into my office over here. I have some things we need to talk about. Shall we?"

He offered them a couple of comfortable chairs in front of his blonde oak desk and then stepped over to his matching cabinet to pull out a file with the Coolidges' names written on its face. As he sat down in his swivel oak chair behind his desk, he took his time looking through their file. "Yes, I remember you...Chantain's your name...such a beautiful name. How did your parent's come up with that name?"

As Chantain played with her hair, she looked up to the ceiling. "It's a long story, actually...before I was born, my mother toasted a glass of champagne to the divorce of my father on New Year's Eve one night when she met another man and—"

Eddie jumped. "I don't think our pastor needs all that kind of detail. The beverage champagne is good enough, honey...sorry Pastor McKoowey."

Pastor McKoowey smiled and continued looking through their file. "That's all right, Eddie...I hear all sorts of stories in my line of work, believe me…okay…so…these are your church records…*hmmm*, let me see here. What can I find?"

By then, Chantain had put Doll down on the floor to wander around and get into things, which he promptly did. He started looking for things he couldn't reach, which happened to be everything on Pastor McKoowey's fine desk. The first things attracting him were the shiniest, prettiest things. One of these just happened to be the beautiful, brass crucifix. Doll wanted it but realized everyone was watching him.

Decisively, he turned away to find something else to play with, which was hard for Doll. Time and again, he sneaked a peek at the statue when nobody else was looking. As Pastor McKoowey observed Doll more than once, he put an end to his efforts by coaxing him closer so that he could hand it to him. However, before he did, he turned to Chantain. "Is it okay that he plays with this?"

Chantain was already smiling. "Oh yes…he won't drop it or hurt it. It's okay."

Before Doll actually accepted it, he turned to Eddie as if needing to know it was okay with him as well. Eddie smiled. "Go ahead…and Doll, don't drop it…it's called 'expensive,' okay?"

Doll gently took it and backed away as he muttered, "Ex-pen-sive?"

Pastor McKoowey noted, "My, he's dexterous. Look, he's trying to pick at Jesus's hands…maybe one of his parents was an artist."

It didn't take long for Doll to notice that something wasn't quite normal with the shiny golden man he was holding. The exemplary figure of Jesus was hung up on iron spikes. Not only that, he was in pain and still alive. Doll then looked out the window, as if he remembered seeing the same empty, life-sized cross that Pastor McKoowey put up outside on the wall, seemingly ready for another body.

Doll's little voice, gasped, "*Ahh no no…noooo.*"

THE TIME TO TELL

Eddie leaned over from his chair. "It's okay, Doll. Not real. No, just a statue."

Doll kept trying to delicately pick out the little spikes out of Jesus's hands and feet, but he couldn't. Shortly after, he walked back over to where Pastor McKoowey was sitting, then, surprisingly, he tried to give it back to him. "Ouchy... take back...it hurts him."

Pastor McKoowey smirked, "Wow. The little guy talks. How old is he?"

Chantain quickly answered, "A little over a year."

The pastor reached over and touched the crucifix hands and feet, saying in a cute, baby-talk voice, "Yay'uh...that's *uh* ouchy alwight. You see dis wittle man in thu wittle cwoss? He's speciawwl. You wanna be speciawwl too? Now you go pway over dere while I twalk to Mommy and Daddy."

Doll looked puzzled—even a little scared. He gave the pastor back his statue in a hurry and scuttled over to hide behind Eddie.

As Pastor McKoowey carefully put the little statue away, he seemed puzzled. "I didn't do anything wrong, did I?"

Eddie picked Doll up. "Oh no, not at all. He just doesn't understand what you said. Just talk normal to him, and he'll be fine with you after that."

Pastor McKoowey rocked back in his chair as if he'd just been insulted. "Really now. I'll remember that...so anyway, I'm sure you know why I called you in."

Eddie flagged his hand. "Yes, I know...it's about donations, and I'm sorry. Chantain and I thought it would be okay if we just came a couple weeks for now. Our money situation isn't all that good with my disability and all."

Pastor McKoowey looked as if he wasn't buying his story, so Eddie turned to Chantain. "Chantain, you do all the bills. Tell him what's going on."

She just looked at her nails in the painstaking silence that suddenly crept in. She whipped her blonde hair in the direction of Pastor McKoowey, then carved a good look at him from top to bottom. "I guess it's true, but he's kind of wrong...we can afford it."

Eddie put Doll back down on the floor. "Afford it? You're the one that keeps saying we're flapjack broke all the time."

Pastor McKoowey stuck his pencil out between them. "That's okay, really. We really don't need to discuss your finances. That's not what I called you in here for anyway...it is God and his finances"

Eddie sat comfortably back in his chair. "What did you call us in here for then?"

As Pastor McKoowey thumbed through their file more intently, he said with regret,, "*Hmmm*, from what I can tell, neither of you have paid a single cent in tithing, even before you left. *Hmmm,* what was that? A couple years ago?"

He then plopped their file on his desk like it was rubbish. While leaning back in his chair, he kept looking at their file as if he'd like to throw it all the way into his trash can. "Why, look, Mr. and Mrs. Coolidge...Chantain's baptism ceremony, the lease on this new church, my time...it all counts. It's all generously given by God...I mean *whew*...if you had a hard spell, I could see beyond all this, but look at what God's given you. I mean *look*...can you see your miracle? The child. He's a living, breathing *child*...a child you might not have been able to have."

Doll scratched his nose, quietly correcting, "Not 'child'...'Doll.'"

Pastor McKoowey talked right over him: "Miracles happen, believe it or not...money is—how can I say it? It's the gift to keep blessings happening. I hate to explain this, Eddie, but—I wish I could—I can't see this going the same way after you coming back. I mean, you're really nice people, but—I'm sure there are other churches out there if that's what you need to do."

Chantain popped up. "*Wait.* Maybe I can volunteer some work around here as...I'm really good for doing anything."

THE TIME TO TELL

Pastor McKoowey tapped his fingers on their file, thinking impressively fast. "Anything? What about the child? The child needs to be cared for somewhere else while you work, I would imagine."

Doll stomped his foot. "It's *Doll*."

In the midst of everyone ignoring Doll, Eddie turned to Chantain with a long look on his face. "No, no, Chantain. I never have had you work a day of your life. It's not right for… you know."

Pastor McKoowey smiled, reaching into his drawer where he swapped his pencil for a pen. He then pulled out a clipboard with a sheet of paper on it. "Yes, I think so. Chantain helping out sounds like a great idea. Her work sounds very good. Child or not, it's right if you don't mind my two cents. Let me see now, what kind of numbers can I come up with…*hmmm*, and you can find a sitter for the child?"

Doll raised his voice. "My name's *Doll*."

Pastor McKoowey heard him this time, but his reaction was similar to smelling something terribly bad. He slowly lifted his pen off his scratch paper, looking at Doll.

Eddie patted Doll on the head. "Oh, sorry…you called him 'child.' Just call him 'Doll,' and he won't bother you."

Pastor McKoowey was surprised. "You're kidding me, right? Okay, Doll. I won't call you anything else now, but don't yell please."

By then, Doll's tiny adventure of scouting around the office was over. He simply crawled up on Chantain's lap where he played with the buttons on her blouse. She slowly brushed back his hair to keep him quiet. In the course of doing so, she spotted Doll's strange black tattoo, which startled her enough to gasp.

Pastor McKoowey lifted his pen. Without actually looking at anyone in particular, he asked, "Something wrong, Chantain?"

Chantain looked as guilty as hiding a little toy devil in her pocket. She patted Doll's hair back down then looked over to Eddie, who had seen what she did. He was fretting more about what she might say or do next. It could have been anyone's guess the way she stewed in her chair about it.

Eddie soon tried to help her along with a couple of subtle hand signals, but that just made her decide all the more quickly. Within the bat of an eye, she snapped out of her frightened state to boldly answer, "Oh, it's nothing...say, *uh*...I was wondering about a part of your talk a little bit ago...You know, your speech."

Pastor McKoowey kept his eyes on his writing. "Oh? What's that? Did you like it?"

"Yes, I *did*...you said something about one of the angels that came down in the last days and spoke with a loud voice, saying if any man were to worship the beast and receive his mark on his hand—or in his head—"

Pastor McKoowey curiously stopped writing, but didn't look up. "Yes. It was the forehead, not the head. What would you like to know?"

"Oh, you mentioned something awful about it...*um*, what kind of—mark is it?"

Eddie could have shot flames from his eyes he glared at her so hard. Unfortunately, Pastor McKoowey looked up just in time to catch this too. He put his pen down and looked at both of them suspiciously. Nothing too revealing came to him, so he leaned back in his chair, pondering the need to try to read their minds.

One thing was clear. Nobody could have read the depth of distress he thought he saw in Eddie. Nevertheless, he answered her question: "Strange you mentioned that, Chantain...you picked up on it...I was going to explain Revelation thirteen through eighteen, which covers the mark of the beast...it's six hundred threescore and six—but everyone started leaving. I cut it short because of it."

Eddie quickly leaned forward in his chair. "It's nothing more than a mark or symbol of six-six-six, isn't it?"

Pastor McKoowey strained a bit then shook his head. "No, it's not...everyone thinks it's the three sixes that's evil. Crazy, isn't it?" He took a deep breath as he went on, "Now that you brought it up, I wish I would've explained my view."

Chantain and Eddie both asked, "Can you tell us?"

"Yes, we'd like to hear about it."

"Well, all right...how can I say this? You see, it's much more complicated than that...it's not a mark at all, as most believe."

Chantain spoke anxiously, "What? That's silly."

Pastor McKoowey sighed. "No, it's not silly at all...the mark in the forehead is a representation of all those evil thoughts in his or her head. The mark in the hand is a representation of actually doing those thoughts too."

As an example, the pastor pointed to his own forehead and then showed his hands and flipped his idea another way. "You know...forehead is thinking....hands are doing...thinking and then—doing. That's the mark the prophet is talking about—"

Chantain tried negating. "But what about the thinking of six-six-six and doing six-six-six? What if it's not what you're saying at all? What if it's—six letters, like—"

"Hush, Chantain, that's enough. Let the man talk."

Pastor McKoowey gave them a peculiar look. "Six letters? I never heard that one before. You're misinterpreting what my thesis was all about...it's about the end of the world." Pastor McKoowey then methodically raised two sets of fingers in front of him, quoting, "The so-called 'six-six-six' is the profound number of times the majority of people of Babylon have committed their heinous acts. They have to do them over and over and over again, like I said in my talk. So many times it's not twice, not triple...it's at least six times, or threefold...that's what the prophet's interpretation of the 'six-six-six' is. There's no such thing as the symbol of the six-six-six…there is no symbol at all. There never was…everyone obsessed with horror just thinks that."

Eddie's mouth dropped. "No kidding? How do you know for sure?"

Pastor McKoowey picked up his Bible off his desk. "Everyone thought the world was flat too…hard to buy my idea because nobody's ever unraveled one of the Devil's biggest secrets of all time. Here, take my Bible a second…I'll show you why I'm talking about just plain old *Halloween*…Go ahead. Pick it up."

Eddie took it and asked, "Have you thought about…I mean, why?"

"You really want to know? I should have gotten an *A* on my thesis so don't get me started. Everyone grades mainstream with a little bit of their bias mixed up with it. Throw my idea out the window if you want, but remember…Satan's in on it too. He's in on it—more than you know."

Eddie asked, "More than I know? What do you mean?"

"Satan himself has the power to get into the minds of our teachers. Another crazy idea you think? Maybe I shouldn't tell any more."

Chantain inched closer to his desk. "No, go on. I want to hear. You sound so…"

"Convincing? It's true…the idea of Satan's symbol is engrained in everyone's heads so much, it's hard to wipe it out of anyone's heads. Go ahead, Eddie. Open my Bible and turn to Revelation thirteen…back up and start with fifteen… it's all there."

Eddie read out loud, "Fifteen. And he had power to give life unto the image of the beast, that the image of the beast should both speak and cause that as many as would not worship the image of the beast should be killed—"

Pastor McKoowey conclusively posed as he smiled. "You see? That's when the beasts reach equal portion in numbers...a critical mass must to be reached...okay now go on."

Eddie continued, "Sixteen. And he causeth all, both small and great, rich and poor, free and bond, to receive a mark in their right hand, or in their foreheads—"

Pastor McKoowey went on, "That means richer or for poorer, free or for bonded...it means basically everyone. Notice the mark being in the *right* hand? That's not with the *right* hand as it says. 'Right' meaning, they have the *right* to choose by hand of doing it. Notice the mark *in* their foreheads, not *on* their foreheads. It says *in* their foreheads because that's where everyone points with their fingers to think. Now, skip to verse eighteen and read the rest of it."

Eddie went on, "Eighteen. Here is wisdom. Let him that hath understanding count the number of a man; and his number is six hundred three score and six."

Pastor McKoowey then carried on with his business of writing again. "There...you see? Two things. It says 'score'... you know...like keeping track? Secondly, it means being guilty, not twofold, not threefold, but many times more.... say, sixfold many times more."

"But—"

"I know what you're thinking, Eddie...it's the Prophet John's wild writing style that gets everyone. It's not only John's unorthodox writing that got me; it was my professor in my advanced religious studies that gave me the terrible grade."

Eddie shook his head, confused. "What's was wrong with your professor? Did he hate you or something? I mean maybe this is dead-on correct."

Pastor McKoowey put his pen down then folded his hands together. He sobered up, looking straight over to Chantain, then dragged his same jaded look to Eddie. "You saw how damning my talk was, didn't you? The women?"

Eddie nodded. "Yes, so who was he?"

"My professor was one of the biggest figures with a monster agenda and an ego bigger than you, me, all men put together as far as I'm concerned."

"His name? I'm curious."

The pastor picked up his pen and started writing again. "You don't give up, do you, Eddie? It makes no difference the name…but my professor was a woman." He then passed a glance to Chantain. "Sorry, Chantain, that's just the way I feel after uncovering all that I did."

Chantain shrugged her shoulders. "Oh, it doesn't bother me. All your stuff, though. It sounds so—so believable."

As the pastor kept writing, he nodded. "*Hu*…I can't find a church out there that knows how to read John's work in Revelations yet. Lots of people think they know…some think he wrote his work in a cave. Rumors claim there were delusionary gases in there. He had to eat and make fires, remember. Who knows what kind of fungus or leaves he ate or burned too."

As he put their file back away, he turned back to them, looking bothered. "So that's it. Just leave it alone. Everyone else does." He then grabbed up his clipboard. "Now where were we? Oh yes…my tithing is usually seven percent of your pay in the church, but you don't make anything, sooooo—I figure about ten hours of Chantain's time per week should do."

Chantain quickly replied, "Are you sure that would cover it? I mean, I don't want to take advantage of you or anything."

Eddie fell back in his chair as if he were in shock.

Pastor McKoowey smiled. "Oh no, you're not taking advantage of me at all. You're helping me help God…how about starting as soon as you can?"

Chantain took her time thinking for a moment like a cool, coy shark. She bit on her pinky nail, surprising Eddie even. Finally, she rambunctiously blurted, "*Um*, okay. I can start tomorrow afternoon."

THE TIME TO TELL

Pastor McKoowey smiled. "Mondays are actually clean-up days...that'll be good." Before anything else was said, he quickly stood, congratulating them and shaking their hands, even though Eddie was much less enthused.

He showed them to the door and led them outside. As he said his final good-byes, the pastor's attention was caught by the unsightly Pribil. As he stood there wondering what it was, the all-too-familiar Pribiling look crept upon on his face. In the midst of his struggle for something to say, Chantain didn't stick around to hear. She immediately darted out into the parking lot, distancing herself.

Eddie, on the other hand, cordially stopped, bidding his good-byes when the pastor's Pribiling question inevitably surfaced. "What in God's righteous name is that?"

Chantain whipped back around from the middle of the parking lot. "Eddie! Pick up Doll and hurry it up, will you?"

Eddie quickly responded, "Excuse me, Pastor. I'll tell you some other time! She really wants to go. I-I'd better go."

After they loaded up, Chantain looked as if her migraine was giving her trouble again. "How embarrassing. Am I really riding in this thing, or am I just dreaming?"

"No dreams, honey. You're riding in it right now."

"Thanks for telling. Do us a favor and try to take off without making any blasted noise."

Eddie reached for the keys. "I'll try—just stop complaining."

After several cranks on the starter, the Pribiling problem struck again before they even moved.

Kirpop!

Chantain covered her face while Eddie drove away slowly. After getting some distance from the church, Chantain broke out, "Can't you fix this thing? I've got to drive it for church work now."

"I'm going to fix it before. I promise—okay?"

Silence prevailed inside the car for a good while, when Eddie decided that he was going to make a move for the radio knob, which caused Chantain to spit out, "Can you just leave it off? I'm getting a headache."

Eddie turned it on anyway. "Never know, it might help your headache…did you hear what Al said?"

"Who cares what he said. It's about the war again. I already know."

"I didn't think you heard him. He said we confiscated flying saucers from Germany."

Chantain looked at Eddie for the first time since leaving the church. "What?"

"Yeah, Al said he heard it on the radio today. Something about us going to the moon with them or something crazy like that."

Chantain lifted her head off her hand. "Really? You just drive…it's getting dark. I'll find it…*hmmm*, looking…*hmmm*, nothing but static, I guess."

Just then a scratchy signal came in.

"*—and we thank the general for his comments just a while ago…J-Devil bringing you up-to-date news as we hear it…here's more news from our exclusive edition of—Wars of the World—*"

Eddie pushed her hand off the radio knob. "Right there, leave it alone."

Chantain dropped back in her seat. "Oh, God…more war crap?"

"Hush, maybe it's something different this time. Listen."

"*—controversy is sprouting from President Harry Truman's speech last August sixth. According to some critics here in America, they now widely believe we were in an arms race with the Germans to produce the first atomic energy. To back it up, President Truman was quoted as saying that the Germans were working feverishly to find a*

THE TIME TO TELL

way to add atomic energy to the other engines of war with which they hoped to enslave the world.

"More accurate critics are now saying that it's not true...I repeat—not true. We now have unconfirmed reports through private findings that the Germans were working on other technological advancements—so advanced that they go beyond the US in aeronautical rocketry and spacecraft technology.

"Already, the US and Russia leaked out evidence of superior rockets and jet aircraft development called the Me 262[30], and the Horton Ho 229[31]. They also leaked out their directional-guided missile capabilities, also known as the V-1 and V-2 rockets[32], but where was their atomic bomb capabilities the President spoke about?

"We are currently waiting to hear more...further questions are creating the buzz: If the Germans were not pursuing atomic bombs as previously thought, then just what were they pursuing that was so advanced? To keep things quiet, the US government has been standing by its story that they were, in fact, pursuing technologies of mass destruction to enslave and massacre the world.

"Here's what to look for next time on JDVL's Wars of the World to support more of the story... a little talk from a brilliant man in the field of rocketry will be coming to you. Aeronautical engineer Roy Fedden has been contacted and has been asked to elaborate on these ideas if he can, so stay tuned."

Click.

Chantain turned off the radio, while tending to Doll as Eddie kept driving. The farther he drove, the more discouraged he looked. "*Shhhhh*, I can't believe it...they didn't find

---

[30] Me 262, also known as "Messerchmitt Schwale" or "Swallow," was the world's first operational jet fighter craft.
[31] Horton Ho 229 was a prototype, designed by Reimair and Walter Horton toward the end of World War II. The first all-continuous, winged craft once described as the "first stealth bomber." The first US B-2 or "Stealth Bomber" built in the early 1980s looks very similar.
[32] V-1 rocket, or *flying bomb* or *Buzz bomb*, was the first Vergeltungswaffen series of bomb or guided missile type of its kind. The V-2 rocket was the world's first long-range, combat-ballistic missile and, arguably, the first human artifact to enter space.

any flying saucers...Al is so full of crap sometimes. I don't know about him."

Chantain thought for a moment. "No, Al was right if that's what he said...rockets and spacecrafts are flying saucers anyway...aren't they?"

"Don't be so gullible, Chantain...flying saucers have never been found. They're supposed to spin and float...jets and rockets don't do that. They blast into space, for Christ sake."

"Then how do flying saucers get into space?"

Eddie looked back and forth at the road and Chantain. "What? You can't be that naïve, can you?"

"No, I guess not. I knew flying saucers were from outer space all along...maybe I was testing you. They're rockets, like I thought."

Eddie stopped holding his breath. "You already believe they exist."

Chantain reached for her pack of cigarettes. She lit up one as fast as she could. She was annoyed until she took her first drag. After calming down, she looked at the tip of her cigarette, softly speaking through her smoke. "Doesn't everybody believe in saucers? You're the weirdo, not me."

"Thanks...that's just great. So I'm the weirdo?"

A piece of cigarette ash fell on top of Doll's head, which didn't seem to bother her much. She took another drag then blew it off with a good dose of smoke. "Are you really going to fix the backfire on this thing because I don't want to be driving back and forth to church sounding like a popcorn machine—"

"I said I would, damn it—leave something alone for once...it'll be fixed—tomorrow, for crying out loud."

Chapter 13

The very next day during the warm afternoon, Eddie lived up to his word, fixing the Pribil. The long, drawn-out problem, which kept backfiring on him time and time again, got the attention it needed right out in front of the Coolidge house.

At least there were two positives going for such an anomaly of a car just then. First, someone, namely Eddie, believed Pribil's were fixable. Second, as uncommon as she was, common music played from her radio as she was being worked on.

Eddie heard a particular tune he liked, so he turned up the volume as he worked on the motor. Only in a Pribil was this possible. The radio was right next to him and the motor was between the seats under a carpet-layered cover. The speaker inside was loud enough to fill the air outside the camper car's open doors and all around the Coolidge parking lot.

One of Bing Crosby's songs was playing with an unexpected, whistling accompaniment. This was Eddie's whistling. He tried staying in tune, but he should have been left whistling to the birds standing on top of the roof.

The birds perched on top of the Pribil were blackbirds. They remained undetected, for the most part. Between the swaying and rocking Eddie caused from his wrenching and jerking, they were content enough to pick at their feathers and scratch their wings. They also seemed comfortable enough to gaze down at the ground at yet another animal.

This being Major, coincidentally wagged his tail to the motion of Eddie's two legs hanging out the passenger door.

And so the music continued with the irrational mix of birds, dog, and a struggling backyard mechanic whistling sporadically to Pribiling car tunes. That was almost all of the entertainment for the entire repair team, except for one more. One other member was just as much into it as the rest of them, and that was Doll. He was hidden further inside the back of the Pribil, given the unspoken role as young apprentice.

For the most part, he simply sat on a small stool while playing with his spinning top by the bed, with a magazine next to him. Every so often he took his eyes off his business just to watch Eddie. So far, nothing exciting had happened, so he went about his job of putting different spins on his top. He had one hand gripped tightly on the toy's handle as he spun the rest of it faster and faster with his other hand. His little game resembled that of a basketball player spinning a ball on his finger. The only difference was that he had a good hold of his spinner by the handle so it wouldn't fall away.

As a result of his spinning, many shapes caught his eye. On one side were the ten little Indians, and on the other were several he couldn't quite make out. He flip-flopped, comparing, but he wasn't done just yet. He compared a third version by holding the top up to compare the fictitious flying saucer on the cover of the science fiction magazine next to him. Every so often he took his eyes off the cover of the magazine while spinning his top for the simple sake of amusement. He seemed entertained by the changes that took place on the face of the disc-shaped top itself. Safe to say, he was not lost by comparison in the coordination of shapes and colors—with ideas.

Eddie didn't see or care too deeply about what Doll was doing as he worked on his Pribil. He did hear his giggling, however, which caused him to poke his head out of the

THE TIME TO TELL

engine bay to jokingly ask, "Hey, Mr. Gemini Lee...what's so funny?"

Doll stopped giggling then extended his bottom lip. "Not Gemin-leo...it's Doll."

"Oh, it's Doll, *huh?* Well, *Doll,* hand me that thing over there."

Eddie pointed, while blindly shaking his finger. "You see it right there where I'm pointing? It's a wrench...do Daddy a favor and give it here, will you?"

Doll cordially stepped over to where the wrench was, picked it up, and handed it over without a problem. After that, he stepped back to his stool and continued with what he was doing.

Suddenly, Eddied popped up with a surprise. "*Awh,* spider! It's got me! It's got meeee!" There he was shaking a mess of black wires in his hand, which actually resembled an awfully big, mutlilegged-looking thing, dripping of gunk. To make matters worse, he even put on a semiconvincing show of panic.

Doll saw it all from the front row of his stool. He gasped and ditched for cover, as if perhaps he thought it really *was* some kind of monster spider.

Eddie keeled over across the car seat. "*Ha ha ha...*it's just a distributor cap and wires *ha ha ha.* Mechanics call this the octopus—*ha ha,* boy that was good...*oh ho...*man. It's really called an octopus. No spiders around here, *ha ha.*"

Eddie wiggled it some more, pressing it against his neck for a ridiculous reprise. "*Awh,* it's got my neck! It's alive! Help me, Doll!"

Doll poked his head out from where he was hiding under the bed, not buying it again. He too laughed. Excitement overwhelmed him so much he rushed over to see the fascinating prank up close.

Eddie held up. "This is what's causing that 'pop' sound down the road, understand? You know, *pop!*"

Doll touched it before backing his hand away. After rubbing his fingers, he got his firsthand experience of what grease was. No problem with that apparently. He proceeded with wiping the sticky black stuff on his shirt, but before he got too far, Eddie caught him. "Oh no-no-no…don't do that. It doesn't come off your clothes. That's called grease, *yuck, cockahh*, nasty…here, let me wipe it off for you."

Eddie cleaned his hand off as Doll looked at the distributor cap lying on the floorboard. "*Kirpop!*"

"Yeah…*kirpop!* We won't be doing that no more. You got it, boy. Maybe you'll be a mechanic someday. What do you think about that?"

Doll inquisitively pronounced, "Mech—mechinananic? *Kirpop* mechanic."

Eddie quickly made time by putting on new parts where the old ones had been. He then wiped his hands and fingers, showing them all to Doll. "*Welp*, all done now."

Suddenly, the screen door to their home slammed shut with a loud crack, catching the Pribiling repair team's undivided attention. Chantain stepped outside in somewhat of a hurry. In fact, by the time Eddie and Doll looked up, she had already made it down the stairs and was headed their way.

Eddie slid out of the Pribil and started hobbling toward her while wiping his hands, talking to himself: "What is she in such a hurry for?"

She walked right past him and on over to the Pribil. "Are the keys in it?"

"Well, aren't you going to ask if I fixed it first?"

Chantain abruptly stopped at the sight of the birds on top of the Pribil. She tried scaring them off with her irritating hand gestures, but they hardly looked convinced enough to even flutter their wings. "*Shoo*, get outta here, you nasty things…Eddie, make them go away."

Pique got the best of her, so she turned to Eddie standing by Doll a few feet back. "No…why should I ask if you fixed it? You've been out here all day, haven't you?"

THE TIME TO TELL

She then glared back at the birds. "What are those ugly blackbirds doing on the car besides crapping out my garden berries?"

"Oh, they've been hanging out with me, the dog, and Doll...they'll fly away when you start up. Don't worry."

Chantain glanced around. "You must have been feeding them my bird seed to keep them hanging around that way. Where'd you put my bag of seed?"

Eddie shrugged his shoulders with one hand in his pocket. "No. They're just hanging out...your bag of bird seed's still on the porch where you left it a week ago."

He pointed with his cane. "See it? Right there—the rats got into it and just about ate it all up."

Chantain opened the driver's door, looking over her shoulder. "You and Doll have to cook your own supper...I'm late for John's."

"John's? Oh, that's right. You threw me there. It's Pastor McKoowey. 'Work,' you mean."

She slammed the door so hard the birds finally got the picture. As she fumbled with the keys to start the car, she yelled out her window, "Smells like grease in here. Better not get any on my new dress. So nice of you to say good-bye."

"Oh, say good-bye to Mommy, Doll."

"'Bye!"

As they watched her speed off without a single backfire, Eddie looked down at Doll, who seemed a little sad and out of place after she left. At about the same time, Major came over to sit by the two of them, waiting for a small pat on his head. He nudged Doll's hand before Doll got the hint. As he gave the dog a pet, he grabbed Eddie's finger. "No, *kirpop*...she come back soon?"

"Yeah, no pop...yeah, real soon, I hope."

Eddie seemed mildly surprised to feel Doll hanging onto his finger. He looked down to Doll, softening up a sad smile. "Well? The old car will run better now, eh, Doll? Now if we can just get the driver to run better too."

As Chantain raced down the street, she caught the Johnsons off guard on their knees pulling weeds. In the last seconds Julie poked her nose and hands above her white fence. "What's going on 'round here? Do I need to hear better or is that bubble thing of Eddie's not backfirin' anymore?"

Al squinted for a better look. "No...no, Eddie musta fixed it. He's pretty good at that stuff if things is goin' good. How 'bout that? He found parts f'r that thing."

Julie looked at Al as if he didn't know what he was talking about. "They make parts for it?"

"Yeah, reckon so."

Eddie stood in the same place back at his home for several moments after Chantain left. After realizing time was wasting, he picked up his deflated smile. "I'm going, Doll. Want something to eat, big boy?"

Doll sagged and sat on the ground and picked meaninglessly at his spinning top with his fingernail.

Eddie couldn't hide his fatherly concern. "Okay, then, I know...you can stay outside a while longer...you gotta eat more, so think about it while I'm in the house...you wanna be a big man someday, don't you?"

Doll pretended not to hear, so Eddie slowly hobbled up to the porch. Concerned still, he turned back to Doll before going inside. "Don't venture out too far, okay? Hey now, keep your chin up. She hasn't been gone that long yet." Doll nodded while trying to push away some of the sadness he was stuck with.

Eddie quickly stepped inside his home and stopped, as if he was expecting something. Nothing came to greet him inside except the quietness of the living room with all the shades pulled down. Slowly, he opened them up one at a time. Loneliness must have prematurely crept inside the door with him, for he looked to be feeling his arms too insecurely. Curiously, he invited the feeling of it as he stood still, taking in the sole sense of quietness that must have taken control all over his home.

Other small noises he might not have been aware of slowly revealed themselves. They let him know he wasn't alone. He turned to his grandfather clock for a moment, just to listen to it tick among other things. A glance carried him across the living room through the partial light cast through the windows, shedding rays on the empty furnishings from corner to corner. For a moment, he looked as if he wanted to speak, but surely he awakened from the fact that the emptiness he saw couldn't speak back.

He broke out of his loneliness suddenly, like the snap of a finger. He looked around as if all he needed to do was create a little self-made company to share his quiet home. There in plain sight before him, he found it. He hobbled over, turned on his cabinet radio and made his way into to the kitchen as he had planned.

The sink was his first stop, offering him the convenience of a quick hand-washing. Seconds later, he looked toward the living room, waiting for the radio to come on, which it finally did. Its old, glass bubble tubes had to warm up enough to function correctly.

The song that came on appeared to improve his mood immensely. He waltzed with the music as he reached for a towel to dry his hands. Playfully, he opened his icebox to take a look at what was inside. It didn't offer much in the way of new food. Blocking his view was a couple bottles of milk, some condiments in glass jars, a block of butter on a chipped saucer, raw bacon wrapped in paper, and a ceramic bowl of eggs.

He reached through the whole mess in front of the icebox and into the far back where he gently pulled out two uncovered beehive bowls filled with leftovers. His appetite slowed down a little when he saw one bowl had cold fried chicken chill-dried together. A quick glance into the other bowl told a similar story. In it was macaroni salad, dried out on top with a thin crust, which he touched before muttering, "*Hmmm,* supper is served I guess."

It was what it was, so he took his food, along with his failing appetite, to the table. With utensils he pulled from a drawer, he made the best of it by stirring a little life back into the macaroni salad first.

All the while, the radio's song ended as a news flash came on:

"—*JDVL is bringing you more up-to-date news regarding the war in Germany. More details were released regarding advanced technologies found since their surrender.*

"*New problems appear to be breaking out by the day. It's now confirmed that the United States and Russia are in a political fist fight as to which country gets to take the technology away from occupied Germany. A technological tragedy appears to be in the making.*

"*According to both countries and maybe the British too, they will end up with just some or part of the Germans' entire top secret developments. Questions now remain about just how useful Germany's secret weaponry and advanced aeronautical rocket developments can be, if such technology can be salvaged separately—*"

Eddie listened intently as he took his loaded plate of leftovers into the living room. As he sat down next to the radio, he glanced through the windows, noticing that Doll was fine. One surprising thing seemed to pass him by, that was Doll was playing with the blackbirds as he kept listening in on the radio story.

"—*even though the United States government hasn't admitted much, it did acknowledge the fact that it was satisfied with the unusual case of dividing up the advanced equipment and materials so far.*

"*US officials have admitted that they did manage to seize the lion's share of the technologies and materials. An unconfirmed*

THE TIME TO TELL

source also said that those who were involved in the actual removal of the seized equipment and materials witnessed much more than just advanced rocketry. Integral parts to them seemed to be missing, they say. Get this, folks…one source, acting anonymously, claimed to have actually seen parts and pieces of flying disc spacecraft and complete saucer-type spacecraft that looked like they could fly."

Eddie nearly choked on his bite of chicken. He wiped his mouth, put down his plate, then turned up the radio.

"—the unconfirmed witness explained that he helped transport actual saucers, which were heavily concealed in tarps encased in wooden-framed bins so that their shapes were disguised. As far as he knew, massive transports are underway and back to the United States, where he presumes they will undergo further studies.

"Military confiscation efforts also wound up with the lion's share of some of the highly sought-after German engineering scientists too. Some of these scientists captured were in underground facilities in undisclosed areas where the United States got to them first. The scientists voluntarily surrendered and mentioned that they even expected to be discovered, they say.

"And now—here's a nationwide story as promised, which we linked to our exclusive news brought to you by—Wars of the World. World famous aeronautical engineer, Roy Fedden, associated with Cosmos Engineering from Bristol, made a visit to the United States on a separate account. Sir Roy Fedden, Chief of the Technical Mission to Germany for the Ministry of Aircraft Production, was asked to comment on wild, fictitious claims of advanced developments in warfare with the Germans. Here's his quote:

"'I have seen enough of their designs and production plans to realize that if they (the Germans) had managed to prolong the war some months longer, we would have been confronted with a set of entirely new and deadly developments in air warfare.'

"Mr. Fedden also made unconfirmed comments afterward that the only craft that could approach the capabilities attributed to flying

saucers were those being designed by the Germans toward the end of the war. Mr. Fedden also added that the Germans were working on a number of very unusual aeronautical projects, though he did not elaborate on his statement."

Eddie muttered, "Wow, I don't believe it."

"—big questions remain now. Can we make use of these new discoveries and—just what were those other unusual projects Mr. Fedden failed to elaborate on? Those are two big questions as we continue to bring you more up-to-date news from JDVL—"

Click.
Eddie turned the radio off, muttering in shock, "Wow, Al was right…that four-eyed, son of a—wait. I've gotta call my dad."

He grabbed his cane, fumbling into the kitchen for the phone, where he fumbled with the receiver and rotor. After dialing, he stared at the wall. "Son of a—pick up someone…hello operator? Put me through to Las Vegas, Nevada. Cambrin and Gayla Coolidge, please."

Someone answered.
Gayla: "Hello, Coolidge residence. This is Gayla."
Eddie: "Hello, Mom? This is Eddie."
Gayla: "My, oh my, Eddieeee. How are you, son?"
Eddie: "I'm fine. Good to hear from you. Sorry for cutting you short, but let me speak to Dad, please."
Gayla: "Slow down. I haven't heard you in so long… what's wrong?"
Eddie: "Nothing's wrong. I just heard something on the radio, and I want to see if Dad's heard anything down at the Army Air Corps Gunnery School.[33] He's still one of the janitors, isn't he?"

---

[33] The Army Air Corps Gunnery School was a US government facility and gunnery school, formerly the McCarran Field, north of Las Vegas. It later became the Nellis Air Force Base.

THE TIME TO TELL

Gayla: "Yes, I don't think I could ever talk Cambrin into transferring. Hold on, I'll go get him."

Cambrin: "Hello, Son. How's that new kid-a-yours?"

Eddie: "Doll's fine...how're things in Las Vegas over there?"

Cambrin: "Things are going downhill here ever since hotel investors started building the Vegas Strip three or four years ago. Gambling's becoming a legitimate business here. Did you know that?"

Eddie: "Gambling? What's next?"

Cambrin: "What's next? Haven't you heard? Gangsters coming in here by the shitloads...you heard-a-that hood named... what name was it...can't think...oh, you heard 'o Bugsy Siegel?"

Eddie: "No...never heard of him. Say, Dad. I was wondering. Can you tell me—?"

Cambrin: "Oh well, it doesn't matter who Bugsy is...whoever allowed gambling here should be taken out the back and shot. You watch. They're going to allow gambling everywhere before we know it."

Eddie: "That can happen? *Um*, Dad. Gambling's not what I called about—"

Cambrin: "It's not that...it's all the other shit that goes with it...prostitution, booze, gangsters, you name it, gambling has it...people pissing on the streets—cats and dogs together, shitt'n on fire hydrants."

Eddie: "Maybe that's why the government let it go out there to Nevada then?"

Cambrin: "I don't trust the government Commies. May as well throw us to the dogs or leave us for dead. May as well gamble in California—Florida. Hell, why not the whole damn country. Rat-infested places are gonna spread like the plague. I mean it."

Eddie: "You're funny. It'll never be that way. You know that...speaking of going to the dogs, your job's hanging in there, I take?"

Cambrin: "How'd you guess? There's talk about the Gunnery School being closed September, next month."

Eddie: "Oh, I didn't mean it that way."

Cambrin: "That's all right...they said I might be outta work temporarily, but they're going to try and keep me working on odd jobs. Maybe one 'o the caretakers. What y' calling about?"

Eddie: "You're not going to stay out there if there's no work are you? Desert heat's gettin' to you—I can tell. You should come back here."

Cambrin: "Me and your mom are going to stick it out here...they're changing stuff so darn fast, there's bound to be something for me to do...don't you worry about me."

Eddie: "*Hmmm*, you think so? Say, Dad, I was calling because—"

Cambrin: "I know so. First it was the Gunner School... then it's the Army Air Force Training Command. Wars never end, you know."

Eddie: "Oh, Dad, you make it sound like you're in war central, for crying out loud."

Cambrin: "No...they should call this place the United States War Center. Something like 'at."

Eddie: "The US Warfare Center? What do you think about calling it that next?"

Cambrin: "No—oh God no...the war's supposed to be over—remember? No, no, no. Now they're talking about naming the place in honor of some bozo. One of the names mentioned was some guy named Nellis."

Eddie: "Who's that? Is he some war general or something?"

Cambrin: "No. Just some lieutenant killed somewhere last year in combat I hear. Nobody big."

Eddie: "Hey, Dad, I hate to bother you, but—"

Cambrin: "I know, I know. You never want to hear my problems. What's on your mind?"

THE TIME TO TELL

Eddie: "Don't take this silly, okay? I just heard that that the United States confiscated German jets, *um*, rockets and—*uh*—you know—*um*—sort of like, *uh*, flying saucers. *Is it true?*"

Cambrin: "*Ho* there. Wait a minute. What did you say?"

Eddie: "You heard me."

Cambrin: "Flyyying—saauucers? What in the...? Is your wife—wait a minute...Chantain getting to you again with her stupid science-fiction trash again?"

Eddie: "No! I mean no. You heard me. I figured you working around the army base over there in Nevada, you might've heard something. You didn't—hear anything did you?"

Cambrin: "*Ha*! Can't say that I have...you did say—*flying saucers?* We're not talking about coffee cups on small, flat plates are we?"

Eddie: "No...it was on the radio...real flying disc gyros. One guy even said he saw our military bringing them to the US from Germany for more studies—then maybe go to the moon with them."

Cambrin: "What? Christ sakes. Is this my son talking? Who heard—I mean who saw this?"

Eddie: "I don't know...they couldn't say the names. Wait, they talked about some guy named Roy Fedden. Some space pro in the field of flying saucers. He said that if any country could do it, it would be the Germans."

Cambrin: "Good God, I am talking to my son...a flying saucer pro? Chantain's been leaving her fiction books around. I just know it. Damn her."

Eddie: "No, she hasn't. What about Roy Fedden then?"

Cambrin: "Roy Fedden. *Hmmm*, yeah I've heard-a-him, I guess. Don't know about saucer pro, but he is a top-notch guy. He designed aircraft engines and things. Roy never said your gyros existed, did he?"

Eddie: "Well—no. Maybe not but—"

Cambrin: "Listen—if there was something out there, believe me, I would've heard it by now. You're just getting caught up in all the hype. If it's not those books, then it's that brand-new news people are getting all caught up with…shit's all over ever since after the war."

Eddie: "You think so? I never heard it."

Cambrin: "That's all it is, just space crap. I'm tellin' you flat out."

Eddie: "Okay, I know what you're saying. My neighbor's into it, I think. *Hmmm,* but what if—"

Cambrin: "This flying saucer stuff is starting to get bad, I'm telling you. It's been buzzing around here even. They're trading junk news after the war is what it is. Everyone's bored."

Eddie: "But—"

Cambrin: "There's no 'buts' about it…you're the butt for believing it. Now how's that kid-a-your's doing? Talk about something productive—normal, for Pete's sake."

Eddie: "*Ah,* okay…he's fine. We just got word from the constable. We get to keep him."

Cambrin: "Keep him? *Ha haaa,* that's wonderful!"

Eddie: "Yeah, I thought that too…just need to let the kid thing sink in with Chantain, that's all."

Cambrin: "Hey, give me a sec will you, Eddie?"

Eddie: "Sure, go on. I can hold."

Cambrin: "Hey, Gayla, honey! *Whoooaaaa….*our son gets to keep the kid!"

Eddie: "Okay, Dad. I don't want to go overboard with it."

Cambrin: "Wait a minute…what about that gold-looking metal thing that was on his ankle. Did you ever find out what it was made of? I remember you being real interested about it."

Eddie: "No…never did. It's pretty hard, though. I know that."

Cambrin: "Well—tell you what. We have lab techs here thinking they're whiz kids. Send me a sample of it. Maybe I can find out what it's made of…see if it's worth anything or not."

Eddie: "You'd do that?"

Cambrin: "Sure, I would. That's what I'm for."

Eddie: "Hey, great. I know gold's in it. I've gotta piece of the chain I can send you. It's all the same-looking stuff."

Cambrin: "That'll do. When do Grandma and Grandpa get to have Doll for a week? Summertime would be best, you know."

Eddie: "Just as soon as he's old enough to ship out on a train and enjoy you two…how's that?"

Cambrin: "I won't hold my breath then. Before you go hangin' up the phone, don't start believing too much about your saucer stuff."

Eddie: "Okay."

Cambrin: "I did hear about your rocket story, though."

Eddie: "You did?"

Cambrin: "Yeah, that much I can give ya. They're keeping it pretty hush-hush around here."

Eddie: "What did you hear, or can you tell me?"

Cambrin: "Suppose it can't hurt. I think I heard them say they were V-1s—and V-2s I heard too. From the sounds of it, sounds like we don't have anything like 'em here in the country."

Eddie: "That's right. Yeah—that's what they said. You think we could eventually go to the moon on them?"

Cambrin: "Haven't seen 'em yet. Of course—anything's possible. Moon's not that far away, come to think. Heard about the gyro stuff during the war, so I'll give you that too."

Eddie: "I remember you telling me, what did you say they were?"

Cambrin: "Don't go repeating, but us guys called them 'Fuckin' Foo Fighters.' Just a bunch of German propaganda was all it was."

Eddie: "You don't have to cuss about it, Dad. I was just—"

Cambrin: "No, that's the name they gave them. Of course, they had to clean it up a little when the name got to the States...shit was designed to scare us. Still is, I guess. You be better off ignoring what I said."

Eddie: "Okay, I'll do that then...rockets was all it is...say, I left Doll outside, so it's been good talking to you."

Cambrin: "Okay, son. Call again sometime. Stay in touch and send me a sample-a-that metal. I've been thinking of ways to keep my job alive."

Eddie: "Okay, 'bye for now."

Cambrin: "'Bye."

Eddie uneasily looked at the receiver before hanging it up. Slowly, he came around to believing in what his father said. Soon enough, he went from spooked to being a believer of spoof. Nonchalantly, he shrugged his shoulders while looking around in the kitchen, mumbling, "The chain... let me see now. Where'd I put it?" He rummaged around in the kitchen drawer before he found the link he had severed from Doll's ankle that one evening. He then wrapped up his little piece of curiosity into a nice envelope.

A funny thing happened as he passed by the living room windows in search of a stamp, however. As he hobbled by the screen door, he got his first solid glimpse of Doll playing with the blackbirds outside. *Again*, he shrugged off Doll's close encounters of the feathered kind. Other matters took priority, so he quickly carried out his business of sealing up his envelope and stamping it for three cents.

Shortly thereafter, he hobbled out onto the porch with every intention of mailing the letter, but as he hobbled to the edge of the porch, he came to a sudden halt. Doll's unique display of feathered friends, perching on his head and shoulders, struck Eddie. Finding no immediate answer for it, he quickly looked around the porch and saw Major. He was pushing himself up against the wall, looking at Doll without answers too.

THE TIME TO TELL

Eddie tried again, squaring up his eyes at the most unusual scene. Sure enough, Doll was still sitting in the middle of the driveway with his arms straight out, giggling at the birds standing all over him as if he were a live scarecrow. Doll had them at the tips of his hands, both shoulders, and arms. He even had two, fluttering for better positions, on the top of his head.

Eddie stumbled off his porch, waving his cane. "*Shoo...shoo*...go on, get outta here! Pesky things, go on, *git!*"

The birds flew off together, but they didn't scare very far. They flew off to the nearest tree, bobbing their beaks with little cause for alarm. Doll stood up, scowling as Eddie approached him with an alarmed look on his face.

"How'd you get them to fly up to you like that?" Eddie went on, "Forget it. Don't answer...gosh, we better get that bird poop off your shoulders before Chantain sees it. She'll have a field day. Bad enough she doesn't wash your clothes...guess I'm gonna be the one that cleans you all the time. Now she's got the excuse she's been waiting for—she's working."

He finished up with Doll and stuck the letter to his father in the mailbox out by the street. On his way back down the driveway, he picked up Doll and continued hobbling back inside. "Boy, you're just full of surprises. What's getting into you? You don't smell like bird food or anything. Is it that new stinky smell I smell? How long since you had a bath, kid? Mommy knows that answer, I bet. It's last week or never."

They stayed inside for the rest of the afternoon while the great outdoors slowly gave up the day. House lights were eventually seen coming on as the sun settled in the east. The distant tree line surrounding the Coolidge place began to turn distinctive shades of gray until nothing but silhouettes remained. The sky too began to change, quickly giving up its bright blues for mystical hues of yellow, orange, and red.

The evening seemed quiet outside while Doll soaked up fun in the bathtub just below the window's view. Eddie hobbled through the kitchen and up close to one of the backyard windows just to gaze at the same colorful cape in the sky that was in Doll's bathroom window. He took the time to recognize peaceful, pleasant things just then, like the scenery. Besides the sunset being a little more beautiful than usual, he stood there long enough to notice yet another change. Darkness came all too quickly, drawing its imaginary black curtain down behind the window he was looking out of.

Like the coming of night, Eddie's face drew darker as well. Sadly so, he still stood there, looking through the dark window where he could no longer see. He moved shortly thereafter, but not far. He gave the clock on the wall a troubled glance. He was bothered deeply by the time. He began to move slowly across the floor. As he hobbled to the center of his home, he swung another uneasy glance around throughout his empty home, turning on no more lights than he needed.

Suddenly, he remembered Doll, who was still in the bathtub alone, being a little too quiet. When he hobbled through the hall to the open bathroom door, he noticed that Doll had dozed off in the shallow water. Eddie spent time gently picking him up, drying him off, and then carrying him to bed to cap the boy's evening. It wasn't quite that simple for him. Sadness rocked him around every corner of his newly appointed, fatherly deeds he thought were for the mother.

He refused to go to bed himself, even though he made small preparations to end his day. Slowly, he began to turn off the lights throughout the house—one by one. Then, while dragging his feet into the kitchen, he thought about sitting at the table. For the moment he stared at the last light still on, above the kitchen table. It hung so low with its heavy shade that it was hard to see the grief that grew upon his shadowy face. He looked at the table as if he were carrying an overloaded, sad hunch. While deflating his breath, he sat down. A soft wisp blew from his cheeks, sounding more like sudden depression than fatigue.

Besides Chantain being gone, his worries seemed less than numerous on the flip side. Yes, she was out of the house, but she was volunteering her time and doing them a favor in tithing. They had left a church he didn't like, and now they were going back to their old church, which he was clearly happy about. Doll was already walking around and smart as a whip. He was even theirs to keep. The house they rented seemed nice enough. Their corny car was even fixed. None of this, however, seemed to be enough to keep him from the sudden bout of emotion he was experiencing.

Somehow, he looked as though he were still chasing the dream of a comfortable life. Time would tell. He let his eyes drift, looking at things throughout the kitchen. He looked at the brass handle of his cane and at his old dog, Major, on his bed in the corner fast asleep. Nothing seemed to change.

What got him the most was the stark silence that surrounded him, with only the ticking of the clock on the wall. He jumped, glancing up quickly at the time it displayed, which didn't register with him immediately. He looked at the clock again, reading the time—which changed everything. Suddenly, he snapped back. Looking straight across the kitchen, he said, "Ten o'clock."

To escape his disheartening thoughts for just a moment, he yawned. Feeling somewhat better, he smacked his lips and looked for something else to sidetrack his mind while he waited for Chantain to come home.

A small paperback book on the table left by Chatain caught his eye. He grabbed it up, flipping it over a time or two for a quick examination. He quickly discovered it was one of her science fiction books. The thing glaring right at him on the cover was hard to miss. It was an awful picture, casting a vivid, colorful scene of numerous flying saucer machines walking on earth, blowing up everything in sight. After getting his eyeful of the artist's shocking rendition of the story, he didn't show much feeling for it.

He fanned the pages to feel the book, killing more time than interest. This went by quickly, so he opened it up to learn a little bit more of what her book was about, without reading the story. He muttered, "Published in 1900? Martians back then? *Pssss*, no way." He shook his exhausted face, spinning the book back onto the table where it twirled to a stop at the edge.

Indeed, as time kept ticking away, he realized he was wasting more of it. Something became clear to him while snooping around in Chantain's stuff as he waited for her—he was becoming more jaded. A few more minutes swept by. He was so bored that Chantain's book, once again, drew his attention. Gravity seemed to hold it there half way off the table quite nicely. While barely moving a muscle, he huffed to himself, using his cane to shove it back to safety. Once he was done, he did little more than grow sleepier by the minute.

Minutes turned into an hour or more before a twin glimmer of headlights made their way through the pitch-black forest outside. The recognizable flickers were short of solid beams, which meant that they belonged only to one vehicle for that neck of the woods. All of her dim six volts barely stayed on as they rose between the trees with the moon in the distance. As they came closer, the moon revealed more of a silvery body of a car that didn't quite look like a car. No doubt who was coming. Chantain was making good use of her newly tuned engine as she crept back toward the home ever so slowly, without a single misfire.

First, the mailboxes out in the street lit up as she turned quietly into the driveway. Just as quietly, she came to a stop and shut her lights off. While being quieter still, she stepped out of the Pribil, revealing only her silhouette as she tiptoed across the driveway and onto the porch.

As she slipped into the home, she tiptoed softly toward the kitchen where she saw that the dim light of the kitchen table was still on. As she peeked in through the kitchen doorway, the first thing that caught her eye was Eddie sitting up in his chair, hands crossed on his cane against his chest, fast asleep.

His being there was not what Chantain wanted to see. She leaned on the edge of the doorway, letting her posture fill with irritation, ready to pop. Suddenly, it did. Without notice, she stomped across the floor in her heels. To bugle her presence even more, she slammed kitchen cabinet doors with no rhyme or reason as to what she was looking for. She saw a coffee cup in the last cabinet, so she grabbed the one in back, clanking it against the others as she pulled it out.

Eddie jumped up as if he dreamed, or even saw a terribly rude ghost. "*AaaaAAaahahahaaaa!*"

He twitched like a poor soul on death row being charged in an electric chair. Between Chantain's cabinets banging and his bad dreams, his mind was left in worse shape than cell divisions. His head-splitting episode didn't end right there. He jolted in his chair as if he tried to shake off some residual pain left inside him somewhere.

He didn't seem to know which of his two worlds to go to apparently. For the moment, he was back in his home, but when he noticed Chantain barreling through the dark kitchen, he must have thought it was something beast-like. He tried to grab for protection, but nothing was there. Finally, the poor man realized what he was doing and spewed a gust of air, much like a tire blowing out.

Only afterward did he politely come around. "Oh, it's you...my God...I think I was having an awful dream."

Chantain smirked. "Oh? What was it?"

"I don't know…these-these…these aliens ending the world or something…wow, *whew*…I guess it was that."

Chantain stopped to pour herself coffee as she listened to his comments from the dark side of the room. She paused, holding up her cup. At that moment, she realized her science fiction book under the light of the table had been moved. "So…you've been checking out my book, I see. Funny—our radio station uses almost the same name."

"What? Oh, 'War of the Worlds?' I know…funny having complete different names by moving one letter."

"The book title isn't what's funny. The war stuff on the radio is…besides, I've read better books before."

"Oh, yes….yes, well, *uh*, I guess that would explain my dream I woke up from."

Chantain already had a cigarette lit, puffing her first smoke as Eddie tried peering through the light of the table. All he could see was her shadowy face, glowing with cigarette embers in the middle of it.

He fumbled a bit before politely pulling a chair out for her. "Here, sit down…tell me about your work at church."

Chantain took her time. While picking up her coffee cup from the counter, she swaggered over to the kitchen table. Hesitation crossed her mind as she lowered herself into the table's light to sit across from him.

Eddie didn't quite know what to think of the guilty look on her face. "Well? It's past eleven o'clock, so, *um*—what happened?"

"Oh, John's got so much to do it's not even funny. He's way behind."

Eddie grabbed up his cane and held it close. "Oh, John? You mean Pastor McKoowey, don't you?"

Chantain tapped her ashes in the tray before looking away. "Pastor, McKoowey, John…whatever. He's all the same guy."

"Are you all right? I mean, you sound like you're in a bad mood."

THE TIME TO TELL

"I'm fine. I just didn't think you'd be waiting up for me—reading my books."

Eddie looked at her book on the table. "Oh, I didn't read a thing, just looked at the cover...I was *um*, just starting to get a little worried about you was all. I guess I fell asleep after that."

Chantain softened up somewhat. "Well, there is some more news now that you mentioned...John needs assistance at all three of his churches now. He decided after tonight that he would like to hire me."

"Oh...hire you?"

"Yeah, two fifty an hour, ten hours a week at each church."

"What? That's three churches times ten. That's...wait... that's thirty hours a week. Did you tell him 'No?' I mean, I don't think we can handle it...you know...working...working wife."

Chantain dumped her ashes, blowing smoke straight up. "Not exactly. Why would I do that? It's forty hours a week."

Eddie scooted his chair closer to the table. "Say forty hours? Where'd that come from? We need to talk some more. Don't you—"

"That's what we're doing, aren't we?" She took a drag of her cigarette, blowing smoke straight into his face. "The extra ten hours involves helping him with books and running around."

"What about...what about Doll? I thought—"

Suddenly, she sweetened up. "Doll? *Um*, look Eddie. You know you wanted to buy this house from the landlord. Listen to me...if I saved my money in a separate house account, we could do it someday."

"Separate account?"

"Yes, my account. This way we know it gets saved and not spent."

"Am I hearing right? Your bank account? Since when do we divide things?"

Chantain rolled her eyes. "Since your money's not going anywhere, that's when...your money can take care of the rest of the bills."

Eddie rubbed his eyes, refocusing through the light. "Excuse me? *Ho...whew*...honey, look what you're saying...I mean, I may have gotten this wrong but—"

"I did Eddie. What do you want me to do? Take charity from our church?"

"No, God no...I'll get a job if that's what you think we need. With my pension, plus whatever I can make on the side. Sounds good, don't you think?"

Chantain toyed with her cigarette. "Wouldn't want it on my conscience."

"Wow...this is too fast for me...I mean this could kill my idea of...*ah*, who cares?"

"Cares what?"

Eddie plopped his hand down. "I can't believe what you're saying...you got any other surprises? Go on...love to hear more."

"Kill what? Finish what you were going to say."

"Okayyy...this kills my idea of a—of a, you know, kids and all."

Chantain put her coffee cup and cigarette down and grabbed his hand from across the table. Eddie thought he saw fluttering signals of love in her eyes. Passionately, she brought her face closer into the light of the table, moistening her red lipstick with the tip of her tongue while being careful not to lick it off. "I know how much you want this house, Eddie. We'll never be able to afford it with your money alone. Don't worry. I can still manage the finances and bills if you like...I'll do my job, and you can watch Doll."

Eddie stroked his jaw, stewing. "I don't know...I wanted Doll for you, so we can grow together."

"Grow? What are you talking about?"

"How can you, you know...see him or help him grow up—if you're not there?" He went on, "I mean, I feel like something's missing between us...I'll never figure it out if you don't do what mothers do."

Chantain came closer. "I still have Doll. Don't you understand? It's the moneyyy...you'll do a great job with him. He needs a father figure too—to grow up with and be a bigger man someday...I mean it's not all about the woman." She clenched his hands tightly as he looked into her beautiful eyes.

"I know, it's about me and a mother...the house means a lot, I have to say. *Hmmm...whew...*I can't believe this."

"Believe it, Eddie."

"This can't work. I mean it's not—"

"Of course, it will, Eddie, honey. Just believe in yourself."

Eddie tried looking away, but couldn't. "If we bought the house afterward, like in a year—would you quit?"

"Of course, I would...you know me."

"*Ah*, don't do this to me, Chantain."

"Come on...you know it'll work."

"I—I know what you're talking about...the money...we can get somewhere maybe."

Chantain quickly got up from the table. "Good. I knew you'd see it my way. I'm going to bed. It's getting late." Without another word, she headed straight out of the kitchen, down the dark hall to their bedroom.

Eddie didn't feel like leaving the table, however. He stayed there for a while, looking and wondering what he had gotten himself into. He picked up her cigarette from the ashtray, which was still lit, and gently put it out. After clearing away her coffee cup, he fell back down into his chair, folding his hands into a dismal knot. Sleeping was the furthest thing from his mind. Slowly, he dropped his forehead onto his thumbs, weeping.

Chapter 14

Almost a week had passed. A brand-new Sunday was upon them, intended for perhaps meaningful discoveries as they approached Pastor McKoowey's establishment and parked the car. Their heads were on swivels as they walked up together to the doors, wide open with an invitation to come on inside. As they stepped in, they couldn't help but stand there with the expectations of what they already knew. After last week's seemingly antic performance by Pastor McKoowey, the psychological damage was still quite clear to see. No doubt about it—they were gazing across pews at a half full house.

Chantain's jaw dropped as she walked through the congregational. "I don't believe it…the people. Where did they go?"

Eddie walked up beside her, gripping his cane. He tapped a little sarcasm all the way down to the bottom of his cane as he rustled with coins in his pocket. "What? You were expecting them to return? Wow…I guess I could say I'm glad…*real* glad I don't have to fight for a place to sit."

Further inside the church, behind closed doors of his office was Pastor McKoowey himself, sitting at his desk and looking like a psychological mess. Carefully, he went over his notes for that day's sermon, but none of it pleased him. Nerves and jitters quickly caused him to shove all of his material aside. As he covered his face, he strained to say in a muffled voice, "Oh God. What's next?"

THE TIME TO TELL

Just then, Sister Thelma opened his door, fanning the sadness away from her face. "Pastor McKoowey, you still have about half who returned. Did you hear me?" She stopped abruptly. "Pastor McKoowey...did you hear what I said?"

Pastor McKoowey looked up. "What?"

Sister Thelma walked back to the door, peeking outside again. "Yes, that's right...I'm surprised any of them came back after last week. Have you been praying because—you got a second chance. I say don't blow it this time."

Pastor McKoowey quickly gathered his notes scattered across his desk. "Blow it? Who said I blew it? Well, well, well... straighten my necktie a little bit here...there...how's my hair?"

Sister Thelma smirked. "You look like you always do, John. You should know that."

He slowly stood up with a sorry face. "Okay, then...I guess I'm ready to show my stuff." He headed to the door opening it. "After you, Sis. Let's get on with the show."

As he took his first step out into the room where everyone was standing, a proud and renewed Pastor McKoowey emerged. He nodded, waved, and greeted almost everyone in his path. Just like a mayor in a town hall, he shook hands practically all the way up to his podium where he then gazed at all his people with smiling faces.

The crowd wasn't quite as jubilant as he was. To garner the pastor's attention among those standing, one might have had to stand out from the crowd. Chantain did precisely that. With her high heels tipping up higher than ever, she held her waving hand up high, waving almost too much.

Pastor McKoowey kindly noted her audacious presence with a return wave of excitement of his own. He blushed and grinned as well, but shortly after, he became all business. Like last time, he went through a few quick, routine preparations: adjusting his tie, running his fingers back in his hair, and then there was his mirror below his podium where he took a quick peek.

As the crowd seated themselves, Chantain was among one of the last to be seated when she quietly slipped up with a dainty whisper, "He likes me."

Eddie leaned his ear over as he sat Doll down between them. "What? You talking to me?"

"Oh no, excuse me. I mean John. He likes to see."

"What? I thought you said—what do you mean?"

"You know—he likes to see some of his people. They're back."

Eddie raised his eyebrow. "I bet he does. Sometimes some of that stuff's good for people to hear. I don't care what anybody thinks."

Chantain stopped smiling. "You kidding me? That speech of his had a man's ego written on it so bad they choked... they're just coming back because they like him, and he's different. That's all."

Eddie brushed his face as if he were bamboozled. "I see. So is that why you want to work for him?"

She stopped in the middle of fluffing her hair. "No... people change. You should know that better than anyone."

"Ouch...well I guess I *do* know better than anyone. Maybe you should try a little bit of that change-o-range-o yourself?"

Chantain pulled out her lipstick and mirror, whispering to herself, "I don't change for nobody."

Pastor McKoowey started off by silently quieting the crowd with his hands. Nobody seemed to be paying attention to him, so he loosened his necktie just a bit to speak loudly. "I am so surprised...hey, I'm surprised to see some of you back tonight. Was there a barbeque last Sunday night? If there was, I didn't get invited to it. Maybe that's what it was?"

Nobody said anything before settling down completely to ready themselves for the pastor's prayer. After his word and the thoughtfulness of a fanciful hymn, he got his notes together and systematically laid them out on top of his podium. They were not wrinkled this time. They looked well

THE TIME TO TELL

prepared. "Tonight's lesson, I promise you, won't be quite as intimidating as last week's...it's a story at the beginning...the beginning of the Bible this time. It's a story in which I have less interpretation. But that doesn't mean I won't tell you what I think."

He continued, "It's a famous story you all know about. What's that? It's about Adam and Eve...The Book of Genesis...the so-called beginning of *mankind*. Let's turn to chapter two of Genesis please."

The soft noise of shuffling pages spread throughout the church. Chantain was one of many who opened her Bible right along with the rest of them. She yawned then whispered toward Eddie, "Oh, I forgot. Your father called the other night."

Eddie shut his Bible glaring. "The other night? I've been waiting all week for his phone call, Chantain."

"Don't be so bothered. It was two days ago...you act like everything's such a big deal."

Eddie opened his Bible up again. As the pastor kept lecturing, he whispered indiscreetly, "What did he say? Wait, I gotta better idea. Just talk to me about it next week, okay?"

Chantain ticked her tongue, closing her Bible. "Real funny...he said you should call, and that's all he said. It's not like he ever has anything important to say."

"Important? What about *your* father? He's a dad missing in action. How could he say anything at all?"

"Don't even go there, Eddie...he doesn't talk because he left me and my mother a long time ago."

"That's not what he said."

"Since when did my dad talk to you? Back when they invented the wheel?"

"Not exactly...back when we first met—if you can remember that far."

Chantain huffed, "Whatever he said is a lie...I told you that. He wouldn't be interested in talking to you."

"Oh, I don't know. Maybe he wanted to warn me."

"I said don't go there...what did he say then? Can't be that bad."

"Hopefully not...he said your mother left him, and I would be next."

"And you believed it?"

"Why don't you tell me? Hard to believe him anyway since you two always mess with each other all the time."

"That's not true...he messes with me...besides, we're friends now."

"So you can't admit it. I see."

"Admit? Admit what?"

Eddie glared. "That all three of you mess with each other since your mother supposedly took off."

"Look, you have no idea...best mind your own business if you know what I mean...none of it matters a hill-a-beans now."

"Oh, it doesn't matter? It does too, honey."

"Okay, pop shot...why would it matter to you?"

"Good gosh, you couldn't see a fly if it landed on your nose."

Chantain rolled her eyes. "You can't come up with a legitimate reason—so shut your mouth."

Eddie whispered, "There's bigger reasons than you know, darling...I'm trying to put a family together with this ring here on my finger, not destroy it like yours."

Chantain looked at his hand. Without saying anything, she put her eyes back to her Bible and pretended to read along with the lecture while he continued. "Of course, you wouldn't know what I'm talking about, would you?"

"Yes, I would...when the going gets tough, I get going, so you better watch it...someday your crap's going to come back and kick you."

"I guess that means you're going to leave me someday. Should I get ready for it?"

THE TIME TO TELL

"Take it any way you wish. You need to be quiet. We're in a church in case you didn't notice."

Eddie delicately placed his Bible up on the shelf on back of the pew then slowly put his hands down on his knees. "Oh, I get it. We argue all the time anyway. What is the difference? Remind me not to go to war with you in a church."

"Gooood God, you and your war stuff again...what's that supposed to mean?"

"Oh, nothing...you're not a comrade, put it that way. You'd be some kind of undercover enemy in my foxhole trying to slash my throat at night."

"Did you hear what you just said? I can't believe you...go comparing me to some murdering war man like yourself."

Eddie smirked. "War?"

"Yeah, war...something you know too much about."

He whispered a little louder, "War? 'War,' she says...you know more about war than I do...you've been cutting me up and throwing me to the dogs our whole marriage."

"Oh God, Eddie, the day I do that, this church'll freeze over."

"You need to start helping us out...'*God,*' you say...you keep slipping grenades in my pockets then running off in the corner for cover...do you hear what I'm saying?"

By this time their arguing carried over to the attention of a couple sitting near them, already looking aggravated.

Chantain whispered more loudly, "Marriage...that's what you're speaking about. My mother always said something about you."

"Oh boy, look out now. Your divorced mother's slipping grenades in our marriage too. *Pshhhh,* see what I mean? *Ah,* forget it. It's a losing battle, I can tell."

"Just leave my mother out of this or I'll start talking about your parents. Bet you wouldn't like that?"

Eddie sneered. "Good luck with that...maybe you forgot. They're still together. You and your mother are way different from my parents...you're cookie cutters—breeding breakups instead of children...no, my parents are better than that."

Suddenly, a few more church members looked over their shoulders, glaring their vivid discontent.

The two of them suddenly became a nuisance for several feet in all directions. Still, they whispered as if nobody was listening.

"That's it, Eddie. You make marriage sound so fun. My mother's brilliant—should have listened to her."

"Doesn't take a rocket scientist to know what your mother said."

Chantain slapped her Bible back on the shelf. "You have no idea the wisdom my mother has."

"Wisdom you say? She's making sure you get rid of me like she did your dad."

Just then a couple church members gasped and then looked over to see what Chantain would say next.

"Maybe it's not a bad idea, Eddie."

"I'll tell you your mom's bad idea, Chantain. Misery loves company, so I'm already gone if you ask about her evil crystal ball."

Chantain stopped whispering. "Shut up. Bad enough... all these church people looking at us. Then you go calling names."

Suddenly, an old couple to their side whispered at them together, "*Shhhhh*, quiet, my granddaughter's next to me listening."

"Please, take it outside if you have to."

Eddie and Chantain immediately grabbed up their Bibles again, thumbing through them to find their places.

The one little member between them who didn't mind their arguing was Doll. He looked as if he were immune to it. Besides, Chantain had given him one of her science fiction books to look at while they were there. As it turned out, the little paperback had another one of those colorful scenes on the cover of rocket ships blasting into outer space.

THE TIME TO TELL

Doll playfully growled, showing his teeth as if pretending that *he* was the one flying the rockets right next to the hideous-looking, green, frog-like creatures in the picture. Incidentally, he opened the paperback up, expecting to find more of what was on the cover, but nothing was there. He got stuck rummaging through page after page, looking at nothing but tiny words. To him, they most assuredly resembled hundreds of thousands of black ants smashed in geometric shapes and lines. His happy, little face drooped. After he flipped through almost every page, his fascination of fun looked like it was hijacked. He then looked at the book as if it were a piece of junk.

For the moment, Doll looked to be getting through his problem by sneaking a pencil out of Chantain's purse. Unfortunately, when he tried to look for a place to scribble inside the book, he was stuck again. There was no place to draw on it either, for all the letters got in his way. Reluctantly, he tugged on Chantain's arm for an explanation, but he was derailed yet again. She whipped her hair around to him, snarling and whispering, "What do you want?"

Doll backed off in shock. Whatever it was about the book she had given him, he wanted no part of it. He dropped it on the pew then took a double take at the creature on the cover as if he were comparing it to Chantain. The looks didn't match, but he might have gotten the picture without reading a word.

Chantain saw the mischief he was into, so she took his pencil away, shoved it back in her purse, and slapped his hand, causing him to pucker up. Before he could shed a tear, she snatched the book away, confounding him even more. Doll sat there, staring at his empty hands as if he'd just lost everything he had, so he held his hands up to Chantain for comfort or her book back. Either one would have been fine.

Chantain scowled straight at him. "Stupid kid. Knock it off or I'll bust your butt."

Eddie whispered, "Hey, easy...you gave your book to him—then you took it away."

"So! Little rat stole my pencil out of my purse then tried to vandalize it."

Eddie looked around before continuing, "You're angry... how can Doll learn if you keep flipping out on him?"

"Flipping out? He's the one pouting about it, not me. Look at him."

Quickly, she grabbed Doll's arm. "Shut up before I take you outside and find a stick."

By this time the old couple next to them had tried to distance themselves, as another couple in front started gossiping into each other's ears, "It's that lady behind us. What do we do?"

"*Shhhh*, just stay seated. Wait, so we can leave."

Eddie put his hand on Chantain's shoulder, whispering, "Look, you're bothering everyone. You gotta stop—right now."

That was all it took. Chantain brushed his hand off, speaking louder, "Take your hand off me, youuuu—"

At the podium Pastor McKoowey detected a little disturbance. However, as he looked toward the far back of his church, he couldn't quite make out who was responsible.

Slowly, Pastor McKoowey got back to business. "*Ahem... excuse me...where was I?*"

Sister Thelma whispered up to him, "Wrapping up Adam and Eve, I think."

He nodded, "Oh yes, thank you, Sister Thelma...that pretty well wraps it up with Adam and Eve, the beginning of all life. Don't forget now...Adam and Eve and all their children were philosophical symbols handed down from the prophets. They existed for the grandiose world of meaning only. They never existed. Pay attention to what our Prophet says about the beginnings of mankind. That's what he wanted you to do. Okay, questions anyone?"

THE TIME TO TELL

Nobody said anything, so he continued, "Now let's move on to how they, our descendants, populated the world. Go to chapter four, verses one and on, in Genesis. We're getting to something interesting now: Adam and Eve's children, or the offspring of mankind. That's us."

Sounds of pages shuffled as he continued, "Eve conceived two children...one was named 'Cain,' who was the tiller of the ground. The second son was named 'Abel,' who was the keeper of the sheep. Abel's work flourished while Cain's didn't do quite so well. Cain's behavior became accountable for a number of small things that you or I wouldn't perhaps notice. First there was anger and jealousy on Cain's part. Then there was his loss of composure and self-control. Vengeance could have been involved afterward.

Anyway, all these ill-fated feelings collected inside Cain, which led to his biggest upheavals of all. You know what that was?"

The crowd stayed silent so McKoowey carried on, "Cain turned against his own flesh and blood—that's one thing. Worse than that...Cain killed someone...he didn't just kill anyone—he killed his brother."

Pastor McKoowey then closed his Bible. He walked out to the front of the stage, leaving his notes behind. "This story isn't what you think. It's a prophet's philosophy told in another wise abstraction. Cain starts with little crimes that you or I might pass off. Here's where his upheavals connect...if one of you plays these little games of mischief or petty crime, they ultimately play out the same if you keep it up. They play out to worse things, then worse, again and again, until...some even reach murder."

He paused then began pacing on stage with a figurative idea on the tip his tongue. "There...you see? All these little things lead to worse things, no exception. If you keep doing them over and over, you soon forget you're doing these things, which makes them worse...how can you stop if you don't know you're doing it?" He paused with his hands in his pockets. "One more thing...you have to have done all the little crimes first, before you get to the bigger ones. Sort of like going to school or practicing before you get to a real job."

He walked back to his podium. "Okay, here's more... chapter four, verses nine through fifteen. I'll sum it up...the Lord received Abel, who was murdered from the ground with his cries. The Lord—*rather*—didn't accuse Cain. Instead, he confronted Cain for an explanation first, to see what he'd say. Cain exposed another vital thing of the stereotypical person that he was. Cain wrote the whole thing off. It's in verse nine. He explained it his way, *'Why or how should he know what happened to Abel? He wasn't his brother's keeper.'* Do you realize what he said? Guesses anyone?"

Nobody guessed. "I'll tell what he said. He said, *'Go bother someone else. I'm not responsible for my brother.'*"

He then tapped his finger on his Bible. "Adam and Eve had more children...they lived on to populate the world. Cain was allowed to live and populate the world too."

Almost everyone in the audience groaned their displeasure as he went on, "Wait now...let me explain...Cain's people live among us right now...they're multiplying. Multiplying by the thousands, now the millions even. These are the criminals, fugitives, vagabonds and murderers. They are vicious to everyone, including their families if they have to be. Where are they, you ask? They hide. They play the same game as us—except they use *lies* to pretend they're normal. Ladies and gentlemen, they care about no one. They could be you or me.. If they're not stopped, they'll take over everything we know, including all that is good."

The audience started riling themselves up as he went on, "It's right here in verses eleven and twelve...it says here that he cursed Cain as a fugitive, a deserter, a traitor...Cain and the descendants of Cain are cursed forever to be fugitives, criminals, murderers, and vagabonds…There's no going back, ladies and gentlemen."

He looked up at his audience, trying not to smile. "I mean it's hard for them to hide once they are caught in the act of a crime committed over and over."

Nobody said a word, so he continued, "Here's the scary part…what about the most clever and wicked of them all? Who are they? Good question since we might be talking millions and millions. Why can't they be found? They don't—get—caught. They learn how to lie better, that's all…it's simple…they continue to build their armies to devour our definition of *good*, so they can rewrite the definition of *good*… why is that? Simple again."

Pastor McKoowey turned away from the crowd to hide his chuckle, then turned back to face them with a serious face. "They don't have to admit they are bad if we're gone…now that, ladies and gentlemen, is evil's finest hour…the wickedest *world war* of all. A war that will end this world in an instant if nobody finds a solution."

He looked at the clock, looking shifty eyed. "Wait…I have something for you. It was given to me by this battle beyond…then you can begone…Cain, who possessed *all* those bad characteristics, was marked, or 'identified' if you will. In verses fourteen and fifteen, it says that Cain's people will hide among us, but they should not be slain by us, the people, as part of his curse. Instead, God has put a mark on them."

He paused briefly. "The final piece to the 'Cain' puzzle I've laid out for you…before I go further…I'll have you know that this book was written as the first book of the Hebrew Bible and Christian Old Testament. These stories were some of the oldest mysteries in the first of five books of the Jewish Torah or Pentateuch. The words have been around since the creation of the world to the birth of Israel and Egypt. What about this book? The book I have here? It's just a book. It's the book of primeval history in other words. It's the Book of—Book of Genesis. This changes things, doesn't it? Genesis is the beginning of the end."

The members throughout the church started to grow restless as he continued, "Wait! It's no physical mark. If we could identify them, it would be nice. Some churches even began thinking that the curse of the mark of Cain was the black skin of people...yes, Negroes."

The only African American couple inside the church gasped as Pastor McKoowey quickly caught on, pointing. "Oh, don't worry, Mr. and Mrs. Holgrim. I don't think it's true, and I'm sure other churches will find their way to better answer it at some point."

He philosophically swirled his hands. "Skin's not it....I said *all* Cain's people have to share one thing in common."

The pastor glanced around, noticing that on the flip of a coin, his audience had begun to grow more restless. Still, he carried on, clearing his throat. "Well...someone will find the answer...excuse me, that will be all."

Suddenly, a buzz of whispers swirled throughout the entire congregation. Some even looked as if they wanted to say something, but they didn't. As Pastor McKoowey began putting away his notes and closing up his Bible, he deviously glanced throughout his audience as if he felt another presence within his church he was not familiar with. Quickly, he cast his ill look aside and nodded a signal for Sister Thelma to take over in a hurry.

Sister Thelma quickly stood up, but before she could announce a closing hymn, the eldest man, Clarence, raised his shaky hand. "Hey, Mr. Preacher! You must have some kinda idea who Cain or Cain's people are, don't ya?"

The audience instantly quieted down to hear what the pastor would say as Clarence spoke a little louder. "Mr. Preacher...what do these mongrels all share 'n common? You gotta tell us more before we go singin' and forget."

THE TIME TO TELL

In the midst of near total silence, Pastor McKoowey suddenly dropped his face, feeling an even stronger presence yet.

A big, bodacious woman, as well as a couple others, speaking, "Yeah, Pastor McKoowey."

"We want to hear your answer."

"You must have an idea. Tell us what it is."

"Yeah, even if it's wrong. What do you say, everyone? We ain't leavin' 'til you say something."

"Yeah, we want to know!"

Pastor McKoowey eased his curious churchgoers with the sweep of his hands. While reluctantly gathering himself, he studdered, "I-I'm sorry…I've tried…maybe it'll come out in the future by someone else—I don't know."

Someone in the audience piped up, "What's going on?"

Pastor McKoowey started to look scared. "Okay…okay then…I've traced links and connections to Abel, and I just—"

Others in his crowd stood up blurting, "No, you said 'Cain.'"

"Yeah, we wanna know about the Cains because they're the bad ones."

"We don't want to know about Abel. I want to know about Cain."

Pastor McKoowey went on, "Okay, quiet down please. You have to believe me…I looked into the names of Adam and Eve's other offspring, but found nothing. Not even a clue…. really…it's gonna take someone whole lot better than me to figure it out if I'm a liar…wait, I-I mean who the liars are."

He went on, shaking his finger. "That's all for now, please."

Others in the audience stood up. "But we haven't got time."

"Wait, the end of the world is what it's about. It's about last week and this week, isn't it? It's all the same, isn't it?"

"It's all connected I bet, isn't it, Mr. Preacher?"

Pastor McKoowey thought before nodding. "Well...they could be...yes, all right then...so now you know. All I can say is—*time will tell.*"

Another person raised her hand, looking irritated, while three others stood up, throwing their hands around. "Hey, wait! I know Cain's people. I got one down the road."

"Yeah, I see 'em dropping their kids everywhere."

"Yeah! Rats is what they are—populating faster than us too!"

"Yeah, how's anyone going to fix it before they take over then?"

The pastor quickly gathered his material off the podium. "That's why it's called 'prophecy.' Nobody knows. I'm sorry."

He then turned to Thelma as he darted away from the podium. "Okay, Sister Thelma, get me out of this...lead the closing song so we can get to our prayer."

Sister Thelma hopped up, turning to the audience. "Gladly. I have a song everyone needs... okay, everyone. Please turn to page twenty-nine of your songbook. The song is called 'They Are Telling.' Everyone, please be ready. First two verses only, skip the third. Here we go."

She began with the stroke of her hand as everyone joined in at different times, out of order.

> *They are tell-ing of a Sav-iour, and a joy that they have found,*
> *They are tell-ing of salvation, let me hear the joyful sound.*
> *Let me hear, let me hear, let me hear the joy that they repeat;*
> *Let me hear, let me hear, let me hear the story sweet.*
> *They are telling of a Sav-iour, they are saying he has come,*
> *That he seeks and saves the lost ones, that he brings the wan-derers home.*
> *Let me hear, let me hear...*
> *Let me hear, let me hear, story sweet.*

Immediately after the song, everyone seated themselves as Pastor McKoowey popped up from the front row, facing everyone with a quick idea. "We're going to do something new tonight. Instead of me giving prayer, I'd like to choose one of you out there. How's this sound for something new? Sound good everyone?"

The audience seemed receptive as he selectively combed his eyes through the pews of people.

"Okay then...*um*...let me see all your faces...*um, ah,* Mr. Coolidge! Won't you please stand up and give us your guidance and blessings tonight?"

Instantly, the shuffling noises of shoes beneath the pews began to shift. Most everyone there knew exactly where Eddie was seated, so they all looked back to him, putting him heavy on the spot.

Eddie looked like he could have crawled down to the floor, whereas Chantain got caught in the crossfire with a little stage fright herself. She skittishly smiled back at everyone then indirectly whispered, "Get up, Eddie—now. Everyone's looking at us."

Eddie sat right where he was—shifting around, not knowing what to do. With no resolution of where to turn, he tried to gather himself up for what everyone was patiently waiting for. Just when he looked like he couldn't do it, he hung his head down—down to the face of Doll.

Pastor McKoowey rustled his notes in his hands, with a tomfoolery tone in his voice. "*Ah*, come on, Mr. Coolidge...surely there's something on your mind tonight. Let's hear it for Mr. Coolidge everyone...give him some encouragement."

Subtle words surfaced from all around him: "It's okay, Eddie."

"Yeah, nobody's here but us."

"Pray for your new kid. That's a good one."

Then a bigger, dirty fellow with grungy hair, sitting back against the wall, cracked open a partial grin. "*He he*, yeah... pray about y'r dolly boy is what I might say."

Eddie's attitude suddenly changed from diffident to defiantly defensive. Without hesitation, he swiped an awfully angry eye back at the man, then turned to Chantain, whispering, "You and that stupid—name."

She barely contained her laughter.

Quite unexpectedly, Eddie rose to the occasion with a mighty big thump of his cane. Before he began to pray, he scanned across the pews as if he silently dared anyone to make fun of "Doll" once more. No one said a thing, so he bowed his head to pray aloud: "Thank you, Lord, for giving me *Doll* and the opportunity to serve you and everyone here with a word. Give *Doll* the strength, courage, and wisdom that he may need to grow up in Devil's. Have mercy on everyone's souls…God bless and amen."

Pastor McKoowey kindly spoke out as the audience began shuffling and gathering up their things to leave. "Very good, Mr. Coolidge. Nice prayer for the gift of a child. Next time, though, please try and make it more general for everyone. Thank you…thanks for coming, everyone."

As everyone slowly shuffled toward the door, Eddie fell in line too, coaxing his family right along. Before they got too far, Pastor McKoowey waved Chantain down to come forward. Chantain lit up like a Christmas tree, tapping Eddie on his back. "You and Doll go ahead home without me. John needs to talk about church work."

Eddie turned around, stopping and holding traffic in the aisle. "What? Oh, well, *uh*, how are you going to get home? I've got the car."

"Don't worry about it. John'll give me a ride."

Eddie hesitated as he glared back up to the pastor. He then dropped his face, muttering to Chantain, "It's not about the arguing, is it? You had this planned, didn't you?"

"No, of course not. Whatever gave you that idea? See you later."

"You've been putting the idea in my head. What is it then?"

THE TIME TO TELL

Chantain huffed, "It's nothing to do with anything. You're overreacting. I'll be home soon. It won't be long."

Eddie flowed back in line with the traffic headed for the doors. "Okay, then...I have to telephone Dad. He's probably wondering why I never called. What should I say?"

As Chantain inched away, she shrugged her shoulders. "Tell him I forgot...oh, and don't forget about supper."

"I know. Food'll be on the stove waiting...come on, Doll. We gotta go."

Eddie carried Doll outside, practically dragging his cane all the way to his camper car, then quickly got in to sit for a few seconds. As he started fumbling with the keys behind the wheel, passing church members walking hand-in-hand caught his attention. Some of them waved their good-byes and some didn't, but most were smiling together as couples, families, and extended families.

Briefly, he aspired to sit and watch them a little longer while they loaded up in their cars and drove off. Their overwhelming smiles didn't rub off on him too well. Those many smiles caused him to lose his own until he looked downright depressed.

Once he began driving away, his depression was relieved. The further he drove down the road, the better he got. The beautiful scenery assisted him. The radio played on with nice warm music too. "Out of sight, out of mind" may have been a kind friend to his sudden sadness. He may as well have enjoyed another old saying too: 'What he doesn't know can't hurt him.' Time was wasting for the better part of his concerns, however.

He and Doll quickly made it back home, parked the car, and headed inside. After greeting Major, the first thing to cross Eddie's mind was to pick up the telephone and get his father on the line.

Cambrin: "Hello, Cambrin here. Your nickel, start talking."

Eddie: "I just got word that you called."

Cambrin: "I was beginning to wonder if you'd ring back."

Eddie: "Yeah, sorry. It's my message lady."

Cambrin: "So Chantain's up to her selective memory lapses again? What's new besides that?"

Eddie: "No, you tell me what's new. You got my stuff in the mail I take?"

Cambrin: "Yes, as a matter of fact I did. That's why I called."

Eddie: "Okay...well what? Lay it on me."

Cambrin: "Funny thing. I'd liked to have never got the metallurgist and lab techs off my tail."

Eddie: "*Huh*? What do you mean?"

Cambrin: "You'd think I had some secret bullshit going on, I tell ya."

Eddie: "What, over a piece of metal?"

Cambrin: "Yeah! After they ran a number of tests, they got curious where the damn stuff came from."

Eddie: "Oh?"

Cambrin: "I had to make up something—like quick."

Eddie: "You didn't tell them about my kid did you? They'll come take him away if—"

Cambrin: "Oh God no...I told'em you used to play with my welding torches and melted a bunch a stuff for jewelry and whatnot."

Eddie: "*Whew*...good. You had me scared there for a second."

Cambrin: "Just one problem...they had a hard time swallowing that."

Eddie: "Why, what's wrong with melting up a pot o' gold and stuff?"

Cambrin: "It's the chemical makeup, they said. I finally said I didn't know what the hell you threw in it."

Eddie: "So tell me what it is. It's got gold in it, right?"

Cambrin: "You're right about that. In fact, it's mostly gold, but there's something else it's mixed with they never seen before. One-a-them said it had uncharacteristic properties."

Eddie: "Uncharacteristic properties? What's that supposed to mean?"

Cambrin: "They called it 'isolative phonetic properties,' if I remember right. Two-a-them agreed. They have no way to test it beyond their current lab. They want to keep working on it."

Eddie: "Isolative phonetics? Isn't phonetics something about the study of speech or sound or something? What's that got to do with anything?"

Cambrin: "I didn't quite understand either. The main guy tried to say, but it went in one hearing aid and out the other. They just begun to study it in a new theory, I think he said."

Eddie: "Theories don't help. You got anything useful?"

Cambrin: "I guess what one said was that it can insulate against just about *anything*."

Eddie: "Insulate against what?"

Cambrin: "That's what he said…anything. Guess that means *anything*."

Eddie: "*Hmmm*. Sounds like you got a lab guy all right. What about the sound thing? What's that?"

Cambrin: "Hate to say, but that ain't helping you either. He tried to describe it in layman's terms."

Eddie: "Oh yeah? Try me."

Cambrin: "See if I get this right now. Okay, people's perception of sound's normally limited to frequencies between about 12 hertz and 20,000 hertz. Animals can get vibrations higher. Then he went off with what I didn't quite follow."

Eddie: "You mean dogs can hear better? I know that. What's so complicated about that?"

Cambrin: "No, no…more weird than that….he said the Earth's atmosphere and everything such as fire, water, and physical stuff like matter, has a frequency with sound."

Eddie: "Okay, now you lost me."

Cambrin: "I told you…okay, I know you're bright, hush up. In gases, sound is way over six hundred miles per hour I think he said. In water, something like three thousand, three hundred miles per hour. In steel or iron it's over thirteen thousand miles per hour. The alloy you gave me tips the scales, I guess, where it is dangerous beyond what they know."

Eddie: "Okayyyy, so what can they do with it?"

Cambrin: "That's what I'm sayin'. They can't test it if they can't identify it."

Eddie: "*Hmmm.*"

Cambrin: "Then I knew I had to get outta there when he said Geronimo's involved with it."

Eddie: "Geronimo? Dad, you've been reading those western magazines I sent you. You like 'em?"

Cambrin: "Oh, sure I do. Can't say it does much for my remembering all the things these guys said, though."

Eddie: "You said, 'anything' didn't you?"

Cambrin: "I did, and for whatever reason that's the word he used. He went off on something else like oscillations through gases, plasma, and liquids, solids—*err, uh* longitudinal, *um*—transverse."

Eddie: "Okay, okay. So they can't find out what it was made of besides gold?"

Cambrin: "They didn't know. Thought I said that. Anyways, they got more confusing if you can believe."

Eddie: "So there's more? Listen, I have to go right now, Dad, because—"

Cambrin: "Physical stuff in the universe mixes with mediums. Mediums, I guess, periodically displace waves or frequency for whatever. Periodically—like it happens every so often."

THE TIME TO TELL

Eddie: "Dad, I gotta—"

Cambrin: "The other lab guy that got involved said your mystery gold challenges anything in existence…that's why I said 'anything.' I didn't make that up."

Eddie: "You sure they're not overeducated? I bet they were bored too."

Cambrin: "Yeah, no shit. So why you in such a hurry to leave your dad?"

Eddie: "It's not you. I've got to tend to Doll and things right now, and—"

Cambrin: "Oh, good then. I can tell you more if you like. Another lab guy kept rambling how impressed they were with mumbo jumbo about acoustics of noise, pressure levels of sound, and their formulas of root-mean-square…the letter p…logarithmic decibel scales—"

Eddie: "Wait, Dad, I think I—"

Cambrin: "You ain't heard nothing yet…how 'bout velocity vectors, frequency, wavelength, amplitudes, intensities, polar bears—*err, uh polarization,* or whatever they said the stuff was."

Eddie: "Okay, okay, I got it. I got it. That's enough for now. I—"

Cambrin: "Oh, you too? I could hardly wait to get out of there myself. Sounded like a pissing contest if you ask me."

Eddie: "Sorry for putting you through it. Sooo—"

Cambrin: "You know, I can't believe it…got some of the best brains in the world working here, and they can't figure out their own heads from a hole in the ground."

Eddie: "*Mmm-hmm*…won't be the first time. What did you do with the piece of chain?"

Cambrin: "Nothing left of it. One-a-them asked if he could get a hold of some more. I said there was no more."

Eddie: "That's fine…I hope you get to keep your job."

Cambrin: "Oh, me too. I'll find work around here no matter what, I suppose…oops, I can hear Gayla calling. Hey, thanks for hangin' out with your dad on the phone a little longer."

Eddie: "No problem, talk to you later, love you and good-bye. Tell Mom I love her too."

Cambrin: "Lots-a-love here. I sure will and take care-a-that new kid."

Eddie: "I will and thanks."

Eddie heard his father hang up. He looked at his receiver then hung up and paused. He was taken aback, but not for long. Reminders caused him to follow up with a grin. Immediately, he picked up his cane and hobbled down the hallway to his bedroom, where he patiently dialed the combination to his safe. Then, without a hitch, he clicked open the heavy door to sneak a peek at what he was thinking about.

There it was, just as shiny as the day he put it there. Doll's medallion lay inside, breathing freely from its sheltered half-ton box of darkness. Oh, but now it gleamed right along with Eddie's proud, curious smile. The light of the window amplified its glorious presence. Until then, it seemingly insulated itself quite well from impenetrable forces roaming just outside. Coincidentally, a small gray cloud nearby expelled what little bit of cover it had, quickly dissipating without a single soul, including Eddie, noticing. He was preoccupied with seeing Doll's medallion for the first time since he had locked it up in there.

He looked at his other personal items scattered around in the safe too: his military-issue Colt .45, a Purple Heart medal, his discharge papers, a couple of cigar boxes of photographs, a quart jar of cash, and a few other miscellaneous items. He touched and felt each item one at a time, yet repeatedly he came right back to Doll's medallion without picking it up. Finally, he did. He caressed it, feeling how smooth it was, yet so sharp around the star's edges. Its craftsmanship and design kept him immensely intrigued.

THE TIME TO TELL

As he continued to admire it, a very coy, young little voice came up from behind. "What you doing, Daddy?"

Instantly, he dropped the medallion back into the safe, closing the door. "Oh, nothing. You startled me. I was just looking at some of our *uh*...family things. That's all."

Doll stepped inside the bedroom, pointing. "The big black thing? What's it for?"

"Oh, it's called a safe...want to see? It opens with this here handle. See this dial with the numbers? It's called a 'combination lock.' Nobody gets in. See, all locked up. Everything is all safe now."

Doll stepped right up to it. "Safe?"

Eddie tugged on the big brass handle, making sure it wouldn't open. "Why, yes...sooo, want something to eat? I see you got your blue star pajamas on."

"No. Not hungry."

Eddie crouched down. "Oh, Doll...I'm concerned about you. You've got to eat more. You want to grow up and be a big man someday, don't you?"

"Not hungry...I'm sleepy."

"You haven't been getting any sleep lately either, have you? Is that why you don't like to eat before bed?"

Doll smiled, but the smiled faded to a frown. "*Um* Daddy? Is okay Major goes to bed?"

"Well, I think he's already in bed...oh, you mean *your* bed—with you again like last night?"

"Yes."

"Of course, Doll. I think he'd sleep with you every night if you let him. Why you ask anyway?"

Doll lowered his head. "Oh—*um*."

"Speak clear...you know what I said about talking...so why is the dog sleeping so much with you lately?"

Doll kept looking to the floor. "A thing...it bothers me... when I sleep."

Eddie looked mildly concerned. He carefully sat down on the side of bed, thinking. He didn't rightfully know what to say, so he offered his open arms. "I see...come jump in my lap and give me a hug...I heard you a few nights ago...you whimper sometimes. Did you know that?"

Doll shook his head, brushing the sniffles from his nose as Eddie continued, "You know...every time I come to your room, you always look too comfortable for me to wake you up, so I let you sleep. *Hmmm*, you know what it's called that you have? They're called 'bad dreams' or 'nightmares'...sure wish Chantain would step up to the plate and help out with you."

"What do you mean?"

"Oh, nothing....Daddy's here...I'm here...Mommy's just going to be busy working all the time, that's all...so remember, they're just dreams."

"They bother me. I want them to go away."

"They don't come all the time, do they?"

"No."

Eddie kept rocking him on his lap. "*Whew*, let me see...how can I make you feel better...*hmmm*, I know...say, didn't you tell me you saw something in your dreams? Tell me what it is. What did you see exactly?"

Doll hid his face in Eddie's shirt. "Dog dreams."

Eddie grabbed Doll's shoulders and looked at him. "A dog? Did he hurt you?"

"No."

"There now...you see? He's like Major."

Doll began rubbing his eyes. "*Um*...no."

"No? What do you mean?"

"He's bigger Major."

Eddie leaned back to look him in the eyes. Then he looked beyond him and out through the window. Carefully, he asked, "Bigger than Major? How much bigger? Have you ever seen a dog bigger than Major before?"

"No...he's way bigger."

"How much bigger?"

THE TIME TO TELL

"It doesn't want to show me...oh, and blue eyes."

"*Ahem*...oh, Doll, dogs don't get much bigger than Major. It's your imagination. Your little brain up there is playing tricks in your sleep...trust me...it won't bother you if you don't think too much."

He kept on, "Tell you what...big strong Daddy says you're safe—like that safe right there. I was a boy once—like you. I know what I'm saying, so here's what you can do...just think of Daddy being there with you, and you'll be okay—okay?"

Doll halfheartedly nodded as Eddie gently slid him off his lap. While playfully ruffling his hair into a mess, he said, "Good. As long as you know that—Daddy's always there with you."

"Daddy? Really? In my dreams?"

"Sure. Daddy's in your dreams...go on now. Get to bed. I've got to get my head straight with Mommy...I think I'm not doing so well with her."

"Mommy? She okay?"

"It's nothing...just grown-up stuff...you've got better things to think about...it's getting late, so shove off to bed, okay?"

Doll smiled. "Wow, Daddy in my dreams."

Eddie nudged him along. "Okay, Champ...my big ball-player star...start exercising those tiny legs and eat big tomorrow. You do that for me?"

"*Ummm*, okay."

"Go on...I'll be right behind you to tuck you in...call Major and see who wins this time."

Doll nodded then spun out into the hallway. "Here, Major!"

After they both wrestled around with the covers, Doll peeked out up at the top of the bed while Major eventually grappled with leaning against the footboard. A minor sense of good times before bed seemed to end—but then again, maybe not. Something else was brewing. Doll held all the clues through his anxious expressions. Something bigger was brewing all right. Nobody would have guessed it either.

Doll hung tight in the covers of his dark bedroom, while keeping a sharp, close eye toward the little bit of light streaming in from the hallway. Total silence crept on for almost a minute before something childishly great was about to begin outside his bedroom. Just like the live set of a haunted house horror scene, it started with a single creak from some far off, distant door. It sounded so creepy it even raised the hair on Major's back. Doll, however, looked as if he were expecting something. Then from a distance came the sound of some wild concoction, destined to grow more sinister by the second.

Eddie playing the part of anyone's fool. He was the ghoul, creeping up with a whole host of jokes mixed in with passions of good, old-fashioned fear. He couldn't be seen and that was the point. The first big bulk of his hidden presence started off with a good dose of shock. Actually, it sounded more like the dropping of someone's quality, heavy-grade bowling ball.

Whammm!

Doll screamed as he ditched under his covers. The blankets he hid under tried to stay still, but they wouldn't stop shaking. Frankly, it was hard to tell if the poor boy was truly scared, or just excited. Either way, he put up a good show of being scared in his deathbed, with nowhere to go.

Joke or not, Major wanted no part of it. The jig was up, so he backed up against the footboard, looking utterly depressed. If anyone could have understood his growls, he or she might have said that Major knew what was going on. Eddie was at it again, morphing into one of those terrible ideas of his. Dogs may have an extra sense, but according to Major's extra sense, Eddie didn't make any sense at all. He even glared at Doll as if he were shocked any human could fall for such a thing every night.

Doll peeked out of his covers, expecting to see more, and he got more. Special effects of shadows loomed out in the hallway in no time and apparently right on schedule, getting larger by the second. Eddie was the one behind the scenes, playing with those black figurines running all over the walls. Shadows from hell they were, distorted and overdone. Doll ditched under the covers again as the tickling terror played out with a tremendously slow thrill of anticipation.

Eddie notched it up a bit with botched sound effects. In all truthfulness, he sounded as if he couldn't make up his mind whether he wanted to be a dumb mummy with a bum foot, or a pathetic pirate dragging a wooden leg. Either way, he was a lame copy of an Eddie-zombie, dragging his cane.

Doll lay waiting, expecting every second of Eddie's draconian dragnet, which was well into the hallway by then. Now, it was inching closer to the edge of his door.

Eerrrrrr, grrrrrr. Kirpunk-skid-draaag.
"Here I come."
Kirpunk-draaag-skid.
"Pegleg's comin' to get you, Dollllll."
Hack-gag....eerrrrr. Kirpunk-drag.
"I'm going to crush youuuu...bones-n-your bodyyyyy."
Kirpunk. Eerrrrraaaaaah. Eerrrrraaaahahaha.

Right when the spoof horror show should have peaked, nothing happened. It ended in a dud of silence. Just like a bomb before the blast that lost its fuse. Doll screamed beneath his covers, "*Ahhhh!*"

Eddie quietly stepped into Doll's doorway with nothing more to hide. Just like that, nothing flat, his groaning ghoul traded places with the stand-up kind of a guy named Eddie. "My gosh, what was that in the hallway? You guys are fast. Who won this time?"

Doll almost died laughing. While gathering himself and poking his head out of his covers, he pointed down to Major who was still utterly unentertained by Eddie's freak fraud.

Eddie chuckled as he hobbled closer. "Well, maybe I should try a three-legged vampire next time. Hey, how about Mr. Dracula? Yeah, Dracula with a stiff leg."

He swiftly straightened Doll's covers and good-humoredly tucked him in bed. "Boy—took me a while to wrestle that monster in the hallway. Did you see him escape?" Doll giggled as Eddie continued, "I saved you, though, didn't I? Oh, come on, you know what to do next. It's bedtime. Game over for the night, big guy."

Doll waited for Eddie's belated call before he moved on to his next routine, which was saying his bedtime prayer. Routine it was. Just like that, he sat up in his bed as if he were anxious to get on with it. Before he did, however, he paused, got serious, and pointed to his nightstand drawer as if he had suddenly become concerned. "*Um*, can I see it?"

Eddie thought for a moment and turned on the lamp. "So you want to see the old book...the one with your prayer inside?" He opened the drawer and all that was inside it was a tattered, old book that looked as if it should have been thrown away decades ago. Eddie took care in pulling it from the drawer, for if he didn't, it may have fallen apart. It was in shambles.

"Okay, here it is." He carefully turned to a certain page. "Okay, prayer's right here. See it?"

Doll held the book in his hands then closed it back up carefully. Tenderly, he felt the weathered cover before he shook his head.

Eddie quickly replied, "That's okay...you'll be able to read when you get older, I promise."

Doll pointed to its small, crumbled face that was barely legible. "*Um*, what that say?"

"Oh, that? That's called the title...you know? It's a name. Name of the book....it says...hard to see...so old. Oh yes, it says, 'New England Primer'...yeah, that's what it says...

it's the first reading primer that was used to teach the first children in America."

"Teach?"

"Yes, teach...it taught little boys and girls which way to go in our country...teaching of the old days, you might say...there are morals in it. Something you don't see very often anymore...book's outdated, but I remember it from when I was young."

"Was it—yours?"

"What? Who, me? No, I got it for, *uh*—free down at the secondhand place because the man...he, *uh*, couldn't sell it, I guess."

Doll looked utterly confused. "Morrral? Free?"

"Oh, forget what I said...I'm talking grown-up talk...you'll learn more when you get older."

Doll pointed below the title. "What's that say?"

Eddie glanced closer. "*Hmmm*, you're testing me, aren't you? You little stinker...okay, after this we say the prayer and go to bed, okay?"

Doll nodded.

"Says here, 'Printed and sold by—*Benjamin Franklin.*'"

Doll blinked to think. "Benjuuumin Frankullin?"

"Franklin Benjamin, yes...he was one of our founding fathers—a gifted man. Not anyone like him anymore. He was a politician, a scientist, a writer, a musician, and a great inventor too. Come to think of it, I wonder what he would do if he saw his country the way it is today."

Eddie then read Doll's face. "*Um hmmm*...you don't understand all I said, did you? Sorry, I don't expect you to know everything too quickly."

Doll twisted his lips. "Politishn—scientisss—musi-shun? Is book for boys like me?"

"Yes, I mean he printed it and gave copies to all the colonies' children."

"Colony?"

"Yes sort of like that. You'll learn all about that when the time comes. You know, Benjamin Franklin was the best. There.. that's good for tonight...maybe you should know that. He was a big, great man...he believed in a lot of things about this country we don't see anymore."

Doll snuggled back down in his covers looking mildly curious. "Country? He live in Devil's? Is he a daddy?"

"Oh no...he's been dead...dead a long time. He was a daddy...soooo, you thinking about being someone special like say—Ben Franklin? Maybe you could become someone important like him." Doll didn't answer, so Eddie kept talking. "Hey, I know something more like you."

"What?"

"How about—you wanna be—*a rocket man?*"

"Rocket man?"

"Yeah, a man that flies rockets...maybe rockets on his feet too...rockets everywhere...I wanted to fly when I was a little boy. How about you?"

Doll grinned. "*Hmmm*, yeah—*rocket man.*" Then Doll thought hard again. "*Um*, can I see what Benjuuumen says too? Can I have—me a book?"

"Sure...you can have all the books you want."

"No—Benjamin book...I want Benjamin book."

Eddie look curious just then. He looked at the old tattered book, then put it back in the drawer, pausing, as if wondering why such a young child would be interested in such a book. Nevertheless, he still seemed to be in the mood to amuse. "Of course, you can. Book's no good to me. Good ol' Benjamin would be proud of you if you kept it... how's that? Now that Benjamin's long gone, maybe you and him can get together in a prayer for wishes to come true. Let's say the prayer in his little book, shall we?"

THE TIME TO TELL

Doll sat up in bed, bowing his head with closed eyes. He clapped his hands together and began:

"Now I lay me down to sleep,
I pray the Lord my soul to keep,
If I should die before I wake,
I pray the Lord my soul to—"

"Wait-wait-wait a second...you said you have this *bad dream*, didn't you?"

Doll seemed like he was already thinking about it before he asked. His worried look just got a little more worrisome as he slowly nodded.

Eddie patted his head. "Okay, I know a prayer—like the one you already know...maybe me and Benjamin can help you in your dreams together."

Doll perked up. "Really?"

"Yes...I'm no witch doctor, but I know a thing or two about prayers. They can be powerful things if you believe in them...it goes like this—so, can you repeat after me?"

"Yes, I want to. I want to."

Eddie spoke slowly with Doll repeating every sentence right behind.

"Now I lay me down to sleep,
I pray the Lord my soul to keep,
May angels protect me through the night.
And keep me in their watchful sight.
Amen."

Eddie grinned. "That one'll keep the bogeyman away."

Doll smiled a big smile, but slowly his frown came back again.

Eddie lifted his chin. "*Ah*, Doll...what's wrong? It's supposed to cheer you up—what's the matter?"

Doll muttered, "Don't know angels…can I say 'Daddy'? You said *Daddy's* in my dreams."

"You mean in place of 'angels' in the prayer? Why, I don't know, *hmmm*." Eddie picked at his fingernails, seriously thinking. "Well, *hmmm*, you got me there…*ah*, okay then…whatever it takes…of course, go ahead. Be my guest. I'm leaving now, though, so good night."

As Eddie started to stand up, Doll grabbed him. "Can I do it now—as often as I want?"

"Of course. Pray away. I'll bow my head too with you—how's that sound?"

Doll adjusted himself up in bed. He took his time preparing for his new prayer as seriously as he could. In doing so, he took in a big deep breath, then blew his fear completely away. When he felt sanguine enough to continue, he closed his eyes, put his honorable little hands together and then spoke softly—except one more thing he added. The strain in is face revealed telltale signs of what he was truly trying to do. Within him, he tried so desperately to believe what he wanted to believe:

> *"Now I lay me down to sleep,*
> *I pray the Lord my soul to keep,*
> *May—Daddy—protect me through the night.*
> *And keep me in his watchful sight.*
> *Amen, amen, amen."*

Eddie smiled. "Wow—looks like you meant it that time. I guess your Daddy's got a big job ahead of him…get some sleep and good night now, all right?"

Eddie then turned off the lamp. As he headed out the door, Doll sprang up from his covers as if a little taste of *real* fear had crawled inside the bed with him. "Wait! How you be my Daddy?"

THE TIME TO TELL

Eddie stopped with his back still turned, as if he didn't want to face him. "Dolllll, not now...I have to start thinking about Mommy now."

Doll hid back in his covers. "Am I okay? Please, am I okay?"

"Doll...they're just dreams."

Doll started weeping. "Big dog's coming. He's coming—my dreams—tonight. I can tell, *ho-ho woo woo*."

Eddie wheezed. "Okay, okay...here's what you do...just keep saying your prayers like you mean it...you meant it just then, didn't you?"

"Yes."

"Good. That's all I can do, really...I've got a ton of problems right now. Daddy'll be there...trust me."

"Okay."

"I'll crack your door and leave the hall light on for you... That should help—good night."

"Good night." Doll wrapped the covers around his face and neck as high as he could, even though the nighttime air wasn't cold in the slightest. Fear kept his glassy eyes locked on Eddie's shadow hobbling slowly back down the dim hallway until he was gone.

"*Ahh!*"

Suddenly, a warm summer breeze came inside through the crack in his window. Strange, it seemed. It was as if the nighttime wind, so uninviting, that moved itself quietly into his room. With ease, it lifted the delicate, ivory lace curtain, reaching in to take a peek inside.

Doll jolted from the drifting presence lifting his hair. By the time he glanced up to the window, the feeble-looking curtain had already gently fluttered down. He tried to look harder, but nothing was there. The only thing he could see was the weathered window sash, framing the picture of the dark sky outside. Beyond it was nothing but the insolent emptiness of black.

Doll gasped, dropping beneath his covers as if he really *did* see something. Quickly, he shuffled down into a little, hollow hiding place; a place where he felt secure. Secure and private it was—and it was there where he whispered, once again, his nightly prayer.

If more was good, a lot would be even better. Again and again, he summoned through his frightened whisper, "Now I lay me down to sleep…Daddy, protect me…now I lay me down to sleep…Daddy, protect me…amen…amen…protect me, Daddy…amen…amen…protect me, Daddy…amen… protect me, Daddy…amen…amen…"

* * *

Eddie pulled a chair out from the table in the kitchen and sat down slowly. He reached over to turn on the little wooden radio beside him as he leaned back in the chair to think. A few seconds later, the news came on with a scratchy signal,

"*…to cap off the hourly news with Wars of the World, stay tuned for a most unusual recording from what is thought to be one of the last German underground labs in an unidentified cave just outside of Berlin in the foothills. A lone survivor was found inside, among a group of fellow scientists who were already dead from taking cyanide pills.*

According to military intelligence, the survivor and the dead men were surrounded by burning debris which had been set on fire just moments before he died. His last words will be translated on this station into English. Please use parental discretion, for you will hear the gunshots that killed the man. Please hold for thirty seconds."

Eddie worked hurriedly to tune the radio more clearly.

"*—Here it is, folks…*"

THE TIME TO TELL

'Hold it right there! Easy now...Don't shoot...come peacefully...Put your gun down...what's your name?'

'It doesn't matter what my name is. He's all that's left now...it is too late...you are too late! Operation Wolfe Cub is imminent. I'm telling you! Alive...yes, alive—in America! Americaaaa!'

BANG!

"That's all we have about the man found inside the mysterious cave. No evidence was recovered about what they were doing in there or what the man was talking about. Perhaps he was insane.

What we can say here at JDVL is—the man was right about one thing. America is alive and well. We don't need to hear about wolves and wolf operations anymore. That's it for now, and I hope you keep enjoying our continuous coverage of wars nonstop...here at—"

Click.

Eddie turned off the radio then hobbled over to the kitchen stove, empty cup in hand. As he poured the coffee, he thought for a moment then mumbled, "Operation Wolf Cub? Pssss...what'll they come up with next? Stupid war's over."

The Time To Tell continues...

AUTHOR BIOGRAPHY

H. C. Wells earned a bachelor's degree in business but still believes in the art of self-teaching, desire, and perseverance. Since childhood Mr. Wells's lifelong passion has not been business, however, but rather the wonderful field of artistry. His crossover into literary art began in 1995 when he became genuinely interested with his idea of creating the series *The Time to Tell*, the first book of which is *Operation Wolfe Cub*. His highest aspiration moving forward with his artistic endeavors is to have a positive impact on the world. Currently, he resides in the beautiful Pacific Northwest with his wife and two rescue dogs, Buddy and Jo.

To learn more about author H.C. Wells and *The Time To Tell* series, visit or email to the following:

http://www.hcwells.com – for newsletter signup, author blog and store.
https://www.facebook.com/pages/HC-Wells-Author

henry@hcwells.com

Made in the USA
San Bernardino, CA
20 November 2013